for plotting and denouement, this will prove surprising and completely satisfying'

SUSIE MAGUIRE, *Scotland on Sunday*

'*A Place of Execution* makes you question your assumptions about the whole crime genre . . . A crime novel about a miscarriage of justice, *A Place of Execution* is a wake-up call to crime writers everywhere. A terrific and original novel, brilliantly executed'

PAUL DAVIES, *Daily Mirror*

'It [*A Place of Execution*] must be in the running for best crime novel of the year. She has propelled herself into the ranks of the very best in the business . . . If you've never read any McDermid, try this. Basically, if you can read at all, try this. Atmosphere, characters, strong plot, tension, menace – it's got the lot'

JANICE YOUNG, *Yorkshire Post*

'Deserves to be the crime novel of the year'   *Prima*

'There is a great deal to admire in this novel . . . above all the book's formal adventurousness and subtle orchestration of different narrative levels, that sets it apart from most thrillers. With *A Place of Execution*, McDermid has wrought a powerful, resonant novel about power and its abuse, about the past's hold on the present, about the nature of knowledge'

LIAM McILVANNEY, *Glasgow Herald*

'Arguably her finest yet . . . Fear infuses every page . . . in this epic tragedy'

ERIC JACKSON, *Manchester Evening News*

'This is an extraordinarily accomplished book . . . the whole affair is a complete success'

F. E. PARDOE, *Birmingham Post*

By the same author

A Darker Domain
The Grave Tattoo
Cleanskin
The Distant Echo
Killing the Shadows

TONY HILL NOVELS
Fever of the Bone
Beneath the Bleeding
The Torment of Others
The Wire in the Blood
The Mermaids Singing

KATE BRANNIGAN NOVELS
Star Struck
Blue Genes
Clean Break
Crack Down
Kick Back
Dead Beat

LINDSAY GORDON NOVELS
Hostage to Murder
Booked for Murder
Union Jack
Final Edition
Common Murder
Report for Murder

NON-FICTION
A Suitable Job for a Woman

VAL McDERMID

A Place of Execution

HARPER

This novel is entirely a work of fiction.
The names, characters and incidents portrayed in it are
the work of the author's imagination. Any resemblance to
actual persons, living or dead, events or localities is
entirely coincidental.

Harper
An imprint of HarperCollins*Publishers*
1 London Bridge Street
London SE1 9GF

www.harpercollins.co.uk

This paperback edition 2010
20

First published in Great Britain by
HarperCollins*Publishers* in 1999

Copyright © Val McDermid 1999

Val McDermid asserts the moral right to
be identified as the author of this work

A catalogue record for this book is
available from the British Library

ISBN: 978-0-00-734466-6

Set in Meridien by Palimpsest Book Production Ltd,
Grangemouth, Stirlingshire
Printed and bound by CPI Group (UK) Ltd, Croydon, CR0 4YY

MIX
Paper from
responsible sources
FSC® C007454

FSC is a non-profit international organization established
to promote the responsible management of the world's forests.
Products carrying the FSC label are independently certified
to assure consumers that they come from forests that are managed
to meet the social, economic and ecological needs
of present and future generations.

Find out more about HarperCollins and the environment at

www.harpercollins.co.uk/green

Acknowledgements

This was not an easy book to write. To delve into a past so recent that it is within many people's living memory is to invite the exposure of one's mistakes. Many people helped me to minimize the opportunities for such embarrassment. Douglas Wynn, true-crime writer, told me the tale that formed the distant seed of inspiration for this book and also helped me with research into historical cases. The staff of the Social Sciences department of Manchester Central Reference Library provided courteous assistance, as did their colleague Jane Mathieson. Without retired inspector Bill Fletcher, I could never have hoped to re-create the world of a county police force in the 1960s. Mark at the *Buxton Advertiser* provided invaluable access to the bound volumes in the cellar, and the *Manchester Evening News* library team also went out of their way to support my quest for authenticity. Dr Sue Black was generous with her forensic experience and Diana Muir supplied crucial assistance that both exposed the fatal flaw in the plot and allowed it to be salvaged. Peter N. Walker also allowed me to pick his brains for period detail and was kind enough to check the finished manuscript for glaring errors. Any remaining mistakes are entirely my responsibility.

I have taken some liberties with the geography of Derbyshire and with the city of Derby itself. The village of Scardale does not exist, although there are several approximations to it in the White Peak.

Writers are a bit like old buildings – we need a lot of shoring up. So thanks to my scaffolding team – Jane and Lisanne, Julia and both Karens, Jai and Paula, Leslie, Mel and, most of all, to Brigid.

To my evil twin; laissez les bon temps rouler, cher.

You shall be taken to the place from whence you came, and thence to a place of lawful execution, and there you shall be hanged by the neck until you be dead, and afterwards your body shall be buried in a common grave within the precincts of the prison wherein you were last confined before your execution; and may the Lord have mercy on your soul.

The formal death sentence of the English legal system

LE PENDU: THE HANGED MAN

Divinatory meaning: The card suggests life in suspension. Reversal of the mind and one's way of life. Transition. Abandonment. Renunciation. The changing of life's forces. Readjustment. Regeneration. Rebirth. Improvement. Efforts and sacrifice may have to be undertaken to succeed towards a goal which may not be reached.

Tarot Cards for Fun and Fortune Telling
S. R. Kaplan

BOOK 1

BOOK I

Introduction

Like Alison Carter, I was born in Derbyshire in 1950. Like her, I grew up familiar with the limestone dales of the White Peak, no stranger to the winter blizzards that regularly cut us off from the rest of the country. It was in Buxton, after all, that snow once stopped play in a county cricket match in June.

So when Alison Carter went missing in December 1963, it meant more to me and my classmates than it can have done to most other people. We knew villages like the one she'd grown up in. We knew the sort of things she'd have done every day. We suffered through similar classes and cloakroom arguments about which of the Fab Four was our favourite Beatle. We imagined we shared the same hopes, dreams and fears. Because of that, right from the word go, we all knew something terrible had happened to Alison Carter, because something we also knew was that girls like her – like us – didn't run away. Not in Derbyshire in the middle of December, anyway.

It wasn't just the thirteen-year-old girls who understood that. My father was one of the hundreds of volunteer searchers who combed the high moorland and

3

the wooded valleys around Scardale, and his grim face when he returned home after a fruitless day scouring the landscape is still sharply etched in my memory.

We followed the hunt for Alison Carter in the news-papers, and every day at school for weeks, someone would be bound to start the speculation rolling. All these years later, I still had more questions for George Bennett than the former policeman could answer.

I have not based my narrative solely on George Bennett's contemporaneous notes and current memories. While researching this book, I made several visits to Scardale and the surrounding area, interviewing many of the people who played a part in the unfolding of Alison Carter's story, gathering their impressions, comparing their accounts of events as they experienced them. I could not have completed this book without the help of Janet Carter, Tommy Clough, Peter Grundy, Charles Lomas, Kathy Lomas and Don Smart. I have taken some artistic licence in ascribing thoughts, emotions and dialogue to people, but these sections are based on my interviews with those of the surviving protagonists who agreed to help me to try to create a truthful picture both of a community and the individuals within it.

Some of what happened on that terrible December night in 1963 will of course never be known. But for everyone who has ever been touched, however remotely, by Alison Carter's life and death, George Bennett's story is a fascinating insight into one of the most heartless crimes of the 1960s.

For too long, it has remained hidden in the shadow of the understandably more notorious Moors Murders. But Alison Carter's fate is no less terrible for coming at the hands of a killer who had but a single victim. And the message of her death is still as important today. If Alison Carter's story tells us one thing, it is that even the gravest of dangers can wear a friendly face.

Nothing can bring Alison Carter back. But reminding the world of what happened to her might prevent others coming to harm. If this book achieves that, both George Bennett and I will feel some satisfaction.

Catherine Heathcote
Longnor, 1998

Prologue

The girl was saying goodbye to her life. And it was no easy farewell.

Like any teenager, she'd always found plenty to complain about. But now that she was about to lose it, this life suddenly seemed very desirable. Now at last she began to understand why her elderly relatives clung so tenaciously to every precious moment, even if it was riven with pain. However bad this life was, the alternative was infinitely worse.

She had even begun to regret things. All the times she'd wished her mother dead; all the times she'd wished that her dream of being a changeling would come true; all the hate she'd expended on the children at school who had called her names for not being one of them; all the fervent longings to be grown up, with these miseries behind her. It all seemed irrelevant now. The only thing that mattered was the uniquely valuable life she was about to lose.

She felt fear, inevitably. Fear of what lay beyond as well as what lay immediately ahead. She'd been brought up to believe in heaven and in its necessary counterweight, hell, the equal and opposite force that held things stable. She had her own very clear ideas of what heaven would be. More than she had ever hoped anything in her short life, she

7

hoped that that was what lay in wait for her, so terrifyingly close now.

But she was desperately afraid that what she was going to was hell. She wasn't so clear about what hell would consist of. She just knew that, compared to everything she'd hated about her life, it would be worse. And given what she knew, that meant it was going to be very bad indeed.

Nevertheless, there was no other possible choice for her. The girl had to say goodbye to her life.

For ever.

PART ONE

The Early Stages

Manchester Evening News,
Tuesday, 10th December 1963, p.3

£100 reward
in boy hunt

Police continued to hunt for 12-year-old John Kilbride today – and hoped that a £100 reward might produce a new lead.

For a local managing director has offered £100 to anyone who gives information which leads directly to the discovery of John who vanished from his home in Smallshaw Lane, Ashton-under-Lyne 18 days ago.

1

Wednesday, 11th December 1963. 7.53 p.m.

'Help me. You've got to help me.' The woman's voice quavered on the edge of tears. The duty constable who had picked up the phone heard a hiccuping gulp, as if the caller was struggling to speak.

'That's what we're here for, madam,' PC Ron Swindells said stolidly. He'd worked in Buxton man and boy for the best part of fifteen years and for the last five, he'd found it hard to shake off a sense that he was reliving the first ten. There was, he reckoned, nothing new under the sun. It was a view that would be irrevocably shattered by the events that were about to unfold around him, but for the moment, he was content to trot out the formula that had served him well until now. 'What seems to be the problem?' he asked, his rich bass voice gently impersonal.

'Alison,' the woman gasped. 'My Alison's not come home.'

'Alison's your lass, is she?' PC Swindells asked, his voice deliberately calm, attempting to reassure the woman.

'She went straight out with the dog when she came

in after school. And she's not come home.' The sharp edge of hysteria forced the woman's voice higher.

Swindells glanced automatically at the clock. Seven minutes before eight. The woman was right to be worried. The girl must have been out of the house near on four hours, and that was no joke at this time of year. 'Could she have gone to visit friends, on the spur of the moment, like?' he asked, knowing already that would have been her first port of call before she lifted the telephone.

'I've knocked every door in the village. She's missing, I'm telling you. Something's happened to my Alison.' Now the woman was breaking down, her words choking out in the intervals between sobs. Swindells thought he heard the rumble of another voice in the background.

Village, the woman had said. 'Where exactly are you calling from, madam?' he asked.

There was the sound of muffled conversation, then a clear masculine voice came on the line, the unmistakable southern accent brisk with authority. 'This is Philip Hawkin from the manor house in Scardale,' he said.

'I see, sir,' Swindells said cautiously. While the information didn't exactly change anything, it did make the policeman slightly wary, conscious that Scardale was off his beat in more ways than the obvious. Scardale wasn't just a different world from the bustling market town where Swindells lived and worked; it had the reputation of being a law unto itself. For such a call to come from Scardale, something well out of the ordinary must have happened.

The caller's voice dropped in pitch, giving the impression that he was talking man to man with Swindells. 'You must excuse my wife. She's rather upset. So emotional, women, don't you find? Look, Officer, I'm sure no harm has come to Alison, but my wife insisted on giving you a call. I'm sure she'll turn up any minute now, and the last thing I want is to waste your time.'

'If you'll just give me some details, sir,' the stolid Swindells said, pulling his pad closer to him.

Detective Inspector George Bennett should have been at home long since. It was almost eight o'clock, well beyond the hour when senior detectives were expected to be at their desks. By rights, he should have been in his armchair stretching his long legs in front of a blazing coal fire, dinner inside him and *Coronation Street* on the television opposite. Then, while Anne cleared away the dishes and washed up, he'd nip out for a pint and a chat in the lounge bar of the Duke of York or the Baker's Arms. There was no quicker way to get the feel of a place than through bar-room conversation. And he needed that head start more than any of his colleagues, being an incomer of less than six months' standing. He knew the locals didn't trust him with much of their gossip, but gradually, they were beginning to treat him like part of the furniture, forgiving and forgetting that his father and grandfather had supped in a different part of the shire.

He glanced at his watch. He'd be lucky to get to the pub tonight. Not that he counted that a great hardship. George wasn't a drinking man. If he hadn't been obliged by his professional responsibilities to keep his finger firmly on the pulse of the town, he wouldn't have entered a pub from one week to the next. He'd much rather have taken Anne dancing to one of the new beat groups that regularly played at the Pavilion

Gardens, or to the Opera House to see a film. Or simply stayed at home. Three months married, and George still couldn't quite believe Anne had agreed to spend the rest of her life with him. It was a miracle that sustained him through the worst times in the job. So far, those had come from tedium rather than the heinous nature of the crimes he encountered. The events of the coming seven months would put that miracle to a tougher test.

That night, however, the thought of Anne at home, knitting in front of the television while she waited for him to return, was far more of a temptation than any pint of bitter. George tore a half-sheet of paper off his scratch pad, placed it among the papers he'd been reading to mark his place, and firmly closed the file, slipping it into his desk drawer. He stubbed out his Gold Leaf cigarette then emptied his ashtray into the bin by his desk, always his last act before he reached for his trench coat and, self-consciously, the wide-brimmed trilby that always made him feel faintly silly. Anne loved it; she was always telling him it made him look like James Stewart. He couldn't see it himself. Just because he had a long face and floppy blond hair didn't make him a film star. He shrugged into the coat, noting that it fitted almost too snugly now, thanks to the quilted lining Anne had made him buy. In spite of the slight straining across his broad cricketer's shoulders, he knew he'd be glad of it as soon as he stepped into the station yard and the teeth of the biting wind that always seemed to be whipping down from the moors through the streets of Buxton.

Taking a last look around his office to check he'd left nothing lying around that the cleaner's eyes shouldn't see, he closed the door behind him. A quick glance showed him there was nobody left in the CID room, so he turned back to indulge a moment's vanity. 'Detective Inspector G. D. Bennett' incised in white letters on a small black plastic plaque. It was something to be proud of, he thought. Not yet thirty, and a DI already. It had been worth every tedious minute of the three years of endless cramming for the law degree that had eased him on to the fast track, one of the first ever graduates to make it to the new accelerated promotion stream in the Derbyshire force. Now, seven years from swearing his oath of allegiance, he was the youngest plain-clothes inspector the county force had ever promoted.

There was no one about to see the lapse of dignity, so he took the stairs at a run. His momentum carried him through the swing doors into the uniformed squad room. Three heads turned sharply as he entered. For a moment, George couldn't think why it was so quiet. Then he remembered. Half the town would be at the memorial service for the recently assassinated President Kennedy, a special Mass open to all denominations. The town had claimed the murdered leader as an adopted native son. After all, JFK had practically been there only months before his death, visiting his sister's grave a handful of miles away in Edensor in the grounds of Chatsworth House. The fact that one of the nurses who had helped surgeons in the fruitless fight for the president's life in a Dallas hospital was a Buxton woman had only strengthened the connection in the eyes of the locals.

'All quiet, then, Sergeant?' he asked.

Bob Lucas, the duty sergeant, frowned and raised

one shoulder in a half-shrug. He glanced at the sheet of paper in his hand. 'We were until five minutes ago, sir.' He straightened up. 'It's probably summat and nowt,' he said. 'A pound to a penny it'll be sorted before I even get there.'

'Anything interesting?' George asked, keeping his voice light. The last thing he wanted was for Bob Lucas to think he was the kind of CID man who treated uniforms as if they were the monkeys and he the organ grinder.

'Missing lass,' Lucas said, proffering the sheet of paper. 'PC Swindells just took the call. They rang here direct, not through the emergency switchboard.'

George tried to picture Scardale on his mental map of the area. 'Do we have a local man there, Sergeant?' he stalled.

'No need. It's barely a hamlet. Ten houses at the most. No, Scardale's covered by Peter Grundy at Longnor. He's only two miles away. But the mother obviously thought this was too important for Peter.'

'And you think?' George was cautious.

'I think I'd better take the area car out to Scardale and have a word with Mrs Hawkin, sir. I'll pick up Peter on the way.' As he spoke, Lucas reached for his cap and straightened it on hair that was almost as black and glossy as his boots. His ruddy cheeks looked as if he had a pair of Ping-Pong balls tucked inside his mouth. Combined with glittering dark eyes and straight black eyebrows, they gave him the look of a painted ventriloquist's dummy. But George had already found out that Bob Lucas was the last person to let anyone else put words in his mouth. He knew that if he asked a question of Lucas, he'd get a straight answer.

16

'Would you mind if I came along?' George asked.

Peter Grundy replaced the phone softly in its cradle. He rubbed his thumb along a jaw sandpaper-rough with the day's stubble. He was thirty-two years old that night in December 1963. Photographs show a fresh-faced man with a narrow jaw and a short, sharp nose accentuated by an almost military haircut. Even smiling, as he was in holiday snaps with his children, his eyes seemed watchful.

Two calls in the space of ten minutes had broken the routine peace of an evening in front of the TV with his wife Meg, the children bathed and in bed. It wasn't that he hadn't taken the first call seriously. When old Ma Lomas, the eyes and ears of Scardale, took the trouble to subject her arthritis to the biting cold by leaving the comfort of her cottage for the phone box on the village green, he had to pay attention. But he'd thought he could wait till eight o'clock and the end of the programme before he did anything about it. After all, Ma might be dressing up the reason for her call as concern over a missing schoolgirl, but Grundy wasn't so sure it wasn't just an excuse to stir things up for the lass's mother. He'd heard the talk and knew there were a few in Scardale as thought Ruth Carter had been a bit quick to jump the broomstick with Philip Hawkin, even if he had been the first man to put roses in her cheeks since her Roy had died.

Then the phone had rung again, bringing a scowl to his wife's face and dragging him out of his comfortable armchair into the chilly hall. This time, he couldn't ignore the summons. Sergeant Lucas from Buxton knew about the missing girl, and he was on his way. As if it wasn't bad enough having Buxton boots tramping all over his ground, he was bringing the Professor with him. It was the first time Grundy or any of his colleagues had ever had to work with somebody that had been to university, and he knew from the gossip on his occasional visits to the sub-division in Buxton that they were none of them comfortable with the idea. He hadn't been slow to join the mutterings about the university of life being the best teacher for a copper. These graduates – you couldn't send them out of a Saturday night on to Buxton marketplace. They'd never have *seen* a pub fight in all their born days, never mind know how to deal with one. As far as Grundy could make out, the only good thing that could be said about DI Bennett was that he could turn a handy bat at cricket. And that wasn't reason enough for Grundy to be happy about him arriving on his patch to upset his carefully nurtured contacts.

With a sigh, he buttoned up his shirt collar. He pulled on his tunic jacket, straightened his cap on his head and picked up his overcoat. He stuck his head round the living room door, a conciliatory smile fastened nervously on his face. 'I've to go to Scardale,' he said.

'Shh,' his wife admonished him crossly. 'It's getting to the exciting bit.'

'Alison Carter's gone missing,' he added, spitefully closing the living room door behind him and hurrying down the hall before she could react. And react she would, he knew only too well. A missing child in Scardale was far too close to home for Longnor not to feel a chill wind on its neck.

*   *   *

George Bennett followed Sergeant Lucas out to the yard where the cars were parked. He'd have far preferred to travel in his own car, a stylish black Ford Corsair as new as his promotion, but protocol demanded he climb into the passenger seat of the liveried Rover and let Lucas drive. As they turned south on the main road through the market square, George tried to stifle the prickle of excitement that had stirred in him when he had heard the words, 'missing lass'. Chances were, as Lucas had rightly pointed out, that it would all come to nothing. More than ninety-five per cent of cases of children reported missing ended in reunion before bedtime, or at worst, before breakfast.

But sometimes, it was a different story. Sometimes, a missing child stayed missing long enough for the certainty to grow that he or she would never come home. Occasionally, that was from choice. More often, it was because the child was dead and the question for the police then became how long it would take them to find a body.

And sometimes, they seemed to vanish as cleanly as if the earth had opened up and gulped them down.

There had been two cases like that within the last six months, both of them less than thirty miles away from Scardale. George always made a careful note of bulletins from outside forces as well as other Derbyshire divisions, and he had paid particular attention to these two missing persons cases because they were just close enough that the children might fetch up on his patch. Dead or alive.

First had been Pauline Catherine Reade. Dark-haired and hazel-eyed, sixteen years old, a trainee confectioner from Gorton, Manchester. Slim build, about five feet tall, wearing a pink and gold dress and a pale-blue coat. Just before eight on Friday, 12th July, she had walked out of the terraced house where she lived with her parents and her younger brother to go to a twist dance. She was never seen again. There had been no trouble at home or at work. She had no boyfriend to fall out with. She had no money to run away with, even if she'd wanted to. The area had been extensively searched and three local reservoirs drained, all without a trace of Pauline. Manchester police had followed up every report of a sighting, but none had led them to the vanished girl.

The second missing child appeared to have nothing in common with Pauline Reade apart from the inexplicable, almost magical nature of his disappearance. John Kilbride, 12 years old, 4ft 10 ins tall with a slim build, dark-brown hair, blue eyes and a fresh complexion. He was wearing a grey check sports jacket, long grey flannel trousers, a white shirt and black, chisel-toed shoes. According to one of the Lancashire detectives George knew from cricket, he wasn't a bright lad, but a pleasant and obliging one. John went to the cinema with some friends on Saturday afternoon, the day after Kennedy died in Dallas. Afterwards, he left them, saying he was going down to the marketplace in Ashton-under-Lyne, where he often earned threepence making tea for the stallholders. The last anyone saw of him, he was leaning against a salvage bin around half past five.

The resulting hunt had been given a last desperate boost only the day before when a local businessman had offered a £100 reward. But nothing appeared to have come of it. That same colleague had remarked to George only the previous Saturday at a police dance, that John Kilbride and Pauline Reade would have left more traces if they'd been abducted by little green men in a flying saucer.

And now a missing girl on his patch. He stared out of the window at the moonlit fields lining the Ashbourne road, their rough pasture crusted with hoarfrost, the dry-stone walls that separated them almost luminous in the silvery light. A thin cloud crossed the moon and in spite of his warm coat, George shivered at the thought of being without shelter on a night like this in so inhospitable a landscape.

Faintly disgusted with himself for allowing his eagerness for a big case to overwhelm the concern for the girl and her family that should have been all that was on his mind, George turned abruptly to Bob Lucas and said, 'Tell me about Scardale.' He took out his cigarettes and offered one to the sergeant, who shook his head.

'I won't, thanks, sir. I'm trying to cut down. Scardale's what you might call the land that time forgot,' he said. In the short spurt of light from George's match, Lucas's face looked grim.

'How do you mean?'

'It's like the Middle Ages down there. There's only one road in and out and it comes to a dead end by the telephone box on the village green. There's the big house, the manor, which is where we're headed. There's about a dozen other cottages and the farm buildings. No pub, no shop, no post office. Mr Hawkin, he's what you might call the squire. He owns every house in Scardale, plus the farm, plus all the land a mile in all directions. Everybody that lives there is his tenant and his employee. It's like he owns them an' all.' The sergeant slowed to turn right off the main

21

road on to the narrow lane that led up past the quarry. 'There's only three surnames in the place, I reckon. You're either a Lomas, a Crowther or a Carter.'

Not, George noticed, a Hawkin. He filed the inconsistency away for later inspection. 'Surely people must leave, to get married, to get work?'

'Oh aye, people leave,' Lucas said. 'But they're always Scardale through and through. They never lose it. And every generation, one or two people do marry out. It's the only way to avoid wedding your cousins. But often as not, them as have married into Scardale come out a few years later looking for a divorce. Funny thing is, they always leave the kids behind them.' He cast a quick glance at George, almost to see how he was taking it.

George inhaled his cigarette and kept his own counsel for a moment. He'd heard of places like this, he'd just never actually been in one. He couldn't begin to imagine what it must be like to be part of a world so self-contained, so limited, where everything about your past, present and future must be information shared with an entire community. 'It's hard to believe a place like that could exist so close to the town. What is it? Seven miles?'

'Eight,' Lucas said. 'It's historical. Look at the pitch of these roads.' He pointed up at the sharp left turn into the village of Earl Sterndale where the houses built by the quarry company to house their workers huddled along the hillside like a rugby scrum. 'Before we had cars with decent engines and proper tarmac roads, it could take you the best part of a day to get from Scardale to Buxton in the winter. That's when the track wasn't blocked with snowdrifts. Folk had to rely on their own. Some places around here, they just never got out of the habit.

'Take this lass, Alison. Even with the school bus, it probably takes her the best part of an hour to get to and from school every day. The county have been trying to get parents to agree to sending children like her as boarders Monday to Friday, to save them the journey. But places like Scardale, they just flat refuse. They don't see it as the county trying to help them. They think it's the authorities trying to take their children off them. There's no reasoning with them.'

The car swung through a series of sharp bends and began to climb a steep ridge, the engine straining as Lucas changed down through the gears. George opened the quarterlight and flicked the remains of his cigarette on to the verge. A draught of frosty air tinged with smoke from a coal fire caught at his throat and he hastily closed the window. 'And yet Mrs Hawkin wasn't slow to call us in.'

'According to PC Swindells, she'd knocked every door in Scardale first, though,' Lucas said drily. 'Don't take me wrong. It's not that they're hostile to the police. They're just . . . not very forthcoming, that's all. They'll want Alison found. So they'll put up with us.'

The car breasted the rise and began the long descent into the village of Longnor. The limestone buildings crouched like sleeping sheep, dirty white in the moonlight, with plumes of smoke rising from every chimney in sight. At the crossroads in the centre of the village, George could see the unmistakable outline of a uniformed officer, stamping his feet on the ground to keep them warm.

'That'll be Peter Grundy,' Lucas said. 'He could have waited indoors.'

'Maybe he's impatient to find out what's happening. It is his patch, after all.'

Lucas grunted. 'More likely his missus giving him earache about having to go out of an evening.'

He braked a little too hard and the car slewed into the kerb. PC Peter Grundy stooped to see who was in the passenger seat, then climbed into the back of the car. 'Evening, Sarge,' he said. 'Sir,' he added, inclining his head towards George. 'I don't like the sound of this at all.'

2

Before Sergeant Lucas could drive off, George Bennett held up one finger. 'Scardale's only two miles away, yes?' Lucas nodded. 'Before we get there, I want to know as much as possible about what we're getting into. Can we give PC Grundy a couple of minutes to give us some more details?'

'A minute or two can't do any harm,' Lucas said, easing the car back into neutral.

Bennett squirmed round in his seat so he could see at least the dim outline of the local man's face. 'So, PC Grundy, you don't think we're going to find Alison Hawkin sitting by the fire getting a tongue-lashing from her mother?'

'It's Carter, sir. Alison Carter. She's not the squire's daughter,' Grundy said with the faint air of impatience of a man who sees a long night of explanations ahead of him.

'Thank you,' George said mildly. 'You've saved me putting my foot in it over that at least. I'd appreciate it if you could give us a quick briefing on the family. Just so I have an idea what we're dealing with.' He held out his cigarettes to Grundy to defuse any idea the man might have that he was being condescended to.

With a quick glance at Bob Lucas, who nodded, Grundy slipped a smoke from the packet and fumbled in his overcoat pocket for a light.

'I've told the inspector the set-up in Scardale,' Lucas said as Grundy lit his cigarette. 'About how the squire owns the village and all the land.'

'Right,' Grundy said through a swathe of smoke. 'Well, until about a year ago, it was Hawkin's uncle who owned Scardale. Old Mr Castleton. There've been Castletons in Scardale Manor as far back as parish records show. Any road, old William Castleton's only son was killed in the war. Flew bombers, he did, but he got unlucky one night over Germany and the last anyone heard was he was missing believed killed in action. His parents had been a good age when young William were born, and there were no other children. So when Mr Castleton died, Scardale went to his sister's son, this Philip Hawkin. A man that nobody in the place had cast eyes on since he was in short trousers.'

'What do we know about him?' Lucas asked.

'His mother, the squire's sister, she grew up here, but she married a wrong 'un when she wed Stan Hawkin. He were in the RAF back then, but that didn't last long. He always claimed he'd taken the rap for one of his senior officers, but the long and short of it was they threw him out for selling tools out the back gate. Any road, the squire took it on himself to see Hawkin right, and he got him a job with an old pal of his, selling cars down south. From all accounts, he never got caught on the fiddle again, but I reckon a leopard never changes its spots, and that's why the family stopped coming up for visits.'

'So what about the son, Philip?' George asked, trying to speed up the story.

Grundy shrugged, his bulk making the car rock. 'He's a good-looking beggar, I'll say that for him. Plenty of charm and smarm, an' all. The women like him. He's always been all right wi' me, but I still wouldn't trust him to hold the dog while I went for a pee.'

'And he married Alison Carter's mother?'

'I was just getting to that,' Grundy said with slow dignity. 'Ruth Carter had been a widow close on six years when Hawkin arrived from down south to take up his inheritance. According to what I've heard, he was right taken with Ruth from the off. She's a fine-looking woman, it's true, but it's not every man who'd be willing to take on another man's child. Mind you, from what I've heard, that were never a problem to him. He never let up on Ruth, though. And she wasn't averse to it, either. He put a sparkle back in her eye and no mistake. They were wed three months after he first showed his face in Scardale. They made a handsome couple.'

'A whirlwind romance, then?' George said. 'I bet that caused a bit of ill feeling, even in a place as tight-knit as Scardale.'

Grundy shrugged. 'I've heard nowt of the sort,' he said. George recognized a stone wall when he saw it. He'd clearly have to earn Grundy's trust before the village bobby would hand over his hard-won local knowledge. That the knowledge was there, George didn't doubt.

'Right then, let's head on into Scardale and see what's what,' he said. Lucas put the car in gear and drove through the village. At a 'no through road' sign, he took a sharp left off the main road. 'Well signposted,' George commented drily.

27

'Anybody that needs to go to Scardale knows the road there, I reckon,' Bob Lucas said as he concentrated on driving up a narrow track that seemed to double back on itself in a series of switchback rises and falls. The twin cones of the headlamps made only a slight impression on the darkness of the road, hemmed in as it was by high banks and uneven dry-stone walls that bulged and leaned at apparently impossible angles against the sky.

'You said when you got in the car that you didn't like the look of this, Grundy,' George said. 'Why's that?'

'She seems like a sensible lass, this Alison. I know who she is – she went to primary school in Longnor. I've got a niece was in the same class and they went on to the grammar school together. While I was waiting for you, I popped in and had a quick word with our Margaret. She reckons Alison were the same as usual today. They came home on the bus together, just like always. Alison were talking about stopping off in Buxton after school one night this week to buy some Christmas presents. Besides, she says, Alison's not one for running. If there's ever owt wrong, she faces it head on. So it looks like whatever's happened to Alison, it's likely not happened from choice.'

Grundy's heavy words sat like a stone in George's stomach. As if to mirror their ominous nature, the roadside walls disappeared, replaced by steep cliffs of limestone, the road weaving through the narrow defile in a route entirely dictated by topography. My God, George thought, it's like a canyon in a Western. We should be wearing stetsons and riding mules, not sitting in a car.

'Just round the next bend, Sergeant,' Grundy said from behind, his breath bitter with tobacco.

Lucas slowed the car to a crawl, following the curve of an overhanging pinnacle of rock. Almost immediately, the road ahead was blocked by a heavy barred gate. George drew his breath in sharply. If he'd been driving, unaware of the obstacle, he'd have crashed, for sure. As Grundy jumped out and trotted to open the gate, George noticed several paint scrapes in a variety of colours along the rock walls on either side of the road. 'They don't exactly welcome strangers with open arms around here, do they?'

Lucas's smile was grim. 'They don't have to. Beyond the gate, technically it's a private road. It's only in the last ten years that it's been asphalted. Before that, nothing that wasn't a tractor or a Land Rover got up or down the Scardale road.' He eased the car forward, waiting on the far side of the gate for Grundy to close up and rejoin them.

They set off again. Within a hundred yards of the gate, the limestone cliffs fell back, sloping away on either side to form a distant horizon. Suddenly they'd emerged from gloom into full moonlight once more. Against the starry sky, it looked to George as if they'd emerged from the players' tunnel into a vast stadium, at least a mile across, with an almost circular ring of steep hills in place of tiers of seats. The arena was no sports field, however. In the eerie light of the moon, George could see fields of rough pasture rising gently from the road that bisected the valley floor. Sheep huddled together against the walls, their breath brief puffs of steam in the freezing air. Darker patches revealed themselves as areas of coppiced woodland as they drove past. George had never seen the like. It was a secret world, hidden and separate.

Now he could see lights, feeble against the moon's silver gleam, but strong enough to outline a straggle of buildings against the pale limestone reefs at the far end of the dale. 'That's Scardale,' Grundy said needlessly from the back seat.

The conglomeration of stone soon resolved itself into distinct houses huddled round a scrubby circle of grass. A single standing stone leaned at an angle in the middle of the green, and a telephone box blazed scarlet at one side, the only vivid splash of colour in Scardale by moonlight. There looked to be about a dozen cottages, none identical, each separated from its neighbours by only a few yards. Most were showing lights behind their curtains. More than once, George caught a glimpse of hands making a gap for faces to peer through, but he refused to be drawn into a sideways look.

At the very back of the green was a sprawl of ill-assorted gables and windows that George assumed must be Scardale Manor. He wasn't sure quite what he'd been expecting, but it wasn't this glorified farm-house that looked like it had been thrown together over several hundred years by people who'd had more need than taste. Before he could say anything, the front door opened and an oblong of yellow light spilled out on to the yard in front of it. Against the light a woman's form was silhouetted.

As the car drew to a halt, the woman took a couple of impulsive steps towards them. Then a man appeared at her shoulder and put an arm round her. Together they waited while the police officers approached, George hanging back slightly to let Bob Lucas take the lead. He could use the time Lucas was taking for the introductions to note his first impressions of Alison Carter's mother and stepfather.

Ruth Hawkin looked at least ten years older than his Anne, which would put her in her late thirties. He reckoned she was about five feet three, with the sturdy build of a woman used to hard work. Her mid-brown hair was pulled back in a ponytail, which emphasized the drawn look around grey-blue eyes that showed signs of recent weeping. Her skin looked weather-beaten but her pursed lips showed faint traces of lipstick in their cracks. She wore an obviously hand-knitted twin set in a blue heather mixture over a pleated grey tweed skirt. Her legs were encased in ribbed woollen stockings, her feet shod sensibly in ankle boots with a zip up the front. It was hard to square what he was seeing with Peter Grundy's description of Ruth as a good-looking woman. George would not have looked twice at her in a bus queue except for her obvious distress, which showed in the tightness of her body, arms crossed defensively across her chest. He assumed it had also drained her attractiveness from her.

The man standing behind her seemed far more at ease. The hand that wasn't lightly touching his wife's shoulder was thrust casually into the pocket of a dark-brown cardigan with suede leather facings. He wore grey flannel trousers whose turn-ups flopped over well-worn leather slippers. Philip Hawkin hadn't been out knocking on village doors with his wife, George noted.

Hawkin was as handsome as his wife was ordinary. A couple of inches under six feet, he had straight dark hair swept back from a widow's peak, lightly brilliantined to hold it in place. His face reminded George of a shield, with a broad, square forehead tapering to a pointed chin. Straight brows over dark-brown eyes were like an heraldic device; a slender nose seemed to point to a mouth shaped so that it appeared always to be on the point of a smile.

All of this George itemized and filed away in his memory. Bob Lucas was still speaking. 'So if we could come in and take some details, we can get a clearer picture of what's happened.' He paused expectantly.

Hawkin spoke for the first time, his voice unmis-takably alien to the Derbyshire Peaks. 'Of course, of course. Come inside, officers. I'm sure she's going to turn up safe and well, but it doesn't hurt to follow the procedures, does it?' He dropped his hand to the small of Ruth's back and steered her back into the house. She seemed numb, certainly incapable of taking any initiative. 'I'm sorry you've been dragged out on such a cold night,' Hawkin added smoothly as he crossed the room.

George followed Lucas and Grundy across the thresh-old and into a farmhouse kitchen. The floors were stone flagged, the walls rough stone brightened with a coat of white distemper that had discoloured unevenly, depending on its proximity to the wood-burning stove and the electric cooker. A dresser and several cupboards of differing heights painted hospital green ranged round the walls, and a pair of deep stone sinks were set under the windows that looked out towards the end of the dale. Another pair of windows gave a view of the vil-lage green, the phone box bright against the darkness. Various pans and kitchen implements hung from the black beams that crossed the room a few feet apart. It smelled of smoke, cabbage and animal fat.

Without waiting for anyone else, Hawkin sat down immediately in a carving chair at the head of a scrubbed wooden table. 'Make the men some tea, Ruth,' he said.

'That's very kind of you, sir,' George interjected as the woman lifted a kettle off the stove. 'But I'd rather we pressed on. Where it's a matter of a missing child, we try not to waste any time. Mrs Hawkin, if you could sit down and tell us what you know.'

Ruth glanced at Hawkin as if seeking his permission. His eyebrows twitched upwards, but he nodded acquiescence. She pulled out a chair and sank into it, folding her arms on the table in front of her. George sat down opposite her, with Lucas beside him. Grundy unbuttoned his overcoat and lowered himself into the carver at the opposite end to Hawkin. He took his pocketbook from his tunic and flipped it open. Licking the end of his pencil, he looked up expectantly.

'How old is Alison, Mrs Hawkin?' George asked gently.

The woman cleared her throat. 'Thirteen past. Her birthday's in March.' Her voice cracked, as if something inside her were splintering.

'And had there been any trouble between you?'

'Steady on, Inspector,' Hawkin protested. 'What do you mean, trouble? What are you suggesting?'

'I'm not suggesting anything, sir,' George said. 'But Alison's at a difficult age, and sometimes young girls get things out of all proportion. A perfectly normal ticking-off can feel like the end of the world to them.

I'm trying to establish whether there are any grounds for supposing Alison might have run away.'

Hawkin leaned back in his seat with a frown. He reached behind him, tipping the chair back on two legs. He grabbed a packet of Embassy and a small chrome lighter from the dresser and proceeded to light a cigarette without offering the packet to anyone else. 'Of course she's run away,' he said, a smile softening the hard line of his eyebrows. 'That's what teenagers do. They do it to get you worried, to get their own back for some imagined slight. You know what I mean,' he continued with a man-of-the-world air that included the police officers. 'Christmas is coming. I remember one year I went missing for hours. I thought my mum would be so glad to see me back home safe that I'd be able to talk her into buying me a bike for Christmas.' His smile turned rueful. 'All I got was a sore backside. Mark my words, Inspector, she'll turn up before morning, expecting the fatted calf.'

'She's not like that, Phil,' Ruth said plaintively. 'I'm telling you, something's happened to her. She wouldn't worry us like this.'

'What happened this afternoon, Mrs Hawkin?' George asked, taking out his own cigarettes and offering them to her. With a tight nod of gratitude, she took one, her work-reddened fingers trembling. Before he could get his matches out, Hawkin had leaned across to light it. George lit his own cigarette and waited while she composed herself to respond.

'The school bus drops Alison and two of her cousins at the road end about quarter past four. Somebody from the village always goes up and picks them up, so she gets in about the half-hour. She came in at the usual time. I was here in the kitchen, peeling vegetables for the tea. She gave me a kiss and said she were off out with the dog. I said did she not want a cup of tea first, but she said she'd been shut in all day and she wanted a run with the dog. She often did that. She hated being indoors all day.' Ambushed by the memory, Ruth faltered then stopped.

'Did you see her, Mr Hawkin?' George asked, more to give Ruth a break than because he cared about the answer.

'No. I was in my darkroom. I lose all sense of time when I'm in there.'

'I hadn't realized you were a photographer,' George said, noticing Grundy shift in his seat.

'Photography, Inspector, is my first love. When I was a lowly civil servant, before I inherited this place from my uncle, it was never more than a hobby. Now, I've got my own darkroom, and this last year, I've become semi-professional. Some portraiture, of course, but mostly landscapes. Some of my picture postcards are on sale in Buxton. The Derbyshire light has a remarkable clarity.' Hawkin's smile was dazzling this time.

'I see,' George said, wondering at a man who could think about the quality of light when his stepdaughter was missing on a freezing December night. 'So you had no idea that Alison had come in and gone out?'

'No, I heard nothing.'

'Mrs Hawkin, was Alison in the habit of visiting anyone when she went out with the dog? A neighbour? You mentioned cousins that she goes to school with.'

Ruth shook her head. 'No. She'd just go up through the fields to the coppice then back. In summer, she'd go further, up through the woodland to where the Scarlaston rises. There's a fold in the hills, you can hardly see it till you're on it, but you can cut through there, along the river bank, into Denderdale. But she'd never go that far of a winter's night.' She sighed. 'Besides, I've been right round the village. Nobody's seen hide nor hair of her since she crossed the fields.'

'What about the dog?' Grundy asked. 'Has the dog come back?'

It was a countryman's question, George thought. He'd have got there eventually, but not as fast as Grundy.

Ruth shook her head. 'She's not. But if Alison had had an accident, Shep wouldn't have left her. She'd have barked, but she wouldn't have left her. A night like tonight, you'd hear Shep anywhere in the dale. You've been out there. Did you hear her?'

'That's why I wondered,' Grundy said. 'The silence.'

'Can you give us a description of what Alison was wearing?' asked the ever-practical Lucas.

'She had on a navy-blue duffel coat over her school uniform.'

'Peak Girls' High?' Lucas asked.

Ruth nodded. 'Black blazer, maroon cardie, white shirt, black and maroon tie and maroon skirt. She's wearing black woolly tights and black sheepskin boots that come up to mid-calf. You don't run away in your school uniform,' she burst out passionately, tears welling up in her eyes. She brushed them away angrily with the back of her hand. 'Why are we sitting here like it was Sunday teatime? Why aren't you out looking for her?'

George nodded. 'We're going to, Mrs Hawkin. But

we needed to get the details straight so that we don't waste our efforts. How tall is Alison?'

'She's near on my height now. Five foot two, three, something like that. She's slim built, just starting to look like a young woman.'

'Have you got a recent photograph of Alison that we can show our officers?' George asked.

Hawkin pushed his chair back, the legs shrieking on the stone flags. He pulled open the drawer of the kitchen table and took out a handful of five-by-three prints. 'I took these in the summer. About four months ago.' He leaned across and spread them out in front of George. The face that looked up at him from five coloured head-and-shoulders portraits was not one he'd forget in a hurry.

Nobody had warned him that she was beautiful. He felt his breath catch in his throat as he looked down at Alison. Collar-length hair the colour of set honey framed an oval face sprinkled with pale freckles. Her blue eyes had an almost Slavic set to them, set wide apart on either side of a neat, straight nose. Her mouth was generous, her smile etching a single dimple in her left cheek. The only imperfection was a slanting scar that sliced through her right eyebrow, leaving a thin white line through the dark hairs. In each shot, her pose varied slightly, but her candid smile never altered.

He glanced up at Ruth, whose face had imperceptibly softened at the sight of her daughter's face. Now he could see what had attracted Hawkin's eye to the farmer's widow. Without the strain that had stripped gentleness from Ruth's face, her beauty was as obvious as her daughter's. With the ghost of a smile touching her lips, it was hard to imagine he'd believed her plain.

'She's a lovely girl,' George murmured. He got to his feet, picking up the photographs. 'I'd like to hang on to these for the time being.' Hawkin nodded. 'Sergeant, if I could have a word outside?'

The two men stepped from the warm kitchen into the icy night air. As he closed the door behind them, George heard Ruth say in a defeated voice, 'I'll make tea now.'

'What do you think?' George asked. He didn't need Lucas's confirmation to know that this was serious, but if he assumed authority now over the uniformed man, it was tantamount to saying he thought the girl had been murdered or seriously assaulted. And in spite of his growing conviction that that was what had happened, he had a superstitious dread that acting as if it were so might just make it so.

'I think we should get the dog handler out fast as you like, sir. She could have had a fall. She could be lying injured. If she's been hit in a rock fall, the dog could have been killed.' He looked at his watch. 'We've got four extra uniformed officers on duty at the Kennedy memorial service. If we're quick, we can catch them before they go off duty and get them out here as well as every man we can spare.' Lucas reached past him to open the door. 'I'll need to use their phone. No point in trying the radio here. You'd get better reception down the bottom of Markham Main pit shaft.'

'OK, Sergeant. You organize what you can by way of a search party. I'm going to call in DS Clough and DC Cragg. They can make a start on a door-to-door in the village, see if we can narrow down who saw her last and where.' George felt a faint fluttering in his stomach, like first-night nerves. Of course, that's exactly what it was. If his fears were right, he was standing on the threshold of the first major case he'd been entirely responsible for. He'd be judged by this for the rest of his career. If he didn't uncover what had happened to Alison Carter, it would be an albatross round his neck for ever.

3

Wednesday, 11th December 1963. 9.07 p.m.

The dog's breath swirled and hung in the night air as
if it had a life of its own. The Alsatian sat calmly on
its haunches, ears pricked, alert eyes scanning Scardale
village green. PC Dusty Miller, the dog handler, stood
by his charge, one hand absently fingering the short
tan and brindle hair between its ears. 'Prince'll need
some clothes and shoes belonging to the lass,' he told
Sergeant Lucas. 'The more she's worn them, the better.
We can manage without, but it'd help the dog.'

'I'll have a word with Mrs Hawkin,' George interjected before Lucas could assign anyone to the task. It
wasn't that he thought a uniformed officer would be
deficient in tact; he simply wanted another chance to
observe Alison Carter's mother and her husband.

He walked into the warm fug of the kitchen, where
Hawkin was still sitting at the table, still smoking. Now
he had a cup of tea in front of him, as did the WPC who
sat at the other end of the table. They both looked up as
he entered. Hawkin raised his eyebrows in a question.
George shook his head. Hawkin pursed his lips and
rubbed a hand over his eyes. George was pleased to see

40

the man finally showing some signs of concern for his stepdaughter's fate. That Alison might be in real danger seemed finally to have penetrated his self-absorption.

Ruth Hawkin was at the sink, her hands among the suds in the washing-up bowl. But she wasn't doing the dishes. She was motionless, staring intently into the unbroken dark of the night. The moonlight barely penetrated the area behind the house; this far down the valley, the tall limestone reefs were close enough to cut off most of it. There was nothing beyond the window but a faint, dark outline against the grey-white of the cliffs. An outbuilding of some sort, George guessed. He wondered if it had been searched yet. He cleared his throat. 'Mrs Hawkin . . .'

Slowly, she turned. Even in the brief time they'd been in Scardale, she seemed to have aged, the skin tightening across her cheekbones and her eyes sinking back into her head. 'Yes?'

'We need some of Alison's clothes. To help the tracker dog.'

She nodded. 'I'll fetch something.'

'The dog handler suggested some shoes, and something she's worn a few times. A jumper or a coat, I suppose.'

Ruth walked out of the room with the automatic step of the sleepwalker. 'I wonder if I could use your phone again,' George asked.

'Be my guest,' Hawkin said, waving his hand towards the hallway.

George followed Ruth through the door and made for the table where the old-fashioned black Bakelite phone squatted on a piecrust table next to a wedding photograph of a radiant Ruth with her new husband. If Hawkin hadn't been so handsomely unmistakable,

George doubted he would have identified the bride.

As soon as he closed the door behind him, he felt icy coldness grip him. If the girl was used to living in temperatures like this, she'd stand a better chance outside, he thought. He could see Ruth Hawkin disappear round the turn in the stairs as he lifted the receiver and began to dial. Four rings, then it was picked up. 'Buxton four-two-two,' the familiar voice said, instantly soothing his anxieties.

'Anne, it's me. I've had to go out to Scardale on a case. A missing girl.'

'The poor parents,' Anne said instantly. 'And poor you, having that to deal with on a night like this.'

'It's the girl I'm worried about. Obviously, I'm going to be late. In fact, depending on what happens, I might not be back at all tonight.'

'You push yourself too hard, George. It's bad for you, you know. If you're not back by bedtime, I'll make up some sandwiches and leave them in the fridge so there's something for you to eat. They'd better be gone by the time I get up,' she added, her scolding only half teasing.

If Ruth Hawkin hadn't reappeared on the stairs, he'd have told Anne how much he loved the way she cared about him. Instead, he simply said, 'Thanks. I'll be in touch when I can,' and replaced the receiver. He moved to the foot of the stairs to meet Ruth, who was clutching a small bundle to her chest. 'We're doing all we can,' he said, knowing it was inadequate.

'I know,' she said. She opened her arms to reveal a pair of slippers and a crumpled flannelette pyjama jacket. 'Will you give these to the dog man?'

George took the clothes, noting with a stab of nameless

emotion how pathetic the circumstances had rendered the blue velveteen slippers and the pink sprigged jacket. Holding them gingerly, to avoid contamination with his scent, George walked back through the kitchen and out into the night air. Wordlessly, he handed the items to Miller and watched while the dog handler spoke soft words of command to Prince, offering the garments to its long nose.

The dog raised its head delicately, as if scenting some culinary delight on the wind. Then it started nosing the ground by the front door, its head swinging to and fro in long arcs, inches above the ground. Every few feet, it gave a snorting snuffle then looked up, thrusting its nostrils towards Alison's clothes and her scent, as if reminding itself what it was supposed to be seeking. Dog and handler moved forward in tandem, covering every inch of the path from the kitchen door. Then, at the very edge of the dirt track that skirted the back of the village green, the Alsatian suddenly stiffened. As rigid as a child playing statues, Prince paused for long seconds, hungrily drinking in the scent from the scrubby grass. Then in one smooth, liquid motion, the dog moved swiftly across the grass, its body close to the ground, its nose seeming to pull it forward in a low lope.

PC Miller quickened his step to keep up with the dog. On a nod from Sergeant Lucas, four of the uniformed men who'd arrived minutes after the dog team fell into step behind them, fanning out to cover the ground with the cones of their torch beams. George followed them for a few yards, not certain whether he should join their party or wait for the two CID officers he'd summoned but who hadn't arrived yet.

Their path touched the village green at a tangent

43

then, via a stone stile, into a narrow salient between two cottages that gave out into a larger field. As the dog led them unwaveringly across the field, George heard a car grumbling down the road into the village. As it pulled up behind the cluster of police vehicles already there, he recognized the Ford Zephyr of Detective Sergeant Tommy Clough. He threw a quick glance over his shoulder at the tracker team. Their torches gave their positions away. It wouldn't be hard to catch up with them. He turned on his heel, strode over to the bulky black car and yanked open the driver's door. The familiar ruddy harvest moon face of his sergeant grinned up at him. 'How do, sir,' Clough said on a wave of beer fumes.

'We've got work to do, Clough,' George said shortly. Even with a drink in him, Clough would still do a better job than most officers sober. The passenger door slammed and Detective Constable Gary Cragg slouched round the front of the car. He'd watched too many Westerns, George had decided the first time the lanky DC had swaggered into his line of vision. Cragg would have looked fine in a pair of sheepskin chaps with matching Colt pistols slung low on his narrow hips and a ten-gallon hat tipped over his hooded grey eyes. In a suit, he had the air of a man who's not quite sure how he got where he is, but wishes with all his heart he was somewhere else.

'Missing girl, is that right, sir?' he drawled. Even his slow voice would have been more at home in a saloon, asking the bartender for a shot of bourbon. The only saving grace, as far as George could see, was that Cragg showed no signs of being a maverick.

'Alison Carter. Thirteen years old,' George briefed

them as Clough unfolded his chunky body from under the steering wheel. He gestured over his shoulder with his thumb. 'She lives in the manor house, stepdaughter of the squire. Her and her mother are Scardale natives, though.'

Clough snorted and clamped a tweed cap over his tight brown curls. 'She'll not have had the sense to get lost, then. You know about Scardale, don't you? They've all been marrying their cousins for generations. Most of them would be hard pressed to find their backsides in a toilet.'

'Alison managed to make it to grammar school in spite of her handicaps,' George pointed out. 'Which, as I recall, is more than we can say for you, Sergeant Clough.' Clough glared at the boss who was three years his junior, but said nothing. 'Alison came home from school at the usual time,' George continued. 'She went out with the dog. Neither of them's been seen since. That was the best part of five hours ago. I want you to do a door-to-door round the village. I want to know who was the last person to see her, where and when.'

'It'll have been dark by the time she went out,' Cragg said.

'All the same, somebody might have seen her. I'm going to try and catch up with the dog handler, so that's where I'll be if you need me. OK?' As he turned away, a sudden chill thought struck him. He looked round the horseshoe of houses huddled round the green, then swung back to face Clough and Cragg. 'And every house – I want you to check the kids are where they should be. I don't want some mother having hysterics tomorrow morning when she discovers her kid's missing too.'

He didn't wait for an answer, but set off for the stile. Just before he got there, he checked his stride and turned back to find Sergeant Lucas in the middle of directing the remaining six uniformed officers he'd managed to rustle up from somewhere. 'Sergeant,' George said. 'There's an outbuilding you can see from the kitchen window of the house. I don't know if anyone's checked it yet, but it might be worth taking a look, just in case she didn't go for her usual walk.'

Lucas nodded and gestured with his head to one of the constables. 'See what you can see, lad.' He nodded to George. 'Much obliged, sir.'

Kathy Lomas stood at her window and watched the darkness swallow the tall man in the mac and the trilby. Illuminated by the headlights of the big car that had just rolled to a halt by the phone box, he'd borne a remarkable resemblance to James Stewart. It should have been a reassuring thought, but somehow it only made the evening's events all the more unreal.

Kathy and Ruth were cousins, separated by less than a year, connected by blood on both maternal and paternal sides. They had grown into women and mothers side by side. Kathy's son Derek had been born a mere three weeks after Alison. The families' histories were inextricably intertwined. So when Kathy, alerted by Derek, had walked into Ruth's kitchen to find her cousin pacing anxiously, chain-smoking and fretting, she'd felt the stab of fear as strongly as if it had been her own child who was absent.

They'd gone round the village together, at first convinced they would find Alison warming herself at someone else's fire, oblivious to the passing of time, remorseful at causing her mother worry. But as they drew blank after blank, conviction had shrivelled to hope, then hope to despair.

Kathy stood at the darkened window of Lark Cottage's tiny front room, watching the activity that had suddenly bloomed in the dismal December night. The plain-clothes detective who had been driving the car, the one who looked like a Hereford bull with his curly poll and his broad head, pushed his car coat up to scratch his backside, said something to his colleague, then started towards her front door, his eyes seeming to meet hers in the darkness.

Kathy moved to the door, glancing towards the kitchen where her husband was trying to concentrate on finishing a marquetry picture of fishing boats in harbour. 'The police are here, Mike,' she called.

'Not before time,' she heard him grumble.

She opened the door just as the Hereford bull lifted his hand to knock. His startled look turned into a smile as he took in Kathy's generous curves, still obvious even beneath her wraparound apron. 'You'll have come about Alison,' she said.

'You're right, missus,' he said. 'I'm Detective Sergeant Clough, and this is Detective Constable Cragg. Can we come in a minute?'

Kathy stepped back and let them pass, allowing Clough to brush against her breasts without complaint. 'The kitchen's straight ahead. You'll find my husband in there,' she said coldly.

She followed them and leaned against the range, trying to warm herself against the cold fear inside, waiting for the men to introduce themselves and settle

47

round the table. Clough turned to her. 'Have you seen Alison since she got home from school?'

Kathy took a deep breath. 'Aye. It was my turn to pick up the kids off the school bus. In the winter, one of us always drives up to the lane end to collect them.'

'Was there anything different about Alison that you noticed?' Clough asked.

Kathy thought for a moment, then shook her head. 'Nowt.' She shrugged. 'She were just the same as usual. Just . . . Alison. She said cheerio and walked off up the path to the manor. Last I saw of her she was walking through the door, shouting hello to her mum.'

'Did you see any strangers about? Either on the road or up at the lane end?'

'I never noticed anybody.'

'I believe you went round the village with Mrs Hawkin?' Clough asked.

'I wasn't going to leave her on her own, was I?' Kathy demanded belligerently.

'How did you come to know Alison was missing?'

'It was our Derek. He's not been doing as well as he should have been at school, so I took it on myself to make sure he was doing his homework properly. Instead of letting him go off with Alison and their cousin Janet when they got home from school, I've been keeping him in.'

'She makes him sit at the kitchen table and do all the work his teachers have set him before she'll let him loose with the girls. Waste of bloody time, if you ask me. The lad's only going to be a farmer like me,' Mike Lomas interrupted, his voice a low rumble.

'Not if I have anything to do with it,' Kathy said grimly. 'I tell you what's a waste of time. It's that record player Phil Hawkin bought Alison. Derek and Janet are never away from there, listening to the latest records. Derek was desperate to get over to Alison's tonight. She's just got the new Beatles number one, "I Want To Hold Your Hand". But it was after tea before I let him out. It must have been just before seven. He came back within five minutes, saying Alison had gone out with Shep and hadn't come home. Of course, I went straight over to see what was what.

'Ruth was up to high doh. I told her she should check with everybody in the village, just in case Alison had popped in to see somebody and lost track of the time. She's always sitting with old Ma Lomas, her and her cousin Charlie keeping the old witch company, listening to her memories of the old days. Once Ma gets going, you could sit all night. She's some storyteller, Ma, and our Alison loves her tales.'

She settled herself more comfortably against the range. Clough could see she was on a roll, and he decided just to let her run and see where her story took them. He nodded. 'Go on, Mrs Lomas.'

'Well, we were just about to set off when Phil came in. He said he'd been in his darkroom, messing about with his photographs, and he'd only just noticed the time. He was going on about where was his tea and where was Alison? I told him there were more important things to think about than his belly, but Ruth dished him up a plate of the hotpot she'd had cooking. Then we left him to it and went knocking doors.' She came to a sudden halt.

'So you never saw Alison again after she got out of the car coming back from school?'

'Land Rover,' Mike Lomas growled.

'Sorry?'

'It were a Land Rover, not a car. Nobody has cars down here,' he said contemptuously.

'No, I've not seen her since she walked in the kitchen door,' Kathy said. 'But you're going to find her, aren't you? I mean, that's your job. You are going to find her?'

'We're doing our best.' It was Cragg who trotted out the formulaic placebo.

Before she could utter the angry retort Tommy Clough could see coming, he spoke quickly. 'What about your lad, Mrs Lomas? Is he where he should be?'

Her mouth dropped open in shock. 'Derek? Why wouldn't he be?'

'Maybe the same reason Alison's not where she should be.'

'You can't say that!' Mike Lomas jumped to his feet, his cheeks flaming scarlet, his eyes tight with anger.

Clough smiled, spreading his hands in a conciliatory gesture. 'Nay, don't take me wrong. All I meant was, you should check in case something's happened to him an' all.'

By the time George got over the stile, the lights from the tracker team's torches were no more than a hazy wavering in the distance. He guessed they had entered some woodland by the way the yellow beams seemed suddenly to disappear and reappear at random. Switching on the torch he'd borrowed from the police Land Rover that had brought some of the men over from Buxton, he hurried across the uneven tufts of coarse grass as quickly as he could.

The trees loomed up sooner than he'd expected. At first, all he could see was undisturbed undergrowth, but swinging the torch to and fro soon revealed a narrow path where the earth was packed hard. George plunged into the woodland, trying to balance haste against caution. The torch beam sent crazy shadows dancing off in every direction, forcing him to concentrate harder on the path than he'd had to do in the field. Frosted leaves crunched under his feet, the occasional twig whipped his face or brushed his shoulder, and everywhere the decaying mushroomy smell of the woodland assailed him. Every twenty yards or so, he snapped off his torch to check his bearings against the lights ahead. Absolute darkness swallowed him, but it was hard to resist the feeling that there were hidden eyes staring at him, following his every move. It was a relief to snap his torch on again. A few minutes into the wood, he realized the lights before him had stopped moving. Putting on a spurt that nearly sent him flying over a tree root, he almost collided with a uniformed constable hurriedly retracing his steps.

'Have you found her?' George gasped.

'No such luck, sir. We have found the dog, though.'

'Alive?'

The man nodded. 'Aye. But she's been tied up.'

'In silence?' George asked incredulously.

'Somebody taped her muzzle shut, sir. Poor beast could barely manage a whimper. PC Miller sent me back to fetch Sergeant Lucas before we did owt.'

'I'll take responsibility now,' George said firmly. 'But go back anyway and tell Sergeant Lucas what's happened. I think it might be wise to keep people out of this piece of woodland until daylight. Whatever's happened to Alison Carter, there might be evidence that we're destroying right now.'

The constable nodded and took off along the path at a trot. 'Bloody mountain goats they breed around here,' George muttered as he blundered on down the path.

The clearing he emerged into was a chiaroscuro of torchlight and strangely elongated shadows. At the far end, a black and white collie strained against a rope tied round a tree. Liquid brown irises stood out against the white of its bulging eyes. The dull pink of the elastoplast that was wound round its muzzle looked incongruous in so pastoral a setting. George was aware of the stares of the uniformed men, looking him over speculatively.

'I think we should put that dog out of its misery. What do you say, PC Miller?' he asked, directing his question to the dog handler, who was methodically covering the clearing with Prince.

'I don't think she'll argue with you on that, sir,' Miller said. 'I'll take Prince out of the way so he won't upset her.' With a jerk on the dog's leash and a word of command, he made for the far side of the clearing. George noticed his dog was still casting around as he'd done outside the house earlier.

'Has he lost the scent?' he asked, suddenly concerned about more important matters than a dog's discomfort.

'Looks like the trail ends here,' the dog handler said. 'I've been right round the clearing twice, and down the path in the opposite direction. But there's nothing.'

'Does that mean she was carried out of here?' George asked, a cold tremor twitching upwards from his stomach.

'Like as not,' Miller said grimly. 'One thing's for sure. She didn't walk out of here unless she turned straight round and walked back to the house. And if that's what she did, why tie up the bitch and muzzle her?'

'Maybe she wanted to creep up on her mum? Or her stepdad?' one of the constables hazarded.

'The dog wouldn't have barked at them, would she? So there'd be no need to muzzle her, or leave her behind,' Miller said.

'Unless she thought one or other of them might be with a stranger,' George said, half under his breath.

'Aye well, my money says she never left this clearing under her own steam.' Miller spoke with finality as he walked his dog down the path.

George approached the dog cautiously. The whimper in the dog's throat turned to a soft grumble. What had Ruth Hawkin called it? Shep, that was it. 'OK, Shep,' he said gently, holding his hand out so the dog could sniff his fingers. The growl died away. George hitched up his trousers and kneeled down, the frozen ground uneven and ungenerous beneath his knees. Automatically, he noticed the elastoplast was the thicker kind, from a roll two inches wide with a half-inch band of lint bulging up the middle of it. 'Steady, girl,' he said, one hand gripping the thick hair at the scruff of the dog's neck to hold her head still. With his other hand, he picked at the end of the elastoplast till he had freed enough to pull clear. He looked up. 'One of you, come over here and hold the dog's head while I get this stuff off.'

One of the constables straddled the nervous collie and grasped her head firmly. George gripped the end of the elastoplast strip and pulled it as hard as he could. Inside a minute, he'd yanked the last of it free, narrowly avoiding the snapping teeth of the collie, panicking in response to having chunks of her fur ripped away with the tape. The constable behind her hastily jumped clear as she swung round to try her chances with him. As soon as she realized her mouth was free, Shep dropped to the ground and began to bark furiously at the men. 'What do we do now, sir?' one of the constables asked.

'I'm going to untie her and see where she wants to take us,' George said, sounding more confident than he felt. He walked forward cautiously, but the dog showed no sign of wanting to attack him. He took out his penknife and sawed through the rope. It was easier than trying to untie it while the dog was straining against it. And it had the advantage of preserving the knot, just in case there was anything distinctive about it. George thought not; it looked pretty much like a standard reef knot to him.

Instantly, Shep lunged forward. Taken by surprise, George gouged a slice out of his thumb as he tried to hold on to the sheepdog. 'Damn!' he exploded as the rope whirled through his fingers, burning the skin where it touched. One of the constables attempted to grab the rope as the dog fled, but failed. George clutched his bleeding hand and watched helplessly as the dog raced down the path Miller and Prince had taken from the clearing.

Moments later, there was the sound of a scuffle and Miller's voice shouting sternly, 'Sit.' Then silence. Then an eerie howling split the night.

Groping in his pocket for a handkerchief, George followed the dog's path. A dozen yards into the wood, he came upon Miller and the two dogs. Prince lay on the ground, his muzzle between his paws. Shep sat on the ground, her head lifted towards the sky, her mouth opening and closing in a long series of heart-stopping wails. Miller held the rope, securing the straining collie. 'She seems to want to go this way,' Miller said, gesturing with his head down the path away from the clearing.

'Let's follow her, then,' George said. He wrapped his bleeding thumb with the handkerchief then took the rope from the handler. 'Come on, girl,' he encouraged the collie. 'Show me.' He shook the rope.

Immediately, Shep bounded to her feet and set off down the trail, tail wagging. They wove through the trees for a couple of minutes, then the track emerged from the trees on to the banks of a narrow, fast-flowing stream. The dog promptly sat down and looked back at him, her tongue hanging out and her eyes bewildered.

'That'd be the Scarlaston,' Miller's voice said behind him. 'I knew it rose in these parts. Funny river. I've heard tell it just sort of seeps out of the ground. If we have a dry summer, it sometimes vanishes altogether.'

'Where does it lead?' George asked.

'I'm not sure. I think it flows either into the Derwent or the Manifold, I can't remember which. You'd have to look at a map for that.'

George nodded. 'So if Alison was carried out of the clearing, we'd lose the trail here anyway.' He sighed and turned away, guiding his torch beam over his watch. It was almost quarter to ten. 'There's nothing more we can do in darkness. Let's head back to the village.'

He practically had to drag Shep away from the Scarlaston's edge. As they made their slow progress back to Scardale, George fretted about Alison Carter's disappearance. Nothing made sense. If someone was ruthless enough to kidnap a young girl, surely they wouldn't show mercy to a dog? Especially a dog as lively as Shep. He couldn't imagine a dog with the collie's spirit meekly submitting to having elastoplast tightly wound round its muzzle. Unless it had been Alison who'd done the deed?

If it had been Alison, had she acted on her own initiative or had she been forced to silence her own dog? And if she'd done it for her own ends, where was she now? If she'd been going to run away, why not take the dog with her for protection, at least until dawn broke? The more he thought about it, the less he understood.

George trudged out of the woods and through the field, the reluctant dog trailing at his heels. George found Sergeant Lucas conferring with PC Grundy in the light of a hurricane lamp hanging from the back of the Land Rover. Briefly, he explained the scenario in the woods. 'There's no point in trampling through there in the dark,' he said. 'I reckon the best we can do is put a couple of men on guard and at first light, we search the woodland inch by inch.'

Both men looked at him as if he'd gone mad. 'With respect, sir, if you're intending to keep the villagers out of the wood, there's not a lot of point in leaving a couple of men to catch frostbite in the field,' Lucas said wearily. 'The locals know the lie of the land far better than we do. If they want to get into those woods, they will, and we'll never know about it. Besides, I don't think there's a soul in the place who hasn't already volunteered to help searching. If we tell them what's what, they'll be the last ones to destroy any possible clues.'

He had a point, George realized. 'What about out-siders?'

Lucas shrugged. 'All we have to do is post a guard on the gate on the road. I don't imagine anybody'll be keen enough to hike in from the next dale. It's a treacherous path up the Scarlaston banks at the best of times, never mind on a frosty winter night.'

'I'm happy to trust your judgement, Sergeant,' George said. 'I take it your men have been searching the houses and outbuildings?'

'That's right. Not a trace of the girl,' Lucas said, his naturally cheery face as sombre as it could manage. 'The building out the back of the manor, it's where the squire develops his photographs. Nowhere for a lass to hide in there.'

Before George could respond, Clough and Cragg appeared from the shadows on the village green. Both looked as cold as he felt, the collars of their heavy winter coats turned up against the chill wind that whistled up the valley. Cragg was flipping back the pages of his notebook. 'Any progress?' George asked.

'Not so's you'd notice,' Clough complained, offer-ing his cigarettes round the group. Only Cragg took one. 'We spoke to everybody, including the cousins she came back from school with. It was Mrs Kathy Lomas's turn to pick them up at the road end, which she did as per usual. The last she saw of Alison, the lass was walking in the kitchen door of the manor. So the mother's telling the truth about the lass getting home in one piece. Mrs Lomas went indoors with her lad and never saw Alison again. Nobody saw hide nor hair of the girl after she came home from school. It's like she vanished into thin air.'

4

Thursday, 12th December 1963. 1.14 a.m.

George looked around the church hall with an air of
resignation. In the pale-yellow light, it looked dingy
and cramped, the pale-green walls adding to the insti-
tutional flavour. But they needed an incident room
large enough to accommodate a CID team as well as
the uniformed officers, and there were precious few
candidates within striking distance of Scardale. Pressed,
Peter Grundy had only been able to come up with either
the village hall in Longnor or this depressing annexe to
the Methodist Chapel that squatted on the main road
just past the Scardale turn-off. It had the advantage
not only of being closer to Scardale, but of having
a telephone line already installed in what claimed,
according to the sign on its door, to be the vestry.

'Just as well Methodists don't go in for vestments,'
George said as he stood on the threshold and surveyed
the glorified cupboard. 'Make a note, Grundy. We'll
need a field telephone as well.'

Grundy added the telephone to a list that already
included typewriters, witness-statement forms, maps
of assorted scales, filing cards and boxes, electoral rolls

and telephone directories. Tables and chairs were no problem; the hall was already well furnished with them. George turned to Lucas. 'We need to draw up a plan of action for the morning,' he said decisively. 'Let's pull up some chairs and see what we need to do.'

They arranged a table and chairs directly below one of the electric heaters that hung suspended from the roof beams. It barely dented the damp chill of the icy night air, but the men were glad of any relief. Grundy disappeared into the small kitchen and returned with three cups and a saucer. 'For an ashtray,' he said, sliding the saucer across the table towards George. Then he produced a Thermos flask from inside his overcoat and plonked it firmly on the table.

'Where did that come from?' Lucas demanded.

'Betsy Crowther, Meadow Cottage,' Grundy said. 'The wife's cousin on her mother's side.' He opened the flask and George stared greedily at the curl of steam.

Fortified by tea and cigarettes, the three men began to plan. 'We'll need as many uniforms as we can muster,' George said. 'We need to comb the whole of the Scardale area, but if we draw a blank there, we'll have to widen the search down the course of the Scarlaston river. I'll make a note to contact the Territorial Army, to see if they can spare us any bodies to help with the searching.'

'If we're spreading the net wider, it might be worth asking the High Peak Hunt if they can help us out,' Lucas said, hunched over his tea to make the most of its warmth. 'Their hounds are used to tracking, and their riders know the land.'

'I'll bear that in mind,' George said, inhaling the smoke from his cigarette as if it could warm his frozen core. 'PC Grundy, I want you to make a list of all the local farmers within, say, a five-mile radius. At first light, we'll send some men out to ask them all to check their land to see if the girl's there. If she was running away, she could easily have had an accident, wandering around in the dark.'

Grundy nodded. 'I'll get on to it. Sir, there was one thing I wanted to bring up?' George nodded. 'Yesterday was Leek Cattle Market and Christmas Show. Fatstock and dairy cattle. Decent prize money, an' all. So that means there would have been a lot more traffic than usual on the roads in these parts. There's a lot go over to Leek for the show, whether they've got cattle entered or not. Some of them will have been doing their Christmas shopping at the same time. They could have been heading for home round about the time Alison went missing. So if the lass was on any of the roads, there's a better than average chance that she'll have been spotted.'

'Good thinking,' George said, making a note. 'You might want to ask the farmers about that when you talk to them. And I'll mention it at the press conference.'

'Press conference?' Lucas asked suspiciously. He'd been reluctantly approving of the Professor this far, but now it looked like George Bennett was planning on using Alison Carter to make a name for himself. It was a move that failed to impress the sergeant.

George nodded. 'I've already been on to headquarters asking them to arrange a press conference here at ten o'clock. We need all the help we can get, and the press can reach people quicker than we can. It could take us weeks to contact everybody who was at Leek Market yesterday, and even then we'd miss plenty. Whereas with press coverage, nearly everybody will know there's a missing girl in a matter of days. Luckily, today's press day for the *High Peak Courant*, so they should be able to get the news on the streets by teatime. Publicity's vital in cases like these.'

'It doesn't seem to have done much for our colleagues in Manchester and Ashton,' Lucas said dubiously. 'Other than waste officers' time chasing down false leads.'

'If she has run away, it'll make it harder for her to stay hidden. And if she's been taken anywhere else, it increases our chances of finding a witness,' George said firmly. 'I spoke to Superintendent Martin, and he agrees. He's coming out here for the press conference himself. And he's confirmed that for now, I'm in over-all charge of the operation,' he added, feeling slightly awkward at his assertiveness.

'Makes sense,' Lucas said. 'You being here from the first shout.' He got to his feet, pushing his chair back and leaning forward to stub out his cigarette. 'So, shall we head back to Buxton now? I don't see there's much we can do here. The day-shift men can set it up when they come on at six.'

Privately, George agreed. But he didn't want to leave. Equally, he didn't want to appear to push his authority by insisting they hang around pointlessly. With some reluctance, he followed Lucas and Grundy out to the car. Little was said on the way back to Longnor to drop Grundy off, still less on the seven miles back to Buxton. Both men were tired, both troubled by their private imaginings.

Back in the divisional headquarters in Buxton, George left the sergeant to type up a list of orders for the day shift and the extra officers drafted in from other parts of the county. He climbed behind the wheel of his car, shivering at the blast of cold air that issued from his dashboard vents when he turned the engine on. Within ten minutes, he was drawing up outside the house that Derbyshire Police decreed was appropriate for a married man of his rank. A three-bedroomed stone-clad semi, it sat in a generous garden, thanks to the sharp bend in the street. From the kitchen and the back-bedroom windows, there was a view of Grin Low woods stretching along the ridge to the beginning of Axe Edge and the grim miles of moorland where Derbyshire blurred into Staffordshire and Cheshire.

George stood in the moonlit kitchen, looking out at the inhospitable landscape. He'd dutifully taken the sandwiches out of the fridge and brewed himself a pot of tea, but he hadn't eaten a bite. He couldn't even have said what the sandwiches contained. There was a thin pile of Christmas cards on the table, left by Anne for his attention, but he ignored them. He cradled the fragile china cup in his broad square hands, remembering Ruth Hawkin's ravaged face when he'd brought the dog back and broken into her private vigil.

She'd been standing by the kitchen sink, staring out into the darkness behind the house. Now he came to think about it, he wondered why she wasn't devoting her attention to the front of the house. After all, if Alison was going to return, she'd presumably come from the direction of the village green and the fields she'd set off towards earlier. And any news would come that way too. Perhaps, George thought, Ruth Hawkin couldn't bear to see the familiar scene criss-crossed by police officers, their presence a poignant and forceful reminder of her daughter's absence.

Whatever the reason, she'd been gazing out of the window, her back to her husband and the WPC who still sat awkwardly at the kitchen table, there to offer a sympathy that clearly wasn't wanted. Ruth hadn't even moved when he'd opened the door. It was the sound of the dog's claws on the stone flags that had dragged her eyes away from the window. When she turned, the dog had dropped to the floor and, whimpering, crawled towards Ruth on her belly.

'We found Shep tied up in the woods,' George had said. 'Someone had taped her mouth shut. With elastoplast.'

Ruth's eyes widened and her mouth twisted in a rictus of pain. 'No,' she protested weakly. 'That can't be right.' She dropped to her knees beside the dog, who was squirming round her ankles in a parody of obsequious apology. Ruth buried her face in the dog's ruff, clutching the animal to her as if it were a child. A long pink tongue licked her ear.

George looked across at Hawkin. The man was shaking his head, looking genuinely bewildered. 'That makes no sense,' Hawkin said. 'It's Alison's dog. It would never have let anybody harm a hair on Alison's head.' He gave a mirthless bark of laughter. 'I lifted a hand to her one time, and the dog had my sleeve in its teeth before I could touch her. The only person who could have done that to the dog was Alison herself. It wouldn't even stand for me or Ruth doing something like that, never mind a stranger.'

'Alison might not have had any choice,' George said gently.

Ruth looked up, her face transformed by the realization that her earlier fears might truly be reflected in reality. 'No,' she said, her voice a hoarse plea. 'Not my Alison. Please God, not my Alison.'

Hawkin got to his feet and crossed the room to his wife. He hunkered down beside her and put an awkward arm round her shoulders. 'You mustn't get into a state, Ruth,' he said, casting a quick glance up at George. 'That won't help Alison. We've got to stay strong.' Hawkin seemed embarrassed at having to show concern for his wife. George had seen plenty of men who were uncomfortable with any display of emotion, but he'd seldom encountered one so self-conscious about it.

He felt enormous pity for Ruth Hawkin. It wasn't the first time George had watched a marriage crack under the weight of a major investigation. He'd spent less than an hour in the company of this couple, but he knew instinctively that what he was witnessing here was not so much a crack as a major fracture. It was hard enough at any time in a marriage to discover that the person you had married was less than you imagined, but for Ruth Hawkin, so recently wed, it was doubly difficult, coming as it did on top of the anxiety of her daughter's disappearance.

Almost without thinking, George had crouched down and covered one of Ruth's hands with his own. 'There's very little we can do just now, Mrs Hawkin. But we are doing everything possible. At first light, we'll have men scouring the dale from end to end. I promise you, I won't give up on Alison.' Their eyes had met and he'd felt the intensity of a clutch of emotions far too complicated for him to separate.

As he stared out towards the moors, George realized there was no way he could sleep that night. Wrapping the sandwiches in greaseproof paper, he filled a flask with hot tea and softly climbed the stairs to pick up his electric razor from the bathroom.

On the landing, he paused. The door to their bedroom was ajar, and he couldn't resist a quick look at Anne. With his fingertips, he pushed the door a little wider. Her face was a pale smudge against the white gleam of the pillow. She lay on her side, one hand a fist on the pillow beside her. God, she was beautiful. Just watching her sleep was enough to make his flesh stir. He wished he could throw his clothes off and slide in beside her, feeling her warmth the length of his body. But tonight, the memory of Ruth Hawkin's haunted eyes was more than he could escape.

With a soft sigh, he turned away. Half an hour later, he was back in the Methodist Hall, staring at Alison Carter. He'd pinned four of Hawkin's photographs of her to the notice board. He'd left the other at the police station, asking for it to be copied as a matter of urgency so it could be distributed at the press conference. The night duty inspector seemed uncertain whether it could be done in time. George had left him in no doubt what he expected.

Carefully, he spread out the Ordnance Survey map and tried to study it through the eyes of a person who'd decided to run away. Or a person who'd decided to steal someone else's life.

Then he walked out of the Methodist Hall and started down the narrow lane towards Scardale on foot. Within yards, the dim yellow light that spilled out of the high windows of the hall was swallowed by the blanketing night. The only glimmers of light came from the stars that broke through the fitful clouds. It took him all his time to avoid tripping over tussocks of grass at the road's edge.

Gradually, his pupils expanded to their maximum extent, allowing his night vision to steal what images it could from the ghosts and shadows of the landscape. But by the time they resolved themselves into hedges and trees, sheep folds and stiles, the cold had sneaked up on him. Thin-soled town shoes were no match for frosty ground, and not even his cotton-lined leather gloves were proof against the icy flurry that seemed to use the Scardale lane as a wind tunnel. His ears and nose had lost all sensation except pain. A mile down the lane, he gave up. If Alison Carter was abroad in this, she must be hardier than him, he decided.

Either that or beyond sensation altogether.

Manchester Evening News, *Thursday, 12ᵗʰ December 1963, p.11*

Boy camper raises hopes in John hunt

POLICE RACE TO LONELY BEAUTY SPOT

By a Staff Reporter

Police investigating the disappearance of 12-year-old John Kilbride of Ashton-under-Lyne rushed to a lonely beauty spot on the outskirts of the town.

A boy had been seen camping out.

Hopes soared when the boy was said to be safe and well. But it turned out to be a false alarm.

The boy they found had been reported missing from home and was about the same age as John – but it was 11-year-old David Marshall of Gorse View, Alt Estate, Oldham.

He had been missing for only a few hours.

After 'getting into trouble' at home, he packed his belongings – and a tent – and went to camp out near a farm in Lily Lanes, on the Ashton-Oldham boundary.

It was another frustrating incident in the 19-day-old search for John, of Smallshaw Lane, Ashton.

Police said today: 'We really thought we were on to something. But at least we are glad we were able to return one boy home safe and well.'

David was spotted at his lonely bivouac by a visitor to the farm who informed the police immediately.

'It shows the public are really cooperating,' said police.

Thursday, 12ᵗʰ December 1963. 7.30 a.m.
Janet Carter reminded George of a cat his sister had once had. Her triangular face with its pert nose, wide eyes and tiny rosebud mouth was as closed and watchful as any domesticated predator he'd ever seen. She even had a scatter of tiny pimples at either end of her upper lip, as if someone had tweezed out her whiskers. They faced each other across the table in the low-ceilinged kitchen of her parents' Scardale cottage. Janet was picking delicately at a piece of buttered toast, small sharp teeth nibbling crescents inwards from

67

each corner. Her eyes were downcast, but every few moments she'd give him a quick sidelong look through long lashes.

Even in his younger years, he'd never been comfortable with adolescent girls, a natural result of having a sister three years older whose friends had regarded the fledgling George first as a convenient plaything and later as a marvellous testing ground for the wit and charms they planned to try on older targets. George had sometimes felt like the human equivalent of training wheels on a child's first bike. The one advantage he'd gained from the experience was that he reckoned he could tell when a teenage girl was lying, which was more than most of the men he knew could manage.

But even that certainty faded in the face of Janet Carter's self-possession. Her cousin was missing, with all the presumptions that entailed, yet Janet looked as composed as if Alison had merely nipped out to the shops. Her mother, Maureen, had a noticeably less sure grip on her emotions, her voice trembling when she spoke of her niece, tears in her eyes when she shepherded her three younger children from the room, leaving George to interview Janet. And her father, Ray, was already up and gone, lending his local knowledge to one of the police search parties looking for his dead brother's child.

'You probably know Alison better than anybody,' George said at last, reminding himself to stick with a present tense that seemed increasingly inappropriate.

Janet nodded. 'We're like sisters. She's eight months and two weeks older than me, so we're in a different class at school. Just like real sisters.'

'You grew up together here in Scardale?'

Janet nodded, another new moon of toast disappearing between her teeth. 'The three of us, me and Alison and Derek.'

'So you're like best friends as well as cousins?'

'I'm not her best friend at school because we're in different classes, but I am at home.'

'What kind of things do you do?'

Janet's mouth twisted and furled as she thought for a moment. 'Nothing much. Some nights Charlie, our big cousin, takes us into Buxton for the roller-skating. Sometimes we go to the shops in Buxton or Leek, but mostly we're just here. We take the dogs for a walk. Sometimes we help out on the farm if they're short-handed. Ali got a record player for her birthday, so a lot of the time me and Ali and Derek just listen to records up in her room.'

He took a sip of the tea Maureen Carter had left for him, amazed that someone could make stronger tea than the police canteen. 'Has anything been bothering her?' he asked. 'Any problems at home? Or at school?'

Janet raised her head and stared at him, her eyebrows coming together in a frown. 'She never ran away,' she said fiercely. 'Somebody must have took her. Ali wouldn't run away. Why would she? There's nothing to run away *from*.'

Maybe not, thought George, startled by her vehemence. But maybe there had been something to run away *to*. 'Does Alison have a boyfriend?'

Janet breathed heavily through her nose. 'Not really. She went to the pictures with this lad from Buxton a couple of times. Alan Milliken. But it wasn't a date, not really. There was half a dozen of them all went together. She told me he tried to kiss her, but she wasn't having any. She said that if he thought paying her in to the pictures meant he could do what he liked, he was wrong.' Janet eyed him defiantly, animated by her outburst.

'So there isn't anybody she fancies? Maybe somebody older?'

Janet shook her head. 'We both fancy Dennis Tanner off *Coronation Street*, and Paul McCartney out of the Beatles. But that's just fancying. There isn't anybody *real* that she fancies. She always says boys are boring. All they want to talk about is football and going into outer space on a rocket and what kind of car they'd have if they could drive.'

'And Derek? Where does he fit in?'

Janet looked puzzled. 'Derek's just . . . Derek. Anyway, he's got spots. You couldn't fancy Derek.'

'What about Charlie, then? Your big cousin? I hear they spent a lot of time together round at his gran's.'

Janet shook her head, one finger straying to a tiny yellow-headed spot beside her mouth. 'Ali only goes round to listen to Ma Lomas's tales. Charlie *lives* there, that's all. Anyway, I don't understand why you're going on about who Ali fancies. You should be out looking for whoever kidnapped her. I bet they think Uncle Phil's got loads of money, just because he lives in a big house and owns all the village land. I bet they got the idea off Frank Sinatra's lad being kidnapped last week. It must have been on the television and in the papers and everything. We don't get television down here. We can't get the reception, so we're stuck with the radio. But even down in Scardale we heard about it, so a kidnapper could easily have known about it and got the idea. I bet they're going to ask for a huge ransom for Ali.' Her lips glistened with butter as the tip of her tongue darted along them in her excitement.

'How does Alison get along with her stepfather?'

Janet shrugged, as if the question couldn't have interested her less. 'All right, I suppose. She likes living in the manor, I'll tell you that for nothing.' A sparkle of malice lit up Janet's eyes. 'Whenever anybody asks her where she lives, she always says, right out, "Scardale Manor", like it's something really special. When we were little, we used to make up stories about the manor. Ghost stories and murder stories, and it's like Ali thinks she's really the bee's knees now she's living there.'

'And her stepfather? What did she say about him?'

'Nothing much. When he was courting her mum, she said she thought he was a bit of a creep because he was always round their cottage, bringing Auntie Ruth little presents. You know, flowers, chocolates, nylons, stuff like that.' She fidgeted in her seat and popped a spot between fingernail and thumb, unconsciously trying to mask the action behind her hand.

'I think she was just jealous because she was so used to being the apple of Auntie Ruth's eye. She couldn't stand the competition. But once they got married and all that courting stuff stopped, I think Ali got on all right with him. He sort of left her alone, I think. He doesn't act like he's very interested in anybody except himself. And taking pictures. He's always doing that.' Janet turned back to her toast dismissively.

'Pictures of what?' George said, more to keep the conversation going than because he was interested.

'Scenery. He spies on people working, too. He says

71

you've got to get them looking natural, so he takes their pictures when he thinks they're not looking. Only, he's an incomer. He doesn't know Scardale like we do. So mostly when he's creeping about trying to stay out of sight, half the village knows what he's doing.' She giggled, then, remembering why George was there, covered her mouth with her hand, her eyes wide.

'So as far as you know, there was no reason why Alison should run away?'

Janet put down her toast and pursed her lips. 'I told you. She never ran away. Ali wouldn't run away without me. And I'm still here. So somebody must have took her. And you're supposed to find them.' Her eyes flicked to one side and George half turned to see Maureen Carter in the kitchen doorway.

'You tell him, Mum,' Janet said, desperation in her voice. 'I keep telling him, but he won't listen. Tell him Ali wouldn't run away. Tell him.'

Maureen nodded. 'She's right. When Alison's in trouble, she takes it head on. If she had something on her mind, we'd all know what it was. Whatever's happened, it's not from Alison's choice.' She stepped forward and swept Janet's teacup away from her. 'Time you and the little 'uns were over to Derek's. Kathy'll run you up to the lane end for the bus.'

'I could do that,' George volunteered.

Maureen looked him up and down, clearly finding him wanting. 'That's kind of you, but there's been enough upset this morning without mucking up their routine any further. Go on, Janet, get your coat on.'

George held his hand up. 'Before you go, Janet, just one more question. Was there any special place you and Alison used to go in the dale? A den, a gang hut, that sort of thing?'

The girl gave her mother a quick, desperate look. 'No,' she said, her voice revealing the opposite of her word. Janet crammed the last of her toast into her mouth and hurried out, waving her fingers at George.

Maureen picked up the dirty plate and cocked her head. 'If Alison was going to run away, she wouldn't do it like this. She loves her mum. They were right close. It comes of being on their own for so long. Alison would never put Ruth through this.'

5

Thursday, 12ᵗʰ December 1963. 9.50 a.m.

The Methodist Hall had undergone a transformation. Eight trestle tables had been unfolded and each was the centre of some particular activity. At one, a constable with a field telephone was liaising with force headquarters. At three others, maps were spread out, thick red lines drawn on them to separate search areas. At a fifth table, a sergeant was surrounded by filing cards, statement forms and filing boxes, collating information as it came to him. At the remaining tables, officers pounded typewriters. Back in Buxton, CID officers were interviewing Alison Carter's classmates, while the dale that surrounded Scardale village and shared its name was being combed by thirty police officers and the same number of local volunteers.

At the end of the hall nearest the door, a semi-circle of chairs faced a proper oak table. Behind it there were two chairs. In front of it, George was finishing his briefing of Superintendent Jack Martin. In the three months since he'd arrived in Buxton, he'd never had personal dealings with the uniformed officer in overall charge of the division. His reports had crossed Martin's desk, he knew, but they'd never communicated directly about a case. All he knew about the man had been filtered through the consciousness of others.

Martin had served as a lieutenant in an infantry regiment in the war, apparently without either distinction or shame. Nevertheless, his years in the army had given him a taste for the minutiae of military life. He insisted on the observance of rank, reprimanding officers who addressed their equals or juniors by name rather than rank. A Christian name overheard in the squad room could raise his blood pressure by several points, according to DS Clough. Martin conducted regular inspections of his uniformed officers, frequently bawling out individuals whose boots failed to reflect their faces or whose tunic buttons were less than gleaming. He had the profile of a hawk, and the eyes to match. He marched everywhere at the double, and was said to loathe what he saw as the sloppy appearances of the CID officers under his nominal charge.

Beneath the martinet, however, George had suspected there was a shrewd and effective police officer. Now he was about to find out. Martin had listened carefully to George's outline of events to date, his salt-and-pepper eyebrows meeting in a frown of concentration. With finger and thumb of his right hand, he rubbed his carefully manicured moustache against the grain then smoothed it back again. 'Smoke?' he said at last, offering George a packet of Capstan Full Strength. George shook his head, preferring his milder Gold Leaf tipped. But he took the overture as permission and immediately lit up himself. 'I don't like the sound of this one,' Martin said. 'It was carefully planned, wasn't it?'

'I think so, sir,' George said, impressed that Martin

had also picked up on the key detail of the elastoplast. Nobody went for a casual walk with a whole roll of sticking plaster, not even the most safety-conscious Boy Scout leader. The treatment of the dog had screamed premeditation to George, though none of his fellow officers had appeared to give it as much weight. 'I think whoever took the girl was familiar with her habits. I think he might have watched her over a period of time, waiting for the right opportunity.'

'So you think it's a local?' Martin said.

George ran a hand over his fair hair. 'It looks that way,' he said hesitantly.

'I think you're right not to commit yourself. It's a popular hike, up Denderdale to the source of the Scarlaston. There must be dozens of ramblers who do that walk in the summer. Any one of them could have seen the girl, either alone or with her friends, and resolved to come back and take her.' Martin nodded, agreeing with himself, flicking a morsel of cigarette ash off the cuff of his perfectly pressed tunic.

'That's possible,' George conceded, though he couldn't imagine anybody forming that sort of instant obsession and hanging on to it for months until the right opportunity presented itself. However, the principal reason for his uncertainty was quite different. 'I suppose what I'm saying is that I can't picture any member of this community doing something so damaging. They're incredibly tight-knit, sir. They've got accustomed to supporting each other over generations. For someone from Scardale to have harmed one of their own children would be against everything they've grown up believing in. Besides, it's hard to imagine how an insider could get away with stealing a child without

76

everybody else in Scardale knowing about it. Even so, on the face of it, it's much likelier to be an insider.' George sighed, baffled by his own arguments.

'Unless everybody's wrong about the direction the girl went in,' Martin observed. 'She may have broken with her usual habits and walked up the fields towards the main road. And yesterday was Leek Cattle Market. There would have been more traffic than usual on the Longnor road. She could easily have been lured into a car on the pretext of giving directions.'

'You're forgetting about the dog, sir,' George pointed out.

Martin waved his cigarette impatiently. 'The kidnapper could have sneaked round the edge of the dale and left the dog in the woodland.'

'It's a big risk, and he'd have had to know the ground.'

Martin sighed. 'I suppose so. Like you, I'm reluctant to see the villain of the piece as a local. One has this romantic view of these rural communities, but sadly we're usually misguided.' He glanced at the hall clock then stubbed out his cigarette, shot his cuffs and straightened up. 'So. Let us face the gentlemen of the press.'

He turned towards the trestle tables. 'Parkinson – go and tell Morris to let the journalists in.'

The uniformed bobby jumped to his feet with a mumbled, 'Yessir.'

'Cap, Parkinson,' Martin barked. Parkinson stopped in his tracks and hurried back to his seat. He crammed his cap on and almost ran to the door. He slipped outside as Martin added, 'Haircut, Parkinson.' The superintendent's mouth twitched in what might have been a smile as he led the way to the chairs behind the table.

The door opened and half a dozen men spilled into the hall, a haze of mist seeming to form around them as their cold shapes hit the airless warmth of the hall. The clump separated into individuals and they settled noisily into their folding chairs. Their ages ranged from mid-twenties to mid-fifties, George reckoned, though it wasn't easy to tell with hat brims and caps pulled low over faces, coat collars turned up against the chill wind and scarves swathed around throats. He recognized Colin Loftus from the *High Peak Courant*, but the others were strangers. He wondered who they were working for.

'Good morning, gentlemen,' Martin began. 'I am Superintendent Jack Martin of Buxton Police and this is my colleague, Detective Inspector George Bennett. As you are no doubt already aware, a young girl has gone missing from Scardale. Alison Carter, aged thirteen, was last seen at approximately four twenty p.m. yesterday afternoon. She left the family home, Scardale Manor, to take her dog for a walk. When she failed to return, her mother, Mrs Ruth Hawkin, and stepfather, Mr Philip Hawkin, contacted police at Buxton. We responded to the call and began a search of the immediate environs of Scardale Manor, using police tracker dogs. Alison's dog was found in woodland near her home, but of the girl herself, we have found no trace.'

He cleared his throat. 'We will have copies of a recent photograph of Alison available at Buxton Police Station by noon.' As Martin gave a detailed description of the girl's appearance and clothing, George studied the journalists. Their heads were bent, their pencils flying over the pages of their notebooks. At least they were all interested enough to take a detailed note. He wondered how much that had to do with the Manchester disappearances. He couldn't imagine that they would normally have turned out in such numbers for a girl missing for sixteen hours from a tiny Derbyshire hamlet.

Martin was winding up. 'If we do not find Alison today, the search will be intensified. We just don't know what has happened to her, and we're very concerned, not least because of the extremely bitter weather we're experiencing at the moment. Now, if you gentlemen have any questions, either myself or Detective Inspector Bennett will be happy to answer.'

A head came up. 'Brian Bond, *Manchester Evening Chronicle*. Do you suspect foul play?'

Martin took a deep breath. 'At this point, we rule nothing out and nothing in. We can find no reason for Alison being missing. She was not in trouble at home or at school. But we have found nothing to suggest foul play at this stage.'

Colin Loftus lifted his hand, one finger raised. 'Is there any indication that Alison might have met with an accident?'

'Not so far,' George said. 'As Superintendent Martin told you, we've got teams of searchers combing the dale now. We've also asked all the local farmers to check their land very carefully, just in case Alison has been injured in a fall and has been unable to make her way home.'

The man on the far end of the row leaned back in his chair and blew a perfect smoke ring. 'There seem to be some common features between Alison

Carter's disappearance and the two missing children in the Manchester area – Pauline Reade from Gorton and John Kilbride from Ashton. Are you speaking to detectives from the Manchester and Lancashire forces about a possible connection to their cases?'

'And you are?' Martin demanded stiffly.

'Don Smart, *Daily News*. Northern Bureau.' He flashed a smile that reminded George of the predatory snarl of the fox. Smart even had the same colouring: reddish hair sticking out from under a tweed cap, ruddy face and hazel eyes that squinted against the smoke from his panatella.

'It's far too early to make assumptions like that,' George cut in, wanting for himself this question that echoed his own doubts. 'I am of course familiar with the cases you mention, but as yet we have found no reason to communicate with our colleagues in other forces over anything other than search arrangements. Staffordshire Police have already indicated that they will give us every assistance should there be any need to widen our search area.'

But Smart was not to be put off so easily. 'If I was Alison Carter's mum, I don't think I'd be impressed to hear that the police were ignoring such strong links to other child disappearances.'

Martin's head came up sharply. He opened his mouth to rebuke the journalist, but George was there before him. 'For every similarity, there's a difference,' he said bluntly. 'Scardale is isolated countryside, not busy city streets; Pauline and John went missing on a weekend, but this is midweek; strangers would be a common sight to the other two, but a stranger in Scardale on a December teatime would put Alison straight on her guard; and, probably most importantly, Alison wasn't alone, she had her dog with her. Besides, Scardale is a good twenty-five, thirty miles away. Anybody looking for children to kidnap would have to pass a lot by before he got to Alison Carter. Hundreds of people go missing every year. It would be stranger if there weren't similarities.'

Don Smart stared a cool challenge at George. 'Thank you, Detective Inspector Bennett. Would that be Bennett with two t's?' was all he said.

'That's right,' George said. 'Any further questions?'

'Will you be draining the reservoirs up on the moors?' Colin Loftus again.

'We'll let you know what steps we're taking as and when,' Martin said repressively. 'Now, unless anyone's got anything more to ask, I'm going to close this press conference now.' He got to his feet.

Don Smart leaned forward, elbows on his knees. 'When's the next one, then?' he asked.

George watched Martin's neck turn as red as turkey wattles. Oddly, the colour didn't rise into his face. 'When we find the girl, we'll let you know.'

'And if you don't find her?'

'I'll be here tomorrow morning, same time,' George said. 'And every morning until we do find Alison.'

Don Smart's eyebrows rose. 'I'll look forward to that,' he said, gathering the folds of his heavy overcoat around his narrow frame and drawing himself up to his full five and a half feet. The other journalists were already straggling towards the door, comparing notes and deciding how they would lead off their stories.

'Cheeky,' Martin pronounced as the door closed behind them.

'I suppose he's only doing his job,' George sighed. He could do without someone as stroppy as Don Smart on his back, but there wasn't much he could do about it except to avoid letting the man needle him too much.

Martin snorted. 'Troublemaker. The others managed to do their job without insinuating that we don't know how to do ours. You'll have to keep an eye on that one, Bennett.'

George nodded. 'I've been meaning to ask, sir. Do you want me to carry on in operational charge here?'

Martin frowned. 'Inspector Thomas will be responsible for the uniformed men, but I think you should take overall command. Detective Chief Inspector Carver won't be going anywhere with his ankle still in plaster. He's volunteered to take care of the CID office in Buxton, but I need a man here on the ground. Can I rely on you, Inspector?'

'I'll do my best, sir,' George said. 'I'm determined that we're going to find this girl.'

Manchester Evening Chronicle, *Thursday, 12th December 1963, p.1.*

POLICE COMB ISOLATED DALE

Dogs in manhunt for missing girl

By a Staff Reporter

Police with tracker dogs were today hunting for a 13-year-old girl missing from her home in the isolated Derbyshire hamlet of Scardale since yesterday teatime.

82

The girl, Alison Carter, vanished from Scardale Manor where she lives with her mother and stepfather after saying she was going to take her collie Shep for a walk.

Alison set off to walk across the fields to nearby woods in the limestone dale where she lives. She has not been seen since.

After her mother alerted police, a search was carried out. The dog was discovered unharmed, but no trace of Alison was found.

Questioning her neighbours and friends at Peak Girls' High School has provided no reason why the pretty schoolgirl should have run away.

Today her mother, Mrs Ruth Hawkin, aged 34, waited anxiously for news as the comb-out of the dale continued. Her husband, Mr Philip Hawkin, aged 37, joined neighbours and local farmers who helped police search the lonely dale.

A senior police official said: 'We can find no reason for Alison being missing. She was not in trouble at home or at school. But we have found nothing to suggest foul play at this stage.'

The search will continue tomorrow if Alison is not found by nightfall.

Don Smart threw aside the early edition of the *Chronicle*. At least they hadn't stolen his line of questioning. That was always the danger of trying something a bit different at a press conference. From now on, he'd try to break away from the pack and dig for his own stories. He had a feeling in his water that George Bennett was going to be great copy, and he was determined that he'd be the one to squeeze the best stories out of the handsome young detective.

He could tell that the man was a bulldog. There was no way George Bennett was going to give up on Alison Carter. Smart knew from past experience that for most of the cops, the disappearance of Alison Carter would be just another job. Sure, they felt sorry for the family. And he'd have bet that the ones who were fathers themselves went home and gave their daughters an extra-tight hug every night they were out on those moors searching for Alison.

But he sensed a difference with George. With him, it was a mission. The rest of the world might have given up on Alison Carter, but George couldn't have been more passionate in her cause if she'd been his own daughter. Smart could sense how intolerable failure would be to him.

For him, it was a godsend. His job in the northern bureau of the *Daily News* was his first on a national newspaper, and he'd been on the lookout for the story that would take him to Fleet Street. He'd already done some of the *News*'s coverage of the Pauline Reade and John Kilbride disappearances, and he was determined to persuade George Bennett or one of his team to link them to Alison Carter. It would be a terrific page lead.

Whatever happened, Scardale was a great backdrop for a dramatic, mysterious story. In a closed community like that, everybody's life would be put under the microscope. Suddenly all sorts of secrets would be forced into the open. It was guaranteed not to be a pretty sight. And Don Smart was determined to witness it all.

*   *   *

Back at the Methodist Hall, George Bennett also threw aside the evening paper. He had no doubt that the morning would bring a less palatable story in the pages of the more sensational *Daily News*. Martin would have apoplexy if there was any suggestion of police incompetence. He stalked out of the Methodist Hall and crossed the road to his car.

Driving down to Scardale in daylight was scarcely less intimidating than approaching at night or in the early-morning darkness. At least blackness obscured the worst of the rock overhangs that George could all too easily imagine splitting off and crushing his car like a tin can beneath a steamroller. Today, though, there was one crucial difference: the gate across the road stood wide open, allowing free passage to vehicles. A uniformed constable stood by it, peering into George's car, then snapping a salute as he recognized the occupant. Poor beggar, George thought. His own days standing around in the cold had been thankfully short-lived. He wondered how the bobbies who weren't on the fast track could bear the prospect of week after week of pounding pavements, guarding crime scenes and, like today, tramping fruitlessly through inhospitable countryside.

The village was no more enhanced by daylight than the road. There was nothing charming about the dour little cottages of Scardale. The grey stone buildings seemed to crouch low to the ground, more like cowed hounds than poised animals ready to spring. One or two had sagging rooflines and most of the wood could have done with a lick of paint. Hens wandered at will, and every car that drove into the village provoked a cacophony of barking from an assortment of sheep and cow dogs tied up to gateposts. What had not changed was the eyes that watched the arrival of every newcomer. As he drove in, George was aware of the watchers. He knew more about them than he had the night before. For one thing, he knew they were all female. Every able-bodied man from Scardale was out with the searchers, adding both determination and local knowledge to the hunt.

George found a space for his car on the far side of the village green, tucked down the side of the wall of Scardale Manor. Time for another chat with Mrs Hawkin, he'd decided. On his way to the house, he paused by the caravan that had arrived that morning from force headquarters. They were using it as a liaison point for searchers rather than an incident room, and a pair of WPCs were occupied with the continuous task of brewing tea and coffee. George pushed the door open and silently congratulated himself on winning his private bet that Inspector Alan Thomas would be settled comfortably in the warmest corner of the caravan, pot of tea to one side of his broad hands, ashtray containing his briar pipe to the other.

'George,' Thomas said heartily. 'Come and park yourself here, boy. Bitter out, isn't it? Glad I'm not out there combing the woods.'

'Any news?' George asked, nodding acceptance at the WPC who was offering him a mug of tea. He sugared it from an open bag and leaned against the bulkhead.

'Not a dicky bird, boy. Everybody's drawn a blank, more or less. The odd scrap of clothing, but nothing that hasn't been there for months,' Thomas said, his Welsh accent somehow rendering the depressing news cheerful.

'Help yourself,' he added, waving a hand towards a plate of buttered scones. 'The girl's mother brought them in. Said she couldn't be doing with sitting about waiting.'

'I'm going to bob in and see her in a minute.' George reached across and grabbed a scone. Not half bad, he decided. Definitely an improvement over Anne's. She was a great cook, but her bakery skills left a lot to be desired. He'd had to lie, say he didn't really like cakes that much. Otherwise he knew that he'd end up praising her because he didn't know how to criticize. And he didn't want to condemn himself to fifty years of heavy sponges, chewy pastry and rock cakes that seemed to have come straight from the local roadstone quarries.

Suddenly, the door crashed open. A red-faced man wearing a heavy leather jerkin over several layers of shirts and jumpers lurched into the caravan, panting hard and sweating. 'Are you Thomas?' he demanded, looking at George.

'I am, boy,' Thomas said, getting to his feet accompanied by a shower of crumbs. 'What's happened? Have they found the girl?'

The man shook his head, hands on knees as he struggled to get his breath back. 'In the spinney below Shield Tor,' he gasped. 'Looks like there's been a struggle. Branches broken.' He straightened up. 'I'm supposed to bring you there.'

George abandoned tea and scone and followed the man outside, with Thomas bringing up the tail. He introduced himself and said, 'Are you from Scardale?'

'Aye. I'm Ray Carter. Alison's uncle.'

And Janet's dad, George reminded himself. 'How

far is this from where we found the dog?' he asked, forcing his legs to full stride to keep up with the farmer, who could move a lot faster than his stocky build suggested.

'Maybe quarter of a mile as the crow flies.'

'It's taken us a while to get to it,' George said mildly.

'You can't see it from the path. So it got missed the first time through the spinney,' Carter said. 'Besides, it's not an obvious place.' He stopped for a moment, turning to point back at Scardale Manor. 'Look. There's the manor.' He swivelled round. 'There's the field that leads to the wood where the dog was found, and to the Scarlaston.' He moved round again. 'There's the way out the dale. And there,' he concluded, indicating an area of trees between the manor and the woodland where Shep had been restrained, 'is where we're heading. On the way to nowhere,' he added bitterly, encompassing the high limestone cliffs and the bleak grey skies with a final wave of his hand.

George frowned. The man was right. If Alison had been in the spinney when she was snatched, why was the dog tied up in a woodland clearing a quarter of a mile away? But if she'd been captured without putting up a fight in the clearing and the struggle had taken place when she'd seen the chance to get away from her captor, what were they doing in the dead end of the dale? It was another inconsistency to file away, he thought, following Ray Carter towards the narrow belt of trees.

The spinney was a mixture of beech, ash, sycamore and elm, more recent planting than the woodland they'd been in the previous night. The trees were smaller, their trunks narrower. They appeared to be too close together, their branches forming a loose-woven screen through which almost nothing could be seen. The undergrowth was heavy between the young trees, too thick to readily provide a way through. 'This way,' Carter said, angling towards an almost invisible opening in the brown ferns and the red and green foliage of the brambles. As soon as they entered the spinney, they lost most of the afternoon light. Half blind, George could see why the first wave of searchers might have missed something. He hadn't fully appreciated how intransigent the landscape was or how easy it could be to miss something as big as, God forbid, a body. As his eyes adjusted to the gloom, he could make out shrubby undergrowth among the trees. Underfoot, the path was slimy with trampled dead leaves. 'I've been telling the squire for months now, this spinney needs thinning out,' Carter grumbled, pushing aside the whiplash branches of a low-growing elder. 'You could lose half the High Peak Hunt in here and never be any the wiser.'

Suddenly, they came upon the rest of the search team. Three PCs and a lad stood in a cluster at a bend in the path. The lad looked no more than eighteen, dressed like Carter in leather jerkin and heavy corduroy trousers. 'Right,' said George, 'who's going to show me and Mr Thomas what's what here?'

One of the constables cleared his throat. 'It's just up ahead, sir. Another team had already been through here this morning, but Mr Carter here suggested we should take another look, on account of the undergrowth being so dense, like.' He waved George and Inspector Thomas through and the others stood back awkwardly to let them pass. The PC pointed to an almost undetectable break in the undergrowth on the south side of the path. 'It was the lad spotted it. Charlie Lomas. There's a very faint track of broken twigs and trampled plants. A few yards in, it looks like there's been a struggle.'

George crouched down and peered at the path. The man was right. There wasn't much to see. It was a miracle that any of them had spotted it. He supposed that the inhabitants of Scardale knew their territory so well that what appeared unobtrusive to him would leap out and hit them between the eyes.

'How many of you trampled over there in your size tens?' Thomas asked.

'Just me and the Lomas lad, sir. We were as careful as we could be. We tried not to disturb anything.'

'I'll take a look,' George said. 'Mr Thomas, could one of your lads phone up to the incident room and get a photographer down here? And I'd like the tracker dogs here as well. Once the photographer's finished, we'll also need a fingertip search of the area.' Without waiting for a response, George carefully held back the branches that overhung the faltering trail and moved forward, trying to keep a couple of feet to the left of the original track. Here, it was even more dim than on the path, and he paused to let his eyes adapt to the gloom.

The PC's description had been admirable in its accuracy. Half a dozen cramped steps, and George found what he'd been looking for. Broken twigs and crushed ferns marked an area about five feet by six. He was no countryman, but even George knew that this was recent damage. The shattered branches and stems looked freshly injured. One evergreen shrub that had been partially crushed was only wilted, not yet entirely dead. If this wasn't connected to Alison Carter's disappearance, it was a very odd coincidence.

George leaned forward, one hand clinging to a tree branch for support. There might be important evidence here. He didn't want to walk over this ground and cause any more harm than the searchers had already done. Even as the thought crossed his mind, his close scrutiny revealed a clump of dark material snagged on the sharp end of a broken twig. Black woolly tights, Ruth Hawkin had said. George's stomach clenched. 'She's been here,' he said softly.

He moved to his left, circling round the trampled area, stopping every couple of steps to examine what lay before him. He was almost diagonally opposite the point where he'd left the path when he saw it. Just in front of him and to the right, there was a dark patch on the startling white bark of a birch tree. Irresistibly drawn, he moved closer.

The blood had dried long since. But adhering to it, unmistakably, were a dozen strands of bright blonde hair. And on the ground next to the tree, a horn toggle with a scrap of material still attached.

6

Thursday, 12th December 1963. 5.05 p.m.

George took a deep breath and raised his hand to knock. Before his knuckles could connect with the wood, the door swung open. Ruth Hawkin stood facing him, her drawn face grey in the evening light. She stepped to one side, leaning against the doorjamb for support. 'You've found something,' she said flatly.

George crossed the threshold and closed the door behind him, determined not to provide the watching eyes with more spectacle than was inevitable. His eyes automatically swept the room. 'Where's the WPC?' he asked, turning to face Ruth.

'I sent her away,' she said. 'I don't need taking care of like a child. Besides, I reckoned there must be something she could do that would be more use to my Alison than sitting on her backside drinking tea all day.' There was an acerbic note in her voice that George hadn't heard there before. Healthy, he thought. This was not a woman who was going to collapse in a whimpering heap at every piece of bad news. He was relieved about that, because he believed he definitely qualified as the bearer of evil tidings.

'Shall we sit down?' he said.

Her mouth twisted in a sardonic grimace. 'That bad, eh?' But she pushed herself away from the wall and dropped into one of the kitchen chairs. George sat opposite, noticing that she was still dressed in the same clothes she'd been wearing the night before. She'd not been to bed, then. Certainly not slept. Probably not even tried.

'Is your husband out searching?' he asked.

She nodded. 'I don't think he was keen. He's a fair-weather countryman, my Phil. He likes it when the sun shines and it looks like one of his picture postcards. But days like today, cold, damp, a touch of freezing fog in the air, he's either sitting on top of the stove or else he's locked in his darkroom with a pair of paraffin heaters. I'll say this for him, though. Today, he made an exception.'

'If you like, we can wait till he comes back,' George said.

'That won't alter what you've got to say, will it?' she said, her voice weary.

'No, I'm afraid not.' George opened his overcoat and removed two polythene bags from the inside poacher's pocket. One contained the soft, fluffy ball of material snagged on the broken twig; the other, the smooth, ridged toggle, its natural shades of brown and bone strange against the man-made plastic. Attached to it by strong navy thread was a fragment of navy-blue felted wool. 'I have to ask you, do you recognize either of these?'

Her face was blank as she reached for the bags. She stared at them for a long moment. 'What's this supposed to be?' she asked, prodding the material with her index finger.

'We think it's wool,' George said. 'Perhaps from tights like Alison was wearing.'

'This could be anything,' she said defensively. 'It could have been out there for days, weeks.'

'We'll have to see what our lab can make of it.' No point in trying to force her to accept what her mind did not want to admit. 'What about the toggle? Do you recognize that?'

She picked up the bag and ran her finger over the carved piece of antler. She looked up at him, her eyes pleading. 'Is this all you found of her? Is this all there is to show?'

'We found signs of a struggle in the spinney.' George pointed in what he thought was the right direction. 'Between the house and the wood where we found Shep, down towards the back of the dale. It's dark now, so there's a limit to what we can achieve, but first thing in the morning, my men will carry out a fingertip search of the whole spinney, to see if we can find any more traces of Alison.'

'But that's all you found?' Now there was eagerness in her face.

He hated to dash her hopes, but he couldn't lie. 'We also found some hairs and a little blood. As if she'd hit her head on a tree.' Ruth clapped her hand to her open mouth, suppressing a cry. 'It really was very little blood, Mrs Hawkin. Nothing to indicate anything but a very minor injury, I promise you.'

Her wide eyes stared at him, her fingers digging into her cheek as if physically holding her mouth closed could somehow contain her response. He didn't know what to do, what to say. He had so little experience of people's responses to tragedy and crisis. He'd always

94

had senior officers or colleagues with more experience to blunt the acuteness of other people's pain. Now he was on his own, and he knew he would measure himself for ever according to how he dealt with this stricken woman.

George leaned across the table and covered Ruth Hawkin's free hand with his own. 'I'd be lying if I said this wasn't grounds for concern,' he said. 'But there's nothing to indicate that Alison has come to any serious harm. Quite the opposite, really. And there is one thing that we can be sure of now. Alison hasn't run away of her own accord. Now, I know that probably doesn't seem like much of a consolation to you right now, but it means that we won't be frittering away our resources on things that are a waste of time. We know that Alison didn't go off on her own and catch a bus or a train, so we won't be devoting officers to checking out bus and railway stations. We'll be using every officer we have to follow lines of inquiry that could actually lead us somewhere.'

Ruth Hawkin's hand fell away from her mouth. 'She's dead, isn't she?'

George gripped her hand. 'There's no reason to think so,' he said.

'Have you got a cigarette?' she asked. 'I ran out a while back.' She gave a bitter little laugh. 'I should have sent yon WPC up to the shop at Longnor for me. That would have been useful.'

Once they were both smoking, he took back the plastic bags and pushed the cigarettes across in their place. 'You keep these. I've more in the car.'

'Thanks.' The tightness in her face slackened momentarily and George saw for the first time the same smile that made Alison's photograph so remarkable.

He let enough time pass for them both to gain some benefit from the nicotine. 'I need some help, Mrs Hawkin,' George said. 'Last night, we had to work against the clock to try and find traces of Alison. And today, we've been searching. All the mechanical, routine things that are often successful, that we have to do. But I've not had a proper chance to sit down and talk to you about what kind of girl Alison was. If someone has taken her – and I won't lie to you, that is looking increasingly likely – I need to know everything I can about Alison so that I can work out where the point of contact is between Alison and this person. So I need you to tell me about your daughter.'

Ruth sighed. 'She's a lovely lass. Bright as a button, always has been. Her teachers all say she could go to college if she sticks in at her books. University even.' She cocked her head to one side. 'You'll have been to university.' It was a statement, not a question.

'Yes. I studied law at Manchester.'

She nodded. 'You'll know what it's like then, studying. She never has to be told to do her homework, you know, not like Derek and Janet. I think she actually likes schoolwork, though she'd cut her tongue out soon as admit it. God knows where that comes from. Neither me nor her dad were ones for school. Couldn't get out soon enough. She's not a swot, mind you. She likes her fun an' all, does our Alison.'

'What does she do for fun?' George probed gently.

'They're all daft about that pop music, her and Janet and Derek. The Beatles, Gerry and the Pacemakers, Freddie and the Dreamers, all that lot. Charlie too, though he's not got the time to be sitting round every night listening to records. But he goes to the dances at

96

the Pavilion Gardens, and he's always telling Alison what records she should get next. She's got more records than the shop, I'm always telling her. You'd need more than two ears to listen to that lot. Phil buys them for her. He goes into Buxton every week and chooses a selection from the hit parade as well as the ones Charlie tells her about . . .' Her voice tailed off.

'What else does she do?'

'Sometimes Charlie takes them into Buxton to the roller-skating on a Wednesday night.' Her breath caught in her throat. 'Oh God, I wish he'd been taking them last night,' she cried, sudden realization felling her. Her head dropped and she drew so hard on her cigarette that George could hear the tobacco crackle. When she looked up, her eyes brimmed with tears and held an appeal that cut directly through his professional defences to his heart. 'Find her, please,' she croaked.

He pressed his lips together and nodded. 'Believe me, Mrs Hawkin, I intend to do just that.'

'Even if it's only to bury her.'

'I hope it won't come to that,' he said.

'Aye. You and me both.' She exhaled a narrow stream of smoke. 'You and me both.'

He waited for a moment, then said, 'What about friends? Who was she close to?'

Ruth sighed. 'It's hard for them, making friends outside Scardale. They never get the chance to join in anything after school. If they get invited to parties or owt, chances are they can't get back home afterwards. The nearest they can get on a bus is Longnor. So they just don't go. Besides, folk in Buxton are set against Scardale folk. They think we're all heathen inbred idiots.' Her voice was sarcastic. 'The kids get picked on. So they stick to their own, by and large. Our Alison's good company, and I hear tell from her teachers that she's well enough liked at school. But she's never really had what you'd call a best friend apart from her cousins.'

Another dead end. 'There's one other thing . . . I'd like to look at Alison's room, if I may. Just to get a sense of what she was like.' He didn't add, 'and to help myself to the contents of her hairbrush so the forensic scientists can compare what we found sticking to the blood on the tree in the spinney.'

She got to her feet, her movements those of a woman far older. 'I've got the heater on up there. Just in case . . .' She left the sentence unfinished.

He followed her into the hall, which was no warmer than it had been the night before. The transition nearly took his breath away. Ruth led the way up a broad flight of stairs with barley-sugar-twist banisters in oak turned almost black by years of polishing. 'One other thing,' he said as they climbed. 'I presume that the fact that Alison is still called Carter means your husband hasn't formally adopted her?'

The tensing of the muscles in her neck and back was so swift George could almost believe he'd imagined it. 'Phil were all for it,' she said. 'He wanted to adopt. But Alison were only six when her dad . . . died. Old enough to remember how much she loved him. Too young to see he was a human being with faults and failings. She thinks letting Phil adopt her would be a betrayal of her dad's memory. I reckon she'll come round in time, but she's a stubborn lass, won't be pushed where she doesn't want to go.' They were on the landing now and Ruth turned to him, face composed and unreadable. 'I persuaded Phil to let it lie for now.' She pointed past George, down a corridor that made a strange dog-leg halfway down where the building had been extended at some indeterminate period. 'Alison's room is the last one on the right. You won't mind if I don't come with you.' Again, it was a statement, not a question. George found himself admiring the way this woman still managed to know her own mind, even under such extreme stress.

'Thanks, Mrs Hawkin. I won't be long.' He walked along the passage, conscious of her eyes on him. But even that uncomfortable knowledge wasn't sufficient distraction to prevent him noting his surroundings. The carpet was worn, but had clearly once been expensive. Some of the prints and watercolours that lined the wall were spotted with age, but still retained their charm. George recognized several scenes from the southern part of the county where he'd grown up as well as the familiar stately historic houses of Chatsworth, Haddon and Hardwick. He noticed that the floor was uneven at the jink in the corridor, as if the builders had been incompetent in all three dimensions. At the last door on the right, he paused and took a deep breath. This might be the closest he'd ever get to Alison Carter.

The warmth that hit him like a blanket seemed curiously appropriate to what was, in spite of its size, a snug room. Because it was on the corner of the house, Alison's bedroom had two windows, increasing the sense of space. The windows were long and shallow, each divided into four by deep stone lintels which revealed the eighteen-inch thickness of the walls. He closed the door and stepped into the middle of the room.

First impressions, George reminded himself. Warm: there was an electric fire as well as the plug-in oil radiator. Comfortable: the three-quarter-sized bed had a thick quilt covered in dark-green satin, and the two basket chairs had plump cushions. Modern: the carpet was thick brown shag pile with swirls of olive-green and mustard running through it, and the walls were decorated with pictures of pop stars, mostly cut from magazines by the looks of their skewed edges. Expensive: there was a plain wooden wardrobe and matching dressing table with a long, low mirror and a vanity stool in front of it, all so unscarred they had to be relatively new. George had seen bedroom suites like that when he and Anne were choosing their own furniture and he had a pretty good idea how much it must have cost. Cheap it wasn't. On a table under the window was a Dansette record player, dark red plastic with cream knobs. A deep stack of records was piled haphazardly underneath. Philip Hawkin was clearly determined to make a good impression on his stepdaughter, he surmised. Maybe he thought the way to her heart was through the material goods she must have lacked as the child of a widow in a community as impoverished as Scardale.

George moved across to the dressing table and folded himself awkwardly on to the stool. He caught his eye in the mirror. The last time his eyes had looked like that had been when he'd been cramming for his finals. And he'd missed a patch of stubble under his left ear, a direct result of the lack of vanity of the Methodist faith. The absence of a mirror in the vestry had forced him to shave in his rear-view mirror. No self-respecting advertising agency would hire him to promote anything except sleeping pills. He pulled a face at himself and got to work. Alison's hairbrush lay bristles upwards on the dressing table, and George expertly removed as many hairs as he could. Luckily, she'd not been too fastidious and he was able to accumulate a couple of dozen, which he transferred to an empty polythene bag.

Then, with a sigh, he began the distasteful search of Alison's personal possessions. Half an hour later, he had found nothing unexpected. He'd even flicked through every book on the small bookcase that stood by the bed. Nancy Drew, the Famous Five, the Chalet School, Georgette Heyer, *Wuthering Heights* and *Jane Eyre* held neither secret nor surprise. A well-thumbed edition of Palgrave's *Golden Treasury* contained only poetry. The dressing table yielded schoolgirl underwear, a couple of training bras, half a dozen bars of scented soap, a sanitary belt and half a packet of towels, a jewellery box containing a couple of cheap pendants and a baby's silver christening bracelet inscribed, 'Alison Margaret Carter'. The only thing he might have expected to find but hadn't was a bible. On the other hand, Scardale was so cut off from the rest of the world, they might still be worshipping the corn goddess here. Maybe the missionaries had never made it this far.

A small wooden box on the dressing table yielded more interesting results. It contained half a dozen black and white snapshots, most of them curled and yellowing at the edges. He recognized a youthful Ruth Hawkin, head thrown back in laughter, looking up at a dark-haired man whose head was ducked down in awkward shyness. There were two other photographs of the pair, arms linked and faces carefree, all obviously taken on the Golden Mile at Blackpool.

Honeymoon? George wondered. Beneath them was a pair of photographs of the same man, dark hair flopping over his forehead. He was dressed in work clothes, a thick belt holding up trousers that looked as if they'd been made for a man much longer in the torso. In one, he was standing on a harrow hitched to a tractor. In the other, he was crouched beside a blonde child who was grinning happily at the camera. Unmistakably Alison. The final photograph was more recent, judging by its white margins. It showed Charlie Lomas and an elderly woman leaning against a dry-stone wall, blurred limestone cliffs in the background. The woman's face was shadowed by a straw hat whose broad brim was forced down over her ears by the scarf that tied under her chin. All that was visible was the straight line of her mouth and her jutting chin, but it was obvious from her awkwardly bent body that she was far too old to be Charlie Lomas's mother. As if they were being captured by a Victorian photographer, held still by dire warnings of moving during the exposure, Charlie stood stony-faced and gazed straight at the camera. His arms were folded across his chest and he looked like every gauche and defiant young lad George had ever seen protesting his innocence in a police station.

'Fascinating,' he murmured. The photographs of her father were predictable, though he'd have expected to see them framed and on display. But that the only other image Alison Carter treasured was one that included the cousin who had made the convenient discovery in the copse was, to say the least, interesting to a mind as trained in suspicion as George's. Carefully, he replaced the photographs in the box. Then, on second thoughts, he removed the one of Charlie and the old woman and slipped it into his pocket.

It was among the records that he found his first examples of Alison's handwriting. On scraps of paper torn from school exercise books, he found fragments of song lyrics that had obviously had some particular meaning for her. Lines from Elvis Presley's 'Devil in Disguise', Lesley Gore's 'It's My Party (And I'll Cry if I Want To)', Cliff Richard's 'It's All in the Game' and Shirley Bassey's 'I (Who Have Nothing)' painted a disquieting picture of unhappiness at odds with the image everyone had projected of Alison Carter. They spoke of the pains of love and betrayal, loss and loneliness. There was, George knew, nothing unusual about an adolescent experiencing those feelings and believing nobody had ever been through the same thing. But if that was how Alison had felt, she'd done a very efficient job of keeping it secret from those around her.

It was a small incongruity, but it was the only one George had found. He slipped the sheets of paper into another plastic bag. There was no real reason to imagine they might be evidence, but he wasn't taking any chances with this one. He'd never forgive himself if the one detail he overlooked turned out to be crucial. Not only might it damage his career, but far more importantly, it might allow Alison's killer to go free. He stopped in his tracks, his hand halfway to the doorknob.

It was the first time he'd admitted to himself what his professional logic said must be the case. He was no longer looking for Alison Carter. He was looking for her body. And her killer.

Thursday, 12th December 1963. 6.23 p.m.

Wearily, George walked down the front path of Scardale Manor. He'd check in at the incident room in the Methodist Hall in case anything fresh had cropped up, then he'd drop off the hair samples at divisional HQ in Buxton and go home to a hot bath, a home-cooked meal and a few hours' sleep; what passed for normal life in an investigation like this. But first, he wanted to have a few words with young Charlie Lomas.

He'd barely made it as far as the village green when a figure lurched out of the shadows in front of him. Startled, he stopped and stared, struggling to believe what he was seeing. His tiredness tripped a giggle inside him, but he managed to swallow it before it spilled into the misty night air. The shape had resolved itself into something an artist might have fallen into raptures over. The bent old woman who peered up at him was the archetype of the crone as witch, right down to the hooked nose that almost met the chin, complete with wart sprouting hairs and black shawl over her head and shoulders. She had to be the original of the photograph he carried in his pocket. The strange suddenness of the coincidence provoked an involuntary pat of the pocket containing her facsimile. 'You'd be the boss, then,' she said in a voice like a gate that creaked in soprano.

'I'm Detective Inspector Bennett, if that's what you mean, madam,' he said.

Her skin crinkled in an expression of contempt. 'Fancy titles,' she said. 'Waste of time in Scardale, lad. Mind you, you're all wasting your time. None of you've got the imagination to understand owt that goes on here. Scardale's not like Buxton, you know. If Alison Carter's not where she should be, the answer'll be somewhere in somebody's head in Scardale, not in the woods waiting to be found like a fox in a trap.'

'Perhaps you could help me find it, then, Mrs . . . ?'

'And why should I, mister? We've always sorted out our own here. I don't know what possessed Ruth, calling strangers to the dale.' She made to push past him on the path, but he stepped sideways to block her.

'A girl's missing,' he said gently. 'This is something Scardale can't sort out for itself. Whether you like it or not, you live in the world. But we need your help as much as you need ours.'

The woman suddenly hawked violently and spat on the ground at his feet. 'Until you show some sign of knowing what you should be looking for, that's all the help you'll get from me, mister.' She veered off at an angle and moved off across the green, surprisingly quick on her feet for a woman who couldn't, he reckoned, be a day under eighty. He stood watching until the mist swallowed her, like a man who has found himself the victim of a time warp.

'Met Ma Lomas, then, have you?' Detective Sergeant Clough said with a grin, looming out of nowhere.

'Who is Ma Lomas?' George asked, bemused.

'Like with Sylvia, the question should be not, "Who is Ma Lomas?" but, "What is she?"' Clough intoned solemnly. 'Ma is the matriarch of Scardale. She's the oldest inhabitant, the only one of her generation left. Ma claims she celebrated her twenty-first the year of Victoria's Diamond Jubilee, but I don't know about that.'

'She looks old enough.'

'Aye. But who the hell in Scardale even knew Victoria was on the throne, never mind how long she'd been there for? Eh?' Clough delivered his punchline with a mocking smile.

'So where does she fit in? What relation is she to Alison?'

Clough shrugged. 'Who knows? Great-grandmother, second cousin once removed, aunt, niece? All of the above? You'd need to be sharper than *Burke's Peerage* to work out all the connections between this lot, sir. All I know is that according to PC Grundy, she's the eyes and ears of the world. There's not a mouse breaks wind in Scardale without Ma Lomas knowing about it.'

'And yet she doesn't seem very keen to help us find a missing girl. A girl who's a blood relative. Why do you suppose that is?'

Clough shrugged. 'They're all much of a muchness. They don't like outsiders at the best of times.'

'Was this the kind of attitude you and Cragg came up against last night when you were asking people if they'd seen Alison Carter?'

'More often than not. They answer your questions, but they never volunteer a single thing more than you've asked them.'

'Do you think they were all telling you the truth about not having seen Alison?' George asked, patting his pockets in search of his cigarettes.

Clough produced his own packet just as George remembered leaving his with Ruth Hawkin. 'There you go,' Clough said. 'I don't think they were lying. But they might well have been hanging on to information that's relevant. Especially if we didn't know the right questions to ask.'

'We're going to have to talk to them all again, aren't we?' George sighed.

'Like as not, sir.'

'They'll have to wait till tomorrow. Except for young Charlie Lomas. You don't happen to know where he is, do you?'

'One of the turnips took him up the Methodist Hall to make a statement. Must be half an hour ago now,' Clough said negligently.

'I don't ever want to hear that again, Sergeant,' George said, his tiredness transforming into anger.

'What?' Clough sounded bemused.

'A turnip is a vegetable that farmers feed to sheep. I've met plenty of CID officers who'd qualify for vegetable status ahead of most uniformed officers I've met. We need uniform's cooperation on this case, and I won't have you jeopardizing it. Is that clear, Sergeant?'

Clough scratched his jaw. 'Pretty much, aye. Though with me not managing to make it to grammar school, I'm not sure if I'll be able to remember it right.'

It was, George knew, a defining moment. 'I tell you what, Sergeant. At the end of this case, I'll buy you a packet of fags for every day you manage to remember it.'

Clough grinned. 'Now that's what I call an incentive.'

'I'm going to talk to Charlie Lomas. Do you fancy sitting in?'

'It will be my pleasure, sir.'

George set off towards his car, then suddenly stopped, frowning at his sergeant. 'What are you doing here, anyway? I thought you were still on night shift till the weekend?'

Clough looked embarrassed. 'I am. But I decided to

come on duty this afternoon. I wanted to give a hand.' He gave a sly grin. 'It's all right, sir, I won't be putting in for the overtime.'

George tried to hide his surprise. 'Good of you,' he said. As they drove up the Scardale lane, George wondered at the sergeant's capacity to confound him. He thought he was a pretty good judge of character, but the more he saw of Tommy Clough, the more apparent contradictions he found in the man.

Clough appeared brash and vulgar, always the first to buy a round of drinks, always the loudest with the dirty jokes. But his arrest record spoke of a different man, a subtle and shrewd investigator who was adept at finding the weakness in his suspects and pushing at it until they collapsed and told him what he wanted to hear. He was always the first to eye up an attractive woman, yet he lived alone in a bachelor flat overlooking the lake in the Pavilion Gardens. He'd called round there once to pick Clough up for a last-minute court appearance. George had thought it would be a dump, but it was clean, furnished soberly and crammed with jazz albums, its walls decorated with line drawings of British birds. Clough had seemed disconcerted to find George on his doorstep, expecting to enter, and he'd been ready to leave in record time.

Now, the man who was always first to claim overtime for every extra minute worked had given up his free time to tramp the Derbyshire countryside in search of a girl whose existence he'd had no knowledge of twenty-four hours previously. George shook his head. He wondered if he was as much a puzzle to Tommy Clough as the sergeant was to him. Somehow, he doubted it.

George put his musings to one side and outlined his

suspicions of Charlie Lomas to his sergeant. 'It's not much, I know, but we've got nothing else at this stage,' he concluded.

'If he's got nothing to hide, it'll do him no harm to realize we're taking this seriously,' Clough said grimly. 'And if he has, he won't have for long.'

The Methodist Hall had a curiously subdued air. A couple of uniformed officers were processing paperwork. Peter Grundy and a sergeant George didn't know were poring over detailed relief maps of the immediate area, marking off squares with thick pencils. At the back of the room, Charlie Lomas's lanky height was folded into a collapsible wooden chair, his legs wound round each other, his arms wrapped round his chest. A constable sat opposite him, separated by a card table on which he was laboriously writing a statement.

George walked across to Grundy and drew him to one side. 'I'm planning on having a word with Charlie Lomas. What can you tell me about the lad?'

Immediately, the Longnor bobby's face fell still. 'In what respect, sir?' he asked formally. 'There's nothing known about him.'

'I know he hasn't got a record,' George said. 'But this is your patch. You've got relatives in Scardale –'

'The wife has,' Grundy interrupted.

'Whatever. Whoever. You must have some sense of what he's like. What he's capable of.'

George's words hung in the air. Grundy's face slowly settled into an expression of outraged hostility. 'You're not seriously thinking Charlie's got something to do with Alison going missing?' His tone was incredulous.

'I have some questions for him, and it would be helpful if I had some idea of the type of lad I'm going to be talking to,' George said wearily. 'That's all. So what's he like, PC Grundy?'

Grundy looked to his right then to his left, then right again, like a child waiting to cross the road correctly. But there was no escape from George's eyes. Grundy scratched the soft patch of skin behind his ear. 'He's a good lad, Charlie. He's an awkward age, though. All the lads his age around here, they go out and have a few pints and try to get off with lasses. But that's not right easy when you live in the back of beyond. The other thing about Charlie is that he's a bright lad. Bright enough to know he could make something of his life if he could bring himself to get out of Scardale. Only, he's not got the nerve to strike out on his own yet. So he gets a bit lippy from time to time, sounding off about what a hard time he has of it. But his heart's in the right place. He lives in the cottage with old Ma Lomas because she doesn't keep so well and the family likes to know there's somebody around to bring in the coal and fetch and carry for the old woman. It's not much of a life for a lad his age, but that's the one thing he never complains about.'

'Was he close to Alison?'

George could see Grundy considering how far he could push it. That was one of the hardest parts of his job, this constantly having to stand his ground and prove himself to his colleagues. 'They're all close down there,' Grundy finally said. 'There was no bad blood between him and Alison that I ever heard.'

However, it wasn't bad blood that George was interested in where the two Scardale cousins were concerned.

Realizing he'd gained all he could from Grundy, he

nodded his thanks and strolled towards the rear of the hall, praying he didn't look as exhausted as he felt. Probably he should wait till morning to interview Charlie Lomas. But he preferred to make his move while the lad was already on the back foot. Besides, there was always the million to one chance that Alison was still alive, and Charlie Lomas might just hold the key to her whereabouts. Even so slim a chance was too much to throw away.

As he approached, George picked up a chair and dropped it casually at the third side of the table, at right angles to both Charlie and the uniformed constable. Without being told, Clough followed his example, occupying the fourth side of the small table and hemming Charlie in. His eyes flicked from one to the other and he shifted in his seat. 'You know who I am, don't you, Charlie?' George asked.

The youth nodded.

'Speak when you're spoken to,' Clough said roughly. 'I bet that's what your gran always tells you. She is your gran, isn't she? I mean, she's not your auntie or your niece or your cousin, is she? Hard to tell down your way.'

Charlie twisted his mouth to one side and shook his head. 'There's no call for that,' he protested. 'I'm helping your lot.'

'And we're very grateful that you've volunteered to come and give a statement,' George said, falling effortlessly into Good Cop to Clough's Bad Cop. 'While you're here, I wanted to ask you one or two questions. Is that OK with you?'

Charlie breathed heavily through his nose. 'Aye. Come ahead.'

'It was impressive, you finding that disturbed spot in the spinney,' George said. 'There had been a whole team through there ahead of you, and none of them so much as picked up a trace of it.'

Charlie managed a shrug without actually releasing any of his limbs from their auto-embrace. 'It's like the back of my hand, the dale. You get to know a place right well, the slightest little thing just strikes you out of place, that's all it were.'

'You weren't the first from Scardale through there. But you were the first to notice.'

'Aye, well, happen I've got sharper eyes than some of you old buggers,' he said, attempting bravado but not even making the halfway line.

'I'm interested, you see, because we find that sometimes people who have been involved in a crime try to include themselves in the investigation,' George said mildly.

Charlie's body unwound as if galvanized. His feet slammed on the floor, his forearms on the table. Startled policemen looked around from the front of the hall. 'You're sick,' he said.

'I'm not sick, but I've got a good idea that somebody around these parts is. It's my job to find out who. Now, if somebody wanted to take Alison away or do anything to her, it would be a lot easier to manage if it was somebody she knew and trusted. Obviously, you know her. She's your cousin, you grew up with her. You tell her what records to get her stepfather to buy her. You sit by the fire with her in your cottage while your granny spins her tales of bygone days in sunny Scardale. You take her to the roller rink in Buxton on Wednesdays.' George shrugged. 'You'd have no trouble persuading her to go somewhere with you.'

Charlie pushed himself away from the table, then thrust his trembling hands into his trouser pockets. 'So?'

George produced the photograph he'd taken from Alison's room. 'She kept a photo of you in her bedroom,' was all he said as he showed it to Charlie.

His face twitched and he crossed his legs. 'She'll have kept it because of Ma,' he said insistently. 'She loves Ma, and the old witch hates having her photo taken. This must be about the only picture of Ma in existence.'

'Are you sure, Charlie?' Clough interjected. 'Because we think, my boss and me, that she fancied you. A nice young lass like that hanging around, worshipping the ground you walk on, not many blokes would say no to that, would they? Especially a lovely lass like Alison. A ripe fruit, ready for the plucking, ready to fall right into your hand. You sure that's not what it was like, Charlie boy?'

Charlie squirmed, shaking his head. 'You've got it all wrong, mister.'

'Has he?' George asked pleasantly. 'So how was it, Charlie? Was it embarrassing for you, having this kid trailing around after you when you went to the roller rink? Did Alison cramp your style with the older girls, was that the problem? Did you meet her in the dale yesterday teatime? Did she push you too far?'

Charlie hung his head and breathed deep. Then he looked up and turned to face George. 'I don't understand. Why are you treating me like this? All I've done is try and help. She's my cousin. She's part of my family. We look out for each other in Scardale, you know. It's not like Buxton, where nobody gives tuppence about anybody else.' He stabbed his finger at each of the policemen in turn. 'You should be out there finding her, not insulting me like this.' He jumped to his feet. 'Do I have to stop here?'

George stood up and gestured towards the door. 'You're free to leave whenever you want, Mr Lomas. However, we will need to speak to you again.'

Clough rose and walked round to George's side as Charlie stalked angrily out of the door, all raw-boned clumsiness and outrage. 'He's not got the gumption,' he said.

'Maybe not,' George said. The two men walked out in Charlie's wake, pausing on the threshold as the youth set off down the Scardale road. George stared after Charlie, wondering. Then he cleared his throat. 'I'll be heading home now. I'll be back before first light in the morning. You're in charge, at least of CID, till then.'

Clough laughed. It seemed to die in a puff of white breath in the oppressive night air. 'Me and Cragg, sir, eh? That'll give the villains something to think about. Was there any line of inquiry in particular you wanted us to pursue?'

'Whoever took Alison must have got her out of the dale somehow,' George said, almost thinking aloud. 'He couldn't have carried her for long, not a normally developed thirteen-year-old girl. If he took her down the Scarlaston valley into Denderdale, he'd have had to hike about four miles before he got to a road. But if he brought her up here to the Longnor road, it's probably only about a mile and a half as the crow flies. Why don't you and Cragg do a door-to-door in Longnor this evening, see if anybody noticed a vehicle parked by the side of the road near the Scardale turn?'

'Right you are, sir. I'll just find DC Cragg and we'll get to it.'

George returned to the incident room and arranged for the tracker dogs to work Denderdale the following morning, spent half an hour in Buxton Police Station filling out requisition forms for the forensic lab on the evidence from the spinney and Alison's hairbrush, then finally set off for home.

The villagers would just have to wait till tomorrow.

7

Thursday, 12th December 1963. 8.06 p.m.

George couldn't remember ever closing his front door with a greater sense of relief. Before he could even take off his hat, the door to the living room opened and Anne was there, taking the three short steps into his arms. 'It's great to be home,' he sighed, drinking in the musky smell of her hair, conscious too that he'd not washed since the previous morning.

'You work too hard,' she scolded gently. 'You'll do nobody any favours if you work yourself into the ground. Come on through, there's a fire on and it won't take me five minutes to warm up the casserole.' She moved back from his embrace and looked critically at him. 'You look worn out. It's a hot bath and bed for you as soon as you've finished your tea.'

'I'd rather have the bath first, if the water's hot.'

'And so you shall. I've had the immersion on. I was going to have a bath myself, but you'd better take the water. You get yourself undressed and I'll run the bath.' She shooed him upstairs ahead of her.

Half an hour later, he was in his dressing gown at the kitchen table, wolfing down a generous helping of beef and carrot stew accompanied by a plate of bread and butter. 'Sorry there's no spuds,' Anne apologized. 'I thought bread and butter would be quicker and I knew you'd need something as soon as you got in. You never eat properly when you're working.'

'Mmm,' he grunted through a mouthful of food.

'Have you found her, then, your missing girl? Is that why you're home?'

The food in his mouth seemed to congeal into an indigestible lump. George forced it down his gullet. It felt like swallowing a hairball the size of a golf ball. 'No,' he said, staring down at his plate. 'And I don't think she'll be alive when we do.'

Anne's face paled. 'But that's awful, George. How can you be sure?'

He shook his head and sighed. 'I can't be sure. But we know she didn't go off of her own free will. Don't ask me how, but we know. She's not from the kind of family where she'd be kidnapped for a ransom. And people who steal children generally don't keep them alive for long. So my guess is she's already dead. And if she's not, she will be before we can find her, because we've got absolutely nothing to go on. The villagers act like we're the enemy instead of on their side, and the landscape is so difficult to search properly it feels like even that's conspiring against us.' He pushed his plate away and reached for Anne's cigarettes.

'That's terrible,' she said. 'How can her mother begin to cope with it?'

'She's a strong woman, Ruth Hawkin. I suppose if you grow up in a place where life is as hard as it is in Scardale, you learn to bend rather than break. But I don't know how she's holding together. She

117

lost her first husband in a farming accident seven years ago, and now this. The new husband's not a lot of use either. One of those selfish beggars who see everything in terms of how it's going to affect them.'

'What? You mean a man?' Anne teased.

'Very funny. I'm not like that. I don't expect my tea on the table when I walk through the door, you know. You don't have to wait on me.'

'You'd soon get fed up if it wasn't.'

George conceded with a shrug and a smile. 'You're probably right. Us men get used to you women taking care of us. But if our child ever went missing, I don't think I'd be demanding my tea before my wife went out looking for her.'

'He did that?'

'According to one witness.' He shook his head. 'I shouldn't be telling you this.'

'Who am I going to tell? The only people I know here are other coppers' wives. And they've not exactly taken me to their bosom. The ones my age are all lower ranks' wives so they don't trust me, especially since I'm a qualified teacher and none of them have ever done anything more challenging than working in a shop or an office. And the officers' wives are all older than me and treat me like I'm a silly girl. So you can be sure I'm not going to be gossiping about your case, George,' Anne said with an edge of acerbity.

'I'm sorry. I know it's not been easy for you to make new friends here.' He reached out to grip her hand in his.

'I don't know how I'd go on if I lost a child.'

Almost unconsciously, her free hand slipped to her stomach.

George's eyes narrowed. 'Is there something you're not telling me?' he asked sharply.

Anne's fair skin flushed scarlet. 'I don't know, George. It's just that . . . well, my monthly visitor's overdue. A week overdue. So . . . I'm sorry, love, I didn't mean to say anything till I was sure, what with it being a missing child case you're on. But yes, I think I might be expecting.'

A slow smile spread across George's face as her words sank in. 'Really? I'm going to be a dad?'

'It could be a false alarm. But I've never been late before.' She looked almost apprehensive.

George jumped to his feet and swung her out of her chair, spinning her around in a whirl of joy. 'It's wonderful, wonderful, wonderful.' They staggered to a halt and he kissed her hard and passionately. 'I love you, Mrs Bennett.'

'And I love you too, Mr Bennett.'

He pulled her close, burying his face in her hair. A child. His child. All he had to do now was figure out how to manage what had been beyond every parent since Adam and Eve: how to keep it safe.

Up to that point, Alison Carter had been an important case to Detective Inspector George Bennett. Now it had symbolic importance. Now it was a crusade.

In Scardale, the mood was as brooding as the limestone crags surrounding the dale. Charlie Lomas's experience at the hands of the police had flashed round the village as fast as the news of Alison's disappearance. While the women checked anxiously and regularly that their children were all in bed asleep, the men had congregated in the kitchen of Bankside Cottage, where Ruth and her daughter had lived until her marriage to Hawkin.

Terry Lomas, Charlie's father, chewed the stem of his pipe and grumbled about the police. 'They've got no right to treat our Charlie like a criminal,' he said.

Charlie's older brother John scowled. 'They've got no idea what's happened to our Alison. They're just making an example of Charlie so it looks like they're doing something.'

'They're not going to let it go at that, though, are they?' Charlie's uncle Robert said. 'They'll go through us one by one if they get no change out of Charlie. That Bennett bloke, he's got a bee in his bonnet about Alison, you can tell.'

'But that's a good thing, isn't it?' Ray Carter chipped in. 'It means he's going to do a proper job. He's not going to settle till he's got an answer.'

'That's fine if it's the right answer,' Terry said.

'Aye,' Robert said pensively. 'But how do we make sure he doesn't get distracted from what he should be doing because he's too busy persecuting the likes of young Charlie? The lad's not tough, we all know that. They'll be putting words in his mouth. For all we know, if they can't get the right man, they'll decide to have Charlie anyway and to hell with it.'

'There's two roads we can go,' Jack Lomas said. 'We can stonewall them. Tell them nothing, except what we need to cover Charlie's back all ways. They'll soon realize they'll have to find another scapegoat then. Or we can bend over backwards to help them. Maybe that way they'll realize that looking at the people who cared about our Alison isn't going to find the lass or whoever took her.'

There was a long silence in the kitchen, punctuated by Terry sucking on his pipe. Eventually, old Robert Lomas spoke. 'Happen we can do both.'

Without George, the work went on. The searchers had given up for the day, but in the incident room, uniformed officers made plans for the following day. Already, they had accepted offers from the local Territorial Army volunteers and the RAF cadets to join the hunt at the weekend. Nobody was voicing their thoughts, but everyone was pessimistic. That didn't mean they wouldn't cover every inch of Derbyshire if they had to.

Up in Longnor, Clough and Cragg were awash with tea but starved of leads. They'd agreed to call it a night at half past nine, a farming community being earlier abed than the townies in Buxton. Just before close of play, Clough struck lucky. An elderly couple had been coming home from Christmas shopping in Leek and they'd noticed a Land Rover parked on the grass at the side of the Methodist Chapel. 'Just before five, it was,' the husband said definitely.

'What made you notice it?' Clough asked.

'We attend the chapel,' he said. 'Normally, it's only the minister who parks there. The rest of us leave our cars on the verge. Anybody local knows that.'

'Do you think the driver parked off the road to avoid being noticed?'

'I suppose so. He wasn't to know that was the one parking place that would make him conspicuous, was he?'

Clough nodded. 'Did you see the driver?'

Both shook their heads. 'It was dark,' the wife pointed out. 'It didn't have any lights on. And we were past it in moments.'

'Was there anything you did notice about the Land Rover? Was it long wheelbase or short wheelbase? What colour was it? Was it a fixed top or a canvas one? Any letters or numbers from the registration?' Clough probed.

Again, they shook their heads dubiously. 'We weren't paying much attention, to be honest,' the husband said. 'We were talking about the fatstock show. Chap from Longnor took one of the top prizes and we'd been invited to join him for a drink in Leek. I think half the village was going to be there. But we decided to come home. My wife wanted to get the decorations up.'

Clough glanced around at the home-made paper chains and the artificial Christmas tree complete with its pathetic string of fairy lights and a garland of tinsel that looked as if the dog had been chewing it since Christmas past. 'I can see why,' he said, dead-pan.

'I always like to get them done the day of the fatstock show,' the woman said proudly. 'Then we feel like Christmas is coming, don't we, Father?'

'We do, Doris, yes. So you see, Sergeant, our minds weren't really on the Land Rover at all.'

Clough got to his feet and smiled. 'Never mind,' he said. 'At least you noticed it was there. That's more than anybody else in the village did.'

'Too busy celebrating Alec Grundy's heifers,' the man said sagely.

Clough thanked them again and left, rendezvousing with Cragg in the local pub. He'd never believed that the rule about not drinking on duty need be strictly applied, especially on night shift. Like high-grade oil to an engine, a couple of drinks always made his mind run more smoothly. Over a pint of Marston's Pedigree, he told Cragg what he'd heard.

'That's great,' Cragg enthused. 'Professor'll like that.'

Clough pulled a face. 'Up to a point. He'll like the fact we've got a pair of witnesses who saw a Land Rover parked where locals knew not to park. He'll like the fact that this unusual piece of parking happened around the same time Alison disappeared.' Then Clough explained what he thought George wouldn't like.

'Bugger,' Cragg said.

'Aye.' Clough took two inches off his pint in a single swallow. 'Bugger.'

Friday, 13th December 1963. 5.35 a.m.

George walked into Buxton Police Station through the front office to find a uniformed constable attaching festive bells of honeycomb paper to the wall with drawing pins. 'Very jolly,' he grunted. 'Sergeant Lucas here?'

'You might just catch him, sir. He said he was going to the canteen for a bacon sandwich. First break he's had all night, sir.'

'The red bell's higher than the green one,' George said on his way out.

The PC glared at the door as it swung shut.

George found Bob Lucas munching a bacon sandwich and staring glumly at the morning papers. 'Seen this, sir?' he greeted him, pushing the *Daily News* across the table. George picked it up and began to read.

Daily News, *Friday, 13th December 1963, p.5*

MISSING GIRL: IS THERE A LINK?

Dogs in manhunt for Alison

By *Daily News Reporter*

Police yesterday refused to rule out a link between missing schoolgirl Alison Carter, 13, and two similar disappearances less than thirty miles away within the last six months.

There are striking similarities between the three cases, and detectives spoke privately of the need to consider whether a joint task force should be set up among the three police forces investigating the cases.

The latest manhunt centres round Alison Carter, who vanished from the remote Derbyshire hamlet of Scardale on Wednesday. She had taken her collie, Shep, for a walk after school, but when she failed to return home, her mother, Mrs Ruth Hawkin, alerted local police at Buxton.

A search led by tracker dogs failed to find any trace of the girl, although her dog was discovered unharmed in nearby woods.

Her mystery disappearance comes less than three weeks after 12-year-old John Kilbride went missing in Ashton-under-Lyne. He was last seen in the town's market at teatime. Lancashire police have so far failed to come up with a single positive sighting of him since.

Pauline Reade, 16, was going to a dance when she left her family home in Wiles Street, Gorton, Manchester in July. But she never arrived and, as with John and Alison, police have no idea what happened to her.

A senior Derbyshire police officer said: 'At this point, we rule nothing out and nothing in. We can find no reason for Alison being missing. She was not in trouble at home or at school.

'If we do not find Alison today, the search will be intensified. We just don't know what has happened to her, and we're very concerned, not least because of the very bitter weather we're experiencing at the moment.'

A Manchester CID officer told the *Daily News*, 'Of course, we hope Alison is found quickly. But we would be very happy to share the fruits of our investigations with Derbyshire if this case drags on.'

'Bloody journalists,' George complained. 'They twist everything you say. Where's all the stuff I said about there being more dissimilarities than there are similarities? I might as well have saved my breath. This Don Smart's just going to write what he wants to write, no matter what the truth is.'

'It's always the same with the Fleet Street reporters,' Lucas said sourly. 'The local lads have to stay on the right side of the truth because they have to come back to us week after week for their stories, but that London lot don't give a monkey's whether they upset the police in Buxton or not.' He sighed. 'Were you looking for me, sir?'

'Just something I wanted you to pass on to the day shift. I think it's time we located any known sex offenders in the area and brought them in for questioning.'

'In the whole division, sir?' Lucas sounded weary.

Sometimes, George thought, he understood exactly why some officers remained locked inside their uniforms for the duration of their careers. 'I think we'll concentrate on the immediate area round Scardale. Maybe a five-mile radius, extending it up on the northern side to include Buxton.'

'Hikers come from miles around,' Lucas said. 'There's no guaranteeing our man isn't from Manchester or Sheffield or Stoke.'

'I know, Sergeant, but we've got to start somewhere.' George pushed his chair back and stood up. 'I'm off to Scardale. I'll be there all day, I expect.'

'You'll have heard about the Land Rover?' Lucas said, his voice as neutral as his face was smug.

'Land Rover?'

'Your lads turned up a pair of witnesses in Longnor last night. Saw a Land Rover parked off the road near the Scardale turn-off round about the time young Alison left the house.'

George's face lit up. 'But that's fantastic news!'

'Not entirely. It were dark. The witnesses couldn't give any description except that it was a Land Rover.'

'But we'll be able to get impressions from the tyres. It's a start,' George said, his irritation with Lucas and the *Daily News* forgotten in his excitement.

Lucas shook his head. 'Afraid not, sir. The spot where the Land Rover was parked? Up the side of the Methodist Chapel. Right where our cars were in and out all night and day yesterday.'

'Bugger,' said George.

Tommy Clough was nursing a mug of tea and a cigarette when George arrived at the incident room. 'Morning, sir,' he said, not bothering to get to his feet.

'You still here?' George asked. 'You can go off duty now, if you like. You must be exhausted.'

'No worse than you were yesterday. Sir, if it's all right with you, I'd rather stop on. This is my last night shift anyway, so I might as well get used to going to bed at the right time. If you're interviewing the villagers, happen I could be some help. I've seen most of them already, I've picked up a fair bit of the background.'

George considered for a moment. Clough's normally ruddy face was paler than usual, the skin around his eyes puffy. But his eyes were still alert, and he had some of the local knowledge that George lacked. Besides, it was about time George established a working partnership with one of his three sergeants that went deeper than the surface. 'All right. But if you start yawning when some old dear decides to tell us her life story, I'm sending you straight home.'

'Fine by me, sir. Where do you want to start?'

George crossed to one of the tables and pulled a pad of paper towards him. 'A map. Who lives where and who they are. That's where I want to start.'

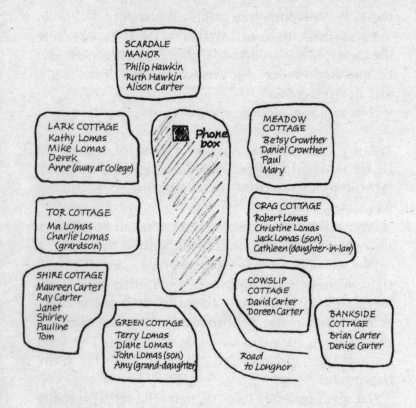

SCARDALE MANOR
Philip Hawkin
Ruth Hawkin
Alison Carter

LARK COTTAGE
Kathy Lomas
Mike Lomas
Derek
Anne (away at College)

Phone box

MEADOW COTTAGE
Betsy Crowther
Daniel Crowther
Paul
Mary

TOR COTTAGE
Ma Lomas
Charlie Lomas (grandson)

CRAG COTTAGE
Robert Lomas
Christine Lomas
Jack Lomas (son)
Cathleen (daughter-in-law)

SHIRE COTTAGE
Maureen Carter
Ray Carter
Janet
Shirley
Pauline
Tom

GREEN COTTAGE
Terry Lomas
Diane Lomas
John Lomas (son)
Amy (grand-daughter)

COWSLIP COTTAGE
David Carter
Doreen Carter

BANKSIDE COTTAGE
Brian Carter
Denise Carter

Road to Longnor

George scratched his head. 'I don't suppose you know how they're all related?' he asked, staring down at the map Tommy Clough had sketched out for him.

'Beyond me,' he confessed. 'Apart from the obvious, like Charlie Lomas is Terry and Diane's youngest. Mike Lomas is the eldest of Robert and Christine's. Then there's Jack who lives with them, and they've got two daughters – Denise, who's married to Brian Carter, and Angela, who's married to a smallholder over towards Three Shires Head.'

George held up his hand. 'Enough,' he groaned.

'Since you've obviously got a natural talent for it, you're officer in charge of Scardale genealogy. You can remind me of who belongs where as and when I need to know it. Right now, all I want to know is where Alison Carter fits in.'

Tommy cast his eyes upwards as if trying to picture the family tree. 'OK. Never mind cousins, first, second or third. I'll stick with just the main relationships. Somehow or other, Ma Lomas is her great-grandmother. Her father, Roy Carter, was David and Ray's brother. On her mother's side, she was a Crowther. Ruth is sister to Daniel and also to Terry Lomas's wife Diane.' Clough pointed to the relevant houses on the map. 'But they're all interconnected.'

'There must be some fresh blood now and again,' George objected. 'Otherwise they'd all be village idiots.'

'There are one or two incomers to dilute the mixture. Cathleen Lomas, Jack's wife, is a Longnor lass. And John Lomas married a woman from over Bakewell way. Lasted long enough for her to have Amy, then she was off somewhere she could watch *Coronation Street* and go out for a drink without it being a military operation. And of course, there's Philip Hawkin.'

'Yes, let's not forget the squire,' George said thoughtfully. He sighed and stood up. 'We could do with finding out a bit more about him. St Albans, that's where he hails from, isn't it?' He took out his notebook and jotted down a reminder. 'Don't let me forget to follow that up. Come on then, Tommy. Let's have another crack at Scardale.'

Brian Carter wiped the teats of the next cow in line and, with surprising gentleness, clamped the milking machine on to her udder. Dawn had still been a few hours away when he'd left the warm bed he shared with his new wife, Denise, in Bankside Cottage, the two-bedroomed house where Alison Carter was born on a rainy night in 1950. Tramping up through the silent village with his father, he'd been unable to avoid thinking bitterly how much his cousin's disappearance had changed his world already.

His had been a simple, uncomplicated life. They'd always been very self-contained, very private in Scardale. He'd grown used to getting called names at school and later in the pubs when folk had had a few too many. He knew all the tired old jokes about inbreeding and secret black magic rituals, but he'd learned to ignore all that and get on with his life.

When there was light, Scardale worked the land and when there wasn't, they were still busy. The women spun wool, knitted jumpers, crocheted shawls and blankets and baby clothes, made preserves and chutneys, things they could sell through the Women's Institute market in Buxton.

The men maintained the buildings, inside and out. They also worked with wood. Terry Lomas made beautiful turned wooden bowls, rich and lustrous, the grain chosen for its intricate patterns. He sent them off to a craft centre in London where they sold for what seemed ridiculous sums of money to everyone else in the village. Brian's father David made wooden toys for a shop in Leek. There wouldn't have been time for the wild pagan rituals that gullible drinkers speculated about in Buxton bars, even supposing anyone had been interested. The truth was, everyone in Scardale worked too bloody hard to have time for anything except eating and sleeping.

There was little need for contact with the outside world on a daily basis. Most of what was consumed in Scardale was produced in the circle of looming limestone – meat, potatoes, milk, eggs, some fruit and a few vegetables. Ma Lomas made wine from elderflowers, elderberries, nettles, dandelions, birch sap, rhubarb, gooseberries and whinberries. If it grew, she fermented it. Everybody drank it. Even the children would get a glass now and again for medicinal purposes. There was a van came on Tuesdays selling fish and greengrocery. Another van came from Leek on Thursdays, a general grocer. Anything else would be bought at the market in Leek or in Buxton by whoever was there selling their own produce or livestock.

It had been strange, the transition from being at school, where he'd gone out of the dale five days a week, to being an adult, working the land and sometimes not leaving Scardale from one month to the next. There wasn't even television to disrupt the rhythm of life. He remembered when old Squire Castleton came back from Buxton with a TV he'd bought for the Coronation. His father and his Uncle Roy had erected the aerial and the whole village had crowded into the squire's parlour. With a flourish, the old man had switched on, and they all stared dumbfounded at a February blizzard. No matter how David and Roy had fiddled with the aerial, all it did was crackle like fat on a fire, and all they could see was interference. The only kind of interference anybody in Scardale had a mind to put up with.

Now it was all changed. Alison had disappeared and all of a sudden, their lives seemed to belong to everybody. The police, the papers, they all wanted their questions answering, whether it was any of their business or not. And Brian felt like he had no natural defences against such an invasion. He wanted to hurt someone. But there was no one to hand.

It was still dark when George and Clough reached the outskirts of the village. The first light they came to spilled out of a half-closed barn door. 'Might as well start here,' George said, pulling the car over on to the verge. 'Who's this going to be?' he asked as they tramped over the few yards of muddy concrete to the door.

'It'll likely be Brian and David Carter,' Clough said. 'They're the cowmen.'

The two men in the barn couldn't hear their approach over the clattering and heavy liquid breathing of the milking apparatus. George waited till they turned round, taking in the strangely sweet smells of dung, sweating animal and milk, watching as the men washed the teats of each cow before clamping the milking machine to her udder. Finally, the older of the two turned. George's first impression was that Ruth Hawkin's careful eyes had been transplanted into an Easter Island statue. His face was all planes and angles, his cheeks like slabs and his eye sockets like a carving in pink wax. 'Any news?' he demanded, his voice loud against the machinery.

George shook his head. 'I came to introduce myself. I'm Detective Inspector George Bennett. I'm in charge of the investigation.' As he walked towards the older man, the younger stopped what he was doing and leaned against the massive hindquarters of one of his Friesians, arms folded across his chest.

'I'm David Carter,' the older man said. 'Alison's uncle. And this is my lad Brian.' Brian Carter gave a stately nod. He had his father's face, but his eyes were narrow and pale, like shards of topaz. He couldn't have been much more than twenty, but the downward cast of his mouth appeared to have been set in stone.

'I wanted to say we're doing everything we can to find out what's happened to Alison,' George said.

'Haven't found her though, have you?' Brian said, his voice sullen as his expression.

'No. We will be searching again as soon as it's light and if you want to join us again, you'd be more than welcome. But that's not why I'm here. I can't help thinking that the answer to what happened to Alison was somewhere in her life. I don't believe that whoever did this acted on the spur of the moment. It was planned. And that means somebody left traces. Whether you know it or not, someone in this village saw something or heard something that will give us a lead. I'm going to be talking to everybody in the village today, and I'll say the same to you all. I need you to search your memories for anything out of the ordinary, anyone you saw that didn't belong here.'

Brian snorted. He sounded surprisingly like one of his cows. 'If you're looking for somebody that doesn't belong here, you don't have to look very far.'

'Who did you have in mind?' George asked.

'Brian,' his father warned.

Brian scowled and fumbled in the pocket of his overall for a cigarette. 'Dad, he doesn't belong here. He never will.'

'Who are we talking about?' George persisted.

'Philip Hawkin, who else?' Brian muttered through a mouthful of smoke. His head came up and he stared defiantly at the back of his father's head.

'You're not suggesting her stepfather had anything to do with Alison's disappearance, are you?' Clough asked, an edge of challenge in his voice that George suspected Brian Carter would find irresistible.

'You didn't ask that. You asked who didn't belong here. Well, he doesn't. Ever since he turned up, he's been sticking his oar in, trying to tell us how to farm our land, as if he's the one been doing it for generations. He thinks if you read a book or an NFU pamphlet, suddenly you're an expert. And the way he courted my Auntie Ruth. He wouldn't leave her alone. The only way she was ever going to get any peace was if she married him,' Brian blurted out.

'Didn't think you minded that,' his father said sarcastically. 'If Ruth and Alison hadn't moved out of Bankside Cottage, you and Denise would have had to start your married life in your old bedroom. I don't know about you, but I could do without the bedhead banging on the wall half the night.'

Brian flushed and glowered at his father. 'You leave Denise out of this. We're talking about Hawkin. And you know as well as me that he doesn't belong here. Don't act like you don't spend half of every day maunging on about what a useless article he is and how you wish the old squire had had more sense than leave the land to an incomer like Hawkin.'

'That doesn't mean he had anything to do with Alison going,' David Carter said, rubbing his hand over his chin in what was clearly a familiar gesture of exasperation.

'Your father's right,' George said mildly.

'Maybe so,' Brian muttered grudgingly. 'But he always has to know best, does Hawkin. If he lays down the law in the house the way he does on the land, then my cousin's got worse than a dog's life. I don't care what anybody says, she can't have been happy living with Hawkin.' He spat contemptuously on the concrete floor then turned away abruptly and stalked off to the far end of the milking shed.

'Take no notice of the lad,' David Carter said wearily. 'His mouth works harder than his brain. Hawkin's an idiot, but according to Ruth, he thought the world of Alison. And I'd take my sister's word ahead of that son of mine.' He shook his head and half turned to watch Brian fiddling with a piece of machinery. 'I thought marrying Denise would knock some sense into him. Too much to hope for, I suppose.' He sighed. 'We'll be out with the searchers, Mr Bennett. And I'll think on what you've said. See if I can think of owt.'

They shook hands. George could feel Carter's cool eyes appraising him as he followed Clough out into the grey-streaked light of dawn. 'No love lost between young Brian and the squire,' George commented as they walked back to the car.

'He's saying nothing that the rest of Scardale doesn't think, according to PC Grundy. We had a chat with him last night after we'd done the door-to-door interviews. He says all the villagers reckon Hawkin's in love with the sound of his own voice. He likes people to be in no doubt who the boss is, and they don't take kindly to that in Scardale. The tradition here has always been that the villagers get on with working the land the way they see fit and the squire collects his rents and keeps his nose out. So you're going to hear a lot of complaints about Hawkin,' Clough said.

He couldn't have been more wrong.

8

Friday, 13th December 1963. 12.45 p.m.
Four hours later, George reckoned he'd seen all the
evidence of heredity he'd ever need. The surnames
might vary according to strict genealogical lines, but
the physical characteristics seemed scattered at random. The slab face of David Carter, the hooked nose
of Ma Lomas, the feline eyes of Janet Carter were all
repeated in various combinations, along with other
equally distinctive features. George felt like a child
playing with one of those books where the pages are
split horizontally and the reader mixes and matches
eyes, noses and mouths.

What the Scardale villagers also had in common was
their complete mystification at Alison's disappearance.
As Clough had predicted, few were willing to volunteer
even the little that Brian Carter had given. Most of the
conversations were an uphill struggle. George would
introduce himself and deliver his little speech. The villagers would look thoughtful, then shake their heads. No,
nothing unusual had happened. No, they hadn't seen any
strangers. No, they didn't think anybody from the village
would touch a hair on Alison's head. And by the way,

137

Charlie Lomas was as good-natured a lad as ever walked, and he didn't deserve being treated like a criminal.

The only point of interest was that not a finger pointed at the squire. Not a word of complaint was uttered about him, not a voice raised against him. True, no one sang his praises, but by the end of the morning, it would have been tempting to think that Brian Carter was the only person in Scardale who thought there was anything about Philip Hawkin worth criticizing.

Finally, George and Clough retired empty-handed to the caravan, uninhabited except for a WPC who jumped to her feet and brewed up as soon as they walked in. 'You were wrong,' George sighed.

'Sir?' Clough opened his cigarette packet and tipped one out for George without bothering to ask.

'You said we'd be hearing a lot of complaints about Hawkin. But we've not had a cheep out of anybody except that young hothead Brian Carter.'

Clough considered for a moment, a frown wrinkling his broad forehead like the skin on a caramel custard. 'Maybe that's why. He's young enough to think it matters in a case like this that Hawkin's not one of them. The others, they're wise enough to understand that there's a hell of a difference between not liking somebody because he tells you how to farm your land and suspecting him of abducting a child.'

George took a cautious sip of his tea. Not so hot it would scald. He drank down half the cup to ease his dry throat; whatever else the people of Scardale were, they weren't generous with their hot drinks. They'd actually been in Diane Lomas's kitchen while the woman had sat with a pot of tea in front of her that she'd never once offered them. 'Maybe. But I don't want to lose sight of the fact that this is a close-knit community. Just the kind of place where they think lynch law's the best way of dealing with their difficulties. It could be that they think Hawkin's behind this and we're too stupid to nail him. Happen they figure the best way to deal with him is to wait for us to give up on Alison and go away. Then a nasty farm accident, and it's goodbye, Squire Hawkin. That gives me two problems. One, there's no reason except prejudice to suspect Philip Hawkin had anything to do with Alison's disappearance. And two, I don't want his blood on my hands, whether he is involved or not.'

Clough looked politely sceptical. 'If you weren't my boss, I'd say you'd been watching too much telly,' he said. 'But seeing as how you are, I'd say, it's an interesting idea, sir.'

George gave Clough a hard stare. 'It's one we'll bear in mind, Sergeant,' was all he said. He held out his mug to the WPC. 'Any more in the pot?'

Before she could give him the refill, the door opened on Peter Grundy. The Longnor bobby gave a satisfied nod. 'Thought I might find you here. Message from Detective Chief Inspector Carver, sir. Will you phone him at Buxton a.s.a.p.?'

George got to his feet, reaching for the tea. He swilled most of it back in moments then signalled Clough to follow. 'We might as well go up to the incident room,' he said, making for his car. Suddenly the door of a Ford Anglia swung open in his path and Don Smart's gingery head popped up.

'Morning, Inspector,' he said cheerily. 'Any luck yet? Anything to report? I was expecting to see you at the ten o'clock press conference, like you said yesterday, but you obviously had better things to be getting on with.'

'That's right,' George said, side-stepping the car door. 'The officers who dealt with you in Buxton this morning were fully briefed on the situation.'

'Did you see our story?'

'I'm in the middle of a major inquiry, Mr Smart. If you want any comment from Derbyshire Police, you'll have to go through the appropriate channels. Now, if you'll excuse me . . .'

Smart's predatory smile appeared. 'If you won't take seriously my suggestion about links to other cases . . . have you considered a clairvoyant?'

George frowned. 'A clairvoyant?'

'It could point you in the right direction. Focus your attention instead of spreading the search so wide.'

George shook his head in wonderment. 'I deal in facts, Mr Smart, not headlines.' He took half a dozen brisk steps away from the journalist, then wheeled round. 'If you really want to do something for Alison Carter rather than your own career, why not print a photograph of her?'

'I take it that means there hasn't been a breakthrough?' Smart said to Clough as George stalked off to his car.

'Why don't you bugger off back to Manchester?' Clough said, his voice low but firm, his face open and smiling. Without waiting to see the effect of his words, he followed George.

'Smart by name thinks he's smart by nature,' George said bitterly as the car toiled up the dale. 'It makes me sick. This isn't a career opportunity, it's a girl's life that's at risk here.'

'He can't afford to think like that. If he did, he'd never be able to write the story,' Clough pointed out.

'That might be better for everyone,' George said. He was still stiff with annoyance when he strode into the Methodist Hall and made straight for the nearest table with a phone. He stood over the constable who was using it, tapping the end of an unlit Gold Leaf against the packet. The PC flashed a glance at him, the whites of his eyes betraying his nervousness.

'That'll be all then, madam, thank you very much,' he gabbled, his hand reaching for the receiver rest to cut off the call even before he'd finished speaking. 'There you go, sir,' he added, thrusting the phone apprehensively at George.

'This is DI Bennett for DCI Carver,' George snapped.

There was a pause, then he heard the nasal Midlands voice of his CID boss. 'Bennett? Is that you?'

'Yes, sir. I got a message that you wanted to speak to me.'

'Took their time delivering it,' Carver grumbled. George had already discovered that after almost thirty years as a police officer, Carver had elevated complaint to an art form. George had spent his first month at Buxton apologizing, his second appeasing. Then he'd noticed how everyone else dealt with Carver's complaints and he too had learned to ignore.

'Have there been some developments, sir?'

'You left instructions for the day shift with Sergeant Lucas,' Carver accused.

'I did, sir.'

'Round up the usual suspects, generally a waste of time for all concerned.'

George waited, saying nothing. The anger from his encounter with Smart was dammed up behind a wall of professional imperturbability, but thanks to Carver's complaints, the weight of his fury was reaching critical mass. The last thing his career needed was for his rage to burst over Carver's head, so he took a deep breath and let it out slowly through his nose.

'This time, though, we might just have come up trumps,' Carver continued. The grudging words came out with grinding slowness. It sounded as if he'd rather the exercise had been a failure, George thought with incredulous bitterness.

'Is that right, sir?'

'Turns out we've got somebody on our books. Indecent exposure to schoolgirls. Lifting women's knickers off their clothes lines. Nothing very terrible, nothing very recent,' Carver added in a dissatisfied aside. 'But the interesting thing about this particular nonce is that he's Alison Carter's uncle.'

George felt his mouth fall open. 'Her uncle?' he managed after a moment.

'Peter Crowther.'

George swallowed hard. He hadn't even known there *was* a Peter Crowther. 'May I sit in on the interview, sir?'

'Why else do you think I was phoning you? I'm in agony with this ankle. Besides, me limping around like Hopalong Cassidy with my leg in a pot is hardly going to put the fear of God into Crowther, is it? You get yourself in here right now.'

'Yes, sir.'

'Oh, and Bennett?'

'Yes, sir?'

'Bring me some fish and chips, will you? I can't be doing with canteen food. Shocking indigestion, it gives me.'

George hung up, shaking his head. He lit a cigarette, screwing up his eyes and turning to scan the room behind him. Clough was leaning negligently against a table, scrutinizing one of the OS maps pinned to the wall. Grundy hovered near the door, uncertain whether he should go or stay. 'Clough, Grundy,' George said through a mouthful of smoke. 'Car, now. We're off to Buxton.'

The doors were barely slammed when George turned in his seat, glared at Grundy and said, 'Peter Crowther.'

'Peter Crowther, sir?' Grundy was trying for innocence and failing, his edgy eyes giving him away.

'Yes, Grundy. Alison's uncle, the one with the record of sex offences. That Peter Crowther,' George said sarcastically, stabbing his foot at the accelerator and jerking them all backwards as he shot up the lane towards Longnor.

'What about him, sir?'

'How come the first I hear about Peter Crowther is from the DCI? How is it that, with all your local knowledge, you didn't get round to mentioning Peter Crowther?' George had abandoned his sarcasm, going for the silky gentleness of the sadistic teacher who lulls his unwary pupils into false security before cutting off at the knees.

'I didn't think it was relevant. I mean, he lives in Buxton, has done for the last twenty years or more. I never gave him a thought,' Grundy said, his ears scarlet.

'That's why you're still a PC, Grundy,' Clough said, swivelling in his seat and giving the constable the hard insolent stare that had catapulted a disturbing number of prisoners into violence that would more

143

than double the sentences for their original offences. 'You don't think.'

'That's true, Clough, but you don't have to have a brain to get stuck on point duty in Derby city centre for a few years,' George said, sweet reason in a shirt and tie. 'Village bobbies, however, are supposed to be able to think for themselves. PC Grundy, unless you truly fancy a change of assignment, I suggest you use the miles between here and Buxton to tell us all you know about Peter Crowther.'

Grundy rubbed his eyebrow with the knuckle of his index finger. 'Peter Crowther is Ruth Hawkin's brother,' he said, like a man working out complicated mental arithmetic. 'Diane's the oldest, that's Terry Lomas's wife Diane. Then Peter, then Daniel, then Ruth. Peter must be a good ten years older than Ruth. That'd make him somewhere around forty-five.

'I never really knew Peter, he was away from Scardale long before I even became village bobby in Longnor. But I'd heard talk about him. Apparently he's not the full shilling. His brother Daniel used to keep an eye on him when he was still living in Scardale, but something happened – I don't know what, nobody outside Scardale does – and they decided they didn't want him in the dale any longer. So they had him shipped out to Buxton. He lives in a single men's hostel up by the golf course at Waterswallows. And he works in that sheltered workshop up the back of the railway yard, the one that makes lampshades and wastepaper baskets. I knew he'd been done for being a Peeping Tom, but it was summat and nowt.'

George sighed heavily. 'You knew all this about

Peter Crowther, and it never crossed your mind to mention it?'

Grundy shifted his weight from one buttock to the other. 'You'll understand when you see him, sir. Peter Crowther's frightened of his own shadow. I don't think he's capable of accosting anyone, never mind abducting them.'

'He wouldn't have had to abduct Alison, though, would he?' Clough butted in, his sarcasm cutting as a whip, his blue eyes cold. 'He was her uncle. She wouldn't be frightened of him. If he said, "Hey, our Alison, I've got a pair of roller-skating boots that'd fit you, d'you want to come and see them?" she'd not have thought twice about going along with him. He might be a bit strange, her Uncle Peter, but it's not like he was a stranger, is it, PC Grundy?' He managed to make the rank sound like an insult.

'He's not got the nerve,' Grundy said stubbornly. 'Besides, when I said they didn't want him in the dale, I meant it. As far as I know, Peter Crowther's not been back to Scardale in nigh on twenty years. And Scardale won't have been near him, neither. I doubt he'd even know Alison if he passed her in the street.'

'We'll see about that,' Clough muttered, his face grim as his eyes narrowed against the smoke from his cigarette.

Janet Carter had begged and pleaded to be kept off school in the wake of Alison's disappearance. She might as well have saved her breath. Back in 1963, kids weren't supposed to have feelings like adults. Grown-ups fed them all sorts of tales to shield them from things, thinking to protect them. The worst crime to

145

the adult mind was disrupting the routine, for nothing would serve as a better signal to the younger generation that something was seriously wrong. So the world could have been about to end back in the dale, but Janet and her cousins still had to be dropped off at the lane end and packed off to school like it was any other morning.

But when she'd arrived at school the morning after Alison's disappearance, it had been unexpectedly exciting. For once, Janet was the centre of attention. Everybody knew Alison had disappeared. The police were at the school, interviewing Alison's classmates and her teachers. There was only one topic of playground conversation, and Janet had the inside track. She was, in her small way, a celebrity. It was enough to make her forget the terror that had kept her awake half the night, wondering where Alison was and what was happening to her.

There was a sort of delicious fear in the air, the sense that something forbidden had taken place that none of the children could quite grasp the significance of. Even those of them who lived on farms. They knew what animals did, but somehow they never quite made the jump across the species barrier. Of course, everyone had heard about girls being 'interfered with', but none of them really knew what that meant, except that it was something to do with 'down there' and the sort of thing that happened if you let a boy 'go too far'. Though none of them really had a clue how far too far was.

So the atmosphere at Peak Girls' High was highly charged when Alison Carter went missing. Although most of her classmates were as scared, anxious and almost as upset as Janet herself, there was a part of them that felt stirred up in a way that was pleasurable even though they knew they shouldn't be feeling like that. With all these emotions churning around, both the Thursday and Friday had been exhausting school days. By the time the final bell went, all Janet could think about was getting home and letting her mother fuss over her with a cup of tea.

She had few reserves left for the shock that awaited her on the school bus. The driver was bursting with the news that Alison's uncle was at the police station, being questioned. Her reaction was instantaneous. It was as if she closed in on herself. She was sitting on the front seat, where she had always sat with Alison, as near to the driver as she could be. 'Which uncle?' Derek asked.

The driver tried the usual sort of joke about everybody being related in Scardale, but he could see Janet wasn't in the mood. So he simply said, 'Peter Crowther.'

Janet frowned. 'It must be some other Crowther, not a Scardale one. Alison doesn't have an Uncle Peter.'

'That's all you know,' he said with a wink. 'Peter Crowther's Alison's mother's daft brother. The one they shipped out of Scardale.'

Janet looked at Derek, who shrugged his shoulders, as baffled and bemused as she was. They had never heard a word about a second Crowther brother. His name had never been mentioned.

All the way back to the lane end, the bus driver kept on about Peter Crowther, how he lived in a hostel and worked in a sheltered workshop for nutters that the council didn't think were daft enough to be locked up, how he supposedly had some dark secret in his past and now the police thought he'd done away with Alison. Janet focused on the back of his thick red neck and wanted him to die.

But she wanted the truth even more. Her father was waiting at the lane end for the bus to drop the children off. He'd been there for ten minutes; nobody in Scardale was taking any more chances. The first thing Janet said when the bus door closed behind them was, 'Dad, who's Peter Crowther? And what did he do?'

Ray Carter, being the kind of man he was, told her. Then she wished he hadn't.

Grundy had been right about one thing at least, George thought as he leaned against the wall of the interview room. Peter Crowther was afraid of his own shadow. And of everyone else's. The first thing that had struck him when he'd walked into the stuffy room was the thin acrid smell of Crowther's fear, an odour quite distinct from the cheesy unwashed reek of his narrow body. 'A chain-smoking interview,' Clough had muttered in an aside, his nose wrinkled fastidiously against Peter Crowther's personal miasma.

'What?' George had mumbled in reply as they stood on the threshold, deliberately sizing up Crowther to lay an even heavier weight of apprehension on the man.

'You have to chain-smoke or you throw up,' Clough illuminated him.

George nodded his understanding. 'You kick off,' he said, moving to stand against the wall and letting Clough drop into the chair facing Crowther. George jerked his head towards the door and the uniformed PC who had been on guard slipped out with a look of relief.

'All right, Peter?' Clough said, leaning forward on his elbows.

Peter Crowther seemed to fold in on himself even more. His head was the colour and shape of a wedge of Dairylea cheese, George decided. Dairylea cheese with a straggle of cress stems across the top. Odd that he should look so greasily pale while he smelled so grubby. He didn't actually look dirty. His clean-shaven pointed chin was tucked in towards his chest, his cat's eyes angled up towards Clough. The man could have served as the illustrated dictionary definition of a cringe. He said nothing in response to Clough's opening, though his lips moved, forming silent words.

'You're going to talk to me sooner or later, Peter,' Clough said confidently, dropping one hand to his pocket and taking out his cigarettes. Nonchalantly, he lit up and blew smoke at Peter Crowther. When the smoke reached him, Crowther's nose twitched as he inhaled it greedily. 'Might as well be sooner,' Clough continued. 'So tell us, what made you decide to go back to Scardale on Wednesday?'

Crowther frowned. He looked genuinely puzzled. Whatever he felt guilty about, it didn't seem to involve Scardale. 'Peter never,' he said, his rising intonation indicating doubt rather than the bluster of the truly guilty. 'Peter lives in Buxton. Waterswallows Lodgings, number seventeen. Peter don't live in Scardale no more.'

'We know that, Peter. But you went back to Scardale on Wednesday night. There's no point in denying it, we know you were there.'

Crowther shuddered. 'Peter never.' This time he was firm. 'Peter can't go back to Scardale. He's not allowed.

He lives in Buxton. Waterswallows Lodgings, number seventeen.'

'Who says you're not allowed?'

Crowther's eyes dropped. 'Our Dan. He says if Peter sets foot in Scardale ever again, he'll cut Peter's hands off. So Peter don't go there, see? Can Peter have a fag?'

'In a minute,' Clough said, negligently blowing more smoke towards Crowther. 'What about Alison? When did you see Alison last?'

Crowther looked up again, his troubled face confused. 'Alison? Peter don't know no Alison. There's an Angela works beside him, she puts the fringes on lampshades. Is it Angela you mean? Peter likes Angela. She's got a leather jacket. She got it off her brother. He works in the tannery at Whaley Bridge. Angela's brother, that is. Peter works with Angela. Peter makes lampshade frames.'

'Alison. Your niece Alison. Your sister Ruth's girl,' Clough said firmly.

At the sound of Ruth's name, Crowther jerked. His knees came up towards his chest and he wrapped his arms tightly round them. 'Peter never,' he gasped. 'Peter never!'

George moved forward and leaned his fists on the table. 'You didn't know Ruth had a daughter?' he asked gently.

'Peter never,' Crowther kept repeating like a talisman.

George unobtrusively signalled to Clough to back off. The sergeant leaned back in his chair and directed his smoke towards the ceiling. George took his own cigarettes out, lit one and held it out to Crowther, who was shivering now as he continued to mutter, 'Peter never. Peter never.' It took a few seconds for Crowther to notice the offering. He looked suspiciously at the cigarette, then at George. One hand snaked out and grabbed it. He held the cigarette cupped inside his hand, the tip pinched between thumb and forefinger, as if he expected it to be hijacked. He inhaled in quick snatches, his eyes flickering and fluttering between George, Clough and the cigarette.

'When did you last speak to anyone from Scardale, Peter?' George asked kindly, slipping into the chair next to Clough.

Crowther gave a knotted shrug. 'Don't know. Sometimes Peter sees family on the market on a Saturday. But family don't speak to Peter. One time, in the summer, Peter was in the paper shop buying smokes and our Diane came in. She nodded, but she didn't say owt. I think she wanted to, but she knew if she did our Dan would hurt Peter bad. Dan always makes Peter scared. That's why Peter never goes back to Scardale.'

'And you really didn't know Ruth had a daughter?' said Clough the sceptic.

Crowther twitched, his face clenching round his cigarette in a tight spasm. 'Peter never,' he moaned. He leaned forward into his knees and began to rock. 'Peter never.'

George looked at Clough and shook his head. He stood up and walked towards the door. 'We'll get somebody to bring you a cup of tea, Peter.' Clough followed him into the hallway. 'He's hiding something,' George said positively.

'I don't think it's anything to do with Alison, though,' Clough said.

151

'I'm not sure,' George said. 'I'm not committing myself till I know why his family threw him out of Scardale. Whatever it was, it must have been bad if his own sister still won't speak to him in passing twenty years later.'

'You want him holding on to, then?' Clough said, unable to keep the doubt out of his voice.

'Oh, I think so. Safest place for him, don't you think?' George said over his shoulder as he walked towards the CID office. 'DCI Carver's convinced he's our man, and it'll take more than my opinion to change his mind. And a police station's always a leaky sieve. Before closing time, half the town will know Peter Crowther's been questioned about Alison's disappearance. I don't think Waterswallows Lodgings, number seventeen, would be the best place for him in those circumstances.' He pushed open the door and contemplated his chief inspector, plastered leg propped on a wastepaper bin, evening paper in front of him. The whole room was still fragrant with the unmistakable aroma of fish and chips soaked with vinegar and wrapped in newspaper.

'Got him to tell you where the girl is yet?' Carver demanded.

'I don't think he knows, sir,' George said, hoping his voice didn't sound as weary as he felt.

Carver snorted. 'Is that what a university education does for you? Unbelievable. I'll give you till morning to get chapter and verse out of that sad sack in the cells.' He caught himself. 'He is still in the cells, I take it? You've not let him walk?'

'Mr Crowther is still in custody.'

'Good. I'm off home now, it's in your hands. If you've

not got the truth out of him by then, I'm taking over, pot leg or no pot leg. He'll cough, believe you me. He'll cough for me.'

'I'm sure he will, sir. Now, if you'll excuse me, I've got to go back out to Scardale.' George withdrew before Carver could offer any further insults to his capabilities.

'Are we?' Clough asked, following George to the car. 'Going back to Scardale?'

'I need to know what Peter Crowther did,' George said bluntly. 'He's not going to tell us, so somebody else will have to. I'm tired of people in Scardale that don't tell us what we need to know.'

9

George was beginning to think he would dream the
road to Scardale for the rest of his life. The car plunged
down the narrow defile in the gathering dusk of a
gloomy winter afternoon. If the sun had made an
appearance through the day's cloud and mist, he'd
certainly missed it, he thought, slowing down as the
village green grew near. Men were milling around the
police caravan, cups of tea sending wisps of steam to join
the wraiths of mist creeping down the dale. The day's
fruitless searching was over with the dying of the light.

Ignoring them, George crossed the green to Tor
Cottage. It was time Ma Lomas stopped behaving like
a character from a Victorian melodrama and started
taking responsibility for what might happen to Alison
if the matriarch and her extended family continued to
keep their mouths shut, he told himself resolutely. As
he rounded the woodpile that almost blocked the path
to her front door, his foot snagged on something and
he pitched forward. Only Clough's quick grasp of his
arm prevented him from an ignominious tumble.

'What the hell . . . ?' George exclaimed, staggering

154

to right himself. He turned and peered through the gathering gloom at Charlie Lomas, sprawled on his back amid a scattered pile of logs, and groaning.

'I think you broke my ankle,' Charlie complained.

'What in the name of God were you doing?' George demanded, crossly rubbing his arm where Clough's strong fingers had dug into the muscle.

'I was just sitting here, minding my own business, trying to get five minutes' peace. It's not a crime, is it?' Charlie squirmed to an upright position. He rubbed the back of his hand fiercely across his face and in a gleam of light from the cottage window, George realized the youth's eyes were bright with tears. He didn't look capable of abducting a kitten, never mind a teenage girl.

'Thinking about Alison?' George said gently.

'It's a bit late to start treating me like a human being, mister.' Charlie's shoulders hunched in defiance. 'What's the matter with you lot? She was my cousin. My family. Ain't you got anybody to care about, that you think it's so bloody strange that we're all upset?'

Charlie's words jolted George's memory. He'd learned early on in his police life that he couldn't do the job as well as he wanted unless his personal concerns were battened down firmly, protected from the raw pain and unpleasantness of so much of his work. Mostly, he managed to keep the Chinese walls intact. Occasionally, like now, the two realities collided. Suddenly George remembered that overnight he'd acquired someone new to care about.

A smile crept over him. He couldn't help it. He could see the contempt in Charlie Lomas's eyes and the

155

puzzlement in Clough's. But the sudden consciousness of the child that Anne was carrying was irresistible.

'What's so bloody funny?' Charlie burst out.

'Nothing's funny,' George said gruffly, dragging himself back into the appropriate state. 'I was thinking about my family. And you're right. I would be devastated if anything happened to them. I'm sorry if I offended you.'

Charlie got to his feet, brushing himself down with his hands. 'Like I said, it's a bit late for that now.' He half turned his head so his eyes were obscured by the shadow. 'You looking for me or my gran?'

'Your gran. Is she in?'

He shook his head. 'She's not come back yet.'

'Back from where?'

'I saw her when we were coming back from looking for Alison. She was walking across the fields, over between where you found Shep and where we were yesterday, when you found that ... stuff.' Charlie frowned as if recalling something half buried. 'It was like she was going over the same road the squire was walking on Wednesday teatime.'

There are times when a particular combination of words shifts the world into slow motion. As the significance of Charlie Lomas's words sank in, George had the strange swimming sensation of a man whose senses have moved into overdrive, leaving the outside world crawling by at a pitiful pace. He blinked hard, cleared his throat then said carefully, 'What did you just say, Charlie?'

'I said my gran was walking over the fields. Like she was heading towards the manor the back way,' he added. He'd obviously decided that in spite of their treatment of him, it was in Alison's interests to be helpful to this strange policeman who didn't behave like any copper he'd ever seen in the flesh or at the pictures in Buxton.

George struggled to keep his self-control. He wanted to grab Charlie by the throat and scream at him but all he said was, 'You said she was walking the same road as the squire on Wednesday teatime.'

Charlie screwed up his face. 'So? Why wouldn't the squire be walking his own fields?'

'Wednesday teatime, you said.'

'That's right. I particularly remember because of all the fuss later on when Alison went missing.'

George exchanged a look with Clough. His incredulity met Clough's rage. 'You were asked if you'd seen anybody in the fields or the woods on Wednesday,' Clough ground out.

'I wasn't,' Charlie said defensively.

'I asked you myself,' Clough said, his lips stretched tight over his teeth, the sibilants hissing.

'No, you never,' Charlie insisted. 'You asked if we'd seen any strangers. You asked if we'd seen anything out of the ordinary. And I didn't. I just saw the same thing I've seen a thousand times before – the squire walking his own land. Anyway, it can't have had anything to do with Alison going missing. Because it was still light enough to see clearly who it was, and according to what you said, Alison didn't go out till it was nigh on dark. So there's no call to take that tone with me,' he added, straightening his shoulders and attempting a maturity he hadn't earned. 'Besides, you were too busy trying to make out I had something to do with it to listen to anything I might have to say.'

George turned away in disgust, his eyes closing momentarily. 'We'll need a statement about this,' he said, his excitement at the possibilities this information opened up overcoming his frustration at the time wasted because the literal minds of Scardale could see no further than the question as asked. 'Get yourself up to the Methodist Hall and tell one of the officers there I sent you. And give him every detail. The time, the direction Mr Hawkin was walking in, whether he was carrying anything, what he was wearing. Do it now, please, Mr Lomas, before I give in to the temptation to arrest you for obstructing a police inquiry.'

He glanced over his shoulder in time to see Charlie's eyes widen in panic. 'I never did,' he said, sounding half his age. 'He never asked me about the squire.'

'I never asked you about the Duke of Edinburgh neither, but if he was walking the fields, I'd expect you to tell me,' Clough snarled. 'Now, don't waste any more time. Get your arse up the road before I decide to let my boot help you.'

Charlie pushed past them and broke into a run, heading across the green to one of the muddy Land Rovers parked opposite. 'Can you believe these people?' George demanded. 'Jesus, I'm beginning to wonder if they want Alison Carter found.' He sighed heavily. 'We'll need to talk to Hawkin about this. He's lied to us, and I want to know the reason why.' He glanced at his watch. 'But I want to find out about Peter Crowther too.'

'Depending on what the squire's got to say for himself, Peter Crowther could be irrelevant,' Clough pointed out.

George frowned. 'You don't seriously think . . . Hawkin?'

Clough shrugged. 'Do I think he's capable of it? I've no idea, I've hardly spoken to the man. On the other hand, he has lied to us.' He enumerated the possibilities on short, strong fingers. 'Either he's got something to hide, or he's covering for somebody else he saw, or else he's criminally absent-minded.'

Before George could respond, the issue was settled by the appearance of Ma Lomas, bundled in a winter coat and headscarf. She cocked her head and said, 'You're blocking my path.'

The two men stepped aside. She carried on towards her door without acknowledgement. 'We need to speak to you,' George said.

'I don't need to speak to you,' she retorted, struggling to fumble a large iron key into the door lock. 'Never had to lock our doors before Ruth Carter brought strangers into the dale.' The lock turned with a jarring screech of metal on metal.

'Don't you care what happens to your own flesh and blood?' George said.

She turned to face him, eyes narrowed. 'You know nowt, you.' Then she opened the door.

'We'll be going to talk to the squire after we've spoken to you,' Clough chipped in as she was about to disappear inside. She stopped on the threshold, still as a mouse below a hovering hawk. 'We know about him walking the field where you've just been. Mrs Lomas, we need to eliminate Peter Crowther from our inquiries if he's an innocent man.'

For a moment she stood thinking, letting the seemingly unconnected sentences settle. Then she nodded, cocking her head and fixing Clough with a calculating stare. 'You'd better come in then,' she said at last. 'Mind you wipe your feet. And no smoking in here. It's bad for my chest.'

They followed her into a parlour no more than nine feet square. A dim room with only one small window, it smelled faintly of camphor and eucalyptus. The stone floor was scattered with faded rag rugs. An armchair sat on either side of a grate flanked by two black iron ovens, each the size of a crate of beer. A kettle sat on one of the ovens, a curl of steam disappearing up the chimney from its spout. A sideboard stood on the opposite side of the room, its surface cluttered with carved wooden animals and roughly polished chunks of limestone containing fossils. In the tiny bay window, three tall ladder-back chairs in black oak loomed above a small dining table, as if threatening it with a beating.

The only decorations were dozens of garish pic-ture postcards of everything from Spanish beaches to Scandinavian baroque town halls. Seeing George's bemused stare, Ma Lomas said, 'They're Charlie's. It's like pen pals, only postcards. He's a dreamer. Thing that makes me laugh is that there's hundreds of people all over the world looking at Squire Hawkin's post-card of Scardale and thinking Derbyshire village life is milk-white sheep in a field full of sunshine.' She hobbled across to the chair facing the door and settled herself down, squirming her shoulders until she was comfortable.

'Can I sit down?' George asked.

'You won't like the armchair,' she told him. With her head, she gestured towards the hard chairs. 'Better for your back, anyway.'

They turned a couple of chairs to face her. They waited while she leaned forward, poking the glowing coals ablaze. 'Peter Crowther's in custody in Buxton,' George said when she'd made herself cosy.

'Aye, I'd heard.'

'Should he be, do you think?'

'You're the copper, not me. I'm just an old woman who's never lived outside a Derbyshire dale.'

'We could waste a lot of time trying to connect Peter Crowther to Alison,' George continued, refusing to be diverted. 'Time that would be better spent trying to find her.'

'I told you before, the trouble with you and your detectives is that you understand nothing about this place,' she said, her voice irritated.

'I'm trying to understand. But people in Scardale seem more interested in hindering than helping me. I've just had the experience of discovering your grandson had omitted to mention something that could be a vital piece of evidence.'

'That's hardly surprising, considering the way you treated the lad. How come none of you had the sense to ask if he could have had owt to do with Alison going missing? Because he couldn't have. When she disappeared, he was here in the house with me. That's what you call an alibi, isn't it?' she demanded scornfully.

'Are you sure about that?' George asked dubiously.

'I might be old, but I've got all me chairs at home. Charlie came in just before half past four and started peeling potatoes. I can't manage them with my arthritis the way it is, so he has to do them. Every night, it's the same routine. He wasn't messing about with Alison, he was here, taking care of me.'

161

George took a deep breath. 'It would have saved us a lot of time if either you or Charlie had seen fit to tell us that. Mrs Lomas, in cases involving missing children, the first forty-eight hours are crucial. That time is almost up and we are no nearer finding a young girl who is one of your relatives.' George's frustration made his voice rise. 'Mrs Lomas, I swear I am going to find Alison Carter. Sooner or later, I am going to know what happened here two days ago. If that means searching every house in this village from roof beam to foundations, I'll do it. If I have to dig up every field and garden in the dale, I'll do it, and to hell with your crops and livestock. If I have to arrest every one of you and charge you with obstruction or even with being accessories, I'll do it.' He stopped abruptly and leaned forward. 'So tell me. Do you think Peter Crowther had anything to do with Alison's disappearance?'

She shook her head impatiently. 'As far as I know, and believe you me, I know most things around Scardale, Peter hasn't set foot in this dale since the war ended. I don't think he even knows Alison exists. And I'd put my hand on the Bible and swear she's never heard his name.' Her lips clamped shut, her nose and chin approaching like the points of an engineer's callipers.

'We can't be sure about that. The lass has been going to school in Buxton. She's got the look of her mother. Don't forget, Mrs Hawkin would have been about Alison's age when her brother last spent much time around her. With somebody who's a bit lacking in the top storey, seeing Alison in the street could have triggered off all sorts of memories.'

Ma Lomas folded her arms tightly across her chest

162

and shook her head vigorously as George spoke. 'I'll not believe it, I'll not,' she said.

'So, should we be interviewing Peter Crowther, Mrs Lomas?' George asked, his voice gentler again in response to her obvious distress.

'If he'd have stepped into the dale, we'd all have known. Besides, he'd have been at work,' she added desperately.

'They get Wednesday afternoons off. He could have been here. Mrs Lomas, what did Peter Crowther do that got him sent away?'

'That's nobody's business now,' she said emphatically. Her eyes were screwed up now, as if the firelight were the noonday sun.

'I need to know,' George persisted.

'You don't.'

Tommy Clough leaned forward, his elbows on his knees, his notepad dangling between his calves. George envied him his ability to appear relaxed even in an interview as tense as this had become. 'I don't think Peter Crowther could hurt a fly,' he said. 'Unfortunately, I'm not the one who makes the decisions. I think it could be a while before Peter sees daylight again. A woman like yourself, Mrs Lomas, who's never lived outside a Derbyshire dale, you'll not have any reason to know what prisoners do with men they think have hurt children. What they do drives sane men mad. They hang themselves from the bars on their windows. They swallow bleach. They'd cut their wrists with butter knives if anybody were daft enough to let them have one. Your Peter will be used and abused worse than a street prostitute in a war zone. I don't think you want that for him. You or anybody else in

Scardale. If you did, you'd have seen to it that he caught what-for twenty years ago. But you let him go. You let him build a bit of a life for himself. What's the point in standing idly by and letting him lose it now?'

It was a persuasive speech, but it had no effect. 'I can't tell you,' she said, her head moving almost imperceptibly from side to side.

George noisily pushed his chair back, the legs shrieking on the stone-flagged floor. 'I haven't the time to waste here,' he said. 'If you don't care about Peter Crowther or about finding Alison, I'll go to someone who will. I'm sure Mrs Hawkin will tell us anything we want to know. After all, he's her brother.'

Ma Lomas's head came up as if someone had yanked at the hair on the back of her head. Her eyes widened. 'Not Ruth. No, you mustn't. Not Ruth.'

'Why not?' George demanded, letting some of his anger out. 'She wants Alison found, she doesn't want us to waste our time on false leads. She'll tell us anything we want to know, believe me.'

She glared at him, her witch's face malevolent as a Halloween mask. 'Sit down,' she hissed. It was a command, not an invitation. George retreated to his chair. Ma Lomas stood up and moved unsteadily across to the sideboard. She opened the door and took out a bottle whose label claimed it contained whisky. The contents, however, were colourless as gin. She filled a sherry glass with the liquid and drank it down in one. She gave two sharp coughs, her shoulders heaving, then she turned back to them, her eyes watering. 'Peter were always a problem,' she said slowly.

'He always had a dirty mind,' she continued, making her way back to her chair. 'Nasty. Mucky. You'd find

164

him out in the fields, staring at any animals that were coupling. The older he got, the worse he got. He'd follow anybody that was courting, his own kith and kin, desperate to see what they were doing. You'd know when the ram were serving the ewes because you'd walk into the wood and find Peter standing with his . . .' She paused, pursed her lips, then continued. 'His *thing* in his hand, eyes on stalks, watching the beasts at their business. He'd been slapped and shouted at, kicked and called for it, but it made no difference to him. After a time, it didn't seem to matter so much. In a place like Scardale, you have to endure what you can't cure.'

She stared into the fire and sighed. 'Then young Ruth started to change from a little girl into a young woman. Peter was like a man obsessed. He followed her around like a dog sniffing after a bitch in heat. Dan caught him a couple of times up a ladder outside the lass's bedroom, watching her through a crack in the curtains. We all tried to make him see sense – she was his own sister, it couldn't go on. But Peter would never take a telling. In the end, Dan made him move out of the house and sleep over here in my cottage.'

Ma Lomas paused and briefly rubbed her closed eyelids. Neither George nor Clough moved a muscle, determined not to break the momentum of the story. 'One night, Dan came back from Longnor. He'd been having a drink. This was during the war, when we were supposed to keep a blackout. As soon as he turned into the dale, he could see a chink of light shining out like a beacon from the village. He pedalled as fast as he could, wanting to tell whoever it was that they had a light showing before the bobby saw it and fined them.

He was a good half-mile away when he realized it must be coming from his own home. Then he really stepped on it. Soon, he recognized the very window – Ruth's bedroom. He knew their Diane was alone with Ruth, and he was convinced something terrible had happened to one or other of them.' She turned to face her spellbound audience.

'Well, he was wrong, and he was right. He came roaring and rushing into the house like a hurricane, up the stairs two at a time, near on hitting his head on the beams. He flung open the door to Ruth's room and there was Peter standing by Ruth's bed, his pants round his ankles, the lantern casting a shadow on the ceiling that made his cock look like a broomstick. The lass had been fast asleep, but Dan bursting in like a madman woke her up. She must have thought she was having a nightmare.' The old woman shook her head. 'I could hear her screaming right across the village green.

'The next thing I heard was Peter screaming. It took three men to drag Dan off him. I thought he was a dead man, covered in blood like a calf that's had a hard birth. We locked him in a lambing shed until his body had started to heal, then Squire Castleton arranged for him to go into the hostel in Buxton. Dan told him if he ever came near Ruth or Scardale again, he'd kill him with his bare hands. Peter believed him then and he believes him now. I know you'll be thinking that what I've told you means he could have seen Ruth in Alison and done something terrible to her. But you're wrong. It means the very opposite. If you want to make Peter Crowther crawl across the floor begging for mercy, just go and tell him Ruth and Dan are looking for him. The last place he'd ever come is Scardale. The last person he'd come near is anybody connected to Scardale. Take my word for it, I know.'

She sat back in her chair, her narrative over. The oral tradition would never die as long as Ma Lomas lived, George thought. She epitomized the village elder who holds the tribal history, its integrity protected only by her personal skills. He'd never expected to encounter one of those in 1963 in Derbyshire. 'Thank you for telling us, Mrs Lomas,' he said formally. 'You've been very helpful. One more thing before we leave you in peace. Charlie said he'd seen Mr Hawkin in the field between the wood and the copse on Wednesday afternoon. He told us you were retracing his steps just now. Did you also see the squire on Wednesday, then?'

She gave him a calculating look, her eye as bright as a parrot's. 'Not after Alison disappeared, no.'

'But before?'

She nodded. 'I'd been having a cup of tea with our Diane. When I came out, Kathy were just getting into the Land Rover to go up to the lane end to pick up Alison and Janet and Derek from off the school bus. I saw David and Brian over by the milking parlour, bringing the cows in. And I saw Squire Hawkin crossing the field.'

'Why didn't you mention this?' George asked, exasperated.

'Why would I? There was nothing out of the ordinary in it. It's his field, why wouldn't he be walking it? He's always out and about, snapping away with his camera when you least expect it. Besides, like I said, Alison wasn't even home from school by then. He'd have had to be a bloody slow walker to still be in the field when she came out with Shep. And this weather, nobody walks slow in Scardale,' she added decisively, as if settling an argument.

George closed his eyes and breathed deeply through his nose. When he opened them again, he could have sworn a smile was twitching the corners of the old woman's mouth. 'I'll have all this typed up into a statement,' he said. 'I expect you to sign it.'

'If it's truthful, you'll get no argument from me. You going to let Peter go now?'

George got up and deliberately tucked his chair back under the table. 'We'll be taking what you've told us into consideration when we make our decision.'

'He's not a violent man, Inspector,' she said. 'Even supposing he had seen Alison, even supposing she'd reminded him of Ruth, all she'd have had to do was push him away. He's a cowardly man. Don't waste your time on Peter and let a guilty man go free.'

'You seem to have made your mind up that whatever's happened to Alison, somebody made it happen,' Clough said, standing up, but making a point of keeping his notebook open.

Her face seemed to close in on itself, eyes narrowing, mouth pursing, nose wrinkling. 'What I think and what you know are very different things. See if you can get them a bit closer together, Sergeant Clough. Then we'll maybe all know what happened to our lass.' She glanced up at the clock. 'I thought you said you were going to talk to Squire Hawkin?'

'We are,' George said.

'Better get your skates on, then. He likes his tea on the table at six sharp and I can't see him changing his ways for you.'

168

They saw themselves out. 'What did you make of that, Tommy?' George asked.

'She's telling us the truth as she sees it, sir.'

'And the alibi for Charlie?'

Clough shrugged. 'She could be lying for him. She would lie for him, I don't think there's any doubt about that. But until we find somebody saying something different, or something more solid to tie him to Alison's disappearance, we've got no reason to doubt her. And I agree with her about Crowther, for what it's worth.'

'Me too.' George ran a hand over his face. The skin felt raw with tiredness, the very bones seeming nearer the surface. He sighed.

'We should let him go, sir,' Clough said, fishing out his cigarettes and passing one to George. 'He's not going to run. He's got nowhere to run to. I could call the station from the phone box and tell them to bail him. They can give him stringent conditions – he shouldn't go within five miles of Scardale, he's got to stay at the hostel, he should report daily. But there's no need to keep him in, surely.'

'You don't think we're exposing him to lynch-mob justice?' George asked.

'The longer we keep him, the worse it looks for him. We could get the duty officer to tip the wink to the newspaper lads that Crowther was never a suspect, just a vulnerable adult relative that we brought in so we could interview him away from the pressures of the outside world. Some sort of rubbish like that. And I could mention the need to spread the same word round the pubs.' There was a stubborn set to Clough's jaw. He had a point, and George was too tired to argue a case he didn't feel passionately about either way.

'All right, Tommy. You call them and say it's my orders. And make sure somebody informs the DCI. He won't like it, but that's his hard cheese. I'll see you in the caravan. If I don't get a brew inside me, I'll be falling off my perch before I can get anything out of the squire.'

George didn't even wait for a response. He walked straight across the green to the police caravan. No prickle of intuition made him turn and stay Detective Sergeant Clough's hand. After all, Clough was convinced he was doing the right thing. Not even Ma Lomas's instincts had cried out against releasing Peter Crowther.

It was a burden of knowledge they would all share equally.

10

Friday, 13th December 1963. 5.52 p.m.

Ruth Hawkin was wiping her hands on her apron as she opened the kitchen door of Scardale Manor. A brief hope flared in her eyes but found nothing in their faces to fan the spark into flame. Hope abandoned, fear wasted no time in taking its place. Judging from the dark circles under her eyes and the pinched look of her pale skin, anxiety had been seldom absent in the previous two days. Seeing her distress, George quickly said, 'We've no fresh news, Mrs Hawkin. I'm sorry. Can we come in a minute?'

Ruth nodded and mutely stepped aside, still rubbing her hands on the rough floral cotton of her wraparound apron. Her shoulders were slumped, her movements sluggish and abstracted. George and Clough trooped past her and stood awkwardly in the middle of the kitchen floor. The unmistakable smell of steak and kidney floated on the air, making both men salivate with hunger. George wondered fleetingly what Anne would have waiting for him if he ever got home. One thing was sure: it would be shrivelled past desirability at this rate. 'Is your husband at home?' he asked. 'It

171

was actually him we needed to have a word with.'

'He's been out searching with your lads,' she said quickly. 'He came in exhausted so he went for a bath. Is it something I could help you with?'

George shook his head. 'It's nothing to worry about. We just need a word with him.'

She glanced at the battered enamel alarm clock on a shelf by the cooker. 'He'll be down for his tea in ten minutes.' She chewed the right-hand corner of her lower lip in an unconscious parade of anxiety. 'It'd be better if you could come back later. After he's eaten. Maybe about half past? I'll tell him to expect you.' Her smile was nervous.

'If you don't mind holding back the tea, Mrs Hawkin, we'll speak to your husband when he comes down,' George said gently. 'We don't want to waste any time.'

The skin round her eyes and mouth tightened. 'You think I don't understand that? But he'll be needing his tea after being out in the dale all afternoon.'

'I appreciate that, and we'll be as quick as we can.'

'As quick as you can about what, Inspector?'

George half turned. He hadn't heard Hawkin open the door behind him. The squire was wearing a shaggy camel dressing gown over striped pyjamas. His skin glowed pink from his bath, his hair even more sleek against his skull than before. He had one hand thrust in his pocket, the other holding a cigarette in a pose that would have passed for debonair in a West End theatre but only managed ridiculous in a Derbyshire farm kitchen. George dipped his head in acknowledgement. 'We need a few minutes of your time, Mr Hawkin.'

'I'm about to eat, Inspector,' he said petulantly. 'As

172

I expect my wife will already have told you. Perhaps you could call back later?'

Interesting, George thought, that Hawkin hadn't even asked if fresh news had brought the police back to his kitchen. Not a mention of Alison, not a hint that he was concerned about anything except filling his belly. 'I'm afraid not, sir. As I've already indicated, in inquiries of this nature, we believe it's vital not to waste time. So if Mrs Hawkin wouldn't mind keeping your dinner warm, we'd like a word.'

Hawkin's sigh was theatrically loud. 'Ruth, you heard the inspector.' He moved forward to the table, his hand snaking out from his pocket and reaching for the back of his chair.

'It might be better elsewhere, sir,' George said.

Hawkin's eyebrows arched. 'I beg your pardon?'

'We prefer to interview witnesses independently of each other. And since your wife has things to attend to in here, it seems sensible for us to go elsewhere. The living room, perhaps?' George was inexorably polite but irresistibly firm.

'I'm not going into the living room. It'll be like a cold store in there and I've no intention of catching pneumonia for your benefit.' He tried to soften his words with a swift triangle of a smile, but George found it unconvincing. 'My study's warmer,' Hawkin added, turning towards the door.

They followed him down the chilly hall to a room that looked like a miniature gentlemen's club. A pair of leather armchairs flanked a grate where a paraffin heater squatted. Hawkin made straight for the one that overlooked the window. A wide desk with a scarred leather top occupied the opposite end of the room, its surface scattered with ornamental paperweights. The walls were lined with mahogany bookshelves crammed with leather-bound volumes, ranging in size from tall ledgers to tiny pocketbooks. A parquet floor, worn uneven with years of use, was partly covered by a frail and faded Turkish rug. By the door was a glazed gun cupboard containing a matching pair of shotguns. George knew nothing about guns, but even he recognized that these were no common farmer's rook controllers. 'Lovely room, sir,' he said, crossing to the armchair opposite Hawkin.

'I don't think my uncle changed anything from his grandfather's day,' he said. 'I shall want to modernize it a bit. Get rid of that tatty old desk and clear out some of these books to make way for something more contemporary. I need somewhere to store my photographic books and my negatives.'

George bit his tongue. He'd have loved a room like this, redolent of a connected past and present, a room he could imagine passing on to a son. If he was lucky enough to have a son. The thought of what Hawkin might do to it was painful, even though he recognized it was none of his business. But it didn't make him like the man any better. He glanced over his shoulder at Clough, who had slipped into the desk chair and had his notebook out, pencil poised. The sergeant nodded. George cleared his throat, wishing for the authority that a few more years would automatically bring. 'Before I get on to the main reason we wanted to see you, sir, I wanted to check that you haven't received any communication asking for a ransom for Alison.'

Hawkin frowned. 'Surely nobody would imagine I

have that kind of money, Inspector? Just because I own a bit of land?'

'People get all sorts of ideas in their heads, sir. And with the Sinatra kidnapping being in the news, it's as well to bear it in mind as a possibility.'

Hawkin shook his head sorrowfully. 'I've had no such thing. Not a letter, not a phone call. We had several letters today from local Buxton people who had heard about Alison's disappearance, but they were all offering sympathy, not asking for money. You're welcome to take a look; they're all on the dresser in the kitchen.'

'If you do, sir, it's important that you let us know. Even if you're warned against telling us, for Alison's sake, you mustn't keep it from us. We need your cooperation in this.'

Hawkin gave a nervous laugh. 'Believe me, Inspector, if anybody thinks they're going to get their hands on my money as well as my stepdaughter, they've got another thing coming. You can rely on me to get right on to you if anyone is foolish enough to think I'm in a position to ransom Alison. Now, what was it you wanted to see me about? I've been out in the dale all afternoon, and I'm famished.'

'We've discovered a small discrepancy between statements. We wanted to clear the matter up. Finding Alison is our highest priority, so any potential misunderstandings need to be sorted out as quickly as possible.'

'Of course they do,' Hawkin said, turning away to crush out his cigarette in the ashtray perched on top of a pile of newspapers next to his chair.

'You stated that on the afternoon Alison disappeared, you were in your darkroom?'

Hawkin cocked his head to one side. 'Yes,' he drawled, caution in his eyes.

'All afternoon?'

'Why does it matter when I went into my darkroom?' he said. 'I don't understand what my afternoon activities had to do with Alison.'

'If you could bear with me, sir, then we can resolve this problem very quickly. Can you tell us when you went through to your darkroom?'

Hawkin rubbed the side of his narrow nose with his index finger. 'We ate lunch at twelve thirty as usual, then I came through here to read the paper. One of the drawbacks of rural living is that the post and the morning paper seldom arrive before lunch. So I have my little ritual after lunch of retiring here to deal with any post and read the *Express*. On Wednesday, I had a couple of letters to answer, so it was probably somewhere in the region of half past two when I went out to the darkroom. It's a small outbuilding at the back of the manor that already had running water. I had it converted. Are you interested in photography, Inspector? I promise you, you won't have seen a private darkroom as well equipped and laid out as mine.' Hawkin's smile was the nearest thing to unguarded candour George had ever seen on his face.

'I'd like to take a look later, if I may.'

'You're welcome. Your uniformed lads were in there the night Alison disappeared, just checking that she wasn't hiding there, but I explained that it's normally kept locked. Because of the valuable equipment. But please don't take their word for it. And if you ever need any professional photographs . . .' Hawkin nodded at the gold ring gleaming on George's finger.

'Perhaps a portrait of you and your wife?'

The thought of Hawkin's lounge-lizard charm focusing on Anne, even mediated by a camera lens, was disproportionately repugnant to George. Masking his distaste, he merely said, 'That's a very kind offer, sir. Now, about Wednesday afternoon. You've told us you went across to your darkroom about half-two. How long did you stay there?'

Hawkin frowned and reached for his cigarettes. 'I had quite a backlog of printing to do. Entries for a competition, so it's important to get the prints just so. I didn't come back indoors until just before dinner time. I found my wife and Kathy Lomas getting themselves in a terrible state in the kitchen about Alison. Does that answer your question, Inspector?'

'It answers my question, but it doesn't resolve my difficulty. You see, sir, we have been told that you were seen walking from the woodland where we found Shep to the spinney where we discovered what we believe to be traces of a struggle involving Alison. The time has been put at about four o'clock on Wednesday afternoon. Can you explain why anyone might think that, sir?'

It was Hawkin's ears that flushed first, turning a deep scarlet that spread along his jaw and up his cheeks. 'Because they are stupid peasants, Inspector?'

George sat up straight in his seat, astonished at the virulence of Hawkin's response. 'I beg your pardon?'

'They've been inbreeding for centuries, Inspector. A village with three surnames? They're not exactly going to win *Top of the Form*, are they? Some of them barely know what year it is, never mind what day it is. Just because one of those halfwits mistook Tuesday for Wednesday ... well, it's hardly something to take *seriously*, is it? Look, Inspector, my uncle ran this village as if it was his personal hobby for a very good reason. He knew that without the protection of a squire, the people of Scardale would never survive. They're just not equipped for the modern world.' Suddenly, Hawkin ran out of vitriol. He ran a hand over his hair and managed one of his neat three-cornered smiles. 'Believe me, Inspector, I never moved out of my darkroom on Wednesday afternoon. Whoever told you otherwise was mistaken.'

Before George could respond, Clough chimed in with the perfect timing that makes comedy duos into stars. Ostentatiously flicking back the pages of his notebook, he spoke apologetically, 'Sir, there were two statements. Two individuals claim they saw you in the same place at about four o'clock on Wednesday. If it was just the one, well, frankly, sir, we've seen enough in the last couple of days to understand exactly what you're getting at. But with two . . . It's a bit more awkward.'

This time, Hawkin's smile appeared genuine. For the first time, George had a flash of what had attracted a Scardale widow like Ruth Carter. When he smiled, Hawkin had the same devilish quality as the young David Niven. And the same smoothness, George added mentally as Hawkin offered both policemen cigarettes with an expansive gesture. 'Thankfully, there's a perfectly reasonable explanation,' he said, his voice straining for lightness.

'And that would be?' George asked, leaning forward to accept a light, his eyes never leaving Hawkin's.

'I'm often out in the dale. I take photographs, I walk my land to make sure everything is as it should be. You have to keep them up to the mark, you know, or the walls would be nothing more than piles of limestone rubble. And as for the gates . . .' Pursed lips, shaken head. 'Anyway, it so happens that on Tuesday I was in the field you mentioned. Obviously a couple of the villagers saw me there. After Alison disappeared, they'll have been arguing about what day it was. Now, if I had been a Carter or a Crowther or a Lomas, I'd have been given the benefit of the doubt and they'd all have agreed it was Tuesday. But I'm an outsider, so they're always ready to think the worst of me. And, let's not forget, they're like children, always playing to the gallery. So if there was any doubt in what passes for a mind among the Carters, the Crowthers and the Lomases, they'd automatically pick the version of events that made them look important and me look bad.' Hawkin leaned back in his seat, crossing one leg over the other to reveal a bony ankle and a few inches of white, hairy skin between pyjama and slipper.

'You're certain it wasn't Wednesday?' George asked.

'I'm positive.'

'And you'd be willing to sign a sworn statement to that effect?' George asked. Nothing Hawkin had said persuaded him Ma Lomas and Charlie were mistaken, but it remained their word against his. And George knew who would make the more convincing witness.

They were back in the kitchen within a couple of minutes. Ruth Hawkin was sitting at the kitchen table, a forgotten cigarette in the ashtray next to her transformed into three inches of marled grey ash. Her hand was clamped over her mouth and her eyes were fixed

179

on the front page of a newspaper on the table in front of her.

'What's the matter?' Hawkin asked, his voice showing more concern for his wife than he ever had in George's hearing before.

Wordlessly, she pushed the paper towards the three men. It was that week's *High Peak Courant*, printed that very afternoon. George stared down at the front page headlines, scarcely able to credit what he was reading.

RELATIVE IN CUSTODY
IN MISSING GIRL HUNT

A man is being questioned by Buxton police in connection with the disappearance of Scardale schoolgirl Alison Carter.

The man assisting police with their inquiries is believed to be a relative of the missing thirteen-year-old who has not been seen since late on Wednesday afternoon.

Alison took her collie Shep for a walk in the woods by the river Scarlaston, as she often did after she came home from school.

Police with tracker dogs have led a massive two-day comb-out of the secluded dale. Local farmers have searched isolated outbuildings and High Peak Mountain Rescue Team have investigated remote gullies where Alison might have fallen.

Further searches are planned for the weekend. Volunteers are asked to assemble at the Methodist Hall on the B8673 south of Longnor at half past eight on Saturday morning.

The man in custody is thought to be a close

relative of Alison Carter, and familiar with the Scardale area, although he has not lived in the dale for twenty years.

He is believed to live in a hostel for single men on the outskirts of Buxton. It is understood that he is employed at a sheltered workshop in the town, where he was met by police when he arrived for work this morning.

A police spokesman refused to confirm or deny the *Courant* story, saying only that wide-ranging inquiries into Alison's disappearance were continuing.

Among those questioned have been Alison's classmates at Peak Girls' High . . .

George could scarcely credit what he was seeing. The glory-hunting Detective Chief Inspector Carver had wasted no time in leaking the story to the local paper. He must have been on the phone to them even before Peter Crowther was in the station. George's heart sank. He thought he and Clough had protected Crowther by arranging for the word to be spread that the man had no connection to his niece's disappearance. They'd reckoned without the Buxton grapevine and the early deadline of the weekly *Courant*. This paper was on the streets of Buxton. And thanks to him, so was Peter Crowther.

Then he caught sight of Ruth Hawkin's stricken face and he reminded himself that his anger would have to wait. 'I'm sorry,' he said. 'There's no reason to suppose he had anything to do with Alison's disappearance. He's been released. That story should never have appeared.'

'What are you talking about?' Hawkin demanded,

sounding genuinely puzzled. He jerked the paper closer and read the first few paragraphs again. 'I don't understand. Who is this relative who's been arrested? Why weren't we informed? And why have you been pestering me with pointless questions when you already have someone in custody?'

'That's a lot of questions, sir,' George said. 'Taking them one at a time, the man the story refers to is your wife's brother, Peter Crowther.'

'No, that's not right. Her brother's called Daniel,' Hawkin protested.

'Mrs Hawkin's other brother is called Peter,' George persisted.

Hawkin glared at his wife. 'What other brother, Ruth?' His voice was as tense as a fishing line holding a salmon.

She was still beyond speech, capable only of shaking her head. George came to her rescue. 'Peter Crowther didn't fit in here, so the family arranged for him to live and work in Buxton. He's not been near Scardale in twenty years, and there's no reason to suppose he was here on Wednesday.'

'But you arrested him!' Hawkin objected.

'The paper doesn't say that,' George said, conscious of his prevarication. 'It relies on innuendo and a few facts to imply that. Peter Crowther was brought to the police station for questioning because my senior officer thought it would provide better circumstances for interviewing him than his place of work or the room he shares with another resident at the hostel. He was questioned, and now he has been released.' He turned back to Ruth, pulling out the chair next to her and sitting down. 'I'm truly sorry about this,

Mrs Hawkin. We do know the circumstances and the last thing we intended was for you to be further upset. Would you like one of us to explain to your husband, or would you rather talk to him yourself?'

She shook her head. Her hand dropped from her mouth and she reached for the dead cigarette, seeming surprised to find nothing there but a filter tip and a finger of ash. Clough had a lit cigarette in her hand before she could find her own. 'Ask Ma,' she said wearily, giving Hawkin a look of tired pleading. 'She'll tell him. Please. I can't.'

Hawkin pushed himself upright. 'Bloody peasants,' he muttered. Turning sharply away from the table, he stalked out of the room, slamming the door behind him.

Ruth sighed. 'Was Peter frightened?' she asked.

'I'm afraid so,' George said.

'Good.' She looked speculatively at her cigarette. 'Bloody good.'

Friday, 13ᵗʰ December 1963. 9.47 p.m.
George had gone home when his eyes could no longer focus on the witness statements. There had been a planning meeting between the uniformed branch and CID to organize the volunteer searches for the morning. A representative from the water board had come along to discuss draining the two moorland reservoirs within four miles of Scardale, one on the bleak Staffordshire uplands, the other in the greener hills between Scardale and Longnor. George had found his eagerness almost ghoulish.

After the arrangements for the morning had been

finalized, he'd suggested a quick drink to Tommy Clough. They'd driven down to the tiny Baker's Arms and settled in the gloomiest corner with a pint apiece. 'I checked with the hostel,' Clough said. 'Crowther went straight back after we cut him loose. He had his tea then went out about an hour later. He didn't say where he was going, but there's nothing unusual in that. The warden reckons he'll have gone out for a pint. Nobody's been there looking for him, though, so it looks like he might have avoided having the finger pointed at him.'

'I hope so. I've got enough to think about without having to feel responsible for what happens to Peter Crowther.'

'Not your fault, sir. If anything does happen, it's down to the DCI and that thick git Colin Loftus from the *Courant*. If ever there was an argument for drowning at birth, it's Loftus.'

'I ordered Crowther's release,' George reminded him.

'And quite right too. We'd no grounds for holding on to him. He's all wrong for it.'

'Assuming there is an "it",' George said morosely.

'We both know there's some sort of an "it". Forty-eight hours and not a sniff except for signs of a struggle and a bit of blood? She's dead, no two ways about it.'

'Not necessarily. Whoever's got her could be holding her captive.'

Clough looked sceptically at his boss. 'With the Lindbergh baby, like as not.'

George stared into his beer. 'I'm going to find her, Tommy. Ideally, alive. But either way, I'm going to find Alison Carter. Whatever it takes, Mrs Hawkin is going to know what happened to her lass.' He downed the rest of his pint in one and stood up. 'I'm going back to read some statements. You're overdue some sleep. And that's an order.'

He'd had to give up on the witness statements when hunger and exhaustion conspired against him. Back home, Anne had been waiting, sitting placidly in her armchair, knitting and watching TV. Within minutes of his weary return, she had a bowl of soup in front of him. He sat at the kitchen table, the monotonous motion of transferring the spoon from the plate to his mouth almost more than he could manage. Behind him, Anne stood at the stove, frying chopped bacon, onions, potatoes and eggs in a kind of hash.

'How are you feeling?' he managed to ask, between finishing his soup and starting his main course.

'I'm fine,' Anne said, sitting down opposite him with a cup of tea. 'I'm expecting, not ill. You're not to worry. It's not a medical condition. I'm more concerned about you, working without proper food or rest.'

George stared at his food, chewing automatically. 'I can't help it,' he said. 'Alison Carter has a mother. I can't leave her not knowing what's happened to her daughter. I keep thinking about how I'd feel if it was my child that was missing, nobody knowing what had happened to her or where she was, nobody seemingly able to do anything to help.'

'For heaven's sake, George, you're taking too much on your shoulders. You're not the only policeman responsible for what's going on out there. You take too much on yourself,' Anne said, a trace of irritation in her voice.

'That's easy to say, but I keep being haunted with the idea that it's a race against time. She could still be alive. While that's still a possibility, I've got to give it everything I can.'

'But I thought you had somebody in custody? Surely you can let up a bit now?' She leaned across the table to refill his teacup.

George snorted. 'You've been believing what you read in the papers again, haven't you?' he said, his voice a grim tease.

'Well, the *Courant* didn't leave much room for doubt.'

'The *Courant* story is a mess of innuendo and inaccuracy. Yes, we picked up Alison Carter's uncle. And yes, he's got convictions for sex offences. And there the similarity ends between the truth and what's in the paper. He's a sad case who's scared of his own shadow. Definitely not got all his marbles. All he's ever been done for is exposing himself, and that was years ago. But when DCI Carver found out about him, he got over-excited and went off like Sputnik.'

'Well, you can't really blame him, George. You're all in a state about this case. It's not surprising if somebody loses his sense of proportion. The uncle must have seemed like an obvious suspect. Poor man,' Anne said. 'He must have been terrified.' She shook her head. 'This case seems full of pain.'

'And there's no sign of it getting better.' He pushed his empty plate away. 'Most cases, you can see a clear way forward. It's obvious who's done what, or at worst, where you should be looking. But not this one. It's full of dead ends and dark corners. They've searched the whole dale and found nothing to lead us to Alison Carter. Somebody must know what happened to her.'

He sighed in exasperation. 'I wish to God I could find out who.'

'You will, darling,' Anne said, pouring him a fresh cup of tea. 'If anyone can, it's you. Now, try to relax. Then tomorrow, you can look at things afresh.'

'I hope so,' George said fervently. He reached for his cigarettes, but before he could extract one from the packet, the phone rang. 'Oh God,' he sighed. 'Here we go again.'

11

Friday, 13th December 1963. 10.26 p.m.
George leaned forward in the passenger seat of Tommy
Clough's Zephyr, staring intently through the windscreen. Outside, shafts of light from streetlamps
illuminated slanted sheets of sleet that swirled in the
wind like net curtains in a draught. It wasn't the
weather that interested George, however. It was the
running battle that swam in and out of the pools of light
outside the single men's hostel at Waterswallows.

'It's hard to credit,' he said, shaking his head. 'You'd
think they'd be glad to get home from the pub on a
night like this. Wouldn't you rather be in front of your
own fireside instead of risking double pneumonia and
a clobbering from a bobby's truncheon?'

'After enough pints of Pedigree, you don't care,'
Clough said cynically. He'd been in the pub himself
when he'd heard that a lynch mob was marching on the
men's hostel at Waterswallows. Pausing only to phone
the station, he'd driven straight to George's house,
knowing his boss would have been alerted. Now they
were watching a team of a dozen uniformed officers
dispersing a mob of about thirty angry drunks with

188

a degree of controlled savagery that was as perfectly choreographed as a ballet. George felt a profound sense of gratitude that it wasn't happening in weather clear enough for anyone to photograph it. The last thing he needed was a bunch of civil libertarians claiming the police were thugs when all they were doing was making sure a bunch of drunken vigilantes didn't get the chance to beat the living daylights out of an innocent man.

Suddenly three struggling men loomed up in front of the car – two uniformed police officers and a man with shoulders a yard wide and a face streaming blood. A truncheon rose and fell across the man's shoulders and he slumped insensible across the bonnet of the Zephyr. 'Oh good. Now we can have him for malicious damage as well,' Clough said ironically as one officer cuffed the man's hands behind his back and left him to slide gently to the ground, trailing blood and mucus.

'I suppose we'd better go and give them a hand,' George said with all the enthusiasm of a man faced with dental treatment without anaesthetic.

'If you say so, sir. Only, us being in plain clothes, we might only cause more confusion.'

'Good point. We'd better hang on till the uniformed lads have got it sorted out.' They watched in silence for another ten minutes. By then, a dozen men were in varying states of consciousness in the back of a paddy wagon. A couple of constables held handkerchiefs to their noses while another searched for the cap he'd lost in the melee. Out of the sleet, Bob Lucas appeared, his overcoat collar turned up against the weather. He pulled open the rear door of the car and dived in.

'Some night,' he said, his voice as bitter as the weather. 'We all know who to blame for this, don't we?'

'The *Courant*?' Clough asked in a butter-wouldn't-melt voice.

'Oh aye,' Lucas said. 'More like, whoever thought the *Courant* should know. If I thought it was one of my lads, I'd skin him alive.'

'Aye, well,' said Clough with a sigh. 'We all know it wasn't one of your lads, Bob. Nobody from uniform would have the nerve to give confidential information to the press.' He softened the veiled insult with a crooked smile over his shoulder. 'You've got them far too well trained for that.'

'Is Crowther safe?' George asked, turning round on the bench seat and reaching over to offer the uniformed sergeant a cigarette.

Lucas nodded his appreciation and helped himself. 'He's not there. After we released him, he came back, had his tea and went out again. They're supposed to be back by nine, that's when the doors get locked. But the warden says Crowther never showed up. He gave him quarter of an hour's grace, knowing what kind of a day he'd had, but then he locked up as usual. He says nobody rang the bell or knocked the door before this lot showed up. Luckily, he had the sense not to open up and they hadn't managed to break the door down before we turned up.'

'So where is he?' Clough asked, inching open his quarterlight so the bitter wind could whip the smoke into the night.

'We've no idea,' Lucas admitted. 'His usual watering hole is the Wagon, so I thought I'd drop by on the

190

way back to the station, see what they had to say for themselves.'

'We'll do it now,' George said decisively, glad to have action to divert him from the constant nagging worry of the investigation.

'I've still got loose ends to sort here,' Lucas protested.

'Fine. You do that, we'll see the landlord at the Wagon.' George's nod was dismissive. Lucas gave him a sour look, took a deep drag of the cigarette and left the car without another word. If he'd been challenged, he'd have said the wind slammed the car door shut.

'You know the landlord?' George asked as Clough cautiously eased the car down the skid pan that Fairfield Road had become.

'Fist Ferguson? I know him.'

'Fist?'

'Aye. He used to be a professional boxer. Then, the story goes, he took a bung to throw a fight, got caught and lost his licence. Then he made a living for a while on the illegal bare-knuckle circuit. Earned enough to buy the pub.'

'Makes you wonder whose application the licensing magistrates would throw out,' George commented as the car slid into the kerb outside the unappetizing Wagon Wheel pub. No lights showed behind the closed doors and curtained windows.

'It's in his wife's name.'

They hurried from the car round the side of the building and huddled in the lee of a stack of beer crates. Clough hammered on the door. 'I don't fancy taking a hand searching tomorrow if this keeps up,' he said, tilting his head back to see the upstairs windows. He banged on the door again.

191

A grimy yellow square appeared above their heads. A bald head popped up, obscuring most of the light. 'Open up, Fist, it's Tommy Clough.'

They heard feet thunder down a flight of stairs. Bolts rattled behind the door, then it opened to reveal a man who filled most of the available space in the narrow corridor. He wore a set of woollen combs that might once have been white but were now the colour of dried snot. 'What the bloody hell do you want this time of night? If it's a drink you're after, you can sling your hook now.' He scratched his balls extravagantly.

'Nice to see you too, Fist,' Clough said. 'A minute of your time?'

Ferguson stepped back reluctantly. They filed inside, George bringing up the rear. 'Who's that, then?' Ferguson demanded, pointing a thick finger at him.

'My guv'nor. Say hello to Detective Inspector Bennett.'

Ferguson made a strange grunting noise that George took to be a laugh. 'Looks young enough to be your lad. What's up, then? Must be a damn sight more than looking for a lock-in if you've brought the organ grinder, Tommy.'

'Peter Crowther drinks here,' Clough said.

'Not after tonight, he doesn't,' Ferguson said, his hands unconsciously bunching into fists. 'I'm not having somebody that interferes with young lasses in my bar.'

'What happened tonight?' George asked.

'Crowther turned up same time as usual. I thought he had more guts than I'd given him credit for, but it turned out he had no idea anybody knew he'd been in the nick all day. I shoved the paper under his nose and he near about burst into tears. I told him if he wanted a drink in Buxton tonight, he'd better find a pub where nobody could read. Then I told him he were barred for life.' Ferguson's chest was puffed out, his shoulders flexed back.

'Very bold of you,' George said drily. 'I take it Mr Crowther left?'

'Of course he bloody left,' Ferguson said indignantly.

'Do you know where he went?' Clough asked..

'I don't know and I don't bloody care,' Ferguson said negligently.

'For the record, Mr Ferguson,' George said, 'Mr Crowther had nothing to do with the disappearance of his niece. The story in this week's *Courant* is a work of fiction. I'd be obliged if you'd lift your ban before your licence comes up for renewal.' He turned on his heel and walked back into weather that suddenly seemed more hospitable than the pub landlord.

'You should pay attention to Mr Bennett,' Clough said as he followed. 'He's going to be around for a very long time.' Ferguson glared at George's back but said nothing.

They sat in the car and stared gloomily at the swirling sleet. 'Better go back to the station and put out a request for patrols to keep a lookout for Crowther,' George sighed. 'Do you think tomorrow's going to be any better than today?'

Saturday, 14th December 1963. 7.18 a.m.
There was little he could contribute to the search plans that the senior uniformed officers were making for the day, so George wandered back upstairs to his office and started the weary task of ploughing through witness

statements in search of something that might produce a lead. He was reading an interview with Alison's English teacher when Tommy Clough stuck his head round the door.

'Have you seen this morning's *Daily News*?' he asked.

'No. The paper shop was still shut when I got in.'

Clough came in and closed the door behind him. 'Train's just in from Manchester. I got one off the driver. I don't think you're going to like it.' He dropped the paper in front of George, folded open to page three.

Clairvoyant joins hunt for missing Alison

By our Staff Reporter

A top French clairvoyant has revealed exclusively to the *Daily News* that missing schoolgirl Alison Carter is still alive.

And she has offered her services in the search for the thirteen-year-old whose disappearance has baffled police.

Madame Colette Charest's clairvoyant powers have amazed police in her native country and she believes she can help find Alison, who vanished from home on Wednesday.

With the permission of Alison's worried parents, a member of our news team phoned Mme Charest and gave her details of Alison's movements after she returned from school to the Derbyshire hamlet of Scardale where she lived with her mother and stepfather.

Safe and well

Mme Charest said she was convinced the girl was still alive.

'She is safe,' she told our staff reporter. 'She went away with somebody that she knew and they travelled in a car.

'She is in a small house, one of a row of many similar houses. I think it is in a city, but it is many miles from her home.

'She has been in danger, but I sense that she is safe for the time being.'

Mme Charest explained that she could not give any more detailed information without a photograph of Alison and a map of the area. These have been sent to Lyons, France, by special air courier and a full report of Mme Charest's conclusions will appear in Monday's *News*.

Police pledge

A police spokesman said, 'We have no plans to consult a clairvoyant, though we do not dismiss Mme Charest's comments out of hand.

'Stranger things have happened.'

Of Mme Charest, French gendarmes have been quoted as saying that her powers were 'uncanny' after she had given assistance in cases where police had no leads.

Weather permitting, members of the public will today join Derbyshire police in further searches of the bleak moors and dales around Scardale.

George screwed the paper into a tight ball and threw it across the room. 'Don bloody Smart,' he swore, his cheeks scarlet against the dark bruises under his eyes. 'Can you believe that? Safe and well?'

'I suppose it's possible.' Clough leaned against a filing cabinet and lit a cigarette.

'Of course it's *possible*,' George exploded. 'It's *possible* that Martin Bormann is alive and well and living in Chesterfield, but it's not bloody likely, is it? What's this going to do to Ruth Hawkin? I can't believe any newspaper could be so irresponsible! And who gave them that bloody silly quote?'

'Nobody, probably. Smart likely invented it.'

'Oh God,' George sighed. 'What's it going to be next, Tommy?' He took a cigarette from the packet lying already open on his desk and inhaled deeply. 'I'll buy you another paper,' he apologized. 'Anything you like except the *News*. Oh God, he'll be at the press conference, grinning like a Cheshire cat.'

'You could get the super to ban him.'

'I wouldn't give him the satisfaction.' George pushed his chair back and stood up. 'Let's go to Scardale. I'm sick of these four walls.'

Smart was there before them. As they pulled up by the village green, they saw him pushing a paper through the letterbox of Crag Cottage. While they looked on, Smart carried on to Meadow Cottage and delivered another copy. 'I'll swing for him,' George said, opening the car door and striding across the green to confront the journalist. With a sigh, Clough climbed out and followed him.

'Congratulations,' George snarled while he was still a few strides away from Smart.

'Good story, wasn't it?' Smart said, his foxy face

pleasantly surprised. 'I didn't think an educated man like you would have appreciated it, though.'

'Oh, I wasn't congratulating you on the story,' George said, now only feet away from the man. 'I was congratulating you on your award.'

'Award?'

Clough couldn't believe Smart had walked straight into it. He bit his lip to keep his smile secret.

'Yes, your award,' George continued with patently false bonhomie. 'The Police Federation Award for Irresponsible Journalist of the Year.'

'Oh dear, Inspector, didn't they teach you at university that sarcasm is the lowest form of wit?' Smart leaned against the wall of Meadow Cottage and folded his arms across his chest.

'Nobody could win the title of lowest form of anything while you're still breathing, Mr Smart. Did you stop for one minute to consider how cruel it is to raise Mrs Hawkin's hopes like that?'

'Are you saying she should give up hope? Is that the official police view?' Smart leaned forward, eyes alert, beard bristling.

'Of course not. But what you held out with that piece of trash this morning was false hope. Grabbing at headlines without thinking about the consequences.' George shook his head in disgust. 'Does she exist, this Madame Charest? Or did you make that up as well as your police quote?'

Now it was Smart's turn to flush with anger. His skin had the mottled look of corned beef. 'I don't make stuff up. I keep an open mind. You might benefit from doing the same thing, Inspector. What if Madame Charest is right? What if Alison is miles from here, locked up in a house in Manchester or Sheffield or Derby? What are you doing to check that out?'

George gave an incredulous gasp. 'Are you saying we should do a door-to-door search of every city in England just on the off chance that some charlatan in France might have struck lucky with her fantasies? You're even more stupid than I thought.'

'Of course that's not what I'm saying. But you could put out an appeal on the news. "Has anybody seen this girl? It's believed that Alison Carter may be staying with somebody she knows. If you know of any house where a teenage girl has appeared in the last few days, or if you know of anyone who has connections to Scardale or Buxton whose behaviour has been at all unusual, please contact Derbyshire Police on this number." That's what I'm going to suggest to your boss at the press conference this morning.' Smart straightened up, his face triumphant. 'Yeah, that's what I'm going to suggest. And see how clever you look sitting beside him when he says what a great idea it is.'

'You're sick, you know that, Smart?' It was the best George could do and he knew it was weak even as he said it.

'You're the one that said you'd do whatever it took to find what had happened to Alison Carter. I took you at your word. I thought you were a bit special, George. But when push comes to shove, you're as set in your ways as the rest of them. Well, God help Alison Carter if you're her best hope.' Smart moved sideways, trying to pass George.

The policeman placed a hand in the middle of Smart's chest. He didn't actually push him, just firmly held him in place. 'I will find out what happened to Alison,' he said, his voice thick with emotion. 'And when I do, you'll be the last to know.' He stepped back and released the journalist, who stood staring back at him.

Then Smart smiled, a tight, sharp sickle that made no impact on the hard glare of his eyes. 'Oh, I doubt that very much,' he said. 'You might not like to think so, George, but you and me, we're two of a kind. Neither of us cares who we upset as long as we get the job done the best it can be done. You might not agree with me right now, but when you go away and talk it over with your pretty wife, you'll know I'm right.'

George inhaled so deeply his physical size actually increased. Hastily, Clough stepped forward and put a hand on his boss's arm. 'I think you'd better be on your way, Mr Smart,' he said. One look at his face and the journalist slid round the two of them and walked briskly to his car.

'How long do you think I'd get if I beat that smile off his face with a truncheon?' George asked through stiff lips.

'Depends if the jury know him or not. Cup of tea?'

They walked together to the caravan where, even this early, the WPCs were brewing up. George stared into a cup of tea and spoke softly. 'I suppose you've worked this kind of case before, Tommy? Full of dead ends and frustrations?'

'Aye, one or two,' Clough admitted, stirring three spoonfuls of sugar into his tea. 'Thing is, sir, you just have to keep plugging away. It might feel like you're battering your head against a brick wall, but as often as not, part of the wall's just cardboard painted to look like the real thing. The breakthroughs generally come sooner or later. And it's early days yet, even though it doesn't feel like it.'

'And what if the breakthrough doesn't come? What if we never find out what happened to Alison Carter? What then?' George looked up, his eyes wide with apprehension about what such a failure would mean, both personally and professionally.

Clough took a deep breath then slowly exhaled. 'Then, sir, you move on to the next case. You take the wife out dancing, you go to the pub and have a pint and you try not to lie awake at night fretting over what you can't change.'

'And is that a recipe that works?' George asked bleakly.

'I wouldn't know, sir, I've not got a wife.' Clough's wry smile didn't mask the knowledge they both shared. If they didn't uncover Alison Carter's fate, it would scar them both.

'Mine's pregnant.' The words were out before George knew he was going to say them.

'Congratulations.' Clough's voice was curiously flat. 'Not the best of times to get the news. How's Mrs Bennett?'

'So far, so good. She's not having morning sickness yet. I just hope . . . well, I just hope she's not in for a difficult time. Because I can't ignore this inquiry, however long it takes.' George stared through the misted windows of the caravan, not registering the gradual lightening of the sky that signalled the start of another day's searching.

'It doesn't go on at this pitch for long, you know,' Clough said, reminding George of what the younger man knew in theory but had little direct experience of. 'If we've not found her after ten days or so, say by next weekend, we'll stop searching. They'll close down the incident room and pull back to Buxton. We'll still be following up leads, but if we're no further forward after a month, it'll be put on the back burner. You and me, we'll have other cases up to our armpits, but we won't close this down. It'll stay open, we'll have reviews every three months or so, but we won't be working it like this.'

'I know, Tommy, but there's something about this one. I worked an unsolved murder when I was a DC in Derby, but it didn't get under my skin like this. Maybe because the victim was in his fifties. It felt like he'd had a life. Now it's looking more and more like we're not going to find Alison alive, and that fills me with rage because she's hardly started living. Even if all she was ever going to do was stop in Scardale and have babies and knit jumpers, it's still been taken from her and I want the law to do the same to whoever did it to her. My only regret is that we don't hang animals like that any more.'

'You still believe in hanging them, then?' Clough asked, leaning forward in his seat.

'Where it's cold-blooded, yes, I do. It's different with spur-of-the-moment killings. I'd just put them away for life, give them plenty of time to regret what they've done. But the kind of monsters who prey on kids, or the animals that murder some innocent bystander because they've got in the way of a robbery, yes, I'd hang them. Wouldn't you?'

Clough took his time answering. 'I used to think so. But a couple of years back I read that book about the Timothy Evans case, *Ten Rillington Place*. When he was tried, everybody believed he was bang to rights. Murdered his wife and his kiddy. The boys in the Met even had a confession. Then it turns out that Evans's landlord murdered at least four other women, so chances are it was him that killed Beryl Evans. But it's too late to go to Timothy Evans and say, "Sorry, pal, we cocked it up."'

George gave a half-smile of acknowledgement. 'Maybe so. But I can't take responsibility for other people's bad practice and mistakes. I don't think I ever have or ever would push an innocent man into confessing and I'm willing to stand by my own results. If Alison Carter has been murdered, like we both probably think by now, then I'd happily watch the man that did it swing from the gallows.'

'You might just do that if the bastard used a gun. They can still hang them for that, don't forget.'

George had no chance to respond. The door to the caravan burst open and Peter Grundy stood framed in the doorway, his face the bloodless grey of the Scardale crags. 'They've found a body,' he said.

12

Peter Crowther's body was huddled in the lee of a dry-stone wall three miles due north of Scardale as the crow flies. It was curled in on itself in a foetal crouch, knees tucked up to the chin, arms curled round the shins. The overnight frost that had turned the roads treacherous had given it a sugar-coating of hoar, rendering it somehow innocuous. But there was no mistaking death.

It was there in the blue-tinged skin, the staring eyes, the frozen drool on the chin. George Bennett looked down at the hull of a human being, recognition chilling him deeper than the bitter weather. He looked up at the miraculously blue sky, oddly surprised that a winter sun was shining as if it had something to celebrate. He certainly didn't. He felt sick, in his spirit as well as his stomach. The bitter taste of responsibility was sharp in his mouth. He hadn't done his job properly, and now a man was dead.

George lowered his head and turned away, leaving Tommy Clough squatting on his haunches by the body, giving it a minute scrutiny. He crossed to the field gate where two uniformed men were stationed to protect the scene until the pathologist arrived. 'Who found the body?' he asked.

'The farmer. Dennis Dearden's his name. Well, technically, it was his sheepdog. Mr Dearden came out at first light to check his stock like he always does. It was the dog that alerted him to the presence of the deceased,' the older constable said.

'Where's Mr Dearden now?' George asked.

'That's his place up the lane. The cottage.' The PC pointed to a single-storey building a few hundred yards away.

'I'll be there if anybody needs me.' George walked up the lane, his step as heavy as his heart. On the threshold of the tiny cottage, he paused, composing himself. Before he could knock, the door opened and a face like a withered apple appeared opposite his, small brown eyes like pips on either side of a nose as shapeless as a blob of whipped cream.

'You'll be the gaffer, then,' the man said.

'Mr Dearden?'

'Aye, lad, there's only me here. The wife's gone to visit her sister in Bakewell. She always goes for a few days in December, buys all the Christmas doings at the market. Come in, lad, you must be freezing out there.' Dearden stepped back and ushered George into a kitchen dazzling with sun. Everything gleamed: the enamel of the cooker, the wood of table, chairs and shelves, the chrome of the kettle, the glassware in a corner cabinet, even the gas fire. 'Set yourself down by the fire, there,' Dearden added hospitably, pushing a carver chair towards George. He lowered himself stiffly into a dining chair and smiled. 'That's better, eh? Get a bit of heat into your bones. By heck, you look worse than Peter Crowther.'

'You knew him?'

'Not to speak to. But I knew who he was. I've done some business with Terry Lomas over the years. I know them all in Scardale. I tell you, though, for a terrible minute out there, I thought it were the lass. She's been on my mind, same as everybody round here, I suppose.' He pulled a briar pipe from his waistcoat pocket and started prodding at it with a penknife. 'What a business. Her poor mother must be half mad with worry. We've all been keeping an eye out, making sure she wasn't lying hurt in some ditch or hiding out in a barn or a sheep shed. So of course, when I saw . . . well, my natural conclusion was that it must be young Alison.' He paused momentarily to fill his pipe, giving George his first real opportunity to speak.

'What exactly happened?' he asked, relieved that at last he was faced with a witness who seemed eager to offer information. After only three days in Scardale, he had developed a fresh appreciation of garrulity.

'As soon as I opened the gate, Sherpa was off like a streak, down the side of the wall. I knew right off something was amiss. She's not a dog that goes off at half-cock, not without cause. Then, halfway along the field, she drops to her belly like she'd been felled. Head down, between her front paws, and I can hear her whimpering half a field away. Like she would if she'd come upon a dead ewe. But I knew it wasn't no sheep, because that field's empty right now. I only opened the gate because it's a short cut to t' bottom piece.' Dearden struck a match and sucked on his pipe.

The tobacco was fragrant and filled the air with the aroma of cherries and cloves. 'Light up yourself, if you've a mind, lad.' He pushed a worn oilskin pouch across the table. 'Me own mixture.'

'I don't, thanks.' George took out his cigarettes and made an apologetic face.

'Aye, you'll not have the time for anything more complicated than fags in your job. You should think about taking up a pipe, though. It does wonders for the concentration. If I'm somewhere I can't smoke, I'm damned if I can finish the crossword.' He gestured with a thumb at the previous day's *Daily Telegraph*. George tried not to show he was impressed. Everybody knew the *Telegraph* crossword was easier than *The Times*, but it was no mean feat to complete it regularly, he knew. Obviously, behind Dennis Dearden's loose tongue was a sharp brain.

'So when I saw the way the dog was behaving, my heart was in my mouth,' Dearden continued. 'There's only one person I knew was missing, and that was Alison. I couldn't bear the thought of her lying dead minutes away from my front door. So I ran up the field as fast as I could, which is not very fast at all these days. I'm ashamed to say, I felt kind of relieved when I saw it were Peter.'

'Did you go right up to the body?' George asked.

'I didn't have to. I could see Peter wasn't going to be waking up much before the last trump.' He shook his head sorrowfully. 'Bloody daft beggar. Of all the nights to take it into his addled head to walk back to Scardale, he had to pick the worst kind. He'd been away from the country too long. He'd forgotten what weather like last night's can do to human beings. The sleet soaks you through to the skin. Then when the sky clears and the frost comes down, you've no resistance. You keep plodding on, but the cold penetrates right to your bones. Then all you want to do is lie down and sleep for ever. That's what Peter did last night.' He drew on his pipe, letting a plume of smoke escape from the corner of his mouth. 'He should have stopped in Buxton. He knew how to keep safe in the town.'

George clamped his mouth tightly round his cigarette. Not any longer, he thought. Peter Crowther had run out of options. His terror of losing only the second place he'd ever felt safe had driven him back, against his fear, to the place that had rejected him. It was exactly what George had dreaded. But in spite of his concerns, he'd let Tommy Clough persuade him to set Crowther free, because it was the most convenient way to deal with the problem. And thanks to a leaky CID and a sensation-hungry local paper, now Peter Crowther was frozen stiff in a Derbyshire sheep field.

'Your farm's a bit off the beaten track for someone coming from Buxton to Scardale, isn't it?' he asked. It was the only thing that gave him any grounds for doubting Dearden's theory of how Crowther had died.

Dearden chuckled. 'You're thinking like a motorist, lad. Peter Crowther thought like a countryman. You go back and look at an Ordnance Survey map. If you drew a line from Scardale to Buxton, avoiding the worst of the ups and downs, it'd go straight through that field. In the old days, before we all got our Land Rovers, there would be somebody from Scardale across my land at least once a day. It's not marked on the map as a footpath, mind you. It's not a right of way. But anybody from round here knows to respect livestock, so it never bothered me, nor my father before me, that the folk from Scardale used it for a short cut.' He shook his head. 'I never thought it'd be the death of any of them.'

George got to his feet. 'Thanks for your help, Mr Dearden. And for the warm. We'll be back to take a formal statement. And I'll make sure somebody lets you know when we've moved the body.'

'That'd be welcome.' Dearden followed him out to the front door. The old man peered past him down the lane at a maroon Jaguar with two wheels up on the verge. 'That'll be the doctor,' he said.

By the time George had walked back up the lane and into the field, the police surgeon was getting to his feet and brushing down his wide-shouldered camel over- coat. He peered curiously at George through square glasses with heavy black frames. 'And you are?' he asked.

'This is Detective Inspector Bennett,' Clough chipped in. 'Sir, this is Dr Blake, the police surgeon. He's just been carrying out a preliminary examination.'

The doctor gave a curt nod. 'Well, he's definitely dead. From the rectal temperature, I'd say he's been that way from somewhere between five and eight hours. No signs of violence or injury. Looking at the way he's dressed – no overcoat, no waterproof – I'd say the likeliest cause of death is exposure. Of course, we won't know for sure till the pathologist's gutted him on the slab, but I'd say this is natural causes. Unless you've found a way of charging the Derbyshire weather with murder,' he added with a sardonic twist of his mouth.

'Thanks, Doc,' George said. 'So, sometime between – what? One and four this morning?'

'Not just a pretty face, eh? Oh, of course, you must be the graduate we've all heard so much about,' the doctor said with a patronizing smile. 'Yes, Inspector, that's right. Once you know who he is, you might even be able to figure out what he was doing wandering round the Derbyshire moors in the middle of the night in a pair of worn-out shoes that would hardly keep out the weather in the town, never mind out here.' Blake pulled on a pair of heavy leather gloves.

'We know who he is and what he was doing here,' George said mildly. He'd been patronized by experts and wasn't about to be riled by a pompous ass who couldn't be more than five years older than him.

The doctor's eyebrows rose. 'Gosh. There you go, Sergeant, the perfect example of how educating our police officers will advance the fight against crime. Well, I'll leave you to it. You'll have my report early next week.' He side-stepped George with a sketchy wave and set off towards the gate.

'Actually, sir, I'd like it tomorrow,' George said.

Blake stopped and half turned. 'It's the weekend, Inspector, and there can be no urgency since you already have an identity for your corpse and a reason for his being here.'

'Indeed, sir. But this death is connected to a larger investigation and I require the report tomorrow. I'm sorry if that interferes with your plans, but that is why the county pays you so handsomely. Sir.' George's smile was pleasant, but his eyes held Blake's without flinching.

The doctor tutted. 'Oh, very well. But this isn't

Derby, Inspector. We're a small community out here. Most of us try to bear that in mind.' He walked briskly away.

'It's obviously my week for making friends,' George remarked as he turned back to Clough.

'He's a lazy sod,' Clough said carelessly. 'About time somebody reminded him who pays for his Jag and his golf club subscription. You'd think he would have been curious about the identity of a body he'd just been on intimate terms with, wouldn't you? He'll be on the blower this afternoon demanding to know what name to put on his report, I bet you.'

'We're going to have to go and break the news to Mrs Hawkin,' George said. 'And fast. The jungle drums will have been beating. She'll know there's a body on the moors, and she's bound to be thinking the worst.' He shook his head. 'It's a bad day when hearing your brother's dead passes for good news.'

Kathy Lomas was feeding her pigs, filling their troughs with a mixture of wilted turnip tops and the vegetable trimmings and leftovers of the village. The thunder of galloping feet over the frozen ground caught her attention and she turned to see Charlie Lomas racing down the back field as if the hounds of hell were after him. He would have run straight past her if she hadn't reached out to grab one of his flailing arms.

His momentum whirled him round and cannoned him into the pigsty wall, where he would have tipped right over into the sty if his aunt hadn't grabbed the back of his heavy leather jerkin.

'What's up, Charlie?' Kathy demanded. 'What's happened?'

Winded, he bent double, hands on knees, chest heaving for breath. At last, he managed to stammer, 'Old Dennis Dearden's dog found a body in one of his sheep fields.'

Kathy's hand flew to her chest. 'Oh no, Charlie. No,' she gasped. 'That can't be right. No, I won't believe it.'

Charlie struggled into a half-erect position, leaning on the wall and panting. 'I was down by the Scarlaston. I've got some illegal traps down there and I wanted to get them cleared out before the searchers got that far up Denderdale. I cut back up through Carter's Copse and I overheard a couple of bobbies talking about it. It's right, Auntie Kathy, they've found a body on Dennis Dearden's land.'

Kathy reached out convulsively for her nephew and clung on to him. They stood in their awkward embrace till Charlie had his breath back. 'You've got to tell Ruth,' she finally said.

He shook his head. 'I can't. I can't. I was going to tell Ma.'

'I'll come with you,' Kathy said firmly, grabbing his arm above the elbow and marching him across the back fields to the manor. 'Those bloody bastards,' she muttered angrily as they went. 'How dare they be tittle-tattling about it before anybody's seen fit to tell our Ruth. Well, I'm damned if I'm going to wait on their pleasure to break the news.'

Kathy dragged Charlie into the manor kitchen without knocking. Ruth and Philip were sitting at the kitchen table over the remains of breakfast. His breakfast, Kathy noticed. She didn't think Ruth had had anything but tea and cigarettes since Alison had disappeared.

'Charlie's got summat to tell you,' she said baldly. She knew the pointlessness of dressing up bad news.

Charlie repeated his stumbling words, anxiously eyeing Ruth. If she hadn't been sitting down already, she'd have collapsed. What colour was left in her face seeped away till she resembled a putty model. Then she started shivering as if she had a fever. Her teeth were chattering and her whole body was trembling. Kathy crossed the kitchen in half a dozen strides and took hold of her, rocking her as she had her children.

Philip Hawkin appeared oblivious to everything around him. Like Ruth, he'd paled at the news. But that was the only common point in their responses. He pushed his chair back from the table and walked out of the room like a man sleepwalking. Kathy was too occupied with Ruth to take it in at first, but Charlie stood staring after him open-mouthed, unable to credit what he'd just seen.

Ruth Hawkin was wearing fresh clothes, George noted. A brown jersey dress under a knobbly heather-mixture cardigan indicated that she had probably gone to bed and tried to sleep for the first time since Alison had vanished. The dark bruises of insomnia told of her failure. She sat at the kitchen table folded in on herself, a cigarette held in shaking fingers. Kathy Lomas leaned against the cooker, arms folded, a frown on her face.

'I don't understand,' Kathy said. 'Why would Peter think of coming back to Scardale now? When all this is going on?'

Ruth Hawkin sighed. 'He won't have been thinking like that, Kathy,' she said wearily. 'Nothing penetrates his head except what affects him directly. He'll have been upset by being at the police station, then when he went for a drink somewhere he thought was safe, he gets terrorized by the landlord. He only knows two places – Buxton and Scardale. But by God, he must have been scared out of his wits if he thought coming back to Scardale was the easy option.' She crushed out her cigarette and rubbed her face in a washing motion. 'I can't bear it.'

'It wasn't your fault,' Kathy said bitterly. 'We all know who to blame.' She pursed her lips and glared at George and Clough.

'No, not Peter. I can bear that. I've no grieving to do for him. It's thinking about Alison I can't bear. When young Charlie came tearing in saying there was a body up on Dearden's farm, I couldn't breathe. It was like I'd been punched in the chest. Everything inside me stopped working.'

She still hadn't been functional when he'd arrived, George thought. Ruth had been sitting at the table, hands clasped over her head, as if she wanted to hear nothing and see nothing. Kathy had been sitting beside her, one arm round her shoulders, the other stroking her hair. There had been no sign of Ruth's husband. When George had asked, Kathy had said bitterly that Philip had gone drip-white when Charlie had brought the news, then he'd walked out of the house. 'He'll not have gone far,' she said. 'Chances are he'll be shut in that darkroom of his. It's where he always goes when anything's going on he doesn't want to be part of.'

George decided Ruth Hawkin had more right to hear the news as quickly as possible than her husband had to share the moment with her. He blurted out his tidings in a single sentence. 'It's a man, the body that we've found.'

Ruth's head jerked back. The look of dazzling joy on her face would have outshone the Christmas lights in Regent Street.

'It's not her?' Kathy exclaimed.

'It's not Alison,' George confirmed. He drew a deep breath. 'I'm afraid it's not all good news. We have tentatively identified the body. It'll have to be confirmed by a member of the family, but we believe the dead man is Peter Crowther.'

There was a long, stunned silence. Ruth simply stared at him, as if she had taken in all she could with the news that the body in the field was not her daughter. Kathy looked aghast. Then she jumped to her feet, disgust on her face. She paced restlessly for a few moments, then had come to rest against the cooker, where she still stood, glowering. She knew who was to blame all right, George thought.

'Now, all I can think is, thank God it's not my Alison,' Ruth continued. 'Isn't that terrible? Peter was a human being too, but I doubt there'll be anyone to mourn him.'

'We shouldn't have to be mourning anybody,' Kathy said, her voice stinging George like a switch of nettles. 'When Ma Lomas started on with her doom and gloom about how we'd all suffer for bringing strangers into the dale, I thought she were gilding the lily as usual. But there was some truth in what she said. You lot haven't managed to find Alison, and now one of ours is dead.'

'Perhaps if you'd treated him more like one of yours when he was alive, he still would be,' a voice from behind said. George turned to see Philip Hawkin. He had no idea how long Hawkin had been standing in the half-open doorway. But he'd clearly heard most of the exchange. 'They hounded him from the village and then the Gestapo hounded him back,' he continued. 'God, the ignorance of people. He was clearly harmless enough. He'd never been violent; never, as far as I know, so much as laid a hand on any female. I can't help feeling sorry for the poor wretch.'

'You must be relieved it wasn't Alison's body,' Clough said, ignoring Hawkin's spleen.

'Of course. Who wouldn't be? I'm bound to say, though, that I'm disappointed in you and your men, Inspector. Two and a half days, and no news of Alison. You can see how distressed my wife is. Your failure is a torment to her. Can't you do something more? Apply your imagination? Search more thoroughly? What about this clairvoyant the newspaper's consulted? Couldn't you pay attention to what she's come up with?' He leaned on his fists on the table, two spots of colour in his pale cheeks. 'We're under a terrible strain, Inspector. We don't expect miracles, we just want you to do your job and find out what's happened to our little girl.'

George tried to keep his frustration behind the mask of his official face. 'We're already doing our best, sir. There are more search parties going out now. We've got hundreds of volunteers from Buxton, Stoke, Sheffield and Ashbourne, as well as local people. If she's out there to be found, we will find her, I promise you.'

'I know you will,' Ruth said softly. 'Phil knows you're doing your best. It's just . . . the not knowing. It's a slow torture.'

215

George dipped his head in acknowledgement. 'We'll keep you informed of any developments.'

Outside, the raw winter air knifed into his lungs as he strode across the green, gulping deep breaths. Almost trotting to keep up, Tommy Clough said, 'There's something about Philip Hawkin that doesn't ring right.'

'His responses are all off-key. Like when you're speaking a foreign language you've learned at evening classes. You might get all the grammar and the pronunciation right, but you never pass for a native speaker because they don't ever have to think about it.' George threw himself into the passenger seat of the car. 'But just because he doesn't fit in doesn't make him a kidnapper or a killer.'

'All the same . . .' Clough started the engine.

'All the same, we'd better go and face the music at the press conference. The superintendent's going to want to nail somebody's hide to the wall over this, and as sure as God made little green apples, you can bet Carver will have got his retaliation in first.' George leaned back and lit a cigarette. He closed his eyes and wondered why he'd chosen the police. He could have taken his law degree to some comfortable firm of solicitors in Derby and become an articled clerk. By now, he might have been on the road to becoming a partner specializing in something calm like conveyancing or probate. Mostly, the idea repelled him. That morning, it was curiously appealing.

He opened his eyes on long chains of men moving across the dale closer than arm's-length to each other. 'Nothing to find there except what the earlier teams dropped,' he said bitterly.

'They'll be using the least fit ones here in the dale,'

Clough said knowledgeably. 'They'll be keeping the top-class lads for the crags and the dales that are off the beaten track. Terrain like this, there's always going to be places we've missed just because we don't know it like the back of our hands.'

'Do you think they'll find anything?'

Clough screwed his face up. 'Depends what there is to find. Do I think they'll find a body? No.'

'Why not?'

'If we've not found the body by now, it's well hidden. That means it's been put where it is by somebody that knows their ground far better than anybody who's out there searching. So no, I don't think we'll find a body. I think we've already found all that we're going to find without something more to go on.'

George shook his head. 'I can't think like that, Tommy. That's tantamount to saying that not only will we not find Alison, we won't find the person who took her and probably killed her.'

'I know it's hard, sir, but that's what our opposite numbers in Cheshire and Manchester have had to deal with. I know you don't want to be reminded of what Don Smart's been writing, but we might have lessons to learn from their experience, even if it's only in how to cope with getting absolutely nowhere.' Clough stopped the car abruptly. There was nowhere to park on the main road as far as the eye could see. Cars, vans and Land Rovers jammed the verges. Where there were gaps, motorbikes and scooters were slotted in. 'Oh, flaming Nora. What am I supposed to do now?'

There was only one sensible solution. George stood by the Methodist Chapel and watched Clough expertly swing the big car round and head back down the lane to Scardale. He straightened his shoulders, took a final drag of his cigarette and flicked it into the road. He had no relish for what awaited him inside the church hall, but there was no point in putting it off.

13

The purgatory of the press conference was over sooner than George had feared, thanks to the brisk military approach of Superintendent Martin. He dealt with Peter Crowther's death with a laconic expression of regret. When one of the reporters had challenged him about unofficial leaks to the *Courant*, Martin had turned his artillery on the man.

'The *Courant*'s reckless speculation was of its own making,' he said in a parade-ground voice that was clearly unaccustomed to dissent. 'Had they checked the rumour they had picked up, they would have been told exactly what every other reporter was told – that a man had been brought to the police station for questioning for his own comfort and had been released without a stain on his character. I will not have my officers turned into scapegoats for the irresponsibility of the press. Now, we have a missing girl to find. I'm taking questions relevant to that inquiry.'

There were a few routine questions, then inevitably Don Smart's foxy features twitched into view as he raised his head from his notebook. 'I don't know if

219

you've seen the story in this morning's *News*?'

Martin's bark of laughter was as harsh as his words. 'Until I met you, sir, the only harlots I had met in peacetime had all been women. Though maybe I'm not so wide of the mark in spite of the whiskers, because all your work is good for, sir, is for filling the columns of the most sensationalist women's magazine. I will not dignify your feeble attempts at stirring up contention with a comment. Except to say that it is rubbish, sir, arrant rubbish. I was tempted to ban you from these press conferences altogether but I have been reluctantly persuaded by my colleagues that to do so would give you the very notoriety you crave. So you may stay, but do not forget that the purpose of our gathering here is to find a young, vulnerable girl missing from home, not to sell more copies of your vile little rag.'

By the end of his tirade, Martin's neck was the scarlet of a rooster's crest. Don Smart merely shrugged and dropped his eyes to his notebook again. 'I'll take that as a "no comment", then,' he said softly.

Martin had brought the conference to a swift end shortly afterwards. As the reporters filed out, muttering among themselves and comparing notes, George braced himself. Now the superintendent had warmed up against Smart, he expected to be shredded and left for dead. Martin fingered the salt-and-pepper bristles of his moustache and stared at George. Without taking his eyes off him, he took his Capstans from his pocket and lit one. 'Well?' he said.

'Sir?'

'Your version of yesterday's events.'

George briefly outlined his personal involvement with Crowther. 'So I instructed Sergeant Clough to tell the duty officer in Buxton that Crowther should be released. We agreed that the duty officer should also be asked to spread the word both to the press and locally through the beat officers that there was no suspicion attaching to Crowther.'

'You had not seen the story in the *Courant*?' Martin demanded.

'No, sir. We'd been out in Scardale all day. The paper doesn't reach there till Saturday and we'd had no opportunity to see the early edition.'

'And the duty officer said nothing to Sergeant Clough about the story?'

'He can't have done. If he had, Clough would have come back to me before authorizing the man's release.'

'You're sure of that?'

'You'd have to check with Clough, sir, but based on my knowledge of him, he'd have regarded any such story as a change in circumstances that might affect the decision I'd taken.' George registered the frown on Martin's face and prepared himself for the onslaught.

It never came. Instead, Martin simply nodded. 'I had a feeling it must have been a breakdown in communication. So. Two black marks against us. One, that one of our officers told the press something they should never have known. Two, that the duty officer failed to give officers in the field information relevant to their decision-making. We should be thankful that Mr Crowther's family is too preoccupied with their other loss to give much thought to our role in his death. What are your plans for today?'

George gestured with his thumb at a short stack of cardboard boxes by one of the trestle tables. 'I arranged for the witness statements from Buxton to be brought over here so I can go through them and still be on the spot if the searches produce anything.'

'They'll be finished searching by four, won't they?'

'Thereabouts,' George said, puzzled by the question.

'If they turn up nothing fresh, I expect you to be home by five.'

'Sir?'

'I'm aware of the way you and Clough have been working this case, and I see no reason why you should kill yourselves. You're both off duty tonight, and that's an order. You have an important day tomorrow, I want you rested for it.'

'Tomorrow, sir?'

Martin tutted impatiently. 'Has no one told you? My God, we need to do something about the communications in this division. Tomorrow, Bennett, we have the pleasure of entertaining two officers from other forces – one from Manchester and one from Cheshire. As you were doubtless aware even before Mr Smart of the *Daily News* drew our attention to the matter, both forces have had recent cases of puzzling disappearances of young people. They are interested in meeting to discuss whether there appear to be any significant connections between their cases and ours.'

George's heart sank. Wasting his time being diplomatic with other forces wasn't going to help him to find what had happened to Alison Carter. Manchester City Police had had over five months to try and find Pauline Reade and Cheshire had been searching for John Kilbride for a good three weeks without any result. The detectives on those cases were simply clutching at straws. They were more concerned with appearing to be pursuing some sort of action on their own dead-ended cases than they were with helping his inquiry. If he'd been a betting man, he'd have put money on the meeting already being the subject of a press release from the other two forces. 'Wouldn't it be better if DCI Carver handled the meeting?' he asked desperately.

Martin eyed his cigarette with a look of distaste. 'Your knowledge of the details of the case is altogether superior,' he said shortly. He turned away and started walking towards the door. 'Eleven o'clock, at divisional HQ,' he said, without turning back or raising his voice.

George stood staring at the door for long moments after Martin's straight-backed exit. He felt a mixture of anger and despair. Already other people were writing off Alison's disappearance as insoluble. Whether it could be connected to the other cases or not, it was clear that his superiors no longer expected him to find her at all, never mind to find her alive. Clenching his jaw, he yanked a chair towards the file boxes and began the task of reading the remaining witness statements. It was probably pointless, he knew. But there was a slim chance it might not be. And slim chances felt like the only ones he had left.

Sunday, 15th December 1963. 10.30 a.m.
For once, one of the papers had got it right. Every copy of the *Sunday Standard* contained a 12" by 19" poster. Extra copies had been distributed to every newsagent in the country, and every one that George had passed on his

223

way to the police station was displaying it prominently.
Under the thick black headline:

HAVE YOU SEEN
THIS GIRL?

the paper had reproduced one of Philip Hawkin's
excellent portraits of Alison. The text beneath read:

> **Alison Carter has been missing from her home
> in Scardale village, Derbyshire, since half past
> four on Wednesday 11th December.**
>
> **Description: 13 years old, 5ft, slim build,
> blonde hair, blue eyes, pale complexion, with
> slanting scar running across right eyebrow;
> wearing navy duffel coat over school uniform
> of black blazer, maroon cardigan, maroon skirt,
> white blouse, black and maroon tie, black wool-
> len tights and black sheepskin boots.**
>
> **Any information to Derbyshire County
> Police office at Buxton or any police officer.**

That was how journalists could help the police,
George thought. He hoped Don Smart had choked
over his breakfast when the poster had slid out of
his copy of the *Sunday Standard*. He also wondered
how many homes in the area would be displaying the
poster by nightfall. He reckoned there would be more
pictures of Alison Carter visible in High Peak windows
than there were Christmas trees.

It was a good start to the day, he thought cheerfully. It had already started well. Since he hadn't had to rush out of the door before first light, he and Anne had had the chance to wake naturally and lie chatting comfortably. He'd brought a pot of tea upstairs and they'd had a rare companionable hour that had set the seal on the evening they'd spent together. If he'd been asked in advance, George would have vehemently denied that he could have put Alison Carter from his mind for more than a minute or two. But somehow, Anne's unfussy company had allowed him to switch off from the frustrations of his investigation. They'd had a candlelit supper, then listened to the radio cuddled up on the sofa together, giving tentative shape to their dreams for their unborn child. It had been too short a respite, but it had left him refreshed, his confidence restored in spite of a restless sleep.

George fixed the poster to the CID notice board with drawing pins borrowed from some of the official notices. It would be a striking reminder to the visiting detectives that his case was very much alive. 'That looks well.' Tommy Clough's voice echoed across the room as the door swung shut behind him. He shrugged out of his overcoat and slung it over the coatstand.

'I'd no idea they were planning this,' George said, tapping the poster with his fingernail.

'It was all fixed up yesterday morning,' Clough said carelessly, fastening the top button of his shirt and tightening his tie as he crossed the room.

George shook his head. 'I wish I was plugged into your grapevine, Tommy. Nothing happens here that gets past you.'

Clough grinned. 'By the time you've been here as long as I have, you'll have forgotten more than I'll ever know. I only found out about the posters because I was walking through the front office when the messenger came to pick up the photo. I meant to tell you, but it slipped my mind. Sorry, sir.'

George turned and offered his cigarettes. 'With us working so closely together on this, you might as well make it George when we're on our own.'

Clough took a cigarette and cocked his head to one side. 'Right you are, George.'

Before they could say more, the door swung open again and Superintendent Martin marched in. He was followed by two men dressed almost identically in navy suits, trilby hats and trench coats. In spite of their similar outfits, there was no prospect of confusing them. One had broad shoulders and a thick torso carried on legs that were almost comically short, barely allowing him to make the height requirement of five feet eight inches. The other topped six feet but looked as if he'd disappear if he stood behind a telegraph pole. Martin introduced them. The burly man was Detective Chief Inspector Gordon Parrott from Manchester City Police; the other, Detective Chief Inspector Terry Quirke from the Cheshire County force.

Martin left them to it, promising to have tea sent up from the canteen. At first, the four men were wary as strange dogs on their best behaviour in an unfamiliar parlour. Gradually, however, as they offered details of their own operations without anyone finding fault, they began to relax. A couple of hours later, all four were agreed that there was almost as much reason to suppose the three missing children had been snatched by one individual as there was to suppose there were three separate perpetrators. 'Which is to say, we haven't got grounds to say anything one way or the other,' Parrott said glumly.

'Except that you don't often get cases where there's nothing at all to show what's happened,' George said. 'Which is what you two have got. At least I've got the dog tied up in one piece of woodland and the signs of a struggle in another. That's the crucial element that separates Alison Carter's disappearance from Pauline Reade and John Kilbride.'

There was a grumble of agreement round the table. 'I tell you something,' Clough added, 'I'd put money on Pauline and John being lifted by somebody in a car. Maybe even two somebodies. One to drive and one to subdue the victim. If the abductor had been on foot, there would have had to have been witnesses. To get into a car, that's a matter of seconds. But in spite of that old couple in Longnor who saw the Land Rover parked up by the chapel, I don't see how that can have happened to Alison. A kidnapper couldn't carry her all the way from Scardale woods to the Methodist Chapel, not unless he was built like Tarzan. And there were no strange vehicles seen in the village that afternoon.'

'And they would have been seen,' George confirmed. 'If a mouse sneezed in Scardale, it'd have half a dozen home-made cold remedies to choose from before it could blow its nose.'

Parrott sighed. 'We've wasted your time.'

George shook his head. 'Funnily enough, you haven't. It's clarified my thinking. I know now what we haven't got. The more I've talked and listened this morning,

227

the more certain I am that we're not dealing with a stranger abduction. Whatever happened to Alison, she knew who she was dealing with.'

Monday, 16th December 1963. 7.40 a.m.
The buoyant mood that had sustained George through another day's fruitless searching vanished with the Monday-morning edition of the *Daily News*. This time, Don Smart's tame clairvoyant had earned him the front page.

LOST GIRL: FRENCH SEER
GIVES DRAMATIC CLUE

Exclusive by a Staff Reporter

Investigations into the disappearance of 13-year-old Alison Carter took a dramatic turn today as a clairvoyant gave police vital new leads to her whereabouts.

Madame Colette Charest has given details of what she believed were Alison's movements when she disappeared five days ago from the tiny Derbyshire hamlet of Scardale.

Speaking from her home in Lyons, France, Mme Charest gave her findings based on an Ordnance Survey map of the district, a photograph of the pretty blonde girl and on newspaper cuttings from the *News*.

Impressed

The details were passed on last night to Detective Chief Inspector M. C. Carver, who heads the team of detectives investigating the mysterious disappearance. He said, 'We cannot afford to ignore anything. Her report looks impressive.'

Mme Charest has amazed French police with her clairvoyant powers which have assisted in previous hunts.

The 47-year-old French widow said she 'saw' Alison walking through woodland with a man she knew. He was aged between 35 and 45, with dark hair.

She said Alison had been waiting for the man by water and that she had been sad and afraid.

Still alive

Most remarkably, Mme Charest persisted in her conviction that Alison is still alive and safe. 'She is living in a city. She is in a house that is one of a row of brick houses on a hill.

'She arrived there in something like a small van. It was night when she arrived and she has not been outside since she got there. She is not free to leave but she is not in pain.

'There is a school playground near the house. She can hear the children playing and that makes her sad.'

Meanwhile, teams of volunteers worked tirelessly with police officers and mountain rescue teams searching the dales and moorland round Scardale.

Dogs and grappling irons were used to check a large expanse of moorland which contains several ponds and wells.

DCI Carver said, 'We are spreading the search as widely as possible.

'The public are cooperating magnificently but we still need positive information about Alison's movements after she left home with her dog on Wednesday afternoon.

'Perhaps this new information might jog somebody's memory. No matter how insignificant it may seem, we want to hear from members of the public who might know something.'

'What does Carver think he's playing at?' he grumbled to Anne. 'The last thing we want is to encourage this sort of thing. We'll be swamped by every half-baked fortune teller in the country.'

Anne placidly buttered her toast and said, 'Most likely they twisted what he said.'

'You're probably right,' George conceded. He folded the paper and pushed it across the table towards his wife as he rose. 'I'm off now. Expect me when you see me.'

'Try and get home at a decent time, George. I don't want you to start getting into the habit of working all the hours God sends. I don't want our baby growing up never knowing who its father is. I've listened to the way the other wives talk about their husbands. It's almost as if they're talking about distant relatives that they don't like very much. It sounds like these men treat their homes as a last resort, somewhere to go when the pubs and clubs are shut. The women say even holidays are a strain. Every year it's like going away with a stranger who spends the whole time fretting and sulking. That or drinking and gambling.'

George shook his head. 'I'm not that sort of man, you know that.'

'I don't suppose most of them thought that's what they were getting into when they were newlyweds,' Anne said drily. 'Yours isn't a job like any other. You don't leave it behind at the end of the working day. I just want to make sure you remember there's more to your life than catching criminals.'

'How could I forget, when I've got you to come home to?' He bent over to kiss her. She smelled sweet, like warm biscuits. It was, he knew now, her particular morning fragrance. She'd told him his odour was faintly musky, like the fur of a clean cat. That's when he'd realized that everybody had their own distinctive scent. He wondered if the memory of her daughter's aromatic signature was yet another of the things that tortured Ruth Hawkin. Stifling a sigh, he gave Anne a quick hug and hurried out to the car before his emotions spilled over.

Swinging by the divisional headquarters to pick up Tommy Clough, George decided to give the morning press conference a miss. Superintendent Martin was far better at handling Don Smart than he'd ever be, and the last thing he needed was to be sucked into the public confrontation his anger made almost inevitable. 'Let's go and talk to the Hawkins,' he said to his sergeant. 'They must know in their hearts that hope's running out. They won't be wanting to admit it, either to themselves or to anybody else. We owe it to them to be honest about the situation.'

The wipers swept the rain off the windscreen with mindless monotony as they headed off over the moors towards Scardale. At last, Clough said gloomily, 'She's not going to be out there in this and still be alive.'

'She's not going to be anywhere and still be alive. It's

not like abducting a little kid that you can terrify and shut up in a cellar somewhere. Keeping a teenage girl in captivity is in a different league altogether. Besides, sex killers don't want to wait for their gratification. They want it now. And if she'd been kidnapped by somebody who was idiot enough to think Hawkin had enough money to make a ransom worthwhile, there would have been a ransom note by now.' George sighed as he raised a hand to greet the dripping constable who still stood guard at the gate into Scardale. 'Never mind the Hawkins. *We've* got to face up to the fact that it's a body we're looking for now.'

The slap of the wipers was all that broke the silence until they pulled up on the village green alongside the caravan. The two men ran through the rain and huddled under the tiny porch waiting for Ruth Hawkin to answer George's knock. To their surprise, it was Kathy Lomas who opened the door. She stood back to let them pass. 'You'd better come in,' she said brusquely.

They filed into the kitchen. Ruth was sitting at the table wrapped in a pink quilted nylon housecoat, her eyes listless, her hair loose and uncombed. Opposite her sat Ma Lomas, layered in cardigans topped with a tartan shawl pinned across her breast with a nappy pin. George recognized the fourth woman in the room as Ruth's sister Diane, young Charlie Lomas's mother. The three younger women were all smoking, but Ma Lomas's chest didn't seem to mind.

'What's to do?' Ma Lomas demanded before George could say anything.

'We've nothing fresh to report,' George admitted.

'Not like the papers, then,' Diane Lomas said bitterly.

'Aye, they've always got something to say for themselves,' Kathy added. 'It'll be a load of rubbish, all that stuff about Alison being stuck in some terraced house in a city. You can't hide somebody in the city that doesn't want to be hid. Them houses, they've got walls like cardboard. Can't you stop them printing that rubbish?'

'We live in a free country, Mrs Lomas. I don't like this morning's paper any more than you do, but there's nothing I can do about it.'

'Look at the state of her,' Diane said, nodding at Ruth. 'They don't think about the effect they'll have on her. It's not right.'

George's lips pursed in a thin line. Eventually, he said, 'That's partly why I've come to see you this morning, Mrs Hawkin.' He pulled out a chair and sat facing Ruth and her sister. 'Is your husband in?'

'He's gone to Stockport,' Ma said contemptuously. 'He needs some chemicals for his photography. O' course, he can come and go as he pleases. Not like them as are Scardale born and bred.' Her words hung in the air like a thrown gauntlet.

George refused to pick it up. His own conscience was giving him enough grief about his part in Peter Crowther's death without allowing Ma Lomas free rein with her sharp tongue. He simply bowed his head in acknowledgement and continued regardless. 'I wanted to tell you both that we will be continuing the search for Alison. But I'd be failing in my duty if I didn't tell you that I think it's becoming increasingly unlikely that we'll find her alive.'

Ruth looked up then. Her face was a mask of resignation. 'You think that's news to me?' she said wearily.

'I haven't expected anything else since the minute I realized she was gone. I can bear that, because I have to. What I can't bear is not knowing what's happened to my child. That's all I ask, that you find what's happened to her.'

George took a deep breath. 'Believe me, Mrs Hawkin, I am determined to do just that. You have my word that I'm not going to give up on Alison.'

'Fine words, lad, but what do they mean?' Ma Lomas's sardonic voice cut through the emotional atmosphere.

'It means we go on looking. It means we go on asking questions. We've already searched the dale from end to end, we've searched the surrounding countryside. We've dragged reservoirs and we've had police divers checking the Scarlaston. And we've not found anything more than we found in the first twenty-four hours. But we're not giving up.'

Ma snorted, her nose and chin almost meeting as she screwed up her face. 'How can you sit there and look Ruth in the eye and say you've searched the dale? You've not been near the old lead mine workings.'

14

Bewildered, George saw his surprise mirrored on the faces opposite him. Ruth's eyebrows furrowed as if she wasn't quite sure she'd heard correctly. Diane looked baffled. 'What old lead mine workings, Ma?' she asked.

'You know, up inside Scardale Crag.'

'First I've heard,' Kathy said, sounding mildly affronted.

'Just a minute, just a minute,' George burst in. 'What are we talking about here? What mine workings are we on about?'

Ma gave an exasperated sigh. 'How much plainer can I make it? Inside Scardale Crag there's an old lead mine. Tunnels and chambers and whatnot. There's not much to it, but it's there.'

'How long is it since it was worked?' Clough asked.

'How would I know?' the old woman protested. 'Not in my lifetime, that's for sure. For all I know, it's been there since the Romans were here. They mined for lead and silver in these parts.'

'I've never heard of a lead mine inside the crag,' Diane insisted. 'And I've lived here all my days.'

235

With difficulty, George resisted the impulse to shout at the women. 'Where exactly is this lead mine?' he asked. Clough was glad he wasn't on the receiving end of this voice that cut like a blade. He'd had no idea that George had such an edge in him, but it confirmed to Clough that this had been the right star to hitch his wagon to.

Ma Lomas shrugged. 'How would I know? Like I said, it's never been worked in my day. All I know is that you get into it some place down the back of the spinney. There used to be a stream ran along there, but it dried up years ago, when I was a lass.'

'So the chances are nobody knows it even exists,' George said, his shoulders falling. What had seemed like a thread worth pursuing was falling apart in his hands, he thought.

'Well, I know about it,' Ma said emphatically. 'The squire showed me. In a book. The old squire, that is. Not Philip Hawkin.'

'What book?' Ruth said, showing the first sign of animation since the two men had arrived.

'I don't know what it were called, but I could probably recognize it,' the old woman said, pushing her chair back from the table. 'Has that husband of yours chucked out the squire's books?' Ruth shook her head. 'Come on, then, let's take a look.'

In Philip Hawkin's absence, the study was as cold as the frigid hall. Ruth shivered and pulled her housecoat tighter across her body. Diane threw herself into one of the chairs and took out her cigarettes. She lit up without offering them, then curled around herself in the chair like a plump tabby cat with a mouse in its paw. Kathy fiddled with a pair of prisms on the desk, holding them up to the light and turning them this way and that. Meanwhile, Ma scrutinized the shelves and George held his breath.

About halfway along the middle shelf, she pointed a bony finger. 'There,' she said in a satisfied voice. '*A Charivari of Curiosities of the Valley of the Scarlaston.*' George thrust out an arm and pulled the volume down. It had clearly once been a handsome volume, now ravaged by time and much use. Bound in faded red morocco, it was about ten inches by eight, almost an inch thick. He laid it on the desk and opened it.

'*A Charivari of Curiosities of the Valley of the Scarlaston in the County of Derbyshire, including the Giant's Cave and the Mysterious Source of the River itself. As retailed by the Reverend Onesiphorus Jones. Published by Messrs. King, Bailey & Prosser of Derby MDCCCXXII,*' George read. '1822,' he said. 'So where's the bit about the mine, Mrs Lomas?'

Her fingers with their arthritic knuckles crept across the frontispiece and flicked over to the contents page. 'I recall it were near the middle,' she said softly. George leaned over her shoulder and quickly scanned the list of contents.

'Is that it?' he asked, pointing to *Chapter XIV – The Secret Mysteries of Scardale Cragg; Ancient Man in the Dale; Fool's Gold and the Alchemist's Base Metal.*

'Aye, I think so.' She stepped back. 'It were a long time ago. The squire liked to talk to me about the history of the dale. His wife were an incomer, you see.'

George was only half listening. He flicked over thick off-white pages flecked with occasional foxing until he came to the section he was looking for. There, accompanied by competent line drawings that entirely lacked atmosphere, was the story of lead mining in Scardale. The veins of lead and iron pyrites had first been discovered in the late Middle Ages but had not been exploited fully until the eighteenth century when four main galleries and a couple of hollowed-out caverns were excavated. However, the seams were less productive than they'd appeared and at some point in the 1790s, the mine had ceased to operate commercially. At the time the book had been written, the mine had been closed off with a wooden palisade.

George pointed to the description. 'Are these directions good enough for us to find the way in to these workings?'

'You'd never find it,' Diane said. She'd come up behind him and was peering round his arm. 'I tell you who could, though.'

'Who?' George asked. It can't have been harder to get lead out of the ground than information out of Scardale natives, he thought wearily.

'I bet our Charlie could,' Diane said, oblivious to his exasperation. 'He knows the dale better than anybody living. And he's fit as a butcher's dog. If there's any climbing or caving to be done, he's your lad. That's who you need, Mr Bennett. Our Charlie. That's if he's willing, after the way you've treated him.'

Monday, 16th December 1963. 11.33 a.m.
Charlie Lomas was as skittery as a young pup straining at the leash with the scent of rabbit in his nostrils. Like George, he'd wanted to race down the dale to the place where river met crag as soon as he'd known

what was afoot. But unlike George, who had learned the virtue of patience, he saw no advantage in waiting for the trained potholers to arrive. As far as Charlie was concerned, being a Scardale man was advantage enough when it came to investigating the mysteries of Scardale Crag. So he'd paced up and down outside the caravan, smoking incessantly, nervously sipping from a cup of tea long after it must have been stone cold.

George stared out of the caravan window, glowering at the village. 'It's not as if we're not used to people withholding information, but there's usually a motive behind it that you can see. Mostly they're either protecting themselves or they're protecting someone else. Or else they're just bloody-minded toerags who take pleasure in frustrating us. But here? It's like getting blood out of a stone.'

Clough sighed. 'I don't think there's any malice in it. They don't even know they're doing it half the time. It's a habit they've got into over the centuries, and I don't see them changing it in a hurry. It's like they think nobody's entitled to know their business.'

'It goes beyond that, Tommy. They've all lived in each other's pockets for so long, they know everything there is to know about Scardale and about each other. They take that knowledge totally for granted and simply forget that we're not in the same boat.'

'I know what you mean. Whenever we uncover something they should have told us, it's as if they're gobstruck that we hadn't already known it.'

George nodded. 'This is the perfect example. Ma Lomas never said at any point, "Oh, did you know there are some old lead mine workings inside Scardale Crag? It might be worth searching there." No, like everybody else, she assumed that we'd know about them and her only intent in mentioning them was to get into my ribs because she thinks the police search has been inadequate.'

Clough got up and paced the narrow confines of the caravan. 'It's infuriating, but there's nowt we can do about it because we never know what it is we don't know until we discover we didn't know it.'

George rubbed his eyes wearily. 'I can't help thinking that if only I was better at getting the locals to tell us what they knew, we might have saved Alison.'

Clough stopped pacing and stared at the floor. 'I think you're wrong. I think by the time the first call was made to Buxton Police Station, it was too late for Alison Carter.' He looked up and met George's eyes. Unable to bear what he saw there, he added, 'But that might just be me whistling in the dark because I can't stand the alternative.'

George turned away and looked again at the text in the nineteenth-century book, trying to marry its description to the large-scale Ordnance Survey map. Tommy Clough, recognizing his limitations, sat down again by the window and watched a pair of blackbirds scrabbling in the dirt under the heavy shelter of an ancient yew tree. There would be work to do soon enough; for now, he'd content himself with sitting and thinking.

The cavers arrived in a Commer van with rows of seats bolted to the floor. *Peak Park Cave Rescue* was painted in an amateur hand across the doors. Half a dozen men spilled out across the green, apparently oblivious to the rain, grabbing handfuls of gear out of the back of the van. One man detached himself from the group and crossed to the caravan. Charlie stopped pacing and stared eagerly at him, like a gun dog on point. The man appeared in the doorway and said, 'Who's the boss man, then?'

George stood up, stooping under the low ceiling. 'Detective Inspector George Bennett,' he said, extending a hand.

'You've got the look of Jimmy Stewart, anybody ever tell you that?' the caver said, pumping George's hand briefly.

George frowned as he caught Clough's grin. 'It's been said. Thanks for turning out.'

'Our pleasure. We've not had a decent rescue for ages. We're champing at the bit for something a bit out of the ordinary. How d'you want to run this?' He sat down on the bench seat, the rubber of his wet suit corrugating across his lean stomach.

'We've got a vague idea where the entrance to these mine workings might be,' George said. He gave a brief outline of what they'd learned from the book and the map. 'Charlie here is a local. He knows the dale, so he can probably give us some pointers on the ground. If we find it, then I want to be with you when you go in.'

The caver looked dubious. 'You done any potholing? Any climbing?'

George shook his head. 'I won't be a liability. I'm fit and I'm strong.'

'You will be a liability, whatever you say. We're a team, we're used to working together and looking out for each other. You'll upset our rhythm. I don't really want to go into an unexplored cave system with somebody that doesn't know what's what.' He rubbed his cheek with his knuckles in a nervous gesture. 'People die in caves,' he added. 'That's why we were set up.'

'You're right,' George said. 'People do die in caves. That's exactly why I have to be there with you. It's possible that you might walk into a crime scene. And I'm not prepared to compromise any potential evidence. You have an area of expertise, I'm not denying that. But so do I. That being the case, you're not going in there without me. Now, have you some spare gear, or am I going to have to get one of your team to strip off and give me his wet suit?'

The caver looked mutinous. 'I'm not putting my team at risk because of your inexperience.'

'I'm not asking you to. I'll stay back, let you go ahead and check out any potential dangers. I'll follow your orders. But I have to be there.' George was implacable.

'I want to come an' all,' Charlie burst out, unable to keep quiet any longer. 'I've been in caves, I've done potholing, and climbing. I'm experienced. I know the terrain. You've got to take me.'

Tommy put a hand on his arm. 'It's not a good idea, Charlie. If Alison's in there, chances are she's not going to be a pretty sight. It'd upset you, and you might destroy evidence without meaning to. My first murder, I thought I was going to be the next victim. I threw up all over the crime scene and the DCI looked like murdering *me*. Trust me. It's better if you just help us find the way in.'

The young man frowned, pushing his hair back from his face. 'She's family, Mr Clough. Somebody should be there for her.'

'You can trust DI Bennett to do his best for her,'

Tommy said. 'You know he wants this sorting as badly as you do.'

Charlie turned away, his shoulders slumped. 'So what are we waiting for now?' he demanded, his bravado betrayed by the break in his voice.

'I need to get changed,' George said. 'I don't know your name,' he added to the caver.

'I'm Barry.' He sighed. 'All right, we've got a spare suit that should fit you. You'll need your own boots, though.'

'I've got wellies in the car. Will they do?'

Barry looked contemptuous. 'They'll have to.'

Twenty minutes later, they made a strange procession down the dale and through the woodland where Charlie had uncovered the site of the struggle with Alison. He led the way, closely followed by George and Clough. Behind them the cavers walked in a clump, laughing, talking and smoking cheerfully as if they faced nothing more demanding than the usual Sunday exploration of some fascinating cave system.

When they reached the base of the crag, the cavers squatted on the ground under the nearest trees and waited for directions. Charlie moved slowly along the edge of the limestone, pushing back undergrowth and occasionally clambering over fallen boulders to check if they were obscuring the remains of a hundred-and-fifty-year-old palisade. George followed where he could, but left most of the quest to Charlie, constantly comparing the topography to the description in the book.

Charlie pushed through a thicket of young trees and dead ferns, then pulled himself over a group of small boulders and dropped down on the other side. He was lost from sight, but his voice carried clearly down the dale to the waiting men. 'There's a gap in the cliff here. Looks like . . . looks like there's been a barricade, but it's rotted away.'

'Wait there, Charlie,' George commanded. 'Sergeant, come with me. We need to see if there are any signs of disturbance other than Charlie's tracks.'

They made their difficult way to the cluster of boulders, trying to avoid being whipped in the face by over-hanging small branches or tripped by the tenacious bramble suckers that criss-crossed the undergrowth. 'It's impossible to tell if anyone's been here,' Clough said, his frustration obvious. 'You could come at it through the woods, or along the dale from the other side. As a crime scene, it's worse than useless.'

They scrambled over the rocks and found Charlie dancing impatiently from foot to foot. 'Look,' he exclaimed as soon as he saw them. 'It's got to be this, hasn't it, Mr Bennett?'

It was hard to reconcile what they could see with the mine entrance whose representation George had been studying all morning. Chunks of rock had fallen away from the mouth of the tunnel, leaving it an entirely different shape. The arch that simple tools had carved out of the soft limestone now looked more like a narrow triangular crack, at least twice as high as it had been. Bracken and ferns reached waist height, while an elder tree camouflaged the higher part of what looked as if it might be the way in. 'See,' Charlie said proudly. 'You can see the remains of the iron spikes they hammered in to support the wooden barricade.' He pointed to a couple of black lumps extruding from the rock at one side. 'And down here . . .' He pulled the bracken to one side to reveal the rotten remains of heavy timber. 'I thought I knew every inch of this dale, but I never knew about this place.'

George looked around with a heavy heart. Charlie had trampled the area like a young elephant. If Alison had passed this way, alone or under restraint, there would be no traces now. He took a deep breath and called, 'Barry? Bring your lads up here, would you?' He turned to Clough. 'Sergeant, I want you and Mr Lomas to go back to the caravan. I'm going to need some uniformed officers down here to cordon this area off. And not a word to the press at this stage.'

'Right you are, sir.' Clough clamped a hand on Charlie's shoulder. 'Time for us to leave it to the experts.'

'I should be in there,' Charlie said, pulling away and making a break for the entrance. George neatly stuck out a foot between his legs. Charlie crashed to the ground and rolled over, staring up at George with a look of injured rage.

'That's us quits now,' George said. 'Come on, Charlie, don't make this harder than it is. I promise, you'll be the first to hear if we find anything.'

Charlie stood up and picked strands of bracken out of his hair. 'I'm going back to tell my gran what I found,' he muttered defiantly.

But George had already turned his attention to the cavers, who swarmed over the fallen boulders as if they were mere undulations in a path. Now there was proper work to be done, they were quiet and methodical, each man checking his equipment carefully. Barry handed George a hard hat with a miner's lamp fixed to the front. 'Here's how it's going to be. You stay back at all times. We don't know what it's going to be like in there. Judging by the state of this, it's not looking to be too promising. Or safe. So we go first, and you follow when I say and not before. Is that clear?'

George nodded, adjusting the strap of the hard hat. 'But if we find anything that looks like recent disturbance, you mustn't interfere with it. And if the girl's in there ... well, we'll just have to come straight back out.'

Barry jerked his head towards one of his fellows. 'Trevor's got a special camera for taking pictures underground. We brought it, just in case.' He looked around. 'Right then. Des, you lead. I'll be at the back to make sure George here does what he's told. You heard him, lads – no messing with anything you find. Oh, and George – it's no smoking down there. You never know what little surprises the earth has in store for you.'

It was like entering the underworld. The crack in the hillside swallowed them, depriving them of light almost as soon as they had passed through its portals. Feeble cones of yellow light splashed against streaked white walls of carboniferous limestone. Patches of quartz glittered; damp drizzles of wet flowstone gleamed momentarily; minerals striped and stippled the rock with their particular colours. George remembered a trip he and Anne had made to one of the show caverns near Castleton, but he couldn't recall the correspondences between the strange markings and their sources. It took him all his time to figure out that he was in a narrow corridor, no more than four feet wide and five and a half feet tall. He had to walk with knees bent to avoid battering the hard hat against the strange excrescences that bloomed from the roof.

The air was damp but strangely fresh, as if it were continually renewed. There was a constant irregular series of splashes as drips from the stalactites became too weighty and their surface tension burst. The ground beneath his feet was uneven and slippery, and George had to shine the beam from his hand torch downwards to prevent tripping over one of the many fledgling stalagmites that dotted the floor of the passageway.

'It's amazing, isn't it?' Barry called over his shoulder, his light briefly blinding George.

'Impressive.'

'Leave it alone for a hundred and fifty years and it's well on its way to becoming a show cave. I tell you, if we don't find anything here today, we'll be back at the weekend to have a proper explore. You know how the Scarlaston just seems to seep out of the ground? That means there's got to be an underground cave system somewhere around here, and this mine might just be the way through to that.' Barry's tone of breathless excitement made George feel slightly queasy. He was far from claustrophobic, but the other man's undisguised desire to spend hours underneath these tons of inimical rock was entirely alien to him. He loved the sun and the air on his skin too much to be attracted by this strange half-world.

Before George could reply, a cry echoed back towards them from ahead, so distorted it was impossible to decipher. He started forward, but Barry's arm barred the way. 'Wait,' the caver ordered him. 'I'll go and see what's what. I'll come right back.'

George stood fretting, trying to make sense of the mutter of voices ahead of him. It felt as if he stood there for ever. But within minutes, Barry appeared before him. 'What is it?' George asked.

'It's not a body,' Barry said quickly. 'But there's some clothes. Up ahead. You'd better come and take a look.'

The cavers pressed against the wall to let George pass. A few yards on, the passage widened into what had obviously been a junction of four passages. The other exits had been blocked with rocks and rubble, leaving a small cavern about ten feet across and seven feet high. On the far side, barely visible by the lights from the cavers' lamps, it was possible to make out what looked like clothing.

'Has anybody got a more powerful light?' George asked.

Hands thrust a heavy lamp towards him. He switched it on and pointed its powerful beam towards the clothes. Something dark was bundled against the rocks. What had at first looked like two dark strips became identifiable as a torn pair of tights. The black cloth near them, George realized with a lurch of pain and disgust, was a ripped pair of knickers.

He forced himself to breathe deeply. 'We're all going to leave now. The man at the back, just turn round and head out. Everyone else, follow him. I'll bring up the rear.' For a moment, no one moved. 'I said, now,' George shouted, releasing a fraction of the pent-up tension that strung his nerves tighter than the top string of a violin.

He stood glowering at them. At last, they turned and walked back, their own sure-footedness a taunt to his stumbling pursuit. When they emerged into daylight, he felt as if they'd been inside for hours, but a glance at his watch revealed it had been less than fifteen minutes. Only now were the two uniformed officers emerging from the woodland path to keep the mine workings safe from prying eyes and destructive feet.

George cleared his throat and said, 'Barry, I'd like your colleague Trevor to stay here with me and take some photographs. The rest of you, I'd appreciate it if you'd wait here until we've got the area properly secured. If you go back to the village now, the word will spread that we've found something and the place'll be mobbed.'

The cavers muttered agreement. Barry fished a packet of cigarettes from a waterproof pouch slung round his neck. 'You look like you could use one of these,' he said.

'Thanks.' George turned to the two uniformed officers and said, 'One of you, go back to the caravan and tell Sergeant Clough we've found some clothing and we need a full team down here to secure a possible crime scene. And for God's sake, man, do it discreetly. If anybody asks, we have definitely not found a body. I don't want a repeat of Friday's newspaper story.'

One of the bobbies nodded nervously and turned on his heel, jogging back up the path towards the heart of the village. 'Your job is to make sure nobody who isn't a police officer comes within twenty yards of this mine entrance,' George told the other PC before turning back to Barry. 'That central area in there – is there any chance that any of the other passages are accessible from there?'

Barry shrugged eloquently. 'It doesn't look like it. But I can't be sure without a proper good look. It's always possible that there was a way through and

249

somebody backfilled the passage behind them to make it look impassable. But this is a mine, not a cave system. Chances are there's only one straightforward way in and one straightforward way out. Anybody that dug themselves into the hill is still going to be there, but they're not very likely to be alive and kicking. I don't think she's in there, lad.' He put a hand on George's arm then turned away to squat on the rocks with his mates.

It took seven hours for a thorough search of the cave. Trevor the caver brought his camera back underground and meticulously photographed every inch of the walls and floor. There was no way in or out other than the narrow passage. None of the blocked passages showed any sign of recent interference. There was no trace of a body having been disposed of in the mine. George couldn't decide whether that should depress or encourage him.

By mid-afternoon, a duffel coat with a missing toggle, a pair of tights ripped with such savagery that the legs were entirely separated, and a pair of navy-blue gym knickers were on their way to the county police laboratory, carefully packaged to preserve any forensic traces. But George didn't need a scientist to tell him that the stains on the damp clothes had a human source.

He'd been a police officer too long not to recognize blood and semen.

Two further discoveries were, if anything, even more disturbing. Embedded in the walls of the cave, one officer had found a distorted lump of metal that had once been a bullet. That had led to an inch-by-inch scrutiny of the fissured limestone. Deep in a crack, a second piece of metal had been found.

This time, there was no mistaking its function. It was, unquestionably, a bullet from a handgun.

PART TWO

The Long Haul

Daily News, *Friday, 20ᵗʰ December 1963, p.5*

Heartbreak Christmas
for lost girl's mother

By Staff Reporter Donald Smart

Mrs Ruth Hawkin is not buying a Christmas present for her daughter, Alison, this year. But Alison's stepfather, Philip, has filled the missing girl's room with gaily wrapped parcels containing records, books, clothes and make-up.

Mrs Hawkin, 34-year-old mother of Alison, cannot face Christmas shopping for her daughter. Nine days ago, she waved goodbye to her daughter as she set out from the family home in the tiny Derbyshire hamlet of Scardale to walk her pet sheepdog.

She has not seen her 13-year-old daughter since.

A relative said, 'If Alison is not found, it will be a very unhappy Christmas for everyone in Scardale.

'We are a very close-knit community and it has hit us very hard. Everybody is baffled by Alison's disappearance. She's a lovely girl and no one can think of any reason why she might have run away.'

Police have questioned thousands of people, combed remote dales and moorland and dragged rivers and reservoirs in vain in the hunt for the pretty blonde schoolgirl.

Two other families will also have a gap at the Christmas table. A month ago, John Kilbride, aged 12, of Smallshaw Lane, Ashton-u-Lyne, disappeared. He was last seen on Ashton Market. Five months ago, 17-year-old Pauline Reade left her home in Wiles-street, Gorton, Manchester, to attend a local dance. Neither has been seen again.

1

It wasn't the Christmas George Bennett had envisaged a few months before. He'd been looking forward to his first Christmas in their own home, just him and Anne. He'd reckoned without the pressures of family. Anne was an only child, so there were no conflicting demands on her parents; and being newlyweds, they automatically became the focus for George's mother and father. Realizing it would be their first and last chance to celebrate alone, Anne had done her best to persuade their families that a Boxing Day get-together would be just the ticket. She had failed. As it was, they'd barely escaped George's sister, his brother-in-law and their three small children.

Still, it had been a wonderful lunch. Anne had been planning and working for weeks ahead to make everything run smoothly. Not even Alison Carter's disappearance could dent her determination that her first Christmas in her own home would be exemplary. And it had been. Once the presents were opened and he'd made the appropriate expressions of delight over socks, shirts, sweaters and cigarettes, George had had little to do except make sure everyone's glass was topped up with sherry and Babycham for the women, bottled beer for the men.

As they'd decided in advance, they revealed Anne's pregnancy after the Queen's speech. The mothers rivalled each other in their excitement and, using the washing-up as an excuse, soon disappeared into the kitchen to give the mother-to-be the benefit of their counsel. Anne's father congratulated George gruffly then settled down with a celebratory brandy and cigar to watch TV. George and his father Arthur remained at the dining table. As usual, they were not entirely comfortable with each other, but the news of the baby had bridged some of the distance a university degree had put between George and his train-driver father.

'You're looking tired, lad,' Arthur said.

'It's been a hard couple of weeks.'

'That missing lass, is it?'

George nodded. 'Alison Carter. We've all been putting the hours in, but we're not a lot further forward than we were the night she went missing.'

'Did I not read somewhere in the papers that you'd found some of her clothes?' Arthur asked, sending a perfect smoke ring heading for the light fitting.

'That's right. In a disused lead mine. But all that's really told us is that she definitely didn't run away. It hasn't brought us any closer to finding out what really happened or where she is now. Except that we also found a couple of bullets embedded in the limestone,' he added. 'One was mangled beyond recognition, but we were lucky with the other one. It went into a crack in the limestone wall, so the forensics boys got it out more or less intact. If we ever find the gun it came from, we'll be able to make a positive identification.'

His father sipped his brandy and shook his head sadly. 'Poor lass. She's not going to be alive when you find her, is she?'

George sighed. 'You wouldn't find a bookie to give you odds on it. It's been keeping me awake nights. Especially with Anne in her condition. It changes things, doesn't it? I'd never given it much thought before. You know how it is – you reckon you'll find the right girl, get married, have a family. It's the way things go if you're lucky. But I'd never sat down and thought about what it would mean to be a father. But knowing that it's going to happen, and finding it out in the middle of an investigation like this . . . Well, you can't help thinking how you'd be feeling if it was your kid.'

'Aye.' His father breathed heavily through his nostrils. 'You're right, George. Having a kid makes you realize how many hazards there are in the world. You'd go mad if you let yourself brood on it. You've just got to tell yourself that nothing's going to happen to your own.' He gave a wry smile. 'You made it through more or less in one piece.'

It was a cue to swap stories of George's childhood brushes with danger. But part of him was immune to the shift of subject. Deep inside, Alison Carter was lodged like a crumb in the windpipe. Eventually, George extinguished his cigar and stood up. 'If you don't mind, Dad, I'm going to pop out for an hour. My sergeant's volunteered for Christmas duty, and I thought I'd nip round to the station and wish him a Merry Christmas.'

'On you go, lad. I'm going to settle down with Anne's dad and pretend to watch the telly.' He winked. 'We'll try not to snore too loud.'

George pocketed a box of fifty cigarettes he'd been given by an aunt and drove across town to the police station. He found Tommy Clough's desk vacant, apart from the ballistics file on the bullets from the mining cavern. His jacket was slung over the back of his chair, so he couldn't be far away, George reasoned. He picked up the familiar file and flicked through it again. One bullet was mashed beyond redemption, but the one that had found a crack in the rock had told a distinct story to the firearms examiner.

'The exhibit is a round-nose full-metalled-jacket lead bullet,' he read. *'The calibre is .38. The bullet reveals seven lands and grooves, the lands narrow and the grooves broad. The grooves demonstrate a right-hand twist. These rifling marks are consistent with a projectile fired from a Webley revolver.'*

The door swung open and Tommy Clough walked in, brow furrowed as he read a telex. 'Merry Christmas, Tommy,' George said, tossing the box of cigarettes across the room.

'Cheers, George,' Clough said, sounding surprised. 'What brings you in? Family at war?' He crossed the room and sat down, shoving the telex in the file.

'I was sitting there with my paper hat on pulling crackers and eating goose and wondering what kind of Christmas they're having at Scardale Manor.'

Clough ripped the cellophane off the cigarettes. Straightening up in his seat, he pushed the file to one side and offered the open box to George. 'I'd say that depends on how bright Ruth Hawkin is. And on whether we show her this telex.'

'Meaning?'

Clough took his time lighting a cigarette. 'Since we

didn't get anywhere through official channels connecting Hawkin to a Webley, I decided to try coming at it sideways. So I sent out a request for information on any reports of stolen Webleys. Amongst the dross, there was one that looked a bit interesting. From St Albans. Two years ago, a Mr Richard Wells reported a break-in at his home. Among the stolen items was a Webley .38 revolver.'

From his air of expectation, George could tell there was more to come. 'And?' he asked.

'Mr Wells lives two doors away from Philip Hawkin's mother. The families used to play bridge together once a week. Mr Wells kept his Webley as a souvenir of the war, and he boasted about it often, according to their CID duty man. They never got anyone for the housebreaking, either. The family was away on holiday, so it could have happened at any time that week.' Clough grinned. 'Merry Christmas, George.'

'That's a better present than a box of fags.'

'Fancy a run out there? Just to take the air?'

'Why not?'

They were silent for most of the drive. As they turned into the lane that led to Scardale, George said, 'Care to elaborate on what you said earlier about their Christmas depending on how bright Mrs Hawkin is?'

'It's nothing we haven't already discussed a dozen times in the last few days,' Clough said. 'First off, we've got the conflict between what Hawkin told us about his movements on the afternoon Alison went missing and what we heard from Ma Lomas and Charlie. Second, we've got the lead mine. Apart from Ma Lomas, everybody in Scardale denies they'd even heard of the old workings, never mind knowing where they were. But the book that details the exact location of the entrance happens to be sitting on a shelf in Philip Hawkin's library.'

'And let's not forget the lab results,' George said softly. The irresistible conclusion of what they had found in the lead mine was that Alison Carter had been raped and almost certainly murdered. The blood that stained the clothing had all been group O, which corresponded with Alison's medical records. Whoever had stained Alison Carter's knickers with semen had been a secretor. Thanks to that, the police now knew her assailant's blood group was A. That was something Philip Hawkin had in common with forty-two per cent of the population. So did three other men in the dale – two of Alison's uncles and her cousin Brian. What separated them from Philip Hawkin was that they all had alibis for the time of her disappearance. One uncle had been in a pub in Leek following the Christmas fatstock market, and her cousin Brian had been milking the cows with his father. If Alison had been attacked by someone from inside the dale, it was beginning to appear that there was only one possible candidate.

'It could have been somebody who came up the Scarlaston valley from Denderdale. Somebody who knew her from Buxton. A schoolteacher or a fellow pupil. Or just some pervert who'd been watching her at school,' Clough said when he returned to the car after closing the gate that obstructed the road into the village.

'They couldn't have got there in time. It's a good hour and a half's walk from the road in Denderdale up the river banks. And they'd never have got back down there in the dark with Alison, alive or dead. They'd both have ended up in the river,' George said positively. 'I agree with you. All the circumstantial evidence points to one man. But we've no body, and we've no direct evidence. Without that, we can't justify bringing him in for questioning, never mind charging him.'

'So what do we do?'

'Damned if I know,' George sighed. The car came to a halt beside the brown patch of grass that marked where the police caravan had stood. On Superintendent Martin's orders, it had been towed back to Buxton on the previous Friday. Searches had effectively ended on the same day. There was nowhere left to look.

George stepped out into the chill evening air. The village looked curiously untouched by what had happened. There was no obvious sign that anything had altered, apart from the newspaper poster pasted to the back of the phone box. Around the green, the houses still huddled. Lights burned behind curtains, the occasional bark of a dog split the silence. There were no Christmas trees visible at any of the windows, it was true. Nor were there any holly wreaths on the cottage doors of Scardale. But George wasn't convinced that there would have been on any other Christmas in Scardale either.

He and Clough leaned against the bonnet of the Zephyr, smoking in silence. After a few moments, a wedge of yellow light spread across the doorway of Tor Cottage. The unmistakable outline of Ma Lomas appeared, silhouetted against the interior. Then the light disappeared as abruptly as it had appeared. His night vision impaired, George blinked hard. The old woman was almost upon them before he realized that she hadn't gone back indoors.

'Have you no home to go to?' she asked.

'He's on duty,' George said.

'What's your excuse?'

'Christmas is for kids, isn't that what they say? Well, there's one kid I couldn't get out of my mind.'

'By heck, a copper with a heart,' Ma scoffed. She opened her voluminous coat and from a poacher's pocket she took out a bottle of the clear spirit she'd drunk when they'd interviewed her at the very beginning of the investigation. From another pocket, she took three thick tumblers. 'I thought you might like something to keep the cold out.'

'That would be an act of Christian charity,' Clough said.

They watched her place the glasses on the car bonnet and pour three generous measures. Ceremoniously, she handed them a glass each, then raised hers in a toast.

'What are we drinking to?' George asked.

'We're drinking to you finding enough evidence,' she said in a voice that was more chill than the night air.

'I'd rather drink to finding Alison,' he said.

She shook her head. 'If you were going to find Alison, you'd have found her by now. Wherever he's put her, she's beyond anything except chance. All that's left for us now is the hope that you can make him pay.'

'Did you have anyone in particular in mind?' Clough asked.

'Same as you, I shouldn't wonder,' she said drily, turning to face the manor house and raising her glass. 'To proof.'

George took a swig of his drink and almost choked. 'About a hundred and sixty proof, I'd say,' he gasped when he could speak again. 'Flaming Nora, what is this stuff? Rocket fuel?'

The old woman chuckled. 'Our Terry calls it Hellfire. It's distilled from elderflower and gooseberry wine.'

'We never found a still when we searched the village,' Clough remarked.

'Well, you wouldn't, would you?' She drained her glass. 'So, what's next? How do you get him?'

George forced himself to swallow the rest of the fiery spirit. When he'd recovered the power of speech, he said, 'I don't know that we can. That said, I'm not giving up.'

'See that you don't,' she said grimly. She held out her hand for the empty glasses then turned her back and returned to her cottage.

'That's us told,' Clough said.

'And a Merry bloody Christmas to you, too.'

The first Monday in February, and George was at his desk by eight. Tommy Clough tapped on the door a few minutes after the hour, a couple of steaming mugs of tea gripped in one large hand. 'How was the weather?' he asked.

'Better than we had any right to expect,' George said. 'It was freezing, but the sun shone every day. We neither of us mind the cold as long as it's dry, and Norfolk's so flat that Anne was able to walk for miles.'

Clough settled down opposite George and lit up. 'You look well on it. More like you'd had a fortnight on the Costa Brava than a week in Wells-next-the-Sea.'

George grinned. 'The Martinet was right, then.' He'd resisted furiously when Superintendent Martin had insisted that he take off some time in lieu of the endless hours he'd expended on the Alison Carter inquiry. Eventually, when Jack Martin had turned his suggestion into an order, he'd given in with ill grace and allowed Anne to book them into a guesthouse in the Norfolk seaside town. They'd been the only residents, pampered by a landlady who believed everyone should eat at least three square meals a day. A week of regular food, fresh air and the undivided attention of his wife had filled George with energy and resolve.

'He's been on at me to do the same,' Clough admitted. 'Maybe I will, now you're back.'

'Any developments?' George asked, blowing gently on his tea.

'Well, I took that new WPC from Chapel-en-le-Frith to see Acker Bilk and his Paramount Jazz Band at the Pavilion Gardens on Friday night, and we had a very nice evening. Think I might ask her if she fancies going to see that Albert Finney film at the Opera House. *Tom Jones*, they call it. Apparently it's a right good film to take a young lady to if you want to get her in the mood.' Clough grinned, without lasciviousness.

'I meant in the case, not in your pathetic love life,' George responded with good humour.

'Funnily enough, there was something. We got a call on Sunday from Philip Hawkin. He said he'd been looking at the Spot the Ball competition in the paper and he could swear that one of the people in the crowd beside the goal was Alison.' He squinted at George through the smoke. 'What do you make of that?'

George felt a strange fluttering in his stomach. 'Go on, Tommy. I'm all ears.' Tea forgotten, he leaned forward and stared intently at his sergeant.

'I went straight out to see what was what. It was the *Sunday Sentinel*, the Nottingham Forest match. As soon as I saw the photo, I could see why he'd rung. Admittedly, it was a tiny photograph, but it did look a lot like Alison. So I got in touch with the newspaper, and they got their lads to blow up the original. They sent it up on the train and it got here Monday teatime.' He didn't need to continue; his face told the rest of the story. Closer examination had proved the girl in the football crowd was someone quite different.

George took a deep breath and closed his eyes moment-arily. 'Thank you, God,' he said softly. He looked at Clough and smiled. 'Do we happen to know whether Philip Hawkin takes the *Manchester Evening News*?'

'Funnily enough, I do know. Kathy Lomas mentioned it when she was running through the kids' routine. Because the daily paper doesn't get to Scardale till lunchtime and Hawkin likes a paper with his breakfast, the newsagent at Longnor leaves an *Evening News* in the mailbox at the end of the lane every morning and whoever does the school run drops it off at the manor afterwards.'

George's smile grew wider. 'I thought as much.' He jumped to his feet and yanked open the drawer of his filing cabinet. He scrabbled among the files, then came up with a large manila envelope. He waved it at Clough and said triumphantly, 'This is what I call leverage.'

Clough caught the file as it sailed through the air towards him. The front of the envelope read, 'Pauline Catherine Reade'. He opened the envelope and a thin bundle of newspaper cuttings spilled across the desk. He frowned as he saw the dates noted in red biro on the edge of the clippings. 'You've been following this from the beginning, back last July. That's four months before Alison went missing,' he said, his voice indicating precisely how strange he found such behaviour.

George pushed his blond hair back from his forehead. 'I always take an interest in stories that might turn up on our patch,' was all he said.

'What am I looking for?' Clough asked, flicking through the cuttings.

'You'll know when you see it.' George leaned against the filing cabinet, arms folded, a cool smile on his lips.

Suddenly, Clough froze. His index finger prodded a single clipping as if it could be provoked into biting. 'Bugger me,' he said softly.

Manchester Evening News, *Monday, 2nd November 1963, p.3*

Picture dashes
mother's hopes

For a few brief hours, hopes of a reunion with her missing 16-year-old daughter were raised for Mrs Joan Reade by a crowd picture in the *Manchester Evening News & Chronicle Football Pink*.

But they were dashed when Mrs Reade was shown a specially enlarged copy of the photograph. Sadly she said at her home in Wilesstreet, Gorton, today, 'That is not Pauline after all.'

Pauline has been missing from home since

July 12, when she went to a dance and did
not return.

Mrs Reade's 15-year-old son Paul spotted
a picture in last Saturday's *Football Pink* of a
section of the crowd at the Lancashire Rugby
League Cup Final at Swinton, and thought it
was Pauline.

Clough looked up. 'He thinks we're thick.'

'You're sure it was Hawkin and not his wife who
spotted the likeness?'

'It was him that rang up and him that took all the
credit. When I asked Mrs Hawkin what she thought of
the likeness, she said she'd been more convinced when
she'd first seen it, but looking at it again, she wasn't
at all sure. He sounded a bit brassed off with her, like
she was supposed to back him up all the way and she
wasn't performing as a dutiful little wife should.'

George reached for his cigarettes and paced while
he talked. 'So we've got him trying to make himself
look good. Why has he done it now?' Clough waited,
knowing he was supposed to let the boss answer his
own question. 'Why? Because he expected that we'd
have given up on Alison long ago and moved on to
the next thing. He's disconcerted because you and I are
still out there in Scardale two or three times a week,
talking to folk, going over the ground, not leaving it
alone. He's not stupid; he must realize we fancy him
for whatever has happened to his stepdaughter. Not
to mention the fact that Ma Lomas thinks he's done
it, and I can't imagine her being any more reticent to
his face than she is behind his back.'

'Except that everybody in that village owes Hawkin

the roof over their head and the bread in their mouths,' Clough reminded him. 'Even Ma Lomas might think twice about telling him to his face she thinks he raped and murdered Alison Carter.'

George acknowledged the point with a dip of his head. 'OK, I'll grant you that. But he must be aware that the villagers suspect him of doing something terrible to Alison, if only because he's the outsider. So when it becomes clear that this is not just going to go away, Hawkin decides it's about time he makes himself look good. And he remembers the story he read in the *Manchester Evening News* about Pauline Reade.' He stopped pacing and leaned on the desk. 'What do you think, Tommy? Is it enough to pull him in for questioning?'

Clough pushed his lips together, in and out like a goldfish. 'I don't know. What are we going to ask him?'

'If he reads the *Evening News*. What his relationship with Alison was like. The usual stuff. All the pressure points. Did she resent him taking her father's place? Did he think she was attractive? Christ, Tommy, we can ask him what his favourite colour is. I just want him in here, under pressure, so we can see what happens. We've given him an easy ride so far because we didn't have a big enough lever to justify not treating him like a worried parent. Well, I think we have now.'

Clough scratched his head. 'You know what I think?'

'What?'

'I think they don't pay us enough to carry the can on a decision like this. I think that's why the DCI and the Martinet get their money. If I was you, I'd go and lay all this out before them and see what they say.'

George dropped into his chair like a sack of coal, his face dispirited. 'Oh, Tommy, don't tell me you think I'm talking bollocks?'

'No, I think you're right. I think Hawkin's the man who knows what happened to Alison. But I don't know if this is the right time to put the pressure on, and I don't want to lose him because we've been too hungry. George, we're too close to this case. We've breathed, slept and dreamed it for nigh on seven weeks. We can't see the wood for the trees. Go and talk to the Martinet. Then if the wheels do come off, they can't use it as a stick to beat us with.'

George's laugh was bitter. 'You really think so? Tommy, if the wheels come off this, we'll be back directing traffic in Derby for the rest of our careers.'

Clough shrugged. 'Better make sure we get it right, then.'

2

Clough walked Hawkin into the interview room where George was already waiting. He was sitting at the table, intently reading the contents of a file folder. When Hawkin walked in, George didn't even look up. He simply carried on, a frown of concentration on his face. It was the first move in a carefully orchestrated process. Silently, Clough indicated to Hawkin that he should sit opposite George. Hawkin, lips compressed, eyes unreadable, did as he was bid. Clough grabbed a chair and swung it round so it stood between Hawkin and the door. His solid legs straddled it, his notebook propped on its back. Hawkin breathed out heavily through his nose but said nothing.

Eventually, George closed the file, placed it precisely on the table in front of him and looked evenly at Hawkin. He took in the expensive overcoat draped over his arm, the tailored tweed sports jacket over the fine-wool polo-neck sweater and the crossed legs in their pale-cream twill. He'd have bet a month's salary that Hawkin had spent a chunk of his inheritance buying his country squire look as a job lot in Austin Reed. It seemed entirely wrong on a man who looked as if he belonged in a bank clerk's cheap navy suit. 'Good of you to come in, Mr Hawkin,' George said, his voice devoid of welcoming inflection.

'I was planning to come into Buxton today anyway, so it was no great hardship,' Hawkin drawled. He looked entirely at ease, his small triangular mouth composed, apparently on the edge of a smile.

'Nevertheless, we're always glad when members of the public recognize their duty to support the police,' George said sanctimoniously. He took out his cigarettes. 'You're a smoker, aren't you?'

'Thank you, Inspector, but I'll stick to my own,' Hawkin said, spurning the offered packet of Gold Leaf with a slight sneer. 'Is this going to take long?'

'That depends on you,' Clough ground out from behind Hawkin's right shoulder.

'I don't think I like your sergeant's tone,' Hawkin said, his voice petulant.

George stared at Hawkin, saying nothing at all. When the older man shifted slightly in his chair, George spoke formally. 'I need to ask you some questions relating to the disappearance of your stepdaughter, Alison Carter, on the eleventh of December last year.'

'Of course. Why else would I be here? I'm hardly likely to be involved in anything criminal, am I?' Hawkin's smirk was self-satisfied, as if he alone held a secret that the others could never guess at.

'While I was away last week, you contacted us because you thought you saw Alison in a Spot the Ball competition photograph.'

Hawkin nodded. 'Sadly, I was mistaken. I could have sworn it was her.'

'And of course you have a photographer's eye for

271

these things. You wouldn't expect to be mistaken,' George continued.

'You're quite right, Inspector.' Hawkin flashed him a patronizing little smile and reached for his cigarettes. He was relaxing now, as George had expected.

'So it was you and not your wife who spotted the likeness?'

By now Hawkin was preening himself. 'My wife has many fine qualities, Inspector, but in our house, I'm the one who notices things.' Then, as if he'd suddenly remembered what the reason for the interview was, he composed his face into an expression of solemnity. 'Besides, Inspector, you must realize that since Alison went out of our lives, my wife has lost the habit of paying attention to the outside world. It's all she can do to maintain some semblance of normality in our domestic life. I insist on that, of course. It's the best thing for her, to keep her mind on routine matters like cooking and keeping house.'

'Very considerate of you,' George said. 'This photograph was in the *Sunday Sentinel*, is that right?'

'Correct, Inspector.'

George frowned slightly. 'What newspapers do you take on a regular basis?'

'We've always had the *Express* and the *Evening News*. And the *Sentinel* on Sundays. Of course, with all the press coverage of Alison's disappearance, I made sure we got all the papers while you were still conducting your daily press conferences. Well, somebody's got to check that they've not got everything wrong, haven't they? I didn't want them writing things about us that weren't true. Plus I wanted to be forewarned. I didn't want Ruth upset by some tactless person telling her what the papers were saying without any advance warning. So I made sure I knew what was what.' He flicked the ash off his cigarette and smiled. 'Dreadful people, those reporters. I don't know how you can bring yourself to deal with them.'

'We have to deal with all sorts in our job,' Clough said insolently.

Hawkin pursed his lips but said nothing. George leaned forward slightly. 'So you do read the *Evening News*?'

'I told you,' Hawkin said impatiently. 'Of course, we get it the morning after it's published, but it's the only newspaper they can deliver in time for breakfast, so I have to make do with its parochial view of the world.'

George opened his folder and took out a clear plastic envelope. Inside it was a newspaper clipping. He pushed it across the table. 'You'll remember this story, then.'

Hawkin did not reach for the clipping. All that moved was his eyes, flickering across the lines of type. The ash on his disregarded cigarette grew, its own weight curving it gently downward. At last, he raised his eyes to George and said slowly and deliberately, 'I have never seen this story before today.'

'It's a strange coincidence, don't you think?' George said. 'A missing girl, a family member spots a likeness in a photograph of a sporting crowd, but their hopes are dashed when it turns out to be a tragic error. And this story appears in a paper that's delivered six days a week to your home.'

'I told you, I have never seen this story before today.'

'It's hard to miss. It was on page three of the paper.'

'Nobody reads the *Evening News* from cover to cover. I must have missed the story. What interest could it possibly have held for me?'

'You are the stepfather of a teenage girl,' George said mildly. 'I'd have thought stories about what happens to teenage girls would have been very interesting for you. After all, this was a relatively new experience for you. You must have felt you had a lot to learn.'

Hawkin crushed out his cigarette. 'Alison was Ruth's business. It's a mother's place, to deal with children.'

'But you were obviously very fond of the girl. I've seen her bedroom, don't forget. Beautiful furniture, new carpet. You've not stinted her, have you?' George persisted.

Hawkin frowned in irritation before he replied. 'The girl had been without a father for years. She'd not had most of the things other girls take for granted. I was good to her for her mother's sake.'

'Are you sure that's all it was?' Clough chipped in. 'You bought her a record player. Every week, you bought her new records. Whatever was in the top ten, you got it for her. Whatever Charlie Lomas told her to ask you for, you got her. If you ask me, that goes above and beyond being good to her for her mother's sake.'

'Thank you, Sergeant,' George broke in repressively. 'Mr Hawkin, how close were you and Alison?'

'What do you mean?' He reached for another cigarette. It took him several tries before his lighter caught. He inhaled the smoke gratefully and repeated the question that had earned him no response. 'What do you mean? How close were we? I've told you, I left Alison to her mother to deal with.'

'Did you like her?' George asked.

Hawkin's dark eyes narrowed. 'What kind of trick question is that? If I say no, you'll say I wanted rid of her. If I say yes, you'll imply there was something unnatural about my feelings for her. You want the truth? I was largely indifferent to the girl. Look . . .' He leaned forward and essayed a man-to-man smile. 'I married her mother for three reasons. First, I found her moderately attractive. Second, I needed someone to look after me and the house and I knew no half-decent housekeeper would want to live in a godforsaken place like Scardale. And third, I wanted the villagers to stop treating me like an alien from outer space. I did not marry her because I had designs on her daughter. That's sick, frankly.' He leaned back in his chair after this outburst, as if defying George to say anything further.

George looked at him with clinical curiosity. 'I never suggested you did, sir. I find it interesting that your mind moves in that direction of its own accord, however. I also find it interesting that when you talk about Alison, you always use the past tense.'

His words hung in the air as palpably as the cigarette smoke. A dark flush coloured Hawkin's cheeks but he managed to keep silent. It was clearly an effort.

'As if you were talking about somebody who was no longer alive,' George continued inexorably. 'Why do you think that might be, sir?'

'It's just a habit of speech,' Hawkin snapped. 'She's been gone so long. It means nothing. Everybody talks about Alison like that now.'

'Actually, sir, they don't. It's something I've noticed in my visits to Scardale. They still talk about Alison in the present tense. As if she's stepped out for a while, but she'll be back soon. It's not just your wife that talks like that. It's everybody. Everybody except you, that is.' George lit a cigarette, trying to display a relaxed confidence he did not feel. When he and Clough had rehearsed the interview, they hadn't been at all certain how Hawkin would react. It was satisfying to see him rattled, but they were still a long way from any useful admissions.

'I think you must be mistaken,' Hawkin said abruptly. 'Now, if you have no further questions?' He pushed his chair back.

'I've hardly begun, sir,' George said, his stern expression accentuating his resemblance to James Stewart. 'I'd like to go back to the afternoon when Alison disappeared. I know we've interviewed you about this already, but I want to go over it again for the record.'

'Oh, for heaven's sake!' Hawkin exploded.

Whatever he was about to say was cut off by a knock at the door. It opened to reveal DC Cragg's sleepy-eyed face in apologetic mode. 'I'm sorry, sir, I know you said not to interrupt, but I've got an urgent call for you.'

George tried not to show the anger and disappointment that flooded through him. The rhythm of the interview had been flowing in his direction and now the mood was shattered. 'Can't it wait, Cragg?' he snapped.

'I don't think so, sir, no. I think you'll want to take the call.'

'Who is it?' George demanded.

Cragg flashed a worried look at Hawkin. 'I . . . uh . . . I can't really say, sir.'

George jumped to his feet, his chair clattering on the

floor. 'Sergeant, stay here with Mr Hawkin. I'll be back as soon as I can.' He strode out of the room, exercising his last ounce of self-restraint in not slamming the door behind him.

'What the bloody hell is going on?' he hissed at Cragg as he stalked down the corridor towards his office. 'I specifically said no interruptions. Don't you understand plain bloody English, Cragg?'

The young detective constable scuttled along behind him, waiting for a gap in the tirade. 'It's Mrs Hawkin, sir,' he finally managed to get out.

George stopped so suddenly that Cragg cannoned into him. He whirled round. 'What?' he said, incredulous.

'It's Mrs Hawkin. She's in a state, sir. Asking for you.'

'Did she say why?' George turned on his heel and practically ran for his phone.

'No, sir, just that she needed to talk to you urgently.'

'Jesus,' George muttered, grabbing for the phone before he was even sitting down. 'Hello? This is DI Bennett.'

'Mr Bennett?' The voice was choked with tears.

'Is that you, Mrs Hawkin?'

'Aye, it is. Oh, Mr Bennett . . .' Her sobs rose in a terrible crescendo.

'What's happened, Mrs Hawkin?' he asked, desperately wondering if there was a WPC on duty.

'Can you come, Mr Bennett? Can you come now?' Her words were gasped out between gulps and sniffs.

'I've got your husband here, Mrs Hawkin. Do you want me to bring him home?'

'No!' It was almost a scream. 'Just you. Please!'

'I'll be there as soon as I can. Mrs Hawkin, try to calm down. Get one of your family to sit with you. I'll be right there.' He slammed the phone down and stood for a moment, stunned by the intensity of the phone conversation. He had no idea why Ruth Hawkin was demanding his presence, but it was clearly something traumatic. She couldn't have found a body . . . He thrust the idea away before it could even form properly.

'Cragg,' he bellowed as he emerged from his office. 'Go and relieve Sergeant Clough. You stay there with Mr Hawkin until we get back. You don't let him leave. You explain politely we've been called away on an emergency and he's to wait for us to get back. If he insists on leaving, you go with him. Don't let him bully you.'

Cragg looked dumbfounded. This wasn't the pace of life he was accustomed to in Buxton CID. 'What if he gets in his car?'

'His car's not here. Sergeant Clough drove him in. Cragg, move!'

George grabbed Clough's overcoat and his own trench coat, jamming his trilby down over his hair. As soon as Clough emerged from the interview room looking bemused, George grabbed him by the arm and hustled him down the stairs. 'It's Ruth Hawkin,' George said before Clough could ask him what was up. 'She rang me in a hell of a state. She wants me to come out to Scardale right away.'

'Why?' Clough said as they hurried out into the station yard and made for his car.

'I don't know. She was too upset to make sense. All I know is she went completely hairless when I asked if she wanted me to bring Hawkin back with me. Whatever it is, it's big.'

Clough gunned the engine. 'Better not hang about, then.'

George had no idea that the journey to Scardale could be completed in so short a time. Clough broke every speed limit and most rules of the road as he threw the big saloon around the bends. They said little on the way, both too tense at the prospect of something that might set the Alison Carter case moving again. As they drew up by the village green, George spoke. 'Time we had a little bit of luck, Tommy. We've got him on the back foot. If Ruth Hawkin's got something for us, this could be it.'

They took the path to the manor at a run. Before either could knock, the kitchen door swung open and Ma Lomas greeted them. 'We've been doing your work for you again,' she said.

Ruth Hawkin sat at the head of the table, her face streaked with tears and make-up, her eyes bloodshot and puffy. Kathy sat next to her. Their work-reddened hands were clasped so tight the knuckles showed white. On the table in front of them was a crumpled bundle of tattersall checked material. It was smudged with dirt, but more ominously, there were extensive patches of rust-red that looked remarkably like dried blood.

'You've found something,' George said, crossing the room and sitting opposite Kathy.

Ruth took a shuddering breath and nodded. 'It's a shirt. And a ... And a ...' Her voice cracked and gave up.

George took out a pen and poked at the material,

separating its folds. It was indeed a shirt, made of fine cotton twill. The maker's name was sewn into a label in the collar. He had seen Philip Hawkin in similar shirts more times than he could count. Lying in the centre of the material was a revolver. George didn't know much about guns, but he'd have bet a year's salary that this was a .38 Webley. 'Where did you find these, Mrs Hawkin?'

Kathy gave him a sharp look. 'Have you still got Phil Hawkin at the police station?'

'Mr Hawkin's still helping us with our inquiries,' Clough said stoutly from the bottom of the table, where he sat with open notebook. 'He's not going to be walking in on us.'

Kathy squeezed Ruth's hands even more tightly. 'It's all right, Ruth. You can tell him.'

'I usually wait till he goes out for the day before I can clean his darkroom. He hates me getting underfoot, so I always hang on till I know he's going to be gone for a few hours,' she blurted out. 'I don't know what possessed me to pull it out . . . I thought I could give the place a proper bottoming for once; I was going fair mad with nowt to keep me occupied . . .'

George waited patiently. Ruth pulled her hands away from Kathy and covered her face. 'Oh God, I need a fag,' she said indistinctly.

George handed her a cigarette and managed to light it in spite of her trembling fingers. He wished he could find some useful words, but knew it was futile to tell Ruth that everything was going to be all right. Nothing would ever be right again for this woman. All he could do was sit quietly and watch her drag smoke into her lungs until the hammer of her heart quietened enough to let her take up her tale again.

When she spoke this time, it was almost dreamily. 'The bench he works at, it's really an old table. It's got drawers in it. I moved it away from the wall. It was a hell of a job, it's really heavy. But I wanted to get behind it, to clean properly. I saw this material sticking out of the hole where one of the back drawers used to be. I wondered what it could be. So I pulled it out.'

'She was screaming like a pig with its throat cut,' Ma Lomas interjected. 'I could hear her all the way over the fields.'

George took a deep breath. 'There could be an innocent explanation for this, Mrs Hawkin.'

'Oh aye?' Ma sneered. 'Let's hear one, then. Take it away and test that blood, lad. Look where the blood is, you daft lump. It's all down the front, right where you'd expect it to be. And the gun? How innocent can a pistol be? You check that gun. I bet it fired the bullet you found up in the mine.' She shook her head in disgust. 'I thought your lot were supposed to have searched this place?'

'I seem to remember Mr Hawkin was very particular about his darkroom,' George said.

'All the more reason to go through it like a dose of salts,' Kathy said grimly. 'Are you going to arrest him now, then?'

'Have you got a paper bag I can put the shirt and the gun in?' George asked.

Ruth gave Kathy a look of mute appeal. She jumped up and rummaged in the cupboard under the sink and came out with a large brown paper sack. George picked the shirt up on the end of the pen and fed it into the bag without touching it. The gun he wrapped meticulously in a clean handkerchief from his pocket and carefully placed it on top of the shirt. 'I have to go back to Buxton,' he said quietly. 'Sergeant Clough will stay here and make sure nobody enters the outhouse where Mr Hawkin's darkroom is situated.' He sighed. 'I'll be sending out a team of officers to conduct a thorough search just as soon as I can arrange the warrant.'

'But are you going to arrest him?' Kathy persisted.

'You'll be kept fully informed of any developments,' George said.

A strange look passed among the women. 'If you don't arrest him you'd better keep him away from here,' Ma Lomas said. 'For the sake of his health.'

George gave her a long, steady look. 'I'm going to pretend I didn't hear that threat, Mrs Lomas.'

He drove Tommy Clough's unfamiliar car back to Buxton with a strange mixture of heaviness and exhilaration in his heart. He parked carefully and walked upstairs to the interview room with an air of quiet determination. He knew he ought to speak to DCI Carver or Superintendent Martin before he acted, but this was his case. George pushed open the door and stared down at Hawkin, whose petulant complaint died on his lips when he saw the inspector's expression.

George took a deep breath. 'Philip Hawkin, I am arresting you on suspicion of murder.'

3

George wasted no time. Hawkin was hustled down to the cells, bleating about trumped-up lies and demanding a lawyer. George turned a deaf ear. There would be plenty of time to deal with Hawkin later. If he was right, nobody would question his actions. If he was wrong, nobody would blame him. Nobody except, possibly, DCI Carver, who saw everything George did as a reproach and would glory in his junior officer's embarrassment and disgrace. But staying in DCI Carver's good books was the last consideration in George's mind right then.

As the door slammed shut on the still protesting Hawkin, George took DC Cragg to one side. 'Cragg, I want you to ring the divisional CID down in St Albans, where Hawkin came from. We know he's not got a record, because Sergeant Clough already checked that. What I want to know is if there was ever any talk. Any rumours, any beat gossip. Any allegations where there was never enough evidence for a charge.'

'You mean sex offences?'

'I mean anything, Cragg. Just get alongside the local lads and sound them out.' He realized he was still clutching the paper sack containing the soiled shirt and the carefully wrapped gun. In his hurry, he'd forgotten the need to get them labelled and sent to the lab. He glanced at his watch. Almost noon. If he hurried, he'd catch one of the justices at the High Peak courtrooms. He was sure he would have no trouble getting a search warrant signed. Everyone wanted Alison Carter's disappearance cleared up, and Hawkin hadn't yet had time to make many influential friends in a town where people from five miles away were still regarded as foreigners. Swiftly, he filled in the application and left the station at a run. Ignoring his car, he raced down Silverlands and cut through the marketplace towards the courts. Ten minutes later, he walked out of Peak Buildings with a signed search warrant in his pocket for Scardale Manor and its out-buildings. As he emerged, so did the sun, illuminating him with a brief shaft of pale winter light. It was hard not to interpret it as some kind of omen.

Back at divisional headquarters, still carrying the paper sack, he was relieved to find Sergeant Bob Lucas on duty. It seemed only fitting that the officer who had first taken him to Scardale should be available to help search on what might possibly be the breakthrough in the case. George gave him a succinct outline of events and finally dealt with the formal paperwork that would send the shirt and gun to the labs, the chain of custody intact. Meanwhile, Lucas put together a small search team of two constables and a cadet, all he could spare from the busy day shift.

The liveried police car followed George's unmarked saloon out of the town and through the washed-out February landscape to Scardale. The word of Ruth's discovery had clearly spread as swiftly as the original report of Alison's disappearance. Women stood at open cottage doorways and men leaned against walls, their eyes never leaving the police officers as they trooped round the side of the manor towards the outbuilding where Philip Hawkin pursued his hobby. Even more unsettling than their stares was their silence.

George found Clough standing outside the door of the small stone outbuilding, arms folded, a cigarette drooping from one corner of his mouth. 'Any problems?' he asked.

Clough shook his head. 'The hardest part was staying outside.'

George opened the door to the outbuilding and took his first look inside Hawkin's darkroom. It was obvious that six officers would struggle to fit inside, never mind search adequately. 'Right,' he said. 'Sergeant Clough and I will take the darkroom. Sergeant Lucas, I'd like your men to take the house. As you all know, it's already been searched. But our concern then was to make sure Alison hadn't left any hidden messages or that there were no signs of an assault or murder on the premises. Now, we're looking for anything that sheds light on Philip Hawkin's relationship with his stepdaughter. Or anything that gives us an insight into the man himself. Without a body, we need every scrap of circumstantial evidence we can find to put pressure on Hawkin. You can make a start in his study.'

'Right you are, sir,' Lucas said grimly. 'Come on, lads. Let's strip this place to the bricks.' The four uniformed men headed for the back door. Through the kitchen window, George could see Kathy Lomas watching. When she caught his eye, she looked away.

'OK, Tommy, let's make a start.' George crossed the threshold and flicked a light switch. Red light flooded the room. 'Great,' he muttered. He glanced at the wall and saw a second switch. When he clicked that, an ordinary electric light came on, replacing the eerie scarlet glow. He looked around him, taking stock of what needed to be searched. Apart from the heavy table that stood at an angle to the wall, everything was uncannily neat and tidy. A pair of heavy stone slop sinks that looked as if they had been there since the Middle Ages stood against the wall, the plumbing mounted on them brand new and gleaming. So was the photographic equipment.

In one corner, a pair of gunmetal filing cabinets stood against the wall. George crossed to them and rattled the drawers. They were locked. 'Bugger,' he said softly.

'Not a problem,' Clough said, moving his boss to one side. He grasped the nearer cabinet, pulled it towards him, then, when it was about five inches clear of the wall, he tipped it backwards. 'Can you hold it like that for me?' he asked. George leaned against the cabinet, keeping it tilted at an angle. Clough dropped to the floor and fiddled around underneath for a minute or so. George heard the slide and click of a lock unfastening, then Clough's grunt of satisfaction. 'There you go, George. Very careless of Mr Hawkin to go out and leave his filing cabinets unlocked.'

'I'll start going through this one,' George said. 'You check the table and the shelves.' He pulled the top drawer open and started on the dozens of suspension files it held. Each one contained strips of negatives, contact sheets and a varying number of prints. Quickly, he checked the other drawers. Each was the same. He groaned. 'This is going to take for ever,' he said.

Clough came over and joined him. 'There are thousands of these.'

'I know. But we're going to have to go through every one of them. If he's ever taken dodgy photographs, they could be mixed up with innocent ones anywhere in these drawers.' He sighed.

'Shall we take a look in the other filing cabinet, just so we have a clear idea of the scale of the problem?' Clough asked.

'Good idea,' George said. 'Same routine again?' This time, he manhandled the cabinet clear of the wall himself, leaving Clough to grope underneath.

'Wait a minute,' Clough said, fumbling beneath the metal base. 'I've caught my sleeve on something.' His hand snaked into his jacket pocket and emerged with his cigarette lighter. A flick of the wheel and the flame lit up the area beneath the filing cabinet. 'Jesus Christ on a bike,' he said softly. He looked up at George. 'You're going to love this, George. There's a hole in the floor with a safe in it.'

George nearly dropped the filing cabinet in shock. 'A safe?'

'That's right.' Clough scrambled clear of the filing cabinet and stood up. 'Let's get this moved and you'll see what I mean.'

They wrestled the heavy steel cabinet out of its slot and walked it across the room to clear enough space for them to study the safe. George crouched down and stared at it. The green metal front was about eighteen inches square, with a brass keyhole and a handle that protruded about an inch above the safe door into the cavity in the base of the filing cabinet. He sighed. 'We're going to need fingerprints out here to dust that handle for Hawkin's prints. I don't want him walking away from the contents of that safe on the spurious grounds that somebody else must have planted whatever's in it.'

'Are you sure?' Clough asked dubiously. 'We'll be lucky if there's as much as a partial on a handle like that. It's what's inside that matters. He won't have worn gloves, his prints'll be all over whatever's in there.'

George sat back on his heels. 'You're probably right. So where's the key?'

'If I was him, I'd have it on me.'

George shook his head. 'Cragg searched him when we put him in the cells. The only keys on him were for his car.' He thought for a moment. 'Go and ask Sergeant Lucas if they've come across any keys that look like they might open a safe. I'll have a look here.'

George sat down at the table and started to go through the two drawers. One was a meticulous collection of useful implements – scissors, craft knives, tweezers, tiny soft brushes and draughtsman's pens. The other was the usual jumble of a junk drawer – pieces of string, drawing pins, a broken nail file, a couple of half-used rolls of Sellotape, candle ends, torch bulbs, matchboxes and odd screws. Neither held a key. George lit a cigarette and smoked it furiously. He felt like a watch wound to the absolute limit of its spring.

All through the investigation, he had forced himself to keep an open mind, knowing how easy it was to develop a fixed idea and to force every subsequent piece of information to fit the preconception. But if he was honest, he'd never had an entirely open mind about Philip Hawkin. The more likely it was that Alison was dead, the more likely it was that her stepfather was the man responsible. That was what the statistics suggested, and it was bolstered by his lack of liking for the man. He had tried to stifle his own instinctive response, knowing prejudice was an enemy of building a solid case, but time and again, Hawkin had crept into his consciousness as the prime suspect if murder became the inevitable conclusion of their inquiry.

Now it beckoned irresistibly. Certainty had dropped into place like the tumblers of a well-oiled lock. The only question was whether he could assemble the evidence that would turn it into a conviction.

George walked out of the darkroom and into the darkening chill of the afternoon. The house lights burned pale yellow and he could see figures moving behind the windows. He glimpsed Ruth Hawkin crossing the kitchen and realized he was dreading the moment when he might have to confirm for her what they all believed now anyway. No matter how much she might have thought herself resigned to losing her daughter, the instant when he told her they were formally treating Alison's disappearance as a murder inquiry would send a blade of pain to her heart.

He lit another cigarette and paced in tight circles outside the darkroom. What was keeping Clough? He couldn't leave the outhouse now the search was under way, for fear of a later defence argument that while it had been unattended, someone had slipped incriminating evidence inside. He didn't want to continue searching either, realizing that with so circumstantial an array of evidence, every crucial find must be witnessed. George forced himself to breathe deeply, rotating his shoulders inside his coat to try to release some of the tension that knotted his neck in taut cords.

As the last light faded behind the western edge of the dale, Clough emerged, a wide grin spread across his face. 'Sorry I took so long,' he said. 'I had to go through all the desk drawers. Nothing. Then I noticed one of the drawers wasn't closing flush. So I pulled it out, and bingo! There was the safe key, stuck to the back of the drawer with elastoplast.' He dangled the key in front of George. 'The same kind of elastoplast that the dog was muzzled with, incidentally.'

'Nice work, Tommy.' He took the key and stepped back inside the darkroom. He crouched over the safe and glanced over his shoulder at his sergeant. 'I'm almost scared to open it.'

'In case there's proof she's dead?'

George shook his head. 'In case there's no proof of anything. I'm convinced now, Tommy. Too many small coincidences. Hawkin's done for Alison, and I want him to swing for it.' He turned to his task and slotted the key into the lock. It turned in smooth silence. He closed his eyes for a few seconds. Five minutes before he'd have called himself an agnostic. Now, he was a zealot.

Slowly he turned the handle and used it to lift open the heavy steel door. There was nothing inside but a thin stack of manila envelopes. George lifted them out almost reverently. He counted them aloud for the benefit of Clough, whose notebook was already open, pencil poised. 'Six brown envelopes,' he said, rising and placing them on the bench. George sat down. He had the feeling he'd need the support. He pulled on his soft leather driving gloves and started work.

The flaps had all been tucked inside. George inserted his thumb and flicked the first envelope open. It contained eight-by-ten photographs. He removed them by pushing the sides of the envelope inwards and letting the photos spill out on to the table, to avoid smudging any fingerprints on the envelope or the pictures. There were half a dozen photos, which he spread out using his pen.

Alison Carter was naked in all of them. Her face was devoid of its natural charm, rendered ugly by fear. Her body somehow expressed her reluctance to adopt poses that would have been lewd in an adult but which were gut-wrenchingly tragic in a child. Unless, of course, the viewer was the sort of paedophile who had taken them. Then, they would doubtless have appeared erotic.

Clough looked over his shoulder. 'Ah, Jesus,' he said, his voice thick with disgust.

George could find nothing to say. He gathered the photographs together and slid them back into the envelope, placing it carefully to one side. The second envelope contained strips of large-format negatives. With the aid of the light box on the table, they were able to establish that these were the negatives the prints had been made from. There were sixteen negatives. Hawkin hadn't bothered printing ten of them. Those were the ones where Alison appeared to be crying.

The third envelope was worse. The poses were even more explicit. This time, however, there was a floppy quality to the girl's head, a distant look in her eyes. 'She's either drunk or drugged,' Clough said. Still George could not speak. Methodically, he replaced the photographs in their envelope then checked that the negatives in the fourth envelope corresponded to the photographs they'd just looked at.

The fifth envelope went beyond anything George could have imagined. This time all sixteen negatives had been printed. This time, Hawkin was in the photographs along with his stepdaughter. The background was unmistakably Alison's bedroom, its very ordinariness an obscene counterpoint to the acts it had contained. It formed an innocent backdrop to experiences no thirteen-year-old should endure. In a series of terrible monochrome images, Hawkin's erect penis thrust into Alison's vagina, anus and mouth. His fingers probed her body with ruthless and repellent efficiency. All the while, he stared into the camera, exulting in his power.

'The fucking bastard,' Clough groaned.

George suddenly thrust himself away from the table, sending the chair crashing to the ground. Pushing past his sergeant, he made it through the door just as the wave of nausea he couldn't contain swept through him. Hands on knees, he vomited until his stomach was in spasm and there was nothing left inside him but pain. He half leaned, half fell against the wall, sweating, tears pouring down his face, oblivious to the chill night wind and the scatter of sleety rain that swept the dale.

He'd rather have found her corpse than endured those images of her violated body. Plenty of motive there for running away. But more motive still for the man who had invaded her if she had finally rebelled and threatened to reveal his vile perversion. George ran a trembling hand over his wet face and struggled upright.

Clough, standing right behind him in the doorway, handed him the cigarette already lit. His beefy face was as pale as the night clouds. George inhaled deeply and coughed as the smoke hit a throat left raw by his retching. 'Still think capital punishment's such a bad thing?' he gasped. The rain plastered his hair to his head, but he failed to react to the drops of icy water coursing down his face.

'I could kill him with my own hands,' Clough growled, his voice coming from deep in his throat.

'Save him for the hangman, Tommy. This one, we do by the book. He doesn't have any accidental falls, he doesn't conveniently get put in a cell with a drunk who hates sex offenders. We bring him to court in one piece,' George said hoarsely.

'It won't be easy. Meanwhile, what do we tell Alison's mum? This . . . this beast's wife? How do you say to a woman, "By the way, love, this man you married – he's raped and buggered your daughter and probably murdered her."?'

'Oh Christ,' George said. 'We need a WPC out here. And a doctor.'

'She won't want a WPC, George. She trusts you. And she's got her family around her. They'll take better care of her than any doctor can. We're just going to have to go in there and find a way to tell her.'

'We better tell the uniforms as well. They can keep an eye out specifically for photographs or negatives.' He shuddered as he breathed in deeply. 'Let's bag and tag those envelopes. Forensic will need to do their stuff with them.'

They forced themselves back into the darkroom

and collected the envelopes with their hellish contents. 'Take these indoors to Sergeant Lucas,' George instructed Clough. 'I don't want to be standing there holding them when I speak to Ruth Hawkin. I'll have a last look here to see if there's anything else obvious. We're going to have to get a team to go through every single one of those negatives. But not tonight.'

Clough disappeared into the night. George checked the room, but could see nothing else deserving his notice. He stepped back outside into the miserable weather and closed the door behind him. He carefully fixed a pair of police seals so that nobody could tamper with the evidence. He'd have to have an overnight guard placed on the outbuilding to protect its contents. Tomorrow, he'd organize a team to strip the place and start the long slog through Hawkin's photographic collection. There would be no shortage of volunteers.

'I've handed the evidence over to Sergeant Lucas,' Clough said, running across from the house.

'Thanks. Now, this is how I want to play it. You take the relatives, I'll speak to Ruth Hawkin on her own. Just tell them we've found evidence that suggests Hawkin may have been involved in Alison's disappearance and that we'll be charging him with at least one serious offence tonight. It's up to Ruth how much more she wants to tell them.'

'They're going to want chapter and verse. Especially Ma Lomas,' Clough warned.

'Let them come to court, then. I'm concerned about Ruth Hawkin. She's my key witness as of this moment, and she's got the right to decide how much her family knows at this point,' George said dismissively. 'Tell them as little as you need to.' He squared his shoulders and flicked his cigarette butt into the night. He ran a hand over his soaking hair, showering Clough with tiny droplets of water. 'Right.' He took a deep breath. 'Let's go.'

They walked through the back door and across the hall into the warm fug of the smoky kitchen. The support team of Ma Lomas and Kathy had been joined by Ruth's sister Diane and Janet's mother, Maureen. The five women's faces sharpened with fear at the sight of the grim expressions on the men's faces. 'We have some news, Mrs Hawkin,' George said heavily. 'I'd like to talk to you alone, if I may. The rest of you ladies, if you'll go with Sergeant Clough, he'll explain what's happening.'

Kathy opened her mouth to argue, but a second look at George's face killed her protest. 'We'll go through to the parlour,' she said meekly.

Ruth said nothing as they filed out. Her face was like a bolted door, tightly secured, her jaw muscles bulging with the effort of silence. She never took her eyes off George as he sat down at the table opposite her. He waited till he heard the door close behind Clough, then he said, 'There's no easy way to say this, Mrs Hawkin. We've found evidence that Philip Hawkin has committed serious sexual assaults against your daughter. There can be no doubt about that, and he will be charged before the day's out.'

A whimper escaped from her lips, but her gaze continued to pin him down. He shifted in his seat and automatically reached for his cigarettes. She shook her head as he offered them, so he left the packet sitting on the table between them. 'When you add that to the evidence of the stained shirt and the gun that you found in the outbuilding, it's hard to resist the conclusion that he very probably murdered her too. I'm really very, very sorry, Mrs Hawkin.'

'Don't call me that,' she said, her voice a series of glottal sobs. 'Don't give me his name.'

'I won't,' George said. 'And I'll do my best to make sure no other police officer does.'

'You're sure, aren't you?' she said through stiff lips. 'In your heart, you're sure she's dead?'

George wanted to be anywhere but in Ruth Carter's kitchen, nailed by her eyes against the truth. 'I am,' he said. 'I can find no reason to think otherwise and a significant amount of circumstantial evidence that leads me to that conclusion. God knows, I don't want to believe it, but I can't not.'

Ruth began rocking to and fro in her chair, her arms clamped across her breasts, hands turned to claws in her armpits. Her head dropped back and she let out an agonized roar, the wordless cry of an animal wounded beyond recovery. Helpless, George sat like a block of wood. Somehow, he knew the worst thing he could do would be to touch her.

The noise stopped and her head fell forward, slack-jawed and flushed. Her eyes glittered with tears unshed. 'You get him hanged,' she said, hard and clear.

He nodded, reaching for his cigarettes and lighting one. 'I'll try my best.'

She shook her head. 'Never mind trying. Do it, George Bennett. Because if you don't make sure he dies, somebody else will and it'll be a damn sight less humane than what the hangman will do to him.' Her vehemence seemed to have used her last reserve of energy. She turned away and said breathlessly, 'Now go.'

George slowly got to his feet. 'I'll be back tomorrow, to take a statement. If you need anything, anything at all, you can reach me at the police station.' He scrabbled in his jacket pocket for his notebook and scribbled his home number on a torn-out sheet of paper. 'If I'm not there, call me at home. Any time. I'm sorry.'

He backed across the room and groped for the door handle. He closed the door behind him and leaned against the wall, cigarette smoke dribbling up his arm in a fragmented swirl. The sound of voices from down the hall led him to the cheerless room where the other Scardale women were besieging Tommy Clough. 'To hell with the monkey, here comes the organ grinder,' Maureen Carter said, catching sight of George. 'You tell us. Are you going to hang that bastard Hawkin?'

'I don't make those decisions, Mrs Carter,' George said, trying not to show how far past arguing he was. 'Can I suggest that you'd be better off spending your time and your energy with Ruth? She needs your support. We'll be leaving shortly, but there will be a guard on the outhouse overnight. I'd appreciate it if you'd all rally round Ruth now, and rack your brains for any little detail that might help us build our case.'

'He's right, leave him be,' Ma Lomas said unexpectedly. 'He's only a lad and he's had a lot to take in for one day. Come on, girls. We'd best see to Ruth.' She shooed them out of the door ahead of her, then turned for the inevitable parting shot. 'We won't let you off this light again, lad. Time to shape up.' She shook her head. 'I blame the old squire. He should have known better. Half an hour with Philip Hawkin and there's one thing you know for certain. Who spared that would drown nothing.' The door closed behind her with a sharp snick.

As if choreographed, George and Clough subsided into chairs opposite each other, their faces as drained as their spirits. 'I never want to have to do that again,' George sighed on an exhalation of smoke. He cast around looking for an ashtray, but none of the orna-ments held out any possibilities. He settled for nipping the hot coal off with his fingers and dropping it in the empty grate.

'Chances are you'll have to before you get your pension,' Clough said. In the hall, a phone began to ring. On the sixth or seventh ring, it was picked up. A murmur of interrogatory speech, then footsteps approached the parlour door. Diane Lomas poked her head round and said, 'It's for the inspector. Somebody called Carver.'

Wearily, George pulled himself out of the armchair and across the room. He lifted the receiver and said, 'DI Bennett.'

'What the bloody hell do you think you're playing at, Bennett? I've got Alfie Naden reading the riot act in here, claiming we've shoved his client in the cells without so much as a by-your-leave, and left him to stew while you go gadding around Derbyshire on another wild-goose chase.'

And how, George wondered, had the town's most expensive lawyer found out that Philip Hawkin was in custody in the first place? Cragg was a useless wassock, but he wouldn't have phoned the solicitor without George's say-so. It looked like Carver hadn't learned the lesson of Peter Crowther's death and was behaving like a law unto himself again. George choked back an angry retort and said, 'I was about to come back to the station and charge Mr Hawkin.'

'With what? Naden said you told Hawkin he was being arrested on suspicion of murder. You've not got a murder to charge him with!' Carver's broad Midlands accent always thickened under pressure. George recognized the signs of a man whose temper was about to burst the dam. That made two of them.

Biting down hard on his anger, he spoke calmly. 'I'll be charging him with rape, sir. For starters. That should give us enough breathing space to ask the Director of Public Prosecutions where we stand on a murder charge with no body.'

There was a moment's stunned silence. 'Rape?' Incredulity stretched the word into three syllables.

'We have photographic evidence, sir. Believe me, this is copper-bottomed. Now, if you'll excuse me, sir, I'll get off. I'll be back in the office in about half an hour and I'll show you my evidence then.' George gently replaced the receiver and turned to see Bob Lucas in the doorway of the study. 'DCI Carver would like us to return to Buxton,' he said. 'And I need to take those envelopes back with me. Can I leave you to sort out an overnight guard on the darkroom?'

'I'll deal with it, sir. Just to say, we've been through every book on the shelves in the study and there's no photographs anywhere. We'll carry on looking, though. Good luck with Hawkin.' His sleek head bobbed in a supportive nod. 'Let's hope he makes it easy on Mrs Hawkin and decides to come clean.'

'Somehow, I doubt it, Bob,' Clough said from the doorway. 'Too cocky by half, that one.'

'While I remember, she doesn't want us calling her

Mrs Hawkin any more. I suppose we call her Mrs Carter,' George sighed. 'Pass the word round.' He ran a hand over his still wet hair. 'Right, then. Let's go and make this bastard suffer.'

4

The photographs silenced Carver. George reckoned it wouldn't be the last time they had that effect. Carver stared as if gazing would somehow erase the images and replace them with the picture-postcard shots of Scardale that Hawkin sold to local shops. Then, abruptly, he turned away. He pointed to a sheet of paper. 'Naden's home number. He'll want to be present when you interview the prisoner.' He stood up and snatched his overcoat from the wall hook behind his desk.

'You're not staying for the interview, sir?' George asked, something like dismay showing in his voice.

'It's been your case from the beginning. You see it through,' Carver said coldly. He shrugged into his coat. 'You and Clough, you do it.'

'But, sir,' George started, then stopped. He wanted to say he'd never done anything as serious as this, that he'd never conducted an interrogation where he had so little to go on, that it was Carver's job as the DCI to take charge in this situation. The words died in his mouth with the realization that Carver thought the wheels were going to come off this case somewhere along the line and he didn't want to be aboard when they did.

'But what?'

'Nothing, sir.'

'So what are you waiting for? I can't lock up my office if you're standing in the middle of the floor like piffy, can I?'

'Sorry, sir,' George said, picking up the sheet of paper from Carver's desk. He turned his back and walked out into the CID room. 'Sergeant,' he called across to Clough. 'Grab your coat. Let's go.'

Surprised, Clough did as he was told. Carver scowled. 'Where are you going? You've got a prisoner to charge and question.'

'I'm going to phone Mr Naden and ask him to be here in an hour's time. Then I'm taking Sergeant Clough home with me for a meal. We've neither of us eaten since breakfast, and a major interrogation needs more to sustain it than nicotine and caffeine. Sir,' George said unapologetically.

Carver sneered. 'Is that what they teach you at university?'

'No, sir, it's something I learned from Superintendent Martin, actually. He says you should never send your forces into battle on an empty stomach.' George smiled. 'Now, if you'll excuse us, sir, we have work to do.' He turned away and picked up the phone. He could feel Carver's eyes burning into his back as he dialled. 'Hello? Mr Naden? It's Detective Inspector Bennett from Buxton CID here. I intend to question your client on suspicion of murder and rape in an hour's time. I'd be much obliged if you could be here then . . . Fine, I'll see you then. Thank you.' He ended the call by depressing the rest then dialled again. 'Anne? It's me.' He turned round and stared pointedly at Carver, who snorted and stalked off towards the stairs.

Precisely an hour later, Alfie Naden was shown into the interview room. He looked the epitome of a prosperous country solicitor, his neat paunch encased in a three-piece suit of irreproachable dark worsted. Gold-framed half-moon glasses perched on a fleshy nose flanked by florid cheeks. His bald head shone under the lights, and his chin was as smooth as if he'd shaved before coming out for this evening appointment. It would have been easy to mistake him for a bumpkin except for his eyes. Small and dark, they glittered like the glass eyes of an antique teddy bear. Seldom still except when he was probing a witness, they missed nothing. He was a shrewd adversary and George wished Hawkin hadn't possessed sufficient local knowledge to engage the man.

Once Clough had brought Hawkin up from the cells, they cantered through the formalities. Hawkin said nothing, his lip curled slightly in distaste. He looked as neat and confident as he had at ten that morning.

George cautioned him, then said, 'Following your arrest this morning on suspicion of murder, I obtained a search warrant from High Peak magistrates.' He handed the warrant to Naden who scrutinized it and nodded briefly. 'My officers and I executed that warrant this afternoon at Scardale Manor. In the course of that search, we discovered a safe sunk into the floor of the outbuilding which you have converted into a photographic darkroom. When that safe was opened with a key concealed in your study inside Scardale Manor, six brown envelopes were discovered.'

'Six?' Hawkin interjected.

'Six envelopes which proved to contain certain photographic prints and negatives. As a result of which, I am charging you, Philip Hawkin, with rape.'

Throughout George's formal speech, Hawkin's face had not changed. So he wasn't going to roll over, George thought. He thinks he's got away with the big one, so he's going to bite his tongue and take his medicine for the rape.

'May we see the evidence?' Naden said calmly.

George looked inquiringly at Hawkin. 'Do you really want your solicitor to see the photographs? I mean, Mr Naden is the best there is. If I was you, I wouldn't take the chance of him walking out.'

'Mr Bennett,' Naden warned.

'He can't defend me if he doesn't know what you bastards have faked up,' Hawkin said. His accent had slipped several notches down the social scale since the morning's condescension.

George opened a folder in front of him. In the hour they'd been gone, Cragg had inserted every print and negative strip into its own individual plastic bag. The night-shift CID man had labelled each one as it had been slid inside the bag by its edges. Tomorrow, the forensic team would have their chance. Eventually, the force's photographers would make copies from the negatives. But tonight, George needed to keep hold of the evidence.

Silently, he placed the first photograph of Alison in front of Hawkin and Naden. Hawkin crossed his legs and said, 'Did you bring me some fags?'

Naden dragged his horrified eyes away from the photograph and looked at Hawkin as if he were a creature from another universe. 'What?' he said faintly.

'Fags. I've run out,' Hawkin said.

Naden blinked a dozen times in quick succession then snapped open his briefcase. He took out a packet of Benson & Hedges, still in their cellophane wrapper, and tossed them in front of Hawkin, who made a point of not looking at any more of the photographs that George methodically put in front of Naden. The solicitor seemed mesmerized by the record of defilement piling up before him. When the final photograph sat in front of him, he cleared his throat.

'They've faked them,' Hawkin said. 'Anybody knows you can fake up photographs. My stepdaughter went missing and they've not been able to find her and now they're framing me to make themselves look good.'

'We've got the negatives as well,' George said flatly.

'You can fake negatives too,' Hawkin said superciliously. 'First you fake the photograph, then you photograph it. Bingo, you've got a negative that you can print from.'

'Are you denying that you raped Alison Carter?' George asked incredulously.

'Yes,' Hawkin said firmly.

'We have also taken possession of a bloodstained shirt which is identical in every particular to the shirts you have made to measure at a London tailor. This was hidden in your darkroom too.'

Hawkin finally looked startled. 'What?'

'The shirt was very heavily stained with blood on the front, the lower sleeves and the cuffs. I expect that when it is tested, it will match the blood previously found on Alison's underwear.'

'What shirt? There was no shirt in my darkroom,' Hawkin exclaimed, leaning forward and jabbing the air with his cigarette to make his point.

'That's where it was found. Along with the gun.'

Hawkin's eyes widened. 'What gun?'

'A Webley .38 revolver. Identical to the one your mother's neighbour Mr Wells had stolen a couple of years ago.'

'I haven't got a gun,' Hawkin gabbled. 'You're making a big mistake here, Bennett. You might think you can get away with framing me for this, but you're not as smart as you think you are!'

George's smile was as icy as the wind that whistled outside. 'You should know that it is my intention to present this information to the Director of Public Prosecutions in the firm belief that he will allow us to charge you with murder,' he continued inexorably.

'This is an outrage!' Hawkin exploded. He shifted in his seat and turned his aggression on his solicitor. 'Tell them they can't do this. All they've got are some poxy faked pictures. Tell them!'

Naden looked as if he wished he'd stayed at home. 'I must advise you to say nothing further, Mr Hawkin.' Hawkin opened his mouth to protest. 'Nothing further, Mr Hawkin,' Naden repeated, a hard edge in his voice that entirely contradicted his benign appearance. 'Mr Bennett, my client will not be making any further statement at this time. Nor will he be answering any of your questions. Now, I require a meeting in private with my client. Other than that, we will see you before the justices tomorrow morning.'

George sat staring at the typewriter. He had to prepare

a brief on the rape charge for the uniformed inspector who dealt with the magistrates' court. It was a straightforward request for a remand in custody, but with Alfie Naden defending the squire of Scardale before a bench of the local great and good, George wanted to take no chances. It didn't help that his head pulsed with a pain so powerful that he had to resist the impulse to close one eye to relieve it.

He sighed and lit another cigarette. 'Reasons to oppose bail,' he muttered.

There was a peremptory knock at his door. At this time of night, it was probably one of the night shift taking pity on him and bringing tea. 'Come in,' he called.

Superintendent Martin pushed the door open, dressed in an immaculate dinner jacket instead of uniform. 'Not disturbing you, am I?' he asked.

'You're a very welcome interruption, sir,' George said, meaning it.

Martin settled himself in the chair opposite George and slipped a silver hip flask from his back pocket. 'Anything to drink out of?' he asked.

George shook his head. 'Not even a dirty cup. Sorry.'

'No matter. We'll just adopt battlefield manners,' Martin said, taking a swig from the flask before wiping the top and handing it to George. 'Go on. I bet you need it.'

Gratefully, George took a mouthful of brandy. He closed his eyes and savoured the burn as it coursed down his throat and warmed his chest. 'I didn't realize you had medical qualifications, sir. That was just what the doctor ordered.'

'I was at a Masonic dinner. So was DCI Carver. He told me what you've been up to.' Martin gave George a level stare. 'I'd rather have heard it from you.'

'Things . . . moved at a bit of a lick today. I was very uneasy about that business of the newspaper photograph last week. I thought it needed further investigation. But I wasn't planning on anything more than questioning Hawkin to see if I could unsettle him and perhaps make him slip up. Then when his wife phoned . . . I did think about coming to you before we searched the manor, but if I had, I would have missed the JPs at court, and you know how difficult some of them can be about signing warrants in what they see as their own time. So . . . I just forged ahead.'

'So where exactly are we up to?'

'I've charged him with rape. He'll be up before the justices in the morning for a remand in custody. I'm just doing the paperwork now. I should tell you that he's got Alfie Naden defending him and he's already preparing the defence that we faked the photographs to make it look as if we hadn't completely failed in the Alison Carter case.'

Martin snorted. 'That'll never fly. I doubt we've got either a photographer or the equipment to concoct something so elaborate. Still, it'll stir up a lot of mud and he might just slide through it and out the other side. You can never tell with juries, and he's a good-looking beggar.' He fished a cigar case out of his inside jacket pocket. He loosened his bow tie and undid the top collar stud in his dress shirt. 'That's better,' he said. 'Cigar?'

'I'll stick with my cigarettes, thanks.' Both men lit up.

Martin exhaled a plume of blue smoke. 'What have we got for murder? Take me through it.'

George leaned back in his seat. 'One, we now know he was interfering with his stepdaughter and taking pornographic photographs of her. Two, on the afternoon she disappeared, he claims he was alone in his darkroom. But we have two witnesses who saw him crossing the field between the wood where Alison's dog was found and the copse where there were signs of a struggle involving her.'

'Suggestive,' Martin commented.

'Three, the dog lived in his household. If anyone could have taped its muzzle shut without being bitten, it was someone that familiar with the dog. We'll have to do a trawl of the local chemists to see if anyone remembers selling him a roll of elastoplast. Four, nobody in the village apart from Ma Lomas admits to ever having heard of the disused lead mine workings. But a book detailing the exact location of the entrance to the mine was found on the shelf in Hawkin's study.'

'Suggestive but circumstantial.'

George nodded. 'It's all circumstantial. But then, how often do we get a corroborated witness account of a murder?'

'True. Let's hear the rest of it.'

George paused for a moment to collect his thoughts. 'OK. Five, Hawkin shared the blood group of the person who deposited semen on Alison's underwear. There was also blood on that clothing that is the same group as Alison's and the blood found on the tree in the copse. We know from the presence of Barr bodies that this blood was female in origin. So it's reasonable to assume that Alison was at least injured if not killed at the hands of a sexual predator. And we know from the photographs that Hawkin fits that category. Six, the supposed identification of Alison from a newspaper photograph of a football crowd. It mirrors exactly a newspaper story about the missing Manchester girl, Pauline Reade. I believe he used this as a means of making himself look like a worried and caring father. Something he'd completely failed to do up to that point, I have to say.

'Seven, two bullets were found in the lead mine. One was sufficiently unmarked to be identified as having been fired from a Webley .38 revolver. A similar gun was stolen from a house where Hawkin was a regular visitor a couple of years ago. A similar gun was found hidden in his darkroom, with the serial number filed off. We don't know yet if the man whose gun was stolen can identify this as the same weapon. And we don't know yet if this is the gun that fired the bullets we found in the mine. But we will.

'And finally, we have the bloodstained shirt. It's identical to the ones he has made to measure in London, right down to the tailor's label on the collar. It's been soaked with blood. If that blood corresponds to the other blood we've circumstantially identified with Alison, it ties Hawkin into an attack on her.' George raised his eyebrows. 'What do you think?'

'If we had a body, I'd say charge him. But we haven't got a body. We've got no direct evidence that Alison Carter isn't alive and well. The DPP will never wear a murder charge without a body.'

'There's precedent,' George protested. 'Haigh, the acid-bath murderer. There was no corpse there.'

'There was evidence that someone's body had been

disposed of and forensic traces that pointed to his victim, if I remember rightly,' Martin said.

'There's another precedent with even less evidence. In 1955. A Polish ex-serviceman who was convicted of the murder of his business partner. The prosecution claimed he'd fed the body to the pigs on their farm. All the prosecution had to go on was that friends and neighbours said the two men had been quarrelling. There were some bloodstains in the farmhouse kitchen and the business partner had vanished without trace, leaving behind his Post Office savings account. We've got a lot more than that. There's been no confirmed sighting of Alison Carter since she disappeared. We've got evidence that she was sexually assaulted and that she lost a considerable amount of blood. It's not likely that she's still alive, is it?'

Martin leaned back and let his cigar smoke dribble towards the ceiling. 'There's a lot of difference between "not likely" and "beyond reasonable doubt". Even with the gun. If he killed her close up, why are there two bullets in the wall?'

'Maybe she got away from him initially and he shot at her to scare her. Maybe she was struggling and he threatened her with the other two shots. To subdue her?'

Martin considered. 'Possible. But the defence will use those two bullets to spread confusion with the jury. And if he killed the girl in the mine workings, why move the body?'

George pushed his hair back from his forehead. 'I don't know. Perhaps he knew an even better place to hide the body. He must have done, mustn't he? Or else we'd have found it by now.'

'So if he knew a better place to dispose of the body, why leave evidence of the sexual assault in the mine?'

George sighed. Frustrated as he was by Martin's questions, he knew the defence lawyers would be a hundred times worse. 'I don't know. Maybe he just didn't have the chance. He had to put in an appearance at the dinner table. He couldn't afford to be late that night of all nights. And by the time he'd had his dinner, the word had gone out about Alison and he couldn't chance going back?'

'It's thin, George.' Martin sat up straight and looked George in the eye. 'It's not enough. You're going to have to find her body.'

PART THREE

Trials and Tribulations

The Remand

It was over in minutes. Looking around the courtroom, George was struck by the astonishment on the faces of the Scardale villagers who had turned up in force. They had come to satisfy some primeval urge, to see the man they cast as villain in the dock. They required ceremony to assuage that urge, but there in a modern courtroom that looked more like a school hall than the Old Bailey of film and television, there was nothing that could satisfy that need.

All the facial variants of Scardale were there in the seven men and eight women who had come along, from Ma Lomas's hooked nose to Brian Carter's slab features. The notable absentee was Ruth Carter herself.

The press, of course, were there, though in nothing like the numbers there would be at the committal and trial. There was so little they were allowed to report at that stage, it was scarcely worth turning up. Because of the rules governing the presumption of innocence, now Hawkin had been charged with something, editors had to tread warily. Any suggestion that Hawkin was being considered for a further charge of murder was taboo.

The prisoner was brought into the courtroom where two men and a woman Justices of the Peace sat on the bench. Alfie Naden was there, ready and waiting. So was the duty court inspector. Hawkin looked more at ease than any of them, his freshly shaved face the picture of clean innocence, his black hair gleaming under the lights. There was a low muttering from the public benches that was silenced by a sharp word from the court usher.

The court clerk stood up and outlined the charge against Hawkin. Almost before he had finished, Naden was on his feet. 'Your Worships, I have a submission to put before the court. As Your Worships are aware, it is the duty of the court under Section thirty-nine of the Children and Young Persons Act to protect the identity of minors who are victims of offences of indecency. With that in mind, it is normal for the court to bar the members of the press from reporting the name of the accused, since that would be an indirect way of identifying the victim where there is a family relationship such as we find in these allegations. I would therefore ask Your Worships to make such an order in this case.'

As Naden sat down, the inspector got to his feet again. He had already discussed this with George and Superintendent Martin. 'I would oppose such a ruling,' he said ponderously. 'Firstly, because of the extreme gravity of the circumstances in this case. We believe this is not the first time the defendant has sexually assaulted children. Publicizing his name may lead to other victims making themselves known to us.' That part of the argument was little more than kite-flying; Cragg's attempts at getting gossip out of St Albans officers had been a signal failure. George planned to

316

send Clough down for a second attempt, but for now, they were only guessing.

'Secondly,' the inspector continued, 'it is the prosecution's view that the victim of this assault is no longer alive and therefore does not merit the protection of the court.'

People gasped. One of the Scardale women made a sound like a small groan. Reporters looked at each other in bafflement. Could they report this statement because it had been made in open court? Would it still be contempt? Would it depend on what the magistrates ruled?

Naden was on his feet. 'Your Worships,' he protested, the very image of outrage. 'This is a scandalous suggestion. It's true that the alleged victim of this alleged assault is presently missing from home but for the police to suggest that she is dead is calculated only to generate calumny against my client. I must urge that you rule that nothing may be reported in the press except the fact a man has been charged with the crime of rape.'

The magistrates went into a huddle with the court clerk. George drummed his fingers impatiently on his knee. To be honest, he didn't much care whether the press named Hawkin or not. All he wanted was to crack on with his investigation.

At last, the chairman cleared his throat. 'We are agreed that for the purposes of a remand hearing, the press is barred from naming the accused. However, this decision need not be binding upon the examining justices at any subsequent committal hearing.'

Naden bowed his acknowledgement. 'I am much obliged,' he said.

When the committal hearing was set for four weeks ahead, Naden bounced to his feet again. 'Your Worships, I would ask you to consider the question of bail. My client is an upstanding member of his local community with no previous convictions nor stain on his character. He runs a large estate and there is no question but that his absence will impose hardship on his tenants.'

'Rubbish!' a voice bellowed from the back of the room. George recognized Brian Carter, his face scarlet with emotion. 'We're better off without him.'

The chairman of the bench looked astonished. 'Remove that man at once,' he said, outraged at such an exhibition of disrespect.

'I'm going anyway,' Brian shouted, jumping to his feet before anyone could reach him. He stormed out, slamming the door behind him. He left a stunned silence.

The chairman took a deep breath. 'If there are any further outbursts, I will clear this court,' he said stiffly. 'Please continue, Mr Naden.'

'Thank you. As I was saying, Mr Hawkin's presence is vital to the smooth running of the Scardale estate. As you have already heard, his stepdaughter is missing from home and he feels his place is at the side of his wife, to offer her comfort and succour. He is no feckless criminal who drifts from place to place. He has no intention of leaving the jurisdiction. I urge you to grant bail in these exceptional circumstances.'

The inspector slowly stood up. 'Your Worships, the police oppose bail on the grounds that the accused has sufficient funds at his disposal to be a flight risk. He has no deep roots in this area, having only moved here on the death of his uncle a little over a year ago. We are also concerned about possible interference with witnesses. Many potential prosecution witnesses are not only his tenants but also his employees and there is a very real risk of intimidation. Also, the police view this as an extremely serious offence and it is likely that further serious charges will be brought against the accused in the near future.'

George was relieved to see the woman magistrate nodding firmly at every point the inspector made. If the others were undecided, he thought her conviction would be enough to sway them. As they retired to discuss their decision, a buzz of conversation started again on the press bench. The Scardale contingent sat stolid and silent, their eyes boring holes in the back of Philip Hawkin's neck. Hawkin himself was deep in conversation with his lawyer.

George wished he could smoke.

Within a couple of minutes, the magistrates trooped back to their dais. 'Bail is refused,' the chairman said decisively. 'Take the prisoner down.'

As he passed George, Hawkin gave him a look of utter loathing. George stared right through him. He'd always believed in keeping his powder dry.

Daily News, *Thursday, 6th February 1964, p.2*

Man appears in court

A man charged with rape was remanded in custody by High Peak magistrates sitting at Buxton yesterday. The man, who cannot be named for legal reasons, lives in the Derbyshire village of Scardale.

The Murder Charge

It was strange, George thought, that all public offices were so similar. Somehow, he'd expected the offices of the Director of Public Prosecutions to be as grand as the title. Although the Regency building in Queen Anne's Gate couldn't have been less like the four-square modern brick hutch that housed the Buxton sub-division, the interior was standard government issue. The barrister he and Tommy Clough had arranged to meet four days after the remand hearing inhabited a space that was so similar to his own office it was almost disorientating. Files were stacked on top of filing cabinets, a handful of legal textbooks occupied the windowsill, and the ashtray needed emptying. The floor was covered in the identical linoleum, the walls painted the same off-white shade.

Jonathan Pritchard ran equally counter to his expectations. In his mid-thirties, Pritchard had the sort of carrot-red hair that is impossible to tame. It stuck out in tufts and angles all over his head, actually rising straight up in a kind of crest at one corner of his forehead. His features were equally unruly. His eyes, the blue-grey of wet Welsh slate, were round and widely spaced with long golden lashes. His long bony nose took a sudden swerve to the left at the end, and his mouth sloped at a wry angle. The only orderly thing about him was his immaculate dark-grey pinstripe suit, his dazzling white shirt and a perfectly knotted Guards tie.

'So,' the lawyer had greeted them, jumping to his feet. 'You're the chaps with no body. Come in, sit down. I hope you're fuelled up in advance because there is absolutely no chance of a decent cup of coffee in these parts.' He stood politely until George and Clough were settled, then subsided into his own battered wooden swivel chair. He opened a drawer, took out another ashtray and pushed it towards them. 'The extent of our hospitality,' he said ruefully. 'Now, who's who?'

They introduced themselves. Pritchard made a note on the pad in front of him. 'Forgive me,' he said. 'But isn't it rather unusual for a case of this magnitude to be run by a detective inspector? Particularly a detective inspector who's only been in post for five months?'

George stifled a sigh and shrugged. 'The DCI had his ankle in plaster when the girl went missing, so I was in operational control, reporting to Superintendent Martin. He's the senior officer in the Buxton sub-division. Anyway, as the case went on, HQ wanted to staff it with one of their more experienced CID officers, but the super resisted. He said he wanted it handled by his own men.'

'Very commendable, but perhaps not something your HQ officers were terribly pleased about?' Pritchard said.

'I don't know about that, sir.'

Clough leaned forward. 'The super served in the

322

army with the Deputy Chief Constable, sir. So the brass know they can trust his judgement.'

Pritchard nodded. 'I was an army lawyer myself. I know the form.' He took a box of Black Sobranie cigarettes from his pocket and lit one. George could only imagine the impression that would make in the lawyers' room at Buxton if Pritchard ended up presenting the case for the prosecution at the committal. Thank God the justices wouldn't be in there too. 'I've read the case papers,' Pritchard said. 'And examined the photographs.' He gave an involuntary shudder. 'They are truly some of the most repugnant I have ever seen. I've no doubt that we'll get a conviction on the rape charge on the basis of those photographs alone. What we need to discuss now is whether we have enough evidence to proceed with a charge of murder. The principal obstacle is, of course, the absence of a body.'

George opened his mouth, but Pritchard raised one warning finger to secure silence. 'Now, we must consider the corpus delicti – not, as most people think, the body of the victim, but rather the body of the crime. Which is to say, the essential elements of a crime and the circumstances in which it has been committed. In the case of murder, it is necessary for the prosecution to establish that a death has occurred, that the dead person is the person alleged to have been killed, and that their death was the result of unlawful violence. The easiest way to demonstrate this is by the presence of a corpse, wouldn't you say?'

'There are precedents for murder convictions in the absence of a body, though,' George said. 'Haigh, the acid-bath murderer, and James Camb. And Michael

Onufrejczyk, the pig farmer. That's the case where the Lord Chief Justice said that the fact of death could be proved by circumstantial evidence. Surely we've got enough of that for it to be worth bringing a prosecution?'

Pritchard smiled. 'I see you've studied the leading precedents. I must say, Inspector Bennett, I'm mightily intrigued by the circumstances of this case. There's no denying that it presents some seemingly intractable problems. However, as you rightly point out, there is a remarkable amount of circumstantial evidence. Now, if we could just review that evidence?'

For two hours, they went through every detail that pointed to Philip Hawkin having murdered his step-daughter. Pritchard questioned them closely and intelligently, probing to try to expose weaknesses in the chain of logic. The barrister gave little away of his personal response to their explanations, but he was clearly fascinated.

'There's something more, something that wasn't in your papers,' Clough concluded. 'We only got the report late yesterday afternoon. The blood on the shirt is the same group as Alison's, and it comes from a female, same as the other blood. But there's also some scorching and powder on the shirt, as there would be if a gun had been fired very close to it. And there's no question that it's Hawkin's shirt.'

'All grist to your mill, Sergeant. Even without this latest piece of evidence, there's little doubt in my mind that Hawkin has killed the girl. But the question remains whether we can put together a case that will satisfy a jury.' Pritchard ran a hand through his hair, rendering it even more chaotic. George could see why he'd chosen to become a barrister; under a horsehair wig, he'd look almost normal. And although there was no denying his upper-class origins, his voice wasn't so pukka that it would alienate a jury.

'Wherever the body is, he's done a good job of hiding it. We're not going to find it unless someone stumbles over it by accident. I don't think we're going to get much more than we've already got,' George said, trying not to sound as despondent as he always felt when Anne's unsettled sleeping woke him to brood in the small hours.

Pritchard swivelled from left to right in his chair. 'Still, it's a fascinating challenge, isn't it? I can't remember the last time I read a set of case papers that got the old juices flowing like this. What a battle of wits in the courtroom! I can't help thinking it would be enormous fun to get this one off the ground.'

'Would you do the prosecuting, then?' Clough asked.

'Because it's clearly going to be controversial, we'd use a QC, both for the committal hearing and the actual trial. But I would certainly be his junior, and I'd be largely responsible for preparing the case. I'm bound to say, I'm in favour of pressing forward with this.' Again he raised an admonitory finger. 'But that doesn't mean you can go ahead and charge. I will have to take this to the Director himself and convince him that we will not be exposing ourselves to ridicule if we pursue this case. I'm sure you know how our betters loathe being laughed at,' he added with an ironic smile.

'So when will we hear?' George asked.

'By the end of the week,' Pritchard said decisively. 'He'll want to sit on it for weeks, but time is of the essence here, I feel. I'll call you on Friday at the latest.' Pritchard got to his feet and held out his hand. 'Inspector, Sergeant.' He shook their hands. 'It's been a pleasure. Fingers crossed, eh?'

Daily News, *Monday, 17th February 1964, p.1*

Missing girl: Murder charge

By a Staff Reporter

In a sensational new development, police last night charged 37-year-old Philip Hawkin with the murder of his stepdaughter, missing school-girl Alison Carter.

The unusual aspect of the charge is that Alison's body has not been discovered. The pretty blonde 13-year-old has not been seen since she left her home in the tiny Derbyshire hamlet of Scardale to walk her dog after school on 11th December last year.

Hawkin will appear before Buxton magistrates tomorrow to be remanded for committal.

Not unique

This is not the first time murder charges have been brought where no body has been found. In the case of John George Haigh, the notorious acid-bath murderer, all that was found of his victim was a gallstone, a few bones and her false teeth.

But this residue was enough to demonstrate that a body had been disposed of and Haigh was hanged for murder.

James Camb, a steward on a luxury liner plying between South Africa and England, was accused of murdering a passenger, the actress Gay Gibson.

He claimed she had died from a fit while he had been alone with her in her cabin. He had panicked, thinking he would be accused of killing her, and pushed her body through a porthole.

His story was not believed and he was found guilty.

A further case occurred on a remote farm in Wales where a Polish war hero was convicted of murdering his business partner and feeding his body to the pigs on the farm they jointly owned.

The Committal

George woke at six on Monday, 24th February. He slipped out of bed, trying not to disturb Anne, and quietly padded downstairs in dressing gown and slippers. He made a pot of tea and carried it through to the living room. Pulling back the curtains to watch the dark give way to dawn, he was astonished to see Tommy Clough's car parked outside. The glowing coal of a cigarette revealed his sergeant was as wide awake as he was.

Minutes later, Clough was sitting opposite George, a steaming china cup nestled in one of his large hands. 'I thought you'd be up bright and early an' all. I hope Hawkin's losing as much sleep as we are,' he said bitterly.

'Between Anne's restlessness and worrying about this committal, I can't remember the last time I had eight hours' sleep,' George agreed.

'How's she doing?'

George shrugged. 'She gets tired easily. We went to see *The Great Escape* at the Opera House on Friday night, and she fell asleep halfway through. And she frets.' He sighed. 'I don't suppose it helps that she never knows when I'm going to be home.'

'Things'll ease up a bit after the trial,' Clough consoled him.

'I suppose so. I can't help worrying that he's going to get away with it. I mean, we've got to show our hand at the committal to get the justices to agree to send him for trial at the assizes. Then he'll have at least a couple of months to construct a defence, knowing exactly what we've got to throw at him. It's not like Perry Mason, where we can suddenly spring a surprise clincher at the last minute.'

'The lawyers wouldn't be going ahead with it if they didn't think they had a good chance of winning,' Clough reminded him. 'We've done our bit. All we can do now is leave it up to them,' he added philosophically.

George snorted. 'Is that supposed to make me feel better? Tommy, I hate this stage of a case. Everything's out of my hands, I can't influence what happens. I feel so powerless. And if Hawkin isn't convicted . . . well, never mind the lawyers, I'm going to feel like *I've* failed.' He leaned back in his chair and lit a cigarette. 'I couldn't bear that, for all sorts of reasons. Mostly because a killer would have walked free. But I'm human enough to take it personally. Can you imagine how happy it would make DCI Carver? Can you imagine the headlines that sewer rat Don Smart would get out of it?'

'Come on, George, everybody knows the way you've sweated this one. If Carver had been in charge, we'd never even have got the evidence for the rape charge. And that's rock solid. It's not possible that he can wriggle out of that, whatever happens over the murder. And you can bet your bottom dollar that any judge who hears the evidence and then gets a jury stupid enough to return "not guilty" on the murder charge is going to use the rape conviction to hit Hawkin with the maximum possible sentence. He's not going to be walking Scardale again in a hurry.'

George sighed. 'You're right. I just wish we could have tied Hawkin more closely to the gun. I mean, how much more unlucky can we get? There's one man who could possibly identify the gun we've got as the Webley that was stolen from St Albans. The previous owner, Mrs Hawkin's neighbour Mr Wells. And where is he? Spending a few months with his daughter who's emigrated to Australia. And not a single one of his friends or neighbours has a forwarding address. They can't even remember exactly when he's due back. Of course, we suspect that Hawkin's mother has all these details at her fingertips, being Mr and Mrs Wells's best friend, but she's certainly not going to tell those nasty policemen who are making those terrible allegations against her loving son,' he added with withering sarcasm.

He got to his feet. 'I'm going to have a wash and a shave. Do you want to make a fresh pot of tea? I'll take Anne a cup when I get dressed. Then I'll buy you a full English at the transport caff.'

'Sounds good to me. We'll need stoking up. It's going to be a long day.'

The town hall clock struck ten, its bass note penetrating the courtroom across the road. Jonathan Pritchard raised his head from the pile of papers in front of him, his eyebrows raised in expectation. Next to him, still absorbed in his notes, was the burly figure of Desmond Stanley, QC. A former Oxford rugby blue, Stanley had avoided running to fat in his forties with a strict regime of exercise that he insisted on conducting wherever he worked. As well as the usual wig, gown and bands of the barrister, Stanley's court bag always contained his dumbbells. In robing rooms up and down the country, he had bent and stretched, performed push-ups and squat thrusts before walking into court and prosecuting or defending the worst criminals the legal system could throw at him.

What was odd was that he never looked healthy. His skin had a naturally sallow cast, his lips were bloodlessly pale and his dark-brown eyes watered constantly. He always had a flamboyantly coloured silk handkerchief tucked into one sleeve so he could make regular dabs at his rheumy eyes. The first time George had met him, he had wondered if Stanley would live long enough to try the case. Afterwards, Pritchard had put him right. 'He'll outlive the lot of us,' he confided. 'Be glad he's on our side and not against us because Desmond Stanley is a shark. Trust me on this.'

Pritchard felt even more grateful to have Stanley on his side when he saw who the opposing barrister was. Rupert Highsmith, QC, had earned his formidable reputation as a surgically precise and ruthless cross-examiner in a series of high-profile cases in the early 1950s, when he was still a young barrister. Another ten years at the bar had not blunted his skills; rather, they had taught him a series of new tricks that left his opponents smarting, so much so that lesser talents grew reluctant to draw shaky material from their witnesses because they feared what he might do to it on cross.

Now, Highsmith was leaning back confidently in his chair, scanning the crowded press benches and public gallery, his profile as sharply geometric as if it had been constructed from a child's set of wooden shapes. Unkind colleagues at the bar whispered that he had had cosmetic surgery to keep his jawline so taut. He always liked to check out his audience, to assess the impact his case was likely to have. It was a good turn-out today, he thought. A good showcase for his talents. He was one of the few defence barristers who shone at committals. Because the committal hearing's only purpose was to decide whether the prosecution had a prima facie case against the accused, usually only the prosecution would put their case before the magistrates. The sole opportunity Highsmith would have to demonstrate his skills was in cross-examining their witnesses. And that was what he did best.

A door at the side of the courtroom opened and Hawkin walked in, flanked by two police officers. On George's instructions, he was handcuffed to neither. The detective was determined to do nothing that might elicit the slightest sympathy for Hawkin. Besides, he knew the defence barrister's first action would be to demand the handcuffs be removed, and the magistrates would probably agree, not least because it would be hard for them not to see landowner Hawkin as one of themselves. And Pritchard had emphasized how important it was psychologically that first blood should not go to the defence.

Eighteen nights behind bars had made little impact on Philip Hawkin's appearance. His dark hair was shorter than usual, since prisoners have no choice of barber but must take what they are given. But it was still glossy and smooth, slicked back from his broad, square forehead. His dark-brown eyes flicked around the courtroom before settling on his barrister. The smile that appeared to hover perpetually on his lips widened in acknowledgement of Highsmith's curt nod. Hawkin took his time entering the dock, carefully adjusting the trousers of his sober dark suit as he settled himself on the bench seat.

The door behind the magistrates' raised bench opened and the court clerk jumped to his feet, calling, 'All rise.' Chairs scraped back on the tiled floor as the three justices filed in. Hawkin was among the first to his feet, his bearing showing a deference that Pritchard noticed and filed away for further reference. Either Hawkin was a good actor, or else he really believed these magistrates had power over him that they would use to his advantage.

The three men who would sit in judgement over the case for the prosecution settled themselves, followed in shuffling disorder by everyone else except the court clerk. He reminded them that the court was in session to consider the proceedings to commit Philip Hawkin of Scardale Manor, Scardale in the county of Derbyshire for trial.

Desmond Stanley got to his feet. 'Your Worships, I appear for the Director of Public Prosecutions in this matter. Philip Hawkin is accused of the rape of Alison Carter, aged thirteen. He is further accused that on a separate occasion, on or about the eleventh of December, nineteen sixty-three, he did murder the said Alison Carter.'

The only person smiling in the courtroom was Don Smart, bent over his shorthand notebook. The ringmaster was on his feet. The circus had begun.

*   *   *

After he'd given his evidence and suffered the whip of Highsmith's incisive cross-examination, George walked out of the witness box and back through the crowded courtroom, his head high, two spots of colour burning in his cheeks. Tomorrow, he'd come back and sit in the body of the court to listen to the rest of the prosecution case. But now, he wanted a cigarette and an hour's peace. He was about to run down the stairs when he heard Clough call his name. He half turned. 'Not now, Tommy. Meet me in the Baker's at opening time.' Using the newel post as a pivot, he swung down the stairs and rushed out of the building.

Within forty minutes, he was panting on the rounded summit of Mam Tor, high on the ridge where limestone meets millstone grit, the White Peak on his right, the Dark Peak on his left. The wind whipped the breath from his mouth, and the temperature was dropping even faster than the sun. George threw back his head and roared his pent-up frustration to the scudding clouds and the indifferent sheep.

He turned to face the dark crouch of Kinder Scout, its intractable moorland blocking any vista north. He swung through ninety degrees and looked along the ridge past Hollins Cross, Lose Hill Pike and the distant pimple of Win Hill, with Stanage Edge and Sheffield invisible beyond. Then another ninety-degree turn to gaze at the white scar of Winnats Pass and the dips and rises of the limestone dales beyond. Finally, he faced east, scanning the roll of Rushup Edge and the gentle descent to Chapel-en-le-Frith. Somewhere out there, Alison Carter was lying, her body prey to nature, her life snuffed out.

He'd done what he could. Now it was up to others. He had to learn to let go.

Later, he found Clough nursing the remains of a pint at a quiet table in the corner of the Baker's Arms. The locals knew enough to leave them in peace, and the landlord had already refused service to three reporters, including Don Smart. He had threatened to complain to the next session of the licensing magistrates. The landlord had chuckled and said, 'They'd give me a medal. You're here and gone – we've all got to live here.'

George walked over with a fresh pint for Clough and one for himself. 'I needed some air,' he said as he sat down. 'If I'd stuck around, you'd have me in the cells on a charge of murdering a QC.'

'What a shit,' Clough said, pretending to spit on the floor.

'I suppose he'd say he's only doing his job.' George took a deep draught of his beer. 'Ah, that's better. I've been up Mam Tor, blowing the cobwebs away. Well, at least now we can see where the defence is coming from. It's a conspiracy by me to frame Philip Hawkin to ensure my future promotions.'

'The magistrates won't fall for that.'

'A jury might,' George said bitterly.

'Why would they? You come over as Mr Nice Guy. You've only got to look at Hawkin and the alarm bells start ringing. He's got that look that women can't resist and men hate on sight. Unless Highsmith can swing an all-female jury, there's no chance of that defence running.'

'I hope you're right. Anyway, cheer me up. Tell me what I missed.'

Clough grinned. 'You missed Charlie Lomas. He cleans up well, I'll say that for him. He managed to wear a suit without looking like he was in a straitjacket. Nervous as a cat in a kennel, but the lad stuck to his guns, I'll give him that. Stanley did a good catch-up on Highsmith's smear job. He got Charlie to talk about the lead mine and how it would have been out of the question for an outsider like you to have made your way there, even with the book. He also got Charlie to explain how, although Hawkin is a relative newcomer to the dale, he's done a lot of exploring for his picture-postcard photographs.'

George gave a sigh of relief. 'How did he get on with Highsmith?'

'He just stuck to his guns. Wouldn't be shifted. Yes, he was sure it was Wednesday he saw Hawkin walking the fields. No, it wasn't Tuesday. Nor Monday neither. He was solid as a rock, was Charlie. He made a good impression on the mags, you could tell.'

'Thank God somebody did.'

'Stop feeling sorry for yourself, George. You did fine. Highsmith tried to make you look bent, but he didn't succeed. Considering how little solid evidence we've got, I'd say we're doing all right in there. Now, do you want the good news?'

George's head came up as if it was on a string. 'There's good news?' he demanded.

Clough grinned. 'Oh aye, I think you could say that.' He took his time getting his cigarettes out and lighting up. 'I had another word with the sergeant down in St Albans.'

'Wells has turned up?' George could hardly contain himself.

'Not yet, no.'

George slumped back in his seat, sighing. 'That's the news I'm holding my breath for,' he admitted.

'Well, this isn't half bad. Turns out our sergeant knows Hawkin. He didn't want to say anything till he'd spoken to one or two other folk and got the nod from them that it was all right to talk to me.' Clough drained his pint. 'Same again?'

George nodded in amused frustration. 'Oh, go on, I know you're enjoying dragging it out. You might as well pay for your pleasure.'

By the time Clough returned, George had smoked half a cigarette with the nervous concentration of a man about to enter a no-smoking train compartment on a long journey. 'Come on then,' he urged, leaning forward and sliding his pint towards him. 'Let's hear it.'

'Sergeant Stillman's wife is a Tawny Owl at one of the local Brownie packs. Hawkin turned up offering to be their official photographer. He'd do pictures at parades, camps, that sort of thing, and sell the pictures back to the Brownies and their families at a knockdown price. In exchange, he said he wanted to take portrait photographs of the girls for his own portfolio. It all seemed above board. It wasn't as if Hawkin was a stranger. Him and his mum were both members of the church the Brownie pack was attached to. And he was always perfectly happy for the girls' mothers to come along when he was taking their pictures.' Clough paused, eyebrows raised.

'So what went wrong?' George asked on cue.

'Time went by. Hawkin got friendly with some of the older girls and started setting up sessions without their mothers. There were a couple of . . . incidents. First time, he denied everything, said the girl was telling lies to get attention. Second time, same thing, only this time he said that the girl was getting her own back because Hawkin wasn't interested in photographing her any more. He said she knew the fuss there had been about the first girl's accusation and threatened to say the same things if he wouldn't give her money for sweets and carry on taking her photograph. Well, nobody wanted any trouble, and there wasn't any real evidence, so Sergeant Stillman had a quiet word with Hawkin. Suggested he should stay away from young girls to avoid any possibility of misunderstanding.'

George let out a low whistle. 'Well, well, well. I thought there must be something somewhere. Child molesters don't suddenly start up at Hawkin's age. Well done, Tommy. At least we know we've not been letting ourselves get carried away with some daft notion. Hawkin is exactly what we think he is.'

Clough nodded. 'The only trouble is, we can't use any of it in court. What Stillman has to say is second-hand hearsay.'

'What about the girls?'

Clough snorted. 'Stillman won't even tell me their names. The main reason it never came to formal charges before was that the mothers were adamant that their little girls weren't going to be put through the ordeal of going to court. If they wouldn't hear of it on an indecency, there's no chance of them being persuaded on a murder that's in the headlines like this one.'

George nodded sad agreement. He couldn't argue with people who wanted to protect their kids, even when the damage was already done. Now he was himself about to become a father, however, he felt for the first time in his life the tug of vigilantism. He couldn't understand why Hawkin was still at large. As a policeman, Stillman had plenty of resources to hand to damage the man, physically and socially. But he hadn't. He'd even been reluctant to tell Clough. 'They obviously do things differently down there,' he said wearily. 'If I knew, as a copper, that some pervert had molested a kid belonging to a friend of mine, I couldn't let him walk away. I'd have to find a way of making him pay. Either through the law or . . .'

'I thought you didn't believe in the dark alleyways of justice?' Clough said ironically.

'It's different with kids, though, isn't it?'

It was the great unanswerable question. They pondered it in silence for the rest of their drinks. When George came back with the third round, he seemed a little brighter. 'We've still got enough, even without the St Albans stuff.'

'I think Stillman feels guilty about not taking more action,' Clough said.

'Good. So he should. Maybe he'll make a point of keeping an eye open for the return of Mr and Mrs Wells.'

'I hope so, George. Even if we get our committal, we're still a long way off home and dry.'

Daily News, *Friday, 28th February 1964, p.1*

Alison: Stepfather
to be tried for murder

The stepfather of missing schoolgirl Alison Carter will stand trial for her murder even

339

though the 13-year-old's body has not been found.

In a dramatic decision yesterday Buxton magistrates committed Philip Hawkin for trial to the Derby Assizes on charges of murder and rape.

Alison has not been seen since she disappeared from the remote Derbyshire village of Scardale on 11th December last year.

During the four-day committal, her mother, who married Hawkin just over a year ago, gave evidence for the prosecution. It was Mrs Carter (as she prefers now to be known) who discovered the gun which prosecuting counsel Mr Desmond Stanley, QC claimed had been used to murder her daughter.

Yesterday the court heard from Professor John Hammond that the absence of blood at the alleged murder scene did not necessarily mean no killing had taken place.

He also testified that blood found on a heavily stained shirt identified as belonging to Hawkin could have come from Alison. *(cont. on p.2)*

The Trial

1

High Peak Courant, *Friday, 12ᵗʰ June 1964*

Peak Murder Trial Next Week

The trial of Scardale landowner Philip Hawkin
begins on Monday at Derby Assizes.

Hawkin is charged with the rape and murder
of his stepdaughter, Alison Carter. At his committal before Buxton justices in February, his
wife was among the prosecution witnesses.

Alison has not been seen since the afternoon of 11ᵗʰ December last year when she
disappeared after taking her collie Shep for a
walk in the dale after school.

The presiding judge at the trial will be Mr
Justice Fletcher Sampson.

The fanfare of trumpets seemed to hang in the air like
the shimmer of a rainbow. In all his scarlet and ermine
glory, Mr Justice Fletcher Sampson had arrived at
the oak-panelled county hall with his mounted police

escort. George Bennett sat in an anteroom, smoking a cigarette at an open window. He imagined the dramatic procession of the judge to his courtroom, to take his appointed place at the judicial rostrum beneath the royal coat of arms. At his side on this, the first day of the Assize Court, would be the High Sheriff of Derbyshire in full ceremonial uniform.

By now, he thought, they'd be in the courtroom, staring down from the rostrum at counsel, arrayed before them in their grey wigs and black gowns, their brilliant white bands and shirt-fronts making them look like strange hybrids of hooded crows and magpies. Behind the barristers, their support staff of solicitors and clerks. Behind them, the ornate but solid dock where Hawkin would sit, flanked by a pair of police officers, dwarfed by the timber and kept firmly in his place by the row of iron spikes that topped the wood. Behind Hawkin, the press benches with their assortment of eager youths desperate to make their marks, and old hacks who needed to feel they'd seen and heard it all. Don Smart's fox-red hair would stand out among them like a blaze. Above and behind the journalists, the public gallery, crammed with the concerned faces of Scardale and the prurient eyes of the others.

And over to one side, just beyond the witness box, the most important people in the place would soon sit. The jury. Twelve men and women who would hold Philip Hawkin's fate in their hands. George tried not to think about the possibility of them rejecting the case he had worked so hard with the lawyers to construct, but he couldn't help the niggle of fear that squirmed inside him in the night when he tried for sleep that miserably eluded him too often. He sighed and flicked the butt into the street below. He wondered where Tommy Clough was. They'd been supposed to meet at the police station at eight, but when George had arrived, Bob Lucas had told him Clough had left a message that he'd see him at court. 'Probably chasing some skirt down Derby way,' Lucas had said with a wink. 'Trying to take his mind off the trial.'

George lit another cigarette and leaned on the window-sill. Now the clerk of the assize would be calling all those who had business before his Lady the Queen's Justices of Oyer and Terminer and General Gaol Delivery for the Jurisdiction of the High Court to draw near and give their attention. God save the Queen. He remembered looking up these strangely grandiose terms in his early days of infatuation with the law. The Commission of Oyer and Terminer literally meant to hear and determine; it was originally the royal writ that empowered the King's Judges and Serjeants to sit in judgement on treason and felonies. By 1964, it had become an archaic phrase to cover the commission granted to circuit judges, giving them authority to hold courts for trial. Under General Gaol Delivery, the custodial authorities were obliged to hand over to the judge all the persons awaiting trial and whose names were listed in the court calendar.

In practice, today that would only apply to Philip Hawkin. The sole scheduled murder trial of the assizes, his case would be heard first.

Two days previously, George had had one last try at persuading Hawkin to confess. He'd visited him behind the grim high walls of the prison, where they'd come face to face in a tiny interview room that was no more appetizing than the cells themselves. Hawkin had lost weight, George was pleased to see. The principle that a man was regarded as innocent until proven guilty never held fast inside a gaol; George knew that Hawkin had already been given a taste of his own medicine behind bars. Prison officers were never quick to intervene when a rapist was on the receiving end of an assault. And they always made sure the other prisoners knew exactly who the child molesters were. While the civilized part of him objected, the prospective father in George was in total sympathy.

They had eyed each other across a narrow table. 'Did you bring some cigarettes?' Hawkin demanded.

Silently, George placed an open packet of Gold Leaf between them. Hawkin snatched one greedily and George lit it for him. Hawkin drew in the smoke and his whole body relaxed. He ran a hand over his hair and said, 'I'll be out of here in a few days. You know that, don't you? My brief is going to tell the world just how bent you bastards are. You know I never killed Alison, and I'm going to make you eat your words, one by one.'

George shook his head, almost admiring the man's defiance. 'You're whistling in the dark, Hawkin,' he said, deliberately condescending. 'However hard you try to make the world believe otherwise, I'm an honest copper. You know and I know that nobody's fitted you up. Nobody had to, because you killed Alison and we caught you.'

'I never killed her,' he said, his voice intense as his eyes. 'You've got me locked up in here, and whoever took Alison is walking around laughing at you.'

George shook his head. 'It's not going to work, Hawkin. It's a good act, but all the evidence stacks up against you.' He took a cigarette from the pack and lit it nonchalantly. 'Mind you,' he continued, 'you still have a choice.'

Hawkin said nothing, but cocked his head to one side, his lips a thin, unsmiling line.

'You can choose whether you do life, with a chance of seeing the outside world again in twenty years or so. Or whether you hang. It's up to you. It's not too late to change your plea. You go guilty and you live. You make us work for it, and you hang. By the neck. Till you are well and truly dead.'

Hawkin sneered. 'They're not going to hang me. Even if they find me guilty, there's not a judge in the land would have the nerve to send me to the gallows. Not on evidence like you've got.'

George leaned back in his seat, his eyebrows raised. 'You think not? If it's good enough for a jury to convict you, it's good enough for a judge to hang you. Especially a hard nut like Fletcher Sampson. He's not scared of the bleeding heart liberals.' He suddenly jerked forward, forearms on the table, gaze locked on Hawkin's. 'Look, do yourself a favour. Tell us where to find her. Put her mother's mind at rest. It'll go down well with the judge. You get a good mitigation from your barrister and you could be out in ten years.'

Hawkin shook his head in frustration. 'You're not hearing properly, George,' he said, turning the name into an insult. 'I don't know where she is.'

George got to his feet, sweeping his packet of cigarettes into his pocket. 'Please yourself, Hawkin. No skin off my nose. I'll get the promotion whether you cough or not. Because we are going to win out there.'

Now, as he watched the people in the street below

about their business, oblivious to the drama unfolding inside the courtroom, he wished he felt as confident as he hoped he had sounded. He turned away from the window and slumped into a chair. By now, the charges would have been read and Hawkin would no doubt have answered, 'Not guilty,' twice.

Stanley would wait until the jury were settled, then make the opening statement for the prosecution. It was, George thought, the most crucial moment of any trial. He believed people were most impressed by what they heard at the start of a trial, when they were fresh and their minds most open to persuasion. If the prosecuting barrister delivered an opening address full of conviction and stated what he intended to prove as if it were already demonstrably incontrovertible fact, it left the defence with a steep mountain to climb. George had every confidence that Stanley could do just that. George didn't expect to give his own evidence until the second day of the trial, but he couldn't stay away.

He just wished Clough would turn up. Then at least he'd have someone to share his restlessness with.

Desmond Stanley rose. 'Your Lordship, I appear for the Director of Public Prosecutions in this matter. Philip Hawkin is accused of the rape of Alison Carter, aged thirteen. He is further accused that on a separate occasion, on or about the eleventh of December, nineteen sixty-three, he did murder the said Alison Carter.'

He paused to let the gravity of the charges sink in. The courtroom was silent; it was as if everyone had stopped breathing the better to hear Stanley's sonorous voice.

'Ladies and gentlemen of the jury, Philip Hawkin

moved to Scardale in the summer of nineteen sixty-two, following the death of his uncle. He inherited a substantial estate – the entire dale, consisting of fertile farmland, extensive stock in the shape of sheep and cattle, Scardale Manor itself and eight cottages comprising the hamlet of Scardale. Everyone who lives and works in Scardale does so solely with his blessing, which you should bear in mind when you listen to the evidence of those who are his tenants. It shows commendable courage and lack of self-interest that those people are prepared to appear as witnesses for the prosecution.

'Not long after he arrived in Scardale, Philip Hawkin began to take an interest in one of the women in the village, Ruth Carter. Mrs Carter had been widowed six years previously and had a daughter, Alison, from that marriage. Alison was then twelve years old. You must consider, as our evidence unfolds, whether Hawkin's primary interest was in the mother or the daughter. It may have been that he sought to divert suspicion from his perverted interest in Alison by marrying her mother. If Alison had accused her tormentor, who would have believed such a tale from the daughter of his new bride? Doubtless she would have been accused of acting out of dislike of her stepfather, or jealousy of the attention he had won from her mother. Whatever his motive, the accused pursued Mrs Carter ruthlessly until eventually she agreed to marry him.

'It is our contention that at some point after the marriage took place, Hawkin began to molest sexually his stepdaughter. You will see photographic evidence of a particularly loathsome kind that demonstrates not only the debauch of his stepdaughter but also proves beyond a scintilla of doubt that Philip Hawkin is guilty of the rape of Alison Carter in the most calculated and disgusting manner.

'The Crown intends to show that Alison was further victimized by a man who owed her the duty of care of a father. We may never know the reason why Philip Hawkin decided to silence her for ever. She may have threatened to reveal his bestial practices to her mother or to someone in authority; she may have refused to cooperate further with his vile demands; he may simply have ceased to find her attractive and wished to dispose of her to leave him free to debauch another child. As I said, we may never know. But what we do intend to prove is that, whichever was his motive, Philip Hawkin abducted Alison Carter at gunpoint, abused her sexually for one last time and then murdered her.

'On the afternoon of the eleventh of December last year, Alison Carter left the family home to take a walk after school with her dog, Shep. It is our contention that Philip Hawkin followed her into a nearby wood, where he forced her to accompany him. Her dog was later found there tied to a tree, its muzzle taped shut with elastoplast identical to that purchased by Hawkin the previous week in a local shop.

'He then took her to a secluded spot, a cave in some disused mine workings whose very existence was unknown to all the other inhabitants of the dale save one. On the way, while passing through another piece of woodland, Alison somehow managed to break free and a struggle took place. She struck her head against a tree in the course of this struggle and Hawkin was then able to transport her to the cave. We will present forensic evidence to support this.

'Once her stepfather had managed to bring her to this isolated spot, safe from prying eyes and ears, he brutally raped her yet again. Then he killed her. Afterwards, he moved the body to another site. Although it has not been found, that is not entirely surprising, for the limestone around Scardale is riddled with underground cave systems and potholes. But he had no time to return to clear away the rest of the evidence, for by the time he returned home in time for tea, the hunt was already afoot for his stepdaughter.

'We know for a fact that shots were fired in that cave by a gun that was later found on Philip Hawkin's property, in a locked outhouse which he used as a photographic darkroom. We know that a shirt belonging to Philip Hawkin was heavily stained with blood which is not his. There is no forensic evidence to contradict the convincing conclusion that Hawkin murdered Alison Carter.

'There is an overwhelming burden of evidence to support the case for the prosecution, which we intend to demonstrate in this courtroom. With Your Lordship's permission, I should like to call my first witness?'

Sampson nodded. 'Please proceed, Mr Stanley.'

'Thank you. I call Mrs Ruth Carter.'

Now the silence in the body of the court was disturbed by a ripple of muttered comments. The only island of silence was the stolid-faced contingent of Scardale villagers. Every adult who was not required as a witness was there, dressed uncomfortably in Sunday best, determined to see the justice they wanted done for their Alison.

Ruth Carter walked through the courtroom with

her eyes fixed firmly ahead of her. Not once did she succumb to the temptation to look at her husband in the dock. She wore a simple black two-piece suit, the collar of her white blouse the only relief from its bleakness. She carried a small black handbag, clutched tightly between her gloved fingers. Once she reached the witness box, she carefully positioned herself so she could not accidentally catch a glimpse of Hawkin. She took the oath without a stumble, her voice low and clear. Stanley mopped his eyes and looked gravely at her. He took her through the formal questions of identity and relationship, then moved straight into the meat of his interrogation. 'Do you remember the afternoon of Wednesday, the eleventh of December last year?'

'I'll never forget it,' she said simply.

'Can you tell the magistrates what happened that day?'

'My daughter Alison came home from school and came into the kitchen where I was getting the tea ready. She went straight out again to take the dog for a walk. She usually did that unless the weather was too bad. She liked to get out into the open after a day in the classroom. The last words she said to me were, "See you in a bit, Mam." I haven't seen her from that day to this. She never came back.' Ruth looked up at the bench of magistrates. 'I've lived in hell ever since.'

Gently, Stanley led Ruth through the events of that evening; her desperate door-to-door search of the village, her emotional call to the police and their arrival at the manor house. 'What was your husband's attitude to Alison's absence?'

Her mouth tightened. 'He took it all very lightly. He kept saying she was doing it on purpose to frighten us

350

so that when she came home, we'd be so glad to see her we'd let her get her own way.'

'Did he agree you should call the police?'

'No, he was very opposed to that. He said there was no need. He said nothing could happen to harm her in Scardale, where she knew every inch of the land and everybody on it.' Her voice shook and she took a small white handkerchief from the black handbag. Stanley waited while she dabbed her eyes and blew her nose.

'Did your husband resent your devotion to your daughter?' Stanley asked. 'I mean in a general way.'

'I never thought so. I thought he spoiled her. He was always buying her things. He bought her an expensive record player, and every week he'd go into Buxton and buy her records. He spent a fortune on doing out her bedroom – more than he ever spent on our room. He always said he was trying to make up for what she'd missed out on, and I was daft enough to believe him.'

Stanley let her words sink in. 'What do you think now?' he asked.

'I think he was buying her silence. I should have taken more notice of how she was with him.'

'And how was that?'

Ruth sighed and looked down at her feet. 'She never liked him. She wouldn't be in the same room alone with him, now I think about it. She was moody in the house, which she'd never been before, though everybody said she was just the same as always when she was away from me and him. At the time, I put it down to her thinking nobody could replace her dad. But I was just kidding myself.' She lifted her eyes and fixed the judge with a pleading gaze. 'I thought I was doing what was best for her as well as me when I married him. I thought she'd come round in time.'

'Did you know your husband took photographs of Alison?'

'Oh aye,' she said bitterly. 'He was always getting her to pose for him. He's a clever beggar, though. Nine times out of ten, it would all be innocent and above board and out there in public. Alison posing with the calves, Alison by the river. So I never questioned the other times when he took her off to one of the barns, or when he'd say he was going to have a session with her when I was out shopping.' She put a hand to her cheek, as if appalled by what she was saying. 'She tried to tell me what was happening, but all I heard was the words, not what was under them. A few times, she said she hated the photography sessions. She didn't like posing for him. But I told her not to be daft, that it was his hobby and it was something they could do together.'

Her words fell like stones in the courtroom. Throughout her testimony, Hawkin sat shaking his head, as if in puzzled wonderment that she could be saying such things about him.

'Moving on, Mrs Carter. Has your husband ever owned a gun?'

She nodded. 'Oh yes. He showed it to me after we were married. He said it was a wartime souvenir of his father's, but it wasn't licensed so I shouldn't tell anybody about it.'

'Did you notice anything distinctive about it?'

'The handle grip was all criss-crossed. But there was a chip out of the bottom corner on one side.'

Stanley made a note, then continued. 'Where did he keep the gun?'

'It was in his study, in a locked metal box.'

'Have you seen that box recently?'

'The police found it when they searched his study the day they arrested him. But it was empty.'

'Can Mrs Carter be shown exhibit . . .' Stanley shuffled his papers. 'Exhibit fourteen.'

The court clerk handed Ruth the Webley, tagged and labelled. 'That's it,' she said. 'The handle's chipped there, on the bottom, like I said.'

Hawkin frowned, casting a glance across at his barrister, Rupert Highsmith, who shook his head almost imperceptibly.

Stanley moved on to the discovery of the shirt and gun in Hawkin's darkroom, taking Ruth through the painful evidence with courtesy and patience. At last, he seemed to have reached the end of his questions. But halfway to his seat, he stopped, as if suddenly struck by something. 'One more thing, Mrs Carter. Have you ever asked your husband to buy elastoplast for you?'

Ruth looked at him as if he'd lost his senses. 'Elastoplast? When we need elastoplast, I buy it off the van.'

'The van?'

'The mobile shop that comes once a week. I never asked *him* to buy elastoplast.'

'Thank you, Mrs Carter. I have no further questions, but you must wait to see if my learned friend wants to ask you anything.' He sat down.

By then, the town hall clock had long since struck noon. Sampson leaned back in his seat and said, 'We'll adjourn now. We shall resume at two o'clock.'

Before the door had closed behind the judge, Hawkin was already being hustled from the court. He threw a look over his shoulder towards his wife and his mask of imperturbability finally slipped to reveal the bitter hatred behind it. Highsmith registered the look and sighed. He wished there was another way for him to exercise his skills to the full, but unfortunately, there was nothing more exacting or enthralling than defending someone he knew in his bones to be guilty. He was often asked how it felt to know he'd helped murderers escape punishment. He would smile and say it was a mistake to confuse the law with morality. It was, after all, the prosecution's job to prove their case, not the defence barrister's.

After lunch, he set out to do what damage he could to the prosecution case. He made no pretence at befriending Ruth. His face stern, he went straight to the heart of the case. 'You've been married before, Mrs Hawkin?' The prosecution might choose to obscure her relationship to the man in the dock, but he would use it against her like a weapon.

Ruth frowned. 'I don't answer to Mrs Hawkin any more,' she said coldly, but without defiance.

Highsmith's eyebrows rose and he angled his head towards the jury. 'But that is your legal name, is it not? You are the wife of Philip Hawkin, are you not?'

'To my shame, I am,' Ruth replied. 'But I choose not to be reminded of the fact and I'd thank you to show me the courtesy of calling me Mrs Carter.'

Highsmith nodded. 'Thank you for making it so clear precisely where you stand, Mrs *Carter*,' he said. 'Now perhaps you would be so good as to answer my question? You have been married before you vowed to love, honour and obey Mr Hawkin?'

'I was widowed when Alison was six.'

'So you'll know what I mean when I speak of a full married life?'

Ruth gave him a mutinous glare. 'I'm not stupid. And I did grow up on a farm.'

'Answer the question, please.' His voice was like a blade.

'Yes, I know what you mean.'

'And did you enjoy a full married life with your first husband?'

'I did.'

'Then you married Philip Hawkin. And you enjoyed a full married life with Mr Hawkin?'

Ruth looked him straight in the face, a dark flush on her cheeks. 'He was up to it, but not as often as I was used to,' she said, then gave a tiny shudder of distaste.

'So you noticed nothing abnormal in your husband's appetites?'

'Like I said, he wasn't that interested, not compared to my first husband.'

'Who was of course much younger than Mr Hawkin. Now, did you ever see your husband in a compromising position with Alison?'

'I don't know what you mean.'

He was impressed. She was holding her own far better than he'd expected. Most women of her class were so intimidated by his handsome, forbidding presence that they crumbled and gave him what he wanted to hear almost immediately. He shook his head and gave her a patronizing smile. 'Of course you do, Mrs

Carter. Did he visit her alone in her bedroom late at night?'

'Not that I ever knew about.'

'Did he enter the bathroom when she was in there?'

'Of course not.'

'Did he even sit with her on his knee?'

'No, she was too big for that.'

'In short, Mrs Carter, you never saw or heard anything that made you in the least suspicious of your husband's relationship with your daughter.' It was so definitely a statement rather than a question that Ruth didn't even appear to consider answering its implications. Highsmith glanced down at his papers. He looked up and cocked his head to one side.

'Now, the gun. You told the court your husband had a gun which he kept in a box in his study. Did you tell anyone else about this gun? Any of your family, your friends?'

'He said I was to keep my mouth shut about it. So I did.'

'So we only have your word for it that the gun was ever there in the first place.' Ruth opened her mouth to speak, but he steamrollered on. 'And of course, it was you who handed the gun over to the police, so you had plenty of opportunity to memorize any distinctive features on this otherwise unidentifiable gun. So we only have your word for it that there is any connection between your husband and the gun, don't we?'

'I didn't rape my daughter, mister. And I didn't shoot her either,' Ruth ground out. 'So I've no call to lie.'

Highsmith paused. He allowed his face to slip from grimness to open sympathy. 'But you want someone to blame, don't you, Mrs Carter? More than anything, you want to believe you know what happened to your daughter, and you want someone to blame. That's why you're so willing to go along with the case the police have concocted. You want your heart put at rest. You want someone to blame.'

Stanley was on his feet, objecting. But it was too late. Highsmith had muttered, 'No further questions,' and sat down. The damage was done.

Sampson frowned down at Highsmith. 'Mr Highsmith, I will not have counsel using the examination of witnesses as an excuse for making speeches. You will have your chance to express your views to the jury. Kindly confine yourself to that. Now, Mr Stanley, am I correct in thinking that your next witness is the chief police witness, Detective Inspector Bennett?'

'Yes, Your Lordship.'

'I think it would be as well to begin with his evidence tomorrow morning. This court has civil matters before it and I am minded to deal with those today.'

'As Your Lordship pleases,' Stanley said, ducking his head in a bow.

On the press benches, Don Smart drew a line across the page with a flourish. Plenty of good stuff for the headlines there. And tomorrow, he could watch George Bennett put the noose round Hawkin's disgusting neck. The door had barely closed behind the judge when he was on his feet and heading for the nearest phone.

Clough still hadn't appeared by the end of the afternoon, though a court usher had brought a phone message from Sergeant Lucas. 'Clough has been held up,' it read. 'He says he will see you tomorrow in Derby before the court convenes.' George wondered fleetingly what the detective sergeant was up to. Probably something to do with another case, he thought. In the weeks since the arrest of Philip Hawkin, both men had had plenty of work to occupy them during any time they had to spare from the construction of the Alison Carter case.

George emerged from the anteroom when he heard the murmuring of noise on the landing outside that told him the court had risen for the day. He caught a glimpse of Ruth Carter surrounded by friends and relatives, but made a point of not catching anyone's eye. Now the case had started, it was important that none of the witnesses conferred before they actually appeared to give their evidence. Instead, George moved against the flow of bodies and made his way into the courtroom. Highsmith and his junior had already left, but Stanley and Pritchard were still sitting at their table, heads together, deep in discussion.

'How was it?' George asked, helping himself to the chair next to Pritchard.

'Desmond was marvellous,' Pritchard said enthusiastically. 'Tremendous opening speech. The jury were transfixed. Highsmith wouldn't even speak to us at lunchtime. You'd have been so impressed, George.'

'Well done,' George said. 'How was Mrs Carter?'

The two barristers exchanged glances. 'A bit emotional,' Pritchard said. 'She broke down a couple of times in the box.' He gathered together the rest of his papers and tucked them into a folder.

'It works to our advantage, of course,' Stanley interjected. 'Nevertheless, I take no pleasure in making a lady cry.'

'She's been through the mill,' George said. 'I can't

begin to imagine how it feels to know you've married a man who's raped and killed your child.'

Pritchard nodded. 'She's bearing up well in the circumstances. She's a good witness. She doesn't back down, and her very stubbornness makes Highsmith look like a bully, which the jury don't like at all.'

'What defence is he going to run? Do you know?' George asked, standing up to let Pritchard and Stanley pick up their briefs and leave the courtroom for the robing room.

'Hard to imagine what he could credibly run, unless he tries to convince the jury that the police have framed his client.'

Stanley nodded. 'And that would be a bad mistake, I think. The British jury, like the British public, resents attacks on the police.' He smiled. 'They think of policemen as they do of Labradors – noble, loyal, good with children, man's protector and friend. In spite of evidence to the contrary, they refuse to admit policemen can be corrupt, sly or untruthful because to do so would be to admit we are on the very verge of anarchy. So by attacking you, Highsmith would be employing a strategy fraught with risk.'

'Needs must when the devil drives,' Pritchard commented drily. 'He'll be struggling with anything else. We might only have circumstantial evidence, but there's so much of it Highsmith needs a coherent counter-theory to undermine it. It won't be enough merely to offer alternative explanations for each and every piece of evidence.'

George was reassured by the calm competence of the two lawyers. 'I hope you're right.'

'We'll see you in the witness box tomorrow,' Pritchard

said. 'Go home to that lovely wife of yours and get a good night's sleep, George.'

He watched them exit through a side door, then slowly walked from the empty courtroom. The last thing he felt like was driving back through the lush green Derbyshire evening. He wished he could find a quiet pub and get drunk somewhere. But he had a wife nearly seven months pregnant at home, and she needed to see his strength, not his weakness. With a sigh, George dug his car keys out of his pocket and walked back into the world.

The Trial

2

George entered the witness room on the second day of Philip Hawkin's trial to find Tommy Clough sprawled in a chair, a bottle of lemonade by his feet, a cigarette in the corner of his mouth and the *Daily News* spread across his lap. He greeted his boss with a nod and waved the paper at him. 'Ruth Carter seems to have made a good impression with the jackals. I reckoned they'd turn her into the scapegoat. You know the kind of thing – The Woman Who Married a Monster,' Clough intoned with mock drama.

'I'm surprised they let her off the hook so lightly,' George admitted. 'I was expecting them to say she must have known what Hawkin was like, what he was doing to Alison. Like you, I honestly thought they'd blame her. But I suppose they saw for themselves the state she's in. That's not a woman who's turned a blind eye or connived at what that bastard did to her daughter.'

'I had breakfast with Pritchard at his fancy hotel,' Clough confided. 'He said she couldn't have been a better witness if they'd been coaching her for months. You've got a hard act to follow, George.'

'Breakfast with the barrister, Tommy? You're mixing

with the toffs. By the way, where did you get to yesterday?'

Clough straightened up in his chair, folding his newspaper shut and tossing it to the floor. 'Thought you'd never ask. I got a phone call late on Sunday night. Do you remember Sergeant Stillman?'

'In St Albans?' George was suddenly alert, leaning forward like a dog straining at a leash.

'The same. He rang to tell me Mr and Mrs Wells were back from Australia. Back two hours, to be precise. So I jumped in the car and drove straight down there. Eight o'clock yesterday morning I was knocking on their front door. They weren't best pleased to see me, but they obviously knew what I'd come for.'

George nodded grimly and threw himself into a chair. 'Hawkin's mother.'

'Aye. Like we thought, she must have had a forwarding address after all. Any road, I acted the innocent. I explained that the description of the Webley he'd had stolen corresponded with a gun used in the commission of a crime up in Derbyshire. I laid it on with a trowel that we were impressed by the accuracy of his description and how it had made the match very likely.'

George smiled. He could imagine Clough's subtle manoeuvring of Mr Wells into a corner he could only get out of with a tunnelling crew. 'So of course, when you showed him the photographs, he couldn't do anything else except identify his gun?'

Clough grinned. 'Got it in one. Anyway, I had to come clean then about Hawkin and the trial this week. Wells got into a right old state then. He couldn't testify against a friend and neighbour, we must have made a mistake, blah, blah, blah.'

362

George lit a cigarette. 'So what did you do?'

'I'd been up half the night. I wasn't in the mood. I arrested him for obstruction.'

George looked appalled. 'You arrested him?'

'Aye, I did. He was really annoying me,' Clough said self-righteously. 'Any road, before I could get the caution finished, he'd rolled over. Agreed to testify, agreed to come back to Derby with me then and there. So we both agreed to forget I'd arrested him. Then he gave his wife a brandy, since she looked like she was going to pass out, got his coat and hat and came back with me like a lamb.'

George shook his head in a mixture of outrage and admiration. 'One day, Tommy, one day . . . So where is he now?'

'In a very comfortable room at the Lamb and Flag. I took a full statement off him yesterday when we got back here, and Mr Stanley wants to put him on first thing this morning.' Clough grinned.

'Ahead of me?' George asked.

'Stanley doesn't want to hang about. He doesn't want to run the risk of Mrs Wells getting hold of Hawkin's mother and warning her that Wells is going to testify. He wants to try to catch Highsmith on the hop if he can.'

'But Mrs Hawkin's up here for the trial.'

'True. But I'd bet a tanner to a gold clock Mrs Wells will know who to ask to find out where Mrs Hawkin's staying.'

'Highsmith will object to a witness who wasn't included in the committal.'

'I know. But Stanley says the judge'll allow it, with Wells having been out of the country at the time.'

Clough got to his feet and dusted off the cigarette ash that had drifted down his grey flannel suit. He straightened his tie and winked at George. 'So I better go into court and see how he does.'

Richard Wells, retired civil servant, had already taken the oath when Clough slipped in to the back of the courtroom. He didn't look the type to have had the sort of war that would leave him with a Webley as a souvenir, the sergeant thought. If ever there was a man made for the Army Pay Corps, it was Richard Wells. Grey suit, grey hair, grey tie. Even his moustache looked timid and boring against the startling ruddiness of skin that had not taken kindly to strong Australian sun.

Hawkin was leaning forward intently in the dock, two vertical lines visible between his eyebrows. Clough found a childish pleasure in his obvious concern. Stanley took Wells through the formalities, then said conversationally, 'Is there anyone in this courtroom you have seen before?'

Wells nodded towards the dock. 'Philip Hawkin.'

'How do you know Mr Hawkin?'

'His mother is a neighbour of ours.'

'Was he familiar with your house?'

'He used to accompany his mother to our house for bridge evenings before he moved away.' Wells's eyes kept flickering away from the QC to the prisoner. He was clearly uncomfortable with his role, in spite of Stanley's easy manner.

'You used to own a Webley .38 revolver, did you not?'

'I did.'

'Did you ever show that gun to Mr Hawkin?'

Clough followed Wells's anguished stare up to the public gallery where it rested on Hawkin's elderly mother. Wells took a deep breath and mumbled, 'I may have done.'

'Think carefully, Mr Wells.' Stanley's voice was gentle. 'Did you or did you not show the Webley to Mr Hawkin?'

Wells swallowed hard. 'I did.'

'Where did you keep the gun?'

Wells relaxed visibly, his shoulders dropping a little from their defensive position. 'In a locked drawer in the bureau in the lounge.'

'And was that where you took it from when you showed it to Mr Hawkin?'

'It would have been.' Each word was dragged out slowly.

'So Mr Hawkin knew where the gun was kept?'

Wells looked down. 'I suppose so,' he mumbled.

The judge leaned forward. 'You must speak clearly, Mr Wells. The jury must be able to hear your answers.'

Stanley smiled. 'I am obliged, my lord. Now, Mr Wells, would you tell us what happened to the gun?'

Wells pressed his lips hard together for a moment then answered in a small, tight voice. 'It was stolen. In a burglary. Just over two years ago. We were on holiday.'

'Not a pleasant homecoming for you and your wife. Did you lose much?' Stanley asked, all sympathy.

Wells shook his head. 'A silver carriage clock. A gold watch and the gun. They didn't go any further than the lounge. The gold watch was in the drawer with the gun.'

'You gave a very good description of the gun to the police. Can you remember what it was that made it distinctive, apart from the serial number?'

Wells cleared his throat and smoothed his moustache. His eyes slid round to Hawkin, whose frown had deepened. 'There was a chip out of the bottom corner of the grip,' he said, his words tumbling over each other.

Stanley turned to the assistant clerk of the court. 'Would you be so kind as to show Mr Wells exhibit fourteen?'

The clerk picked up the Webley from the exhibits table and carried it across the courtroom to Wells. He turned the gun over so the witness had the opportunity to see both sides of the criss-crossed butt. 'Take your time,' Stanley said softly.

Wells looked up at the public gallery again. Clough saw Mrs Hawkin's face crumple as the weight of realization struck. 'It's my gun,' he said, his voice empty and flat.

'You're certain of that?'

Wells sighed. 'Yes.'

Stanley smiled. 'Thank you for coming here today, Mr Wells. Now, if you would stay where you are, my learned friend Mr Highsmith may have some questions for you.'

This would be interesting, Clough thought. There was almost nothing Highsmith could ask that wouldn't dig a deeper hole for his client. Hawkin, who had been scribbling desperately during the last few exchanges, passed a note to his solicitor, who gave it a swift glance then thrust it at Highsmith's junior, who placed it in front of Highsmith himself.

The barrister was on his feet now, the sharp lines of his face broken up in a smile. He looked briefly at the note then began to question Wells even more genially than Stanley had done. 'When your house was burgled, you were on holiday, is that right?'

'Yes,' Wells said wearily.

'Did you leave a key with any of your neighbours?'

Wells raised his head, a glimmer of hope in his eyes. 'Mrs Hawkin always had a key. In case of emergencies.'

'Mrs Hawkin always had a key,' Highsmith repeated, his eyes scanning the jury to make sure they'd taken his point. 'Did the police take fingerprints after your burglary?'

'They tried, but whoever broke in wore gloves, they said.'

'Did they ever indicate to you whether they had an idea who might be responsible?'

'No.'

'Did they ever say anything that might have suggested they suspected Mr Hawkin?'

Even as Wells said, 'No,' Stanley was on his feet.

'My lord,' he protested. 'My learned friend is not only leading the witness, but he is leading him down the path of hearsay.'

Sampson nodded. 'Members of the jury, you will disregard the last question and the answer to it. Mr Highsmith?'

'Thank you, my lord. Mr Wells, did you ever suspect Mr Hawkin of having burgled your home?'

Wells shook his head. 'Never. Why would Phil do a thing like that? We were his friends.'

'Thank you, Mr Wells. I have no further questions.'

So that was the way the wind was blowing, Clough thought to himself as he edged out of the courtroom. He slipped into the witness room ahead of the usher. George jumped to his feet, his expression an eager question.

'The defence didn't question the ID – I think their line's going to be that Hawkin bought the gun in a pub, not realizing it was the one stolen from Wells.'

George sighed. 'And I found the gun and used it to frame him. So it doesn't change anything.'

'It does,' Clough said earnestly. 'It ties Hawkin to the gun. Ordinary people don't have guns, George. Remember?'

Before George could reply, the door opened and the court usher said, 'Detective Inspector Bennett? They're ready for you now.'

It was one of the longest walks of his life. He could feel the eyes on him, making him conscious of every step he took. When he reached the witness box, he turned quite deliberately and stared at the impassive face of Philip Hawkin. He hoped Hawkin felt he was looking at his nemesis.

Stanley waited while the clerk administered the oath, then rose to his feet, delicately dabbing at his moist eyes. 'Can you state your name and rank for the record, Inspector?'

'I am George Bennett, Detective Inspector with Derbyshire Constabulary, based at Buxton.'

'I'd like to take you right back to the beginning of this case, Inspector. When did you first hear of Alison Carter's disappearance?'

At once, George was back in the squad room on that bitter December night, hearing from Sergeant

Lucas that there was a girl missing in Scardale. He began his evidence with the clarity of a man who can slip back into the scenes of memory with the immediacy of the present. Stanley almost smiled in his relief at having such an impressive police witness. In his experience, it was a lottery with officers of the law. Sometimes he trusted them less than the shifty individuals in the witness box. But George Bennett was handsome and clean cut. He looked and sounded as honest as a film star playing the decent cop.

Stanley wasted no time, and by the end of the morning he had covered the initial report of Alison's disappearance, George's first interview with her mother and stepfather, the preliminary searches and the discovery of the dog in the woodland.

Then, for a further hour and a half in the afternoon, Stanley took him meticulously through the key discoveries in the investigation. The blood and garment traces in the copse; the book in Hawkin's study detailing the old workings inside the crag; the stained clothes and the bullets in the lead mine; the bloody shirt and the gun; the appalling photographs and negatives in the safe.

'It is unusual to charge a man with murder when there is no body,' Stanley said towards the end of the afternoon.

'It is, sir. But in this case, we felt the evidence was so overwhelming that there was no other conclusion that could be drawn.'

'And of course, there are other cases where men have been found guilty of murder in the absence of a body. Inspector Bennett, given the seriousness of the charges, do you have any lingering doubts about your correctness in charging Mr Hawkin?'

'Anyone who has seen the photographic evidence of what he did to his stepdaughter when she was alive would know this was a man who would stop at nothing. So, no, I have no doubts at all.' It was the first time George had let his emotions surface and Stanley was happy to see the jurors seemed impressed with his passion.

He gathered together his papers. 'I have no further questions for the witness,' he said.

He had never wanted a cigarette more, George thought as he waited for Rupert Highsmith to finish fiddling with his papers and begin his attack. Stanley's questions had been thorough and probing, but there had been nothing he had not been well prepared for. Highsmith had tried suggesting to the judge that they leave the cross-examination till the morning, but Sampson was in no mood to wait.

Highsmith leaned negligently against the rail behind him. 'You won't forget you're still under oath, Inspector? Now, tell the court how old you are.'

'I'm twenty-nine years old, sir.'

'And how long have you been a police officer?'

'Nearly seven years.'

'Nearly seven years,' Highsmith repeated admiringly. 'And you've already reached the lofty heights of detective inspector. Remarkable. So you won't have had much time to gain experience of complicated, serious cases?'

'I've done my share, sir.'

'But you're on an accelerated promotion scheme for graduates, aren't you? Your promotions haven't come because of your brilliant performances in the field of detection, but simply because you have a university degree and you were promised rapid promotion regardless of whether you had investigated murder or shoplifting. Isn't that the case?' Highsmith frowned, as if genuinely puzzled by the thought.

George took a deep breath and exhaled through his nose. 'I did enter the force as a graduate. But it was made plain to me that if my performance did not match up to certain expectations, I would not automatically progress through the ranks.'

'Really?' If Highsmith had used that tone in the cricket club, George would have flattened him.

'Really,' he echoed, then clamped his mouth shut.

'It's very unusual for so junior an officer to head an investigation of this seriousness, isn't it?' Highsmith pressed on.

'The detective chief inspector in the division was incapacitated with a broken ankle. At the outset, we had no idea how serious the investigation might prove to be, so Superintendent Martin asked me to take charge. Once it began to appear more serious, it made sense to maintain continuity rather than hand over to someone from headquarters who would have to start from scratch. I was at all times under the direct supervision of Detective Chief Inspector Carver and the divisional chief, Superintendent Martin. Sir.'

'Prior to this, had you in fact ever been involved in investigating a case involving a missing child?'

'No, sir.'

Highsmith cast his eyes upwards and sighed. 'Had you ever led a murder inquiry?'

'No, sir.'

Highsmith frowned, rubbed the bridge of his nose with his index finger and said, 'Correct me if I'm wrong, Inspector, but this is the first major criminal investigation you have *ever* been in charge of, isn't it?'

'In charge of, yes. But I've –'

'Thank you, Inspector, you need only answer the question asked,' Highsmith cut brutally across him.

George flashed him a look of frustration. Then, from somewhere, he found a twitch of a smile, acknowledging that he knew what was being done to him.

'You've taken a strong personal interest in this case, haven't you?'

'I've done my job, sir.'

'Even after the initial search was called off, you still visited Scardale several times a week, didn't you?'

'A couple of times a week, yes. I wanted to reassure Mrs Carter that the case was still open and we hadn't forgotten her daughter.'

'You mean Mrs Hawkin, don't you?' Highsmith's use of Ruth's current married name was clearly directed at the jury, a device to remind them of her relationship to the man in the dock.

George was proof against such provocative play. He smiled. 'Not surprisingly, she prefers to be known by her previous married name. We're happy to abide by that preference.'

'You even abandoned your family, including your pregnant wife, to visit Scardale on Christmas Day.'

'I couldn't help thinking how Alison's disappearance must have affected the way people in Scardale were feeling at Christmas. I went over with my sergeant for a very brief visit, just to show our faces, to show we sympathized.'

'To show you sympathized. How very commendable,' Highsmith said patronizingly. 'You often visited the manor, didn't you?'

'I dropped in, yes.'

'You knew the study?'

'I've been in it, yes.'

'How many times, would you say?'

George shrugged. 'Hard to put an exact figure on it. Before we executed the search warrant, maybe four or five times.'

'And were you ever alone in there?'

The question came fast as a whip and with the same sting. Now it was clear what Highsmith was planning. 'Only briefly.'

'How many times?'

George frowned. 'Twice, I think,' he said cautiously.

'How long for?'

Stanley was on his feet. 'Your Lordship, this is supposed to be cross-examination. My learned friend seems intent on a fishing expedition.'

Sampson nodded. 'Mr Highsmith?'

'Your Lordship, the prosecution is relying heavily on circumstantial evidence, some of which was found in my client's study. I think it only reasonable that I be allowed to establish that other people had opportunity to have left it there.'

'Very well, Mr Highsmith, you may continue,' the judge grudgingly allowed.

'How long were you left alone in the study?'

'On one occasion, a minute or two at the most. On the second occasion, I must have been in the room for about ten minutes before Mr Hawkin appeared,' George said reluctantly.

'Long enough,' Highsmith said, apparently to himself as he picked up another pad and flicked over a page or two. 'Can you tell us what your hobbies are, Inspector?' he asked pleasantly.

'Hobbies?' George demanded, caught off his stride.

'That's right.'

George looked at Stanley for guidance, but the barrister could only shrug. 'I play cricket. I like to go fell-walking. I don't have time for many hobbies,' he said, sounding as baffled as he felt.

'You've missed one out,' Highsmith said, his voice cold again. 'One that has particular relevance to this case.'

George shook his head. 'I'm sorry, I don't know what you're talking about.'

Highsmith picked up a thin bundle of photostats. 'Your Lordship, I would like these papers entered as defence exhibits one to five. Exhibit one is from Cavendish Grammar School for Boys school magazine for 1951. It is the annual report of the school Camera Club, written by the secretary, George Bennett.' He handed the top sheet to the court clerk. 'The other exhibits are from the newsletter of the Camera Club of Manchester University, where Detective Inspector Bennett was an undergraduate. They contain articles on photography written by one George Bennett.' He handed over the papers to the court clerk.

'Inspector Bennett, do you deny that you wrote these articles on photography?'

'Of course I don't.'

'You are in fact something of an expert in matters photographic?'

George frowned. He could see the trap. To deny it

would make him look like a liar. To admit it might fatally undermine the prosecution case for a committal. 'Any knowledge I had is well out of date,' he said carefully. 'Apart from family snaps, I haven't handled a camera for five or six years.'

'But you would know where to go to find out how to fake photographs,' Highsmith said.

George was wiser than Ruth Carter in the ways of barristers. He knew better than to leave a statement unanswered. 'No more than you would, sir.'

'Photographs can be faked, can't they?' he asked.

'In my experience, not nearly as neatly as this,' George said.

Highsmith pounced on the uncharacteristic slip. 'In your experience? Are you telling the court you have experience of faking photographs?'

George shook his head. 'No, sir. I was referring to attempts at faking that I have seen, not that I have produced.'

'But you do know how photographs can be faked?'

George took a deep breath. 'As I said earlier, my knowledge of photography is well out of date. Anything I know about any aspect of photography has probably been overtaken by changes in technique and technology.'

'Inspector, please answer the question. Do you or do you not know how photographs can be faked?' Highsmith sounded exasperated. George knew it was assumed to make him look shifty, but there was nothing he could do to alter that impression, short of admitting to being a skilled forger of photographs.

'I have some theoretical knowledge, yes, but I have never –'

'Thank you,' Highsmith said loudly, cutting him off. 'A simple answer will always suffice. Now, these negatives which the prosecution has entered into evidence. What kind of camera would you need to take them?'

Beneath the level of the witness box, where the jury could not see them, George clenched his fists till his nails left weals on his palms. 'You'd need a portrait camera. A Leica or a Rolleiflex, something like that.'

'Do you possess such a camera?'

'I have not used my Rolleiflex for at least five years,' he said, knowing he sounded devious even as he spoke.

Highsmith sighed. 'The question was whether you possess such a camera, not when you last used it, Inspector. Do you possess such a camera? Yes or no will serve.'

'Yes.'

Highsmith paused and flicked through his papers. Then he looked up. 'You believe my client is guilty, don't you?'

George turned his head towards the jury. 'What I believe doesn't matter.'

'But you do believe in my client's guilt?' Highsmith persisted.

'I believe what the evidence tells me, and so yes, I do believe Philip Hawkin raped and murdered his thirteen-year-old stepdaughter,' George said, emotion creeping into his voice in spite of his intention to keep it battened down.

'Both of which are terrible crimes,' Highsmith said. 'Any reasonable man would be appalled by them and would want to bring to justice the person who had committed them. The problem is, Inspector, that there is no solid evidence that either of these crimes was ever committed, is there?'

'If there was no evidence, the magistrates would never have committed your client for trial and we would not be here today.'

'But there is an alternative explanation for every piece of circumstantial evidence before us today. And many of those explanations lead us firmly to your door. It is your obsession with Alison Carter that has brought us here today, isn't it, Inspector?'

Stanley was on his feet again. 'My lord, I must protest. My learned friend seems determined to make speeches rather than ask questions, to cast aspersions rather than to make direct accusations. If he has something to ask Detective Inspector Bennett, well and good. But if his sole intent is to deliver slurs and innuendo to the jury, then he should be stopped.'

Sampson glowered down from the bench. 'He's not the only one making pretty speeches out of turn, Mr Stanley.' He looked over his glasses at the jury like a short-sighted mole. 'You should bear in mind that what you are here to listen to is the evidence, so you must disregard any comments that counsel make in passing. Mr Highsmith, please continue, but to the point.'

'Very well, my lord. Inspector, bearing in mind you should answer yes or no, are you an ambitious man?'

Stanley intervened again. 'My lord,' he exclaimed indignantly. 'This has nothing to do with the matter before the court.'

'It speaks to his motivation,' Highsmith said briskly. 'The defence contends that much of the evidence against my client has been concocted. Inspector Bennett's motivation therefore becomes an issue for the defence.'

Sampson thought for a moment then said, 'I am minded to allow the question.'

George took a deep breath. 'My only ambition is to contribute to justice being done. I believe that somewhere out there is the body of a girl who was monstrously abused before she was killed and I believe the man who did it is sitting in the dock.' Highsmith was trying to stop him, but he kept on to the end regardless. 'I'm here to try and make sure he pays for what he's done, not to further my career.' He came to an abrupt halt.

Highsmith shook his head in apparent disgust. 'Yes or no, that was what I asked for.' He sighed. 'I have no further questions of this witness,' he said, his face – turned towards the jury and away from the judge – showing a contempt that was absent from his voice.

George stepped down from the witness box. He could no longer escape from the sight he'd been deliberately trying to avoid all the time he'd been in the witness box. Hawkin stared at him with a look that bordered on the triumphant. The smile that often appeared to hover on his lips was back and he sat as casually in the dock as if he were in his own kitchen. With murder in his heart, George strode past the dock and straight out of the courtroom. Behind him, he heard the judge announcing the close of business for the day. He hurried on, down the corridor to the Gents. He dived into the cubicle, slammed the bolt home and bent over the bowl. He barely made it in time. The hot vomit splattered against the porcelain, the thin acrid smell rising to make him gag again.

He jerked the chain then leaned against the wall of the toilet, cold sweat on his face. For a terrible moment in the courtroom, he had felt the horror of what Highsmith's insinuations and accusations might do to him. All it would take would be a couple of gullible jurors with a grudge against the police, and not only would Hawkin walk free, but he'd take George's career and reputation with him. It was an unbearable notion, the stuff of three a.m. nightmares and bowel-churning panics. He had stuck his neck out for this prosecution. Now, for the first time, he was allowing himself to understand how easily he could become the agent of his own destruction. No wonder Carver had been so magnanimous in his insistence George see the case through himself. He hadn't so much been handed the poisoned chalice as wrestled it out of everyone else's hands.

But what else could he have done? Even as he stood there with the throat-rasping smell of bleach making his watering eyes sting, George knew there had never been any real choice for him.

When he emerged, Clough was waiting, the familiar cigarette drooping from the corner of his mouth. 'I know a good pub on the Ashbourne road,' he said. 'We'll have a jar on the way home.'

He was, George thought, a remarkable lieutenant.

The Trial

3

For the rest of the week, George sat at the back of the court, always contriving to arrive a few minutes after each session began and slipping away as soon as the court rose. He knew he was being ridiculous, but he couldn't escape the idea that everyone was looking at him because they were wondering whether he was corrupt, or, even worse, because they'd already decided he was. He hated the thought of being taken for one of those coppers who made up their minds to have somebody for a crime, regardless of the evidence. But he couldn't stay away.

The third day of the trial saw the Scardale witnesses appear. Charlie Lomas managed to repeat his unflustered performance at the committal, impressing the jury with his open manner and his obvious unhappiness about the disappearance of his cousin.

Next was Ma Lomas, dressed for the occasion in a rusty black coat with a spray of white heather pinned to the collar. She admitted her name was Hester Euphemia Lomas. It was clear she held the court in neither awe nor deference, responding to the two QCs precisely as she would have done to George in the comfort of her own living room. She insisted on a chair and a glass of water, then proceeded to ignore both. Stanley treated her with exaggerated courtesy, which she returned with utter indifference.

'And you are absolutely certain that it was Mr Hawkin you saw crossing the field?' Stanley asked.

'I only need glasses for reading,' the old woman said. 'I can still tell a kestrel from a sparrowhawk at a hundred yards.'

'How can you be sure it was the Wednesday?'

She looked at him with exasperation. 'Because that's the day Alison went missing. When something like that happens, everything else that happened that day sticks in your memory.'

Stanley obviously found nothing to argue with in that. He took her on through her knowledge of the lead mine from the book in the study of Scardale Manor. 'Did Squire Castleton often talk to you about local history?' he eventually asked.

'Oh aye,' she said, off hand. 'I'd known him since he was a little lad. He never lorded it over his tenants, not the *old* squire. We'd often sit and talk, him and me. We always said, when we went, half the dale's history would go with us. He was always on at me to write it all down, but I couldn't be bothered with owt like that.'

'But that's how you knew where to find the book?'

'That's right. Many's the time we've sat and looked at that book, the old squire and me. I was able to put my hand on it right away.'

'Why didn't you mention the old lead mine to the police earlier?' Stanley asked, apparently casually.

She scratched her temple with a finger lumpy with

arthritis. 'I don't rightly know. I forget sometimes that not everybody knows the dale like I do. I've lain awake often since, wondering if it would have made any difference to poor Alison if I'd have mentioned the lead mine to Inspector Bennett the night she went missing.' She sighed. 'It's a terrible burden to me.'

'I have no more questions for you, Mrs Lomas, but my colleague Mr Highsmith will need to ask you some things. So if you would wait there?' Stanley gave the matriarch a slight bow before sitting down.

This time, Highsmith waited for a few moments before he rose. 'Mrs Lomas,' he began. 'It must be hard for you to see the nephew of your old friend in the dock here today.'

'I never thought I'd be glad Squire Castleton were dead,' she said in a low voice. 'This would have broke his heart. He loved Alison like she was his own granddaughter.'

'Indeed. If I might trouble you with a few questions, I'd be very grateful.'

She looked up and George, sitting at the back of the court, caught the wicked gleam in her eye. He winced. 'Questions are no trouble to me,' she snapped. 'Tell truth and shame the devil. I've nothing to fear from your questions, so ask away.'

Highsmith looked momentarily taken aback. Her docile responses to Stanley's questions had not prepared him for Ma Lomas in combative mood. 'How can you be certain it was Mr Hawkin you saw cross the field that afternoon?'

'How can I be certain? Because I saw him. Because I know him. The way he looks, the way he walks, the clothes he wears. There's nobody in Scardale you could confuse with him,' she said, her voice outraged. 'I might be old but I'm not daft.'

A snigger stuttered round the press benches and the Scardale contingent allowed themselves tight smiles. Ma would show this London lawyer what was what.

'That much is obvious, ma'am,' Highsmith squeezed out.

'You don't have to "ma'am" me, lad. Ma'll do.'

Highsmith blinked hard. The point of his pencil snapped against the pad in his hand. 'This book in the study at the manor. You say you knew exactly where to look for it?'

'Well remembered, lad,' Ma said grimly.

'So it was where it should have been?'

'Where else would it have been? Of course it was where it should have been.'

Highsmith pounced. 'No one had moved it?'

'I can't say that, can I? How can I know that? It wouldn't be hard to put it back in the right place – them shelves are full. When you take a book out, it leaves a gap. So you put it back in the same place. Automatic,' she said scornfully.

Highsmith smiled. 'But there was no sign that anyone had done that. Thank you, Mrs Lomas.'

The judge leaned forward. 'You're free to go now, Mrs Lomas.'

She turned to Hawkin and smiled pure malicious triumph. George was relieved she had her back to the jury. 'Aye, I know,' she said. 'More than he can say, isn't it?' She paraded across the room like the royalty she was in her village and settled in a specially vacated chair at the heart of her family.

The following day was taken up with an assortment

of specialists who could testify on particular matters of fact. Hawkin's tailor had travelled up from London to confirm that the stained shirt hidden in the darkroom was one of a batch the accused had had made to measure less than a year before. An assistant from Boots the Chemist revealed he had sold Philip Hawkin two rolls of elastoplast which corresponded to both the tape found on the muzzle of Alison's dog and the short section fixing the safe key to the back of the drawer in the study.

A fingerprint officer revealed that Philip Hawkin's prints were on the photographs and the negatives found in the safe. However, there were no prints on the Webley, and the cover of the antiquarian book had been impossible to retrieve prints from.

The final witness of the day was the firearms expert. He confirmed that one of the bullets found in the cave was clearly identifiable as a .38 fired from the gun that Ruth Carter had found hidden in her husband's darkroom.

Through all of this testimony, Highsmith asked little, except to attempt to demonstrate that there were alternative explanations to all the statements made by the prosecution. Anyone, he argued, could have obtained a shirt belonging to Hawkin. They could even have stolen one from the manor washing line. Hawkin might not have been buying the elastoplast on his own account, but may have been running an errand for someone else. Of course his prints were on the pictures and the negatives – the police had thrown them at him across an interview room table before they were encased in plastic, before his solicitor had ever arrived at the police station. And the only person who had made any connection between the gun and Hawkin was, of course, his wife, who was so desperate to find an explanation for her daughter's disappearance that she was even prepared to turn on her husband.

The jury sat impassively, offering no clue as to their opinion of his performance. At the end of the third day, the court adjourned till morning.

On Friday morning, George's mind was jolted out of his own concerns. There, in the *Daily Express*, was a story that harrowed him.

Tracker dogs join hunt for lost boy

Eight policemen with two tracker dogs searched railway sidings, parks and derelict buildings today for short-sighted schoolboy Keith Bennett, missing from home for nearly three days.

Said a senior police officer: 'If we do not find him today, the search will be intensified. We just don't know what has happened to him. We do not suspect foul play yet, but we can find no reason for him to be missing.'

Twelve-year-old Keith of Eston Street, Chorlton-on-Medlock, Manchester, disappeared on Tuesday night on his way to visit his grandmother.

His home is in an area of Manchester where several murders have occurred and missing persons have gone untraced.

Home-loving

Left behind at home are the thick-lensed spectacles – with one lens broken – without which he has difficulty in seeing.

Keith's mother, Mrs Winifred Johnson, aged 30, who has five other children and is expecting her seventh in two weeks, wept today as she talked of her missing son.

She said: 'He has never done anything like this before. He's a home-loving lad. He can hardly see without his spectacles.'

Said his grandmother, Mrs Gertrude Bennett, aged 63, of Morton Street, Longsight, Manchester: 'We can not eat, sleep or do anything for worrying about him.'

The police search party is made up of a sergeant, five constables and two dog handlers. They are searching an area within a mile of Keith's home.

George stared at the paper. The thought of another mother going through what Ruth Carter had experienced was agonizing for him. But in a corner of his mind, he couldn't help thinking that if it had to happen, it could not have come at a more opportune moment. For any member of the jury reading the paper, Winifred Johnson's anguished plight could only reinforce Ruth Carter's agony and diminish any inclination to believe Hawkin.

A sudden wave of shame washed over him. How could he be so callous? How could he even think about exploiting the disappearance of another child? Disgusted with himself, George crumpled the paper and tossed it into the bin.

That afternoon, as he made his way up the stairs towards the courtroom, he saw a familiar figure waiting by the door. Spotless in his dress uniform, Superintendent Martin stood fiddling with his soft black leather gloves. As George approached, he looked up. 'Inspector,' he greeted him, his face inscrutable. 'A word, please.'

George followed him down a side corridor to a small room that smelled of perspiration and cigarettes. He closed the door behind them and waited.

Martin lit one of his untipped cigarettes and said abruptly, 'I want you back in the office next week.'

'But, sir –' George protested.

Martin held up a hand. 'I know, I know. The prosecution should finish today and then it'll be the defence case next week. And that's precisely why I want you back in Buxton.'

George's head came up and he glared at his station commander. 'This is my case, sir.'

'I know. But you know as well as I do what defence Highsmith's going to run. He's got no choice. And I will not have one of my officers sit in a courtroom and hear his character traduced by some slick lawyer who doesn't care what damage he does to a decent man.' The telltale scarlet tide was rising up Martin's neck. He began to pace to and fro.

'With respect, sir, I can take anything Highsmith throws at me.'

Martin stopped pacing and eyed George. 'You think so, do you? Well, even if you can, I'm not having you at the mercy of the press. If you're not willing to take cover for your own sake, you ought to do it for that wife of yours. It'll be bad enough if she has to read reports that accuse you of all sorts of mischief without her being treated to photographs of you skulking in and out of cars as if you were the one on trial.'

George ran a hand through his hair. 'I'm due some leave.'

'And I'm refusing you permission to take it,' Martin snapped. 'You will stay away from Derby until this trial is over. And that is an order.'

George turned away and lit a cigarette. It was hard not to see his banishment as the gods' retribution for his response to Keith Bennett's disappearance. 'At least let me be here for the verdict,' he said indistinctly.

Professor John Patrick Hammond recited the qualifications that made him one of the leading forensic experts in the north of England. His was a name that ranked alongside that of Bernard Spilsbury, Sydney Smith and Keith Simpson in the public imagination as one of that handful of men who could apply their scientific knowledge to a scatter of traces and draw from them incontrovertible evidence of guilt. It had been Pritchard from the DPP who had insisted on bringing a high-profile expert into the case. 'When we've got so little to go on, we should defend it with the big guns,' he'd said, and Superintendent Martin had agreed.

Hammond was a small, precise man whose head was too big for his body. He compensated for his faintly ridiculous appearance with a solemn and portentous manner. Juries loved him because he could translate scientific jargon into layman's language without ever making them feel talked down to. Stanley had the good sense to keep his questions to a minimum, allowing Hammond to explain for himself.

Hammond made sure the jurors fully appreciated the key points. The blood on the tree in the copse, on the torn underwear in the cave, and on the stained shirt was all from a female with blood group O, which was also Alison's blood group. The amount of blood on the shirt was consistent with a serious wound. The semen on the shirt had been deposited by a secretor with blood group A. The accused was a secretor with blood group A.

He also explained that forensic examination had revealed scorch marks on the shirt that were entirely consistent with a gun having been fired close to the material. Hammond demonstrated by holding the shirt against himself. George noticed Ruth Carter's head fall into her hands. Kathy Lomas put an arm around her and pulled her close.

'As you will see, Your Lordship,' Hammond explained, 'the gunshot residue is present on the right cuff and also on the right front of the shirt. If someone wearing this shirt were to have held a gun at fairly close quarters, this is exactly what we'd expect to find. There is no other explanation consistent with this particular arrangement of scorching and staining.'

Highsmith rose for the cross-examination feeling faintly frustrated. This case had not been one of the most successful performances of his life so far. There was so little to get a grip of, and what there was seemed so flimsy. Here at last was something concrete to attack. 'Professor Hammond, can you tell us what proportion of the population have blood group A?'

'Approximately forty-two per cent.'

'And what percentage of the population are secretors whose blood group is present in their other bodily fluids?'

'Approximately eighty per cent.'

'Forgive me, mathematics has never been my strong point. What percentage of the population are group A secretors?'

Hammond's eyebrows flicked up and down. 'About thirty-three per cent.'

'So all we can say is that these semen stains could have been left by a third of the male population of this country?'

'That is correct, yes.'

'So rather than pointing specifically to my client, the best you can say is that these tests do not rule him out.' It was not a question and Hammond did not respond. 'Moving on to this stained shirt. Is there anything that would indicate that the accused was the person wearing this shirt when a shot was fired next to it?'

'In forensic terms, no.' Hammond sounded reluctant, as he always did when forced to admit his science could not answer every question.

'So, anyone could have been wearing the shirt?'

'Yes.'

'And the person wearing the shirt need not have been the person who deposited the semen on the other pieces of clothing?'

Hammond paused for a moment. 'I consider it rather unlikely, but I suppose it is possible.'

'The amount of blood on the other clothing was significantly less. Would that be consistent with the sort of bleeding that can occur when the hymen is breached?'

'It's impossible to say. Some women lose a considerable amount of blood when they lose their virginity. Others none at all. But if the bloodstains on the shirt came from that source, then this woman was haemorrhaging on a potentially fatal scale.'

'And yet there was no blood at the supposed scene of the crime. Surely if someone had been fatally shot in that cavern, there would have been blood everywhere? Pooled on the floor, splashed on the walls, spattered on the roof? How is it possible that there was no blood except what stained the various garments?'

'Are you asking me to speculate?' Hammond asked crisply.

'I'm asking if, in your experience, it would be possible for someone to be fatally shot in that cavern without the scene exhibiting bloodstains,' Highsmith said, his words enunciated slowly and clearly.

Hammond frowned and thought for a moment, casting his eyes upwards in the act of memory. At last, he said, 'Yes. It would be possible.'

Highsmith frowned. But before he could speak, Hammond continued. 'If, say, the girl was held close and the gun was jammed under her ribs. A bullet travelling with an upward trajectory would destroy the heart, but it might well lodge behind the shoulder blade. If there was no exit wound, there would be no forward spatter of blood. And if she was held close, the back spatter would be absorbed in the larger bloodstain on the shirt.'

Highsmith recovered quickly. 'So, of all the possible scenarios for this putative murder, you can come up with only one that would explain the absence of blood at the scene?'

'Always supposing the girl was killed in the cavern? Yes, I can only come up with that one explanation.'

'One possibility out of dozens, hundreds, even. Not what one could call a probable scenario, then?'

Hammond shrugged. 'I have no idea.'

'Thank you, Professor.' Highsmith sat down. He'd retrieved more than he'd expected. He was confident he could baffle a jury with science and so confuse them that acquittal was the only reasonable option.

'That concludes the case for the prosecution,' Stanley announced as Professor Hammond gathered his papers together and left the witness box.

'I shall adjourn until next week,' Sampson announced.

The Trial

4

Manchester Guardian, *Monday, 22nd June 1964*

New clue to missing boy

Police last night switched their hunt for a near-blind boy missing for five days after one of his schoolfriends had told them: 'He used to boast he had a super-secret den somewhere.'

The search was switched from around twelve-year-old Keith Bennett's home in Eston Street, Longsight, Manchester, to nearby parkland.

A police spokesman said: 'The boy may have a hideout and could have stocks of food. Wherever his hideout, it is a good one.'

Russia admitted its space satellites could spy on its enemies; a heart attack ended Nehru's leadership of India; Rhodesia's new leader Ian Smith was sabre-rattling; The Searchers and Millie and the Four Pennies slugged it out for the top spot in the pop charts. But all George was aware of were the newspaper reports of Philip Hawkin's trial. He tried to keep the papers away from Anne, but she walked to the newsagent every day and bought her own copies. She had to mix with the wives of the other officers; she wanted to know what was being said about her man so she knew how best to strike back on his behalf if anyone was foolish enough to break the solidarity of the police under pressure.

The only defence witness apart from Hawkin himself was his former boss who gave him an anodyne and blameless reference. He was hardly passionate in Hawkin's cause, but he did testify that he had never heard anything against the former draughtsman.

When Hawkin went into the box, the fireworks had started. The headlines had screamed the following morning: **POLICE FRAMED ME, MAN ACCUSED OF MURDER CLAIMS.** *EVIDENCE IN MURDER TRIAL WAS MANUFACTURED.* **LIES, LIES AND MORE LIES, DEFENDANT SAYS.** *ALISON'S KILLER IS STILL AT LARGE, COURT HEARS.*

George sat in his office and stared bitterly at the words in front of him. Never mind that they would wrap tomorrow's fish and chips. The mud was slung and some of it would stick. Whatever happened after this case, he was going to ask for a transfer.

Hawkin had, by all accounts, put up a dazzling performance in the box, protesting his innocence at every possible opportunity. Highsmith had given him plenty of those. For every piece of evidence against him he had found a rebuttal, some carrying more conviction than others. He had spoken frankly and faced the jury throughout, appearing open and candid.

He had even admitted possession of the Webley, though not of having stolen it from Richard Wells. His version was that he had bought the gun from a former workmate, since conveniently deceased. He had always fancied owning a gun, he confessed rather shame-facedly. The man had offered it for sale before Hawkin had even heard about the burglary. Afterwards, he had made the connection but had been afraid to speak up in case he was suspected of having committed the burglary himself. And yes, he had shown the gun to his wife. He was now bitterly ashamed of his behaviour, he'd added. According to the papers, his testimony had seemed fearless. Hawkin had said several times that even though he had been betrayed by the police, he was still putting his faith in British justice and the good sense of a British jury.

'Laying it on with a trowel,' George growled, reading the extensive report under Don Smart's by-line in the *Daily News*.

Clough stuck his head round the door. 'You ask me, he's trying too hard. There's nothing a jury hates more than feeling like they're being flattered. You can butter them up all you like as long as they don't realize it. But he's burying them in flannel and they'll choke on it.'

'Nice try, Tommy,' George sighed. 'I wish I was there today to hear Stanley cross-examine.'

'He'll probably do a better job knowing you're not.'

Manchester Evening News, *Wednesday, 24th June 1964*

Missing boys – and 2
mothers who wait

By a Staff Reporter

Two sad-eyed women, who both know the numbing mental agony of a mother whose child is lost, met at Ashton-under-Lyne today for the first time.

Mrs Sheila Kilbride and Mrs Winifred Johnson sat at a table at Mrs Kilbride's council house in Smallshaw Lane, Ashton, and talked of their sons who have disappeared.

John Kilbride, missing from home since last November, was 12 years old. So was Keith Bennett, from Eston Street, Chorlton-on-Medlock, Manchester, whose mother is Mrs Johnson. Keith disappeared seven days ago.

Both are the first-born of big families. And both disappeared without trace.

'A NIGHTMARE'

Mrs Kilbride and Mrs Johnson talked quietly with the air of women who could not quite believe that it had happened to them.

Said Mrs Kilbride: 'Even after all this time, it is still like a nightmare.'

As time went by, she said, she learned to live with the false hopes and the moments of heart-in-the mouth suspense whenever a car drew up outside.

But the sleepless nights go on, and so do the days of deep despair.

She told Mrs Johnson: 'You've got to keep going. We are a big family like you, and we find we don't even mention John's name much now.'

THE HOAXERS

Mrs Kilbride warned of the cranks and hoaxers who, with their trickery, brought pain.

'I have learned to be suspicious of everybody who comes calling,' she said.

'If they claim to be police or reporters and I don't know them, I ask to see their identity cards.'

Mrs Kilbride, the wife of a building labourer, has seven children, including John. Mrs Johnson, whose husband is an unemployed joiner, has six and is expecting a baby on July 5.

POLICE HUNT

Police are still looking for their boys. Keith's description has been circulated all over the country.

A spokesman in Manchester said: 'We are naturally concerned for his safety. It is an unusual case in that this boy has never wandered away before, and has left his glasses, without which he can see very little.

'He had only one shilling in his pocket. We usually pick such lads up quickly. We have no leads, but are doing all in our power.'

The Trial

5

Extracts from the official transcript of R v Philip Hawkin; Desmond Stanley, QC, delivers his closing speech to the jury on behalf of the prosecution.

Ladies and gentlemen of the jury, I would like to thank you for your patience during this difficult trial. It is always distressing to contemplate the desecration of childhood, as you have had to do in this case. I will try to be as brief as I can, but I must first respond to the suggestions made by my learned friend during his conduct of the defence.

You have seen and heard Detective Inspector George Bennett for yourselves. You have also seen and heard the accused, Philip Hawkin. Now, *I* know Inspector Bennett to be an officer of irreproachable integrity, but you do not have the benefit of my acquaintance with him. So you must rely on those facts we have before us. Inspector Bennett's good reputation came into this courtroom ahead of the man himself. We heard Mrs Carter, the wife of the accused, sing his praises. Later, we heard Mrs Hester Lomas and Mr Charles Lomas speak with great warmth of his support for the villagers of Scardale who had lost one of their young, and of his tireless commitment to uncovering what had happened to Alison Carter.

Mr Hawkin, on the other hand, is, by his own admission, a man who would buy an illegal firearm and keep it in a house where a teenage girl was living.

Those are facts, ladies and gentlemen. Not conjecture, but fact. In spite of what my learned friend has implied, there are many other facts in this case. It is a fact that Philip Hawkin owns the Webley .38 revolver which was fired inside an isolated cavern where clothing identified by her own mother as belonging to Alison Carter was discovered. It is a fact that Philip Hawkin owns a book which meticulously describes the location of this cavern whose existence had been forgotten by everyone except one elderly woman. It is a fact that Philip Hawkin is capable of having produced the semen found on the torn remains of Alison Carter's school knickers.

It is a fact that Philip Hawkin's gun was wrapped in a bloodstained shirt and concealed in Philip Hawkin's darkroom, an outhouse where no one went other than the accused. It is a fact that that shirt belongs to Philip Hawkin. It is a fact that the blood on that shirt, the copious amount of blood on that shirt, could have come from Alison Carter. It is a fact that there exists a perfectly reasonable explanation for the absence of blood in the cavern.

Furthermore, it is a fact that the obscene photographs of Alison Carter and the negatives from which they were printed have Philip Hawkin's fingerprints all over them, not Inspector Bennett's. It is a fact that some of those photographs were taken in Alison

Carter's bedroom, not abstracted from some pornographic magazine. It is a fact that Philip Hawkin possessed all the photographic equipment necessary to take those photographs and process them. Inspector Bennett may have a camera that could take those photographs, but he has no convenient darkroom at the bottom of his garden. He does not possess developing trays, enlargers, a stock of photographic paper or any of the other paraphernalia he would have needed to perpetrate so elaborate a fraud. Come to that, he has not the time.

It is a fact that the photographs were well hidden in a safe whose key was concealed in Philip Hawkin's study. It is a fact that Hawkin had that safe installed when he had the outhouse converted into a darkroom.

Facts, ladies and gentlemen, are not in short supply in this case. Those facts are evidence, and the evidence points overwhelmingly to one conclusion. That there is no body does not mean that no crime has been committed. It may be of some help to you to know that you are not being asked to make a decision that has no precedent. Juries have previously convicted defendants of murder where no body had been found. If you are satisfied on the basis of the evidence laid before you and on your judgement of the witnesses that the crimes of rape and murder were committed against Alison Carter by the accused, then you must carry out your duty and return a guilty verdict.

There is, as I have said, a clear pattern to events in this case, and it points inescapably to one conclusion. Philip Hawkin arrived in Scardale with power and wealth at his disposal for the first time in his life. For the first time in his life, he could see the

400

prospect of indulging his perverted appetite for young girls.

To disguise his real desires, he paid court to Ruth Carter, a woman who had been widowed six years before. Not only was he persuasive and attentive, but he seemed relaxed about the prospect of taking on another man's child. In secret, he was not relaxed; he was ecstatic at the prospect that lay ahead of him if he could only persuade the mother that his interest was in her and not her attractive little girl. He succeeded. And that is when Alison Carter's childhood ended.

When she became Philip Hawkin's stepdaughter, she also became his prey. Living under the same roof, there was no escape. He took pornographic photographs of her. He debauched her. He raped her. He sodomized her. He forced her to commit oral sex. He terrorized her. We know this because we have seen it with our own eyes, in photographs that show no sign of being faked and every indication of being real. Hideous, vile, degrading and without a shadow of a doubt, a record of what really happened to Alison Carter at the hands of her stepfather.

What went wrong we will never know, since the accused has refused the opportunity to put Mrs Ruth Carter out of her misery and tell us how he disposed of her daughter and why he did it. Perhaps Alison had had enough and threatened to tell her mother or another adult. Perhaps he had grown tired of her and he wanted rid of her. Perhaps a sick sexual game got out of hand. Whatever the reason – and it is not hard to imagine motive in a case as darkly barbaric as this – Philip Hawkin decided to kill his stepdaughter. So, in a dark, damp cave, he raped her one final time and then he pulled the trigger on his Webley revolver and murdered this poor thirteen-year-old schoolgirl.

Then when he was confronted with his villainy, he had the effrontery to attempt to wriggle off the hook by smearing the good name of an honest police officer.

Philip Hawkin owed Alison Carter a duty of care. Instead, he used his position to exploit her sexually then, when something went wrong, he shot her dead. Then he disposed of her body, imagining that without a body, there could be no prosecution, no finding of guilt.

Ladies and gentlemen of the jury, you can be guided by the evidence and prove him wrong. Philip Hawkin is guilty as charged, and I urge you to bring the appropriate verdict back to this courtroom.

The Trial

6

Extracts from the official transcript of R v Philip Hawkin;
Rupert Highsmith, QC, delivers his closing speech to the jury
on behalf of the defence.

Ladies and gentlemen of the jury, yours is the most
important task in this courtroom. In your hands lies
the life of a man accused of the rape and murder of
his stepdaughter. It is the job of the prosecution to
prove beyond reasonable doubt that he committed
those crimes. It's my job to demonstrate to you all
the points in their case where they have failed to do
that. I believe that when you have heard what I have
to say, you will not be able to find it in your heart to
convict Philip Hawkin of any crime whatsoever.

The first thing the prosecution has to show is that a
crime has in fact taken place. Now, this case presents
some unusual problems right at the outset. There is no
complainant. Alison Carter is missing, so she is unable
to present an accusation of rape, unable to identify
any assailant – if indeed there was an assailant, for the
prosecution have not been able to produce any third
party to whom Alison complained that she had been
assaulted. No one witnessed the alleged rape. Philip

Hawkin did not come home bruised and bleeding, as if he'd been involved in a violent struggle. The only evidence of rape is the photographs. I will return to the photographs in due course. All I will say at this stage is that you should bear in mind that the camera can indeed lie.

You might think that the discovery of underclothes identified as belonging to Alison and stained with blood and semen are indications of rape. Not so, ladies and gentlemen. Sexual activity takes many shapes and forms. Distasteful though it is for you to have to consider it, these include the wearing of schoolgirls' outfits by older women to indulge male fantasies. They also include the pretence of violence. So, in and of themselves, these exhibits prove nothing.

Which brings us to the second charge, that of murder. But again, there are no witnesses. The prosecution has been unable to find one single person who will testify that Philip Hawkin was a violent man. Not one single witness has come forward to say that Hawkin was anything other than normal in his behaviour towards his stepdaughter. Not only are there no witnesses, there is no body. Not only is there no body, there is no blood at the alleged scene of the crime. The first shooting in the history of forensic science that has left no traces in the place where it is supposed to have taken place. For all the prosecution knows, Alison Carter is a runaway, surviving somehow on the fringes of society. In the absence of blood, in the absence of a body, how can they charge Philip Hawkin with murder? How dare they charge him with murder?

All they have is a chain of circumstantial evidence.

It's well known that a chain is only as strong as its weakest link. What then are we to make of a chain that consists solely of weak links? Let us look at this evidence, piece by piece, and test its weakness. I am convinced, ladies and gentlemen of the jury, that when we have done that, you will find it impossible to convict Philip Hawkin of either of these two terrible crimes of which he stands accused.

You have heard two witnesses testify that on the afternoon of Alison's disappearance, they saw Philip Hawkin in the field between the wood where Alison's dog was found and the copse where a disturbance was later discovered to have taken place. I am not suggesting for one moment that either or both of those witnesses are lying. I think they have both convinced themselves that they are telling nothing less than the truth.

However, I submit that in a small farming community such as Scardale, one winter afternoon is very much like another. It would not be difficult to confuse Tuesday with Wednesday. Now, bear in mind that everyone in Scardale was puzzled and upset by Alison Carter's disappearance. If someone in authority, such as a police officer, were to suggest strongly that a mistake had been made, and that correcting that mistake would help to solve the conundrum, is it so very surprising that witnesses might find themselves going along with the suggestion? Especially since it would mean fixing the blame outside their own tight-knit community and on to the man they all perceived as an outsider, their new and much resented squire, Philip Hawkin? Let us not forget, ladies and gentlemen, that if Philip Hawkin goes to the gallows, Scardale and all it contains will pass to his wife, who is very much one of their own.

Next, we come to the evidence of Mrs Hawkin herself. And whatever she says to the contrary, let us not forget that Mrs Hawkin she remains. You might think that the very fact that she is willing to testify against her husband speaks for itself. After all, what could induce a bride of less than eighteen months to support her husband's prosecution other than compelling evidence? Does it not tell us something about the accused that she gave evidence against him when the prosecution case is so weak?

No, ladies and gentlemen, it does not. What it does tell us is that there is nothing stronger for a woman than the bond of motherhood.

Mrs Hawkin's daughter went missing on Wednesday the eleventh of December. She is frantic. She is distraught. She is bewildered. The one person who seems to offer her any hope is a young detective inspector who throws himself into the case with passion and commitment. He is always there. He is compassionate and dedicated. But he is getting nowhere. Eventually, he forms a suspicion that the woman's husband may have had a hand in Alison's disappearance. And he becomes determined to establish his theory as fact. Imagine what this does to a woman in Mrs Hawkin's unstable frame of mind. Of course she is suggestible. And what he says to her makes perfect sense. Because she wants answers. She wants an end to this terrible uncertainty. It is better to blame her husband than to live in constant fear of what might have happened to her daughter.

And so, ladies and gentlemen of the jury, you must

treat Mrs Hawkin's evidence with extreme scepticism.

As for the so-called physical evidence, not a single piece on its own points to Philip Hawkin. Somewhere around six million men in the country share the same blood group features as Philip Hawkin and whoever left semen stains in that lead mine. How does that point to him? There are four hundred and twenty-three volumes in Squire Castleton's study and no sign that the single book that details the lead mine had been touched by any hand, including those of Hester Lomas or Detective Inspector Bennett. How does that point to him? Boots the Chemist in Buxton sells between twenty and thirty rolls of elastoplast every week, two of which were sold to Philip Hawkin, who lives in a farming community, where cuts and grazes are hardly an unusual feature of life. How does that point to him being a rapist or a murderer?

It does not, of course. But weak as these circumstantial links are, it cannot be denied that when they are all dumped in one side of the balance, it does appear to tip against Mr Hawkin. So if it was not his behaviour that produced this undoubted effect, whose was it?

There is one aspect of this job that every barrister hates. While the vast majority of our police officers are honest and incorruptible, from time to time, things go wrong. And from time to time, it falls to us to expose the rotten apples in the barrel. What is even worse, to my mind, than the officer who falls by the wayside out of greed is the one who takes the law into his own hands out of zeal.

What has brought us here today is not Philip Hawkin's evil but Detective Inspector George Bennett's zeal. His desire to solve the disappearance of Alison Carter has led him instead to pervert the course of justice. There can be no other explanation for events. It is truly terrible what a man will do when he is blinded by conviction, even if that conviction is utterly mistaken.

When we examine the circumstantial evidence, it becomes clear that one man had motive, means and opportunity to put Philip Hawkin in the frame. He is a young and inexperienced officer who was frustrated by his failure in this case. He must have felt the eyes of his superiors were on him and he was determined that he would find a culprit and win a conviction.

George Bennett was left alone in Mr Hawkin's study on more than one occasion, certainly for long enough to find a gun, to examine a book, even to discover the hiding place of a safe key. George Bennett had Mrs Hawkin's confidence, and he had the run of Scardale Manor long before he ever had a search warrant. Who was better placed to remove one of Mr Hawkin's shirts? He won the confidence of the villagers. Who was better placed to persuade Mrs Lomas and her grandson that they were mistaken about the day on which they saw Mr Hawkin walking in his own field?

And finally, the photographs. George Bennett shares a hobby with Philip Hawkin. He doesn't just take holiday snaps with a Box Brownie like most of us. He was secretary of his school Camera Club, he wrote articles on aspects of photography when he was an undergraduate, he owns a portrait camera of the type that must have been used to manufacture these photographs. He knows what is possible in the world of photography. He knows about faking pictures. Philip Hawkin has dozens of photographs of Alison in his files, many taken spontaneously. In some of them, she is angry or upset. He also has photographs of himself. With such material as these, and access to the sort of confiscated pornography that many police stations hold, George Bennett could have created these supposedly incriminating photographs.

At worst, we have uncovered a terrifying conspiracy resulting from one man's arrogant conviction that he knew where justice lay. At best, we have established that the prosecution's case is most certainly not proven beyond reasonable doubt. Ladies and gentlemen, I place Philip Hawkin in your hands. That you will acquit him on both counts is my firm and abiding conviction. Thank you.

The Trial

7

Extracts from the official transcript of R v Philip Hawkin; Mr Justice Fletcher Sampson sums up for the jury.

Ladies and gentlemen of the jury, it is the task of the prosecution to prove beyond a reasonable doubt that the accused is guilty as charged. It is the job of the defence to discover whether there are sufficient weaknesses in their case to render it susceptible to doubt. Some of you may be expecting me to indicate to you at this point whether I think the accused is innocent or guilty. But that is not my role. It is your responsibility and you must not seek to shirk it. My role is to see fair play, and in order to ensure that justice is seen to be done, it is my task to sum up the case and advise you on points of law.

The case before us is a difficult one in the main because of the absence of Alison Carter, either alive or dead. Were she alive, the second charge, the murder charge, would obviously fail, but she would be the most valuable witness as to the first charge, that of rape. Had her body been discovered, it would have had a tale to tell our forensic experts and would inevitably have provided us with considerable amounts of evidence.

But she is not here to give us her testimony, and so we are forced to rely on other sources of evidence.

First, I must tell you that the prosecution does not need to produce a corpse for there to be a presumption of murder. Men have been found guilty of murder where no corpse has ever been found. I will give you two examples which in some respects correspond to this case.

An actress called Gay Gibson was returning home by ship from South Africa to this country when fellow passengers reported her missing. There was a search of the ship, and the captain even turned about and made a search. But no trace of Miss Gibson was found. A deck steward named James Camb came under suspicion because he had been seen by a fellow crew member in the doorway of Miss Gibson's cabin in the middle of the night. He was arrested when the ship docked and he admitted having been in the cabin, although he claimed she had invited him there for the purpose of sexual intercourse.

He further claimed that during intercourse, she had a fit and died. In the course of her fit, she had gone into spasms and clutched at him, scratching his back and shoulders. According to his story, he panicked and pushed her body out of the porthole and into the open sea. The prosecution argued that he had strangled her in the course of raping her and that if events had transpired as he described there would have been no reason for him not to seek medical help for her when she had her fit.

James Camb was found guilty of murder.

Then there was the case of Michael Onufrejczyk. A Pole who earned a distinguished service record in the

Second World War, he became a farmer in Wales in partnership with a fellow Pole, Stanislaw Sykut. A routine police check on resident aliens revealed Mr Sykut was missing. Onufrejczyk claimed his partner had sold out his share of the farm and returned to his native land.

However, when police investigated, they discovered none of Sykut's friends knew anything of such a plan. His bank account was untouched, and the friend Onufrejczyk claimed had lent him the money to buy the farm denied any such thing. Further inquiries revealed the men had quarrelled and that threats had been made. Bloodstains were found in the farmhouse and no satisfactory explanation was forthcoming.

At his trial, it was claimed that Onufrejczyk had fed his partner's body to the farm pigs, hence the absence of any trace of his body. In his judgement at the appeal against conviction, the Lord Chief Justice himself indicated that it was possible to demonstrate the fact of death by means other than the presence of a body.

So you see, under the law of the land, it is not necessary for there to be a body for a finding of murder to be arrived at by a jury. If you are persuaded by the prosecution that there is sufficient evidence here and it points inexorably to one conclusion, you are within your rights to bring in a guilty verdict. Equally, if the defence has managed to shake your certainty, you must bring in a verdict of not guilty.

Now, as to the evidence in this case . . .

The Verdict

George was pretending to read a report on a break-in at a licensed grocery when the phone rang. 'Jury's out,' Clough said tersely.

'I'm on my way,' George said, slamming the phone down and jumping to his feet. He grabbed his coat and hat and ran out of his office. He didn't stop running till he threw himself behind the wheel of the car. As he skidded round the gatepost of the car park, he caught a glimpse of Superintendent Martin at his office window and wondered if he'd had the same message.

He roared through the town and out on to the old Roman road that cut through green fields and off-white dry-stone walls like a blade across a patchwork quilt. With his foot flat to the floor, the needle on the speedo climbed past fifty, past sixty and trembled on the wrong side of seventy. Whenever anything appeared ahead of him, a long blare of his horn made sure they pulled over towards the verge to let him pass.

He had no eyes for the simple beauty of the summer afternoon. His focus was all on the road spooling out ahead of him. He passed the Newhaven crossroads

413

and was forced to slow down as the Roman road disappeared to be replaced by a more winding country route that bounced him up and down hills, round tight corners and through speed-defying chicanes. All he could think about was the ten men and two women cooped up in the jury room. Eventually, he cleared the small market town of Ashbourne and the road opened up before him again.

Would they have reached their decision by the time he got there, George wondered. Somehow, he didn't think so. Much as he wanted to believe he'd supplied Stanley with enough bullets to shoot Hawkin down in flames, he knew they'd taken collateral damage from Highsmith.

As he turned down the side street by the county hall building that housed the assizes, someone pulled out of a parking place right by the side door. 'It's a good omen,' George muttered as he swung the car into the space. He burst into the building, bemused to find it almost empty. The doors to the courtroom stood open, the place empty except for an usher sitting on a chair reading the *Mirror*.

George walked up to him and said, 'Is the jury still out?'

The man looked up. 'That's right.'

George ran a hand through his hair. 'Do you know where I'll find the prosecution team?'

The usher frowned. 'They'll probably be in the residents' lounge at the Lamb and Flag. Just across the square. The canteen's shut, you see.' He frowned. 'You were here last week,' he said accusingly. 'You're Inspector Bennett.'

'That's right,' George said wearily.

'Your pal's been in court today,' the usher continued. 'The one that looks like a prop forward.'

'Do you know where he's gone?'

'He said if I saw you to tell you he'd be in the Lamb and Flag an' all. It's the only place you can be sure of hearing when the jury's coming back, you see.'

'Thanks,' George said over his shoulder as he headed out of the front door and across the square to the old coaching inn. He almost tripped over Clough's legs as he swung through the main entrance. The detective sergeant was stretched out in a chintz armchair in the reception area, a large Scotch in his fist and a cigarette smouldering in a pedestal ashtray next to him.

'I hope Traffic didn't catch you,' Clough said, straightening up. 'Pull up a chair.' He gestured at the half-dozen armchairs that loomed over tiny round tables, filling the cramped area in front of the glassed-in reception desk. The loose covers with their designs of pink and green cabbage roses clashed violently with the rich reds and blues of the traditional Wilton carpet, but neither man noticed nor cared.

George sat down. 'How did you manage that?' he asked, gesturing at the Scotch. 'They're not open for another hour at least.'

Clough winked. 'I got to know the receptionist when I brought Wells up from St Albans. Do you want one?'

'I wouldn't say no.'

Clough crossed to the wood-veneered reception desk and leaned over. George heard the murmur of voices, then his sergeant was back at his side. 'She'll bring one over.'

'Thanks. How was the summing-up?'

'Very even-handed. Nothing to get the Appeal Court excited there. The judge laid out the evidence, fair and square. He made you sound like a wronged maiden one minute, then next minute he said someone had to be lying and they had to decide who. He went on a lot about the difference between fanciful doubt and reasonable doubt. The jury were looking very glum as they went out, I have to say.'

'Thanks for coming down,' George said.

'It's been interesting.'

'I know, but it is your day off.'

Clough shrugged. 'Aye, but the Martinet didn't ban me from coming, did he?'

George grinned. 'Only because he didn't think of it. Where are all the press boys, by the way?'

'They're upstairs in Don Smart's room with a bottle of Bell's. One of the local-paper lads drew the short straw. He's over at the court, ready to phone through soon as there's any sign of the jury. The lawyers are all in the residents' lounge. Jonathan Pritchard's pacing up and down like an expectant father on hot bricks.'

George sighed. 'I know just how he feels.'

'Speaking of which, how is Anne?'

As he lit a cigarette, George raised his eyebrows. 'Upset by what she reads in the papers. This warm weather's getting her down too. She says she feels like she's lugging a sack of spuds round on her stomach.' He nervously chewed the skin on the side of his thumb. 'Between her expecting and this case, I haven't got a nerve left in my body.' He jumped to his feet and walked over to the nearest window. Staring across the square towards the court, he said, 'What am I going to do if they go "not guilty"?'

'Even if he gets away with the murder, they're still going to have him for the rape,' Clough said reasonably. 'They're not going to believe you faked those photographs, no matter what Highsmith tried to make out. I think the worst that can happen is they might decide you got carried away when you found the pictures and decided to have Hawkin for murder as well.'

'But Ruth Carter found the gun before I found the pictures,' George protested, staring at Clough in outrage.

'"So you say," the jury might be thinking,' Clough pointed out. 'Look, whatever they think, they are not going to give him the benefit of the doubt on the rape charge. Come on, you were in court when they saw those photographs. The jury took against Hawkin then. Believe me, they'll be dying to find a way to find him guilty on both charges. Now come on, your drink's here. Sit down and stop fretting. You're making me nervous,' he added, trying vainly to jolly George out of his worries.

George crossed to the table and picked up his drink, then walked back to the window, pausing to stare unseeingly at a luridly coloured Victorian hunting print. 'How long has it been now?' he asked.

'An hour and thirty-seven minutes,' Clough said with a glance at his watch. Suddenly, the phone at reception rang. George swung round and stared at the young woman behind the desk.

'Lamb and Flag reception,' she said in a bored voice. She looked across at George. 'Yes, we do. What was the name?' She paused and stared down at the hotel register. 'Mr and Mrs Duncan. What time will you be arriving?'

417

With a frustrated sigh, George turned back to his study of the county hall building. 'I've never understood why juries take so long,' he complained. 'They should just take a vote and go with the majority. Why does it have to be unanimous? How many criminals walk out of court because one stubborn juror won't be persuaded? It's not like they're all Brain of Britain, is it?'

'George, they could be out for hours. They could be out all night and all tomorrow, so why don't you sit down and drink your drink and smoke your fags? Otherwise we're both going to end up in Derby Royal Infirmary with high blood pressure,' Clough said.

George sighed heavily and dragged himself back to his chair. 'You're right. I know you're right. I'm just on pins.'

Clough pulled a pack of cards out of his jacket pocket. 'D'you play cribbage?'

'We've not got a board,' George objected.

'Doreen?' Clough called. 'Any chance of getting the cribbage board from the public bar?'

Doreen cast her eyes upwards in the universal, exasperated, 'Men!' gesture, then disappeared through a door at the rear of the reception area. 'You've got her well trained,' George commented.

'Always leave them wanting more, that's my motto.' Clough cut the cards then dealt. Doreen returned and slid the cribbage board between them. 'Thanks, love.'

She tutted. 'Watch who you're calling love, you,' she said, with a toss of her head as she tottered back behind her desk on too-high heels.

'I'm watching,' Clough said, just loud enough for her to hear. Normally the banter would have amused

George, but today, it only served to irritate. He forced himself to concentrate on the cards in his hand, but every time the phone rang, he jumped like a man stung by a wasp.

They played cribbage in a tense silence, broken only by scoring claims and the sound of flint on steel as one or other of them lit a cigarette. By half past six, they'd smoked nearly twenty cigarettes between them and swallowed four large Scotches apiece. As they reached the end of a rubber, George stood up. 'I need some fresh air,' he said. 'I'm going to walk round the square.'

'I'll keep you company,' Clough said. They left their cards and glasses on the table, Clough telling Doreen they'd be back.

It was a warm summer evening, the city centre empty now except for the occasional person kept late at the office by some pressing task. It was still too early for any cinema-goers to be about, and the two men had the square more or less to themselves. They paused under a statue of George II, leaning against the plinth while they smoked yet another cigarette. 'I've never felt so tense in all my life,' George said.

'I know what you mean,' Clough said.

'You? You're as relaxed as a three-toed sloth, Tommy,' George protested.

'It's all show, George. Inside, my stomach's tying itself in knots too.' He shrugged. 'I'm just better at hiding it than you. You know you were saying earlier you didn't know what you'd do if Hawkin gets off? Well, I know exactly what I'm going to do. I'm going to hand my papers in and get a job that doesn't give me ulcers.' He tossed his cigarette butt away with a vicious sweep of his arm and folded his arms across his chest, his mouth a thin line in his broad face.

'I . . . I had no idea,' George stammered.

'What? That it bothered me this much? You think you're the only one that lies awake wondering about Alison Carter?' Clough asked belligerently.

George rubbed both hands over his face, pushing his hair awry. 'No, I don't think that.'

'She's got nobody else to fight her corner,' Clough said angrily. 'And if he walks out of that courtroom tonight, we've let her down.'

'I know,' George murmured. 'You know something else, Tommy?'

'What?'

George shook his head and turned away. 'I can't believe I'm even thinking like this, never mind saying it out loud. But . . .'

Clough waited. Then he said, 'Thinking like what?'

'The more I read in the papers that I was supposed to be this bent copper who fitted up Hawkin, the more I kept thinking that maybe I should have done what I could to make the whole thing more watertight,' he said bitterly. 'That's how much this bloody case has got to me.'

Before Clough could reply, both men realized there was an exodus from the Lamb and Flag, led by the barristers, their gowns swooping around them like black wings in the speed of their passage. Behind them, journalists were tumbling through the doors, some still pulling on their jackets and cramming their hats on their heads. Clough and George looked at each other, both taking a deep breath. 'This is it,' George said softly.

'Aye. After you, boss.'

Suddenly the square was alive with people. Carters, Crowthers and Lomases were approaching from the west, where a café owner had realized it was a profitable idea to stay open for as long as Scardale wanted to drink tea and eat chips. Hawkin's mother appeared from the south with Mr and Mrs Wells from St Albans. Everyone converged at the side entrance to county hall, where the bottleneck forced them into uncomfortable proximity. George could have sworn Mrs Hawkin took the opportunity to give him a sharp dig in the ribs, but he was past caring. Somehow, they all squeezed through and into their allotted places in the courtroom. As they settled like a flock of birds in city trees at sunset, Hawkin was led in between the same two police officers who had stood beside him for every day of his trial. He looked sombre and more tired than he had the week before, George noticed. Hawkin looked around him and managed a little wave for his mother in the public gallery. This time, there was no smile for George, just a cold inscrutable stare.

Everyone shuffled raggedly to their feet for the return of the judge, resplendent in his scarlet and ermine, and the High Sheriff. Then, at last, the moment everyone had been dreading for their own particular reasons. The jury filed in, studiously looking at no one. George tried to swallow, but his mouth had gone dry. The conventional wisdom was that a jury who wouldn't look at the accused were going to bring a guilty verdict. His own experience was that no jury ever looked at the accused when they returned to the box. Whatever the verdict, it appeared there was something shaming about having sat in judgement on a fellow member of society.

The elected foreman, a middle-aged man with a narrow face, pink cheeks and horn-rimmed glasses, remained standing when the others took their seats. He kept his eyes firmly fixed upon the judge.

'Members of the jury, are you agreed upon your verdict?'

The foreman nodded. 'We are.'

'And how say you on Count One?'

'Guilty.'

A collective sigh seemed to whisper through the air of the court. George felt the knot in his stomach begin to relax.

'Count Two?'

The foreman cleared his throat. 'Guilty,' he said.

A rising mutter filled the air like the buzz of bees round the hive at evening. George felt no shame at the pleasure Hawkin's devastated expression gave him. The colour had drained from those handsome features, leaving his face as stark as a pen and ink drawing. His mouth opened and closed as if he was gasping for air.

George peered through the animated Scardale crowd, looking for Ruth Carter. At that moment, she turned to him, her eyes filled with tears, her mouth a gash of relief. He saw her lips form the words, 'Thank you,' before she turned away towards the welcoming arms of her relatives.

'Silence in court,' the clerk thundered.

The murmuring died away and everyone turned to the bench. Mr Justice Fletcher Sampson was grim-faced. 'Philip Hawkin, have you anything to say before sentence is passed on you according to the law?'

Hawkin got to his feet. He gripped the edge of the

422

dock. The tip of his tongue appeared at either corner of his mouth. Then, with desperate intensity he said, 'I never killed her. Your Lordship, I'm an innocent man.'

For all the effect of his words on Sampson, he might as well have saved his breath. 'Philip Hawkin, the jury by their verdict have found that you raped your step-daughter Alison Carter, a girl of only thirteen years, and that you subsequently murdered her. That you used a gun in the commission of this crime permits me to pronounce the sentence which the law allows and justice requires.' In absolute hush, he reached for the square of black material and carefully draped it over his wig. Hawkin staggered slightly, but the policeman on his right gripped him by the elbow and forced him upright.

Sampson glanced down at the card in front of him that held the fateful words. Then he looked up and met the frantic eyes of Alison Carter's killer. 'Philip Hawkin, you shall be taken to the place from whence you came, and thence to a place of lawful execution, and there you shall be hanged by the neck until you be dead, and afterwards your body shall be buried in a common grave within the precincts of the prison wherein you were last confined before your execution; and may the Lord have mercy on your soul.'

There was a stunned silence in the courtroom. Then a woman's voice screamed, 'No!'

'Officers, take the prisoner down,' Sampson ordered.

They almost had to carry Hawkin from the court-room. Shock seemed to have destroyed his ability to walk. George could understand the reaction. His own legs seemed unwilling to support him. Suddenly, he found he was at the centre of a group of people who all wanted to shake his hand. Charlie Lomas, Brian Carter, even Ma Lomas were shouting their congratulations. All the buttoned-up restraint he'd come to associate with Scardale villagers had dissipated with the judgement and sentence on Hawkin.

Pritchard's face swam into view. 'Phone your wife and tell her you're staying in Derby,' he shouted. 'We've got champagne across the road.'

'All in good time,' Ma Lomas shouted back. 'He's drinking with Scardale first. Come on, George, we're not letting you out of our sight until you've had a drink off each and every one of us. And bring that big ox of a sergeant of yours along with you.'

His head spinning, his stomach swimming, George Bennett was carried off into the night. Against all odds, he'd triumphed. He'd given Alison Carter the justice she had demanded of him. He had challenged his bosses, the tenets of the English legal system and the vile slanders of the press, and he had triumphed.

A Place of Execution

On the evening of Thursday, 27th August 1964, two
men descended from the train at Derby station, each
carrying a small suitcase. None of their fellow passengers had given them a second glance, but a police car
stood ready to carry them through the streets to the
prison where Philip Hawkin sat in a cell with the two
prison warders appointed to the death watch. Later
that evening, the older of the two men slid open the
oiled flap that allowed him to look into the condemned
cell. He saw a moderately tall man whose medium
frame had clearly shed every spare ounce of flesh.
He was restlessly pacing the floor, a cigarette burning
between his fingers. He saw nothing to contradict the
calculations he had already made based on the piece
of paper he had been handed which said, 'Five feet
ten inches, nine stone ten.' A seven-foot drop would
do nicely.

Hawkin spent the night awake, devoting some of
the time to writing a letter to his wife. According to
Detective Sergeant Clough, who was shown the letter
by Ruth Carter, it maintained his innocence. *Whatever
wrongs I may have done you, killing your beloved daughter*

was not one of them. I have committed many sins and crimes in my life, but not murder. I should not hang for something I have not done, but my fate is sealed now because other people have lied. My blood is on their conscience. I do not hold it against you that you were taken in by their lies. Believe me when I say I have no idea what happened to Alison. I have nothing left to lose now except my life and that will be taken from me in the morning, so there is no reason for me to lie now. I am sorry that I was not a better husband.

Less than five miles away on the other side of the city, George Bennett was also awake. He stood smoking at the open bedroom window of the house that had been their home since his transfer from Buxton a month before. But it was not Philip Hawkin's destiny that was interfering with his sleep. At seven fifty-three the previous evening, Anne had straightened up in her chair and gasped with pain. She had staggered to her feet, George at her side with breathtaking swiftness. It was clearly the moment he'd been anticipating for the two weeks since Anne's due date had passed without a sign of labour. Everyone had told him first babies were often late, but that hadn't made it any easier. Now, before they had reached the living room door, suddenly, mystifyingly to George, clear liquid was pouring out of her. She'd stumbled to the bottom of the stairs and slumped down, reassuring him that this was perfectly normal, but that it was time to take her to the hospital. She'd pointed to the small suitcase, packed and ready in a corner of the hall.

Half-crazy with worry and concern, George helped Anne out to the car and ran back for the suitcase. Then he drove like a maniac through the quiet streets, attracting sharp glances from respectable gardeners and admiring ones from lads lounging on street corners. By the time they reached the infirmary, Anne was shrieking with pain every couple of minutes.

Almost before he could register what was happening, Anne was whisked away from him into the alien world of the maternity wing, a place where no man who lacked a stethoscope would ever be heeded. In spite of his protests, George was firmly herded to the reception area where he was told by a staff nurse who wouldn't have been out of place in Superintendent Martin's regiment that he might as well go home since he was neither use nor ornament to his wife or the medical staff.

Stunned and bemused, George found himself outside in the car park without quite knowing how he'd got there. What was he supposed to do now? Anne had been busily reading books about how to prepare for motherhood, but nobody had told George what he was supposed to do. Once the baby was born, that was all right. He knew about that. Cigars all round for the lads in the office, then down to the pub to wet the baby's head. But how was he to fill the time until that moment? Come to that, how long would it take?

With a sigh, he got back into the car and headed home. When he reached the smart little semi, the identical twin of the one in Buxton except that it lacked the advantage of a corner garden, his first act was to grab the phone and call the hospital.

'Nothing's going to happen for hours yet,' a nurse told him crossly. 'Why don't you have an early night and call us in the morning?'

George clattered the phone back into its cradle. He

didn't even know anybody well enough in the city CID to ring them up and suggest a drink. He was about to raid the bottle of whisky in the sideboard when the phone rang, startling him so much he dropped one of the crystal tumblers they'd been given for a wedding present. 'Damn!' he exclaimed as he picked the phone up.

'Bad moment, George?' Tommy Clough's bantering tone was as welcome to his ears as the confession of a grass.

'I've just taken Anne to the maternity ward, but apart from that, I'm fine. What can I do for you?'

'I've just managed to swap my shift for tomorrow. I thought I'd come down and make sure they hang that bugger in the morning. And then I thought we could go out and get drunk as skunks. But it sounds like you're otherwise engaged.'

George clutched the phone like a drowning man would a life belt. 'Come down. I could use the company. Those nurses act like men have got nothing to do with babies.'

Tommy chuckled. 'There's an answer to that, but you're a married man so I won't sully your ears with it. I'll be there in an hour or so.'

George filled some of the time by walking down to the local pub and buying bottles of beer to supplement the whisky. In the event, they'd drunk very little, both affected in their different ways by the magnitude of the events that were unfolding around them.

Some time after midnight – and George's fourth call to the maternity ward – Clough had bedded down in the spare room. But it wasn't the soft grumble of his snoring that kept George awake. As the long night unfurled into dawn, he found the images of Alison Carter's ordeal intermingling with what he imagined Anne was enduring until he could no longer separate the sufferings. Eventually, as the eastern sky lightened, he dozed off, curled like a foetus in one corner of the bed.

The alarm roused him at seven and his eyes snapped open, his mind fully conscious. Was he a father? He uncoiled his legs and half ran across the room, almost tripping as he hurried downstairs to the phone. The tone was the same, even though the accent was different. No news. The subtext: stop *bothering* us.

Clough's tousled curls and bleary eyes appeared over the banister. 'Any news?'

George shook his head. 'Nothing.'

'Seems weird,' Clough yawned. 'Anne going into labour now.'

'Not really. She was already two weeks overdue. Anxiety can sometimes bring on labour, according to one of her books. And she's had more than her fair share of anxiety out of this case,' George said, walking back upstairs. 'First she has to cope with me working all the hours God sends on the initial inquiry, then she has to read all that stuff in the papers about how I'm so corrupt I'd send an innocent man to the gallows, then she had to read it all over again after the appeal, and now she's had to think about a man hanging because I've done my job.' He stood on the landing and shook his head, his rumpled fair fringe swinging with the movement. 'It's a miracle she's not lost it.'

Clough put a hand on his shoulder. 'Come on. Let's get dressed. I'll buy you breakfast. There's a café not far down the road from the prison.'

George froze. 'Are you going to the prison?'

'Were you not?'

George looked surprised. 'I'm going to the office. Somebody'll phone me when it's all over.'

'You're not coming to the prison? They'll all be there, the Lomases and the Carters and the Crowthers. You're the man they'll want to see.'

'Am I?' George said with an edge of bitterness in his voice. 'Well, they'll just have to make do with you, Tommy.'

Clough shrugged. 'I've always reckoned if I've done my bit to send a man to the gallows, I should take the consequences.'

'I'm sorry, I've not got the stomach for it. I'll buy you breakfast in the police canteen, then you can go over there if you've a mind.'

'Aye, fine.'

George turned away and made for the bathroom.

'George?' Clough said softly. 'There's no shame in it, either way. There's nothing worse in this job, not even telling a mother her child's dead. But you have to survive it. I've got my way, and you're finding your way. Never mind breakfast. I'll catch up with you later, and we'll go out tonight and get slaughtered.'

Eight fifty-nine, and George watched the second hand of his watch stutter round the dial. The priest would be finished with Hawkin now. George wondered how Hawkin would be. Terrified, for sure. He thought he'd probably try for dignity.

The hand swept up towards twelve and the nearby church clock boomed out the first stroke of nine o'clock. The double doors in the condemned cell would be swung open and Hawkin would walk the last twenty feet of his life. The hangman would be wrapping the leather strap round his wrists.

The second stroke. Now the executioner is walking ahead of Hawkin, his assistant behind, keeping the pace as even as possible, the official killers trying to act as if this were another stroll in the park.

The third stroke. Hawkin is on the drop now, feet planted one on each side of the double doors of the trap that will fall away and take his life with it.

The fourth stroke. The hangman will be turning to face the condemned man, holding out his hands to halt his progress while his assistant squats and straps Hawkin's legs together.

The fifth stroke. The linen bag appears as if by a magic trick. The hangman drops it over Hawkin's head with the ease of practice. Now it's faster because nobody has to look at the man who will be dead inside a minute, his eyes have ceased to implore them, to stare with the wall-eyed panic of the condemned animal. The hangman pulls the bag down and smooths it round the neck so the linen won't catch in the eye of the noose.

The sixth stroke. The hangman slips the noose over his head, checking that the brass eye which had replaced the traditional slip-knot is positioned behind Hawkin's ear for maximum speed in the fracture and dislocation process that makes hanging theoretically swift and relatively painless.

The seventh stroke. The hangman steps back, signals to his assistant. The assistant pulls out the cotter pin that acts as a safety measure in the gallows mechanism. Then, almost in the same instant, the hangman pulls the lever.

The eighth stroke. The trap falls away, Hawkin plunges down in the fatal drop.

The ninth stroke. It is over.

George knew there was sweat on his lip. He could see his hand tremble as it reached for his cigarettes. Tiny human gestures lost to Hawkin now, as they had been lost earlier to Alison Carter.

Only with the release of his breath did he realize he'd been holding it. He rubbed a hand over his face, feeling the rough skin with something like gratitude.

When the phone rang, he jumped.

Within the same five minutes, Philip Hawkin had left the number of the living and Paul George Bennett had joined them.

Tommy Clough and George never did get together for that drink.

BOOK 2

PART ONE

10th August 1998

Dear Catherine,

I am writing about a very important matter that is of great concern for both of us. This is not an easy letter for me to write, all the more so since I cannot give you an explanation for what I am asking of you. I can only apologize and ask you to continue to give me your trust as you have done over the past six months while we have been working together on A Place of Execution.

Catherine, you must halt the publication of this book. It cannot go ahead. I beg of you to do whatever it takes to stop it ever appearing. I know that you have only recently delivered your finished manuscript to the publisher, so they cannot have proceeded very far with the job. But no matter what the inconvenience to them, they must be made to understand that this book must never be published.

I know that this must seem outrageous to you, especially since I am asking you to do it without explaining why. All I can say is that fresh information has come to me that makes it imperative that this book should not be left as the definitive record of the Alison Carter case. I cannot tell you what that information is, because it affects people other than me. My fear is that if the book is published, the case will attract a great deal of publicity and that in turn could have terrible, terrible consequences for innocent people. I beg of you not to inflict those consequences on their heads because they have done nothing to deserve it.

The only person who should have to pay for my mistakes is me. I understand that the publishers' advance must be repaid, and it is my intention to repay the whole amount, your share included. You deserve to be recompensed for the work you have done, and I will not add insult to injury by expecting you to refund the money you have already had.

I know this is a terrible thing to ask of a professional writer, but I beg you to forget this book, to forget this case and to turn your back for ever on the story of Alison Carter and Philip Hawkin. You have what it takes to find the truth, but for the sake of your sanity, I urge you to abandon this project, however painful it may be.

Catherine, I know you will try to talk me out of this decision, but it is final. If you attempt to persist with the book, I will have to employ whatever legal steps it takes to stop you. I would hate to have to do that, because I feel a friendship has grown up between us in the course of this work that I would be sorry to see finish. But it is a measure of how serious I am about putting a stop to this book that I would sacrifice our friendship to prevent it ever seeing the light of day.

I am more sorry about this than I can express. Recent events have turned my life upside down and I can barely think straight. The one thing I can be certain of is that you must ensure that our book is never published.

Yours truly,

George Bennett

BOOK 2

PART TWO

1

February 1998

Even a pale winter sun made the White Peak dramatic. The chill blue of the sky contrasted with the tired green of the fields, which seemed to have picked up a tinge of grey from the dry-stone walls. There were more shades of grey than seemed possible; the off-white of limestone cliffs, striated and stippled with a spectrum that ranged from dove through battleship to almost black; the darker tones of the barns and houses that dotted the landscape; the flat matt-grey of slate roofs, splashed with the white of hoarfrost where the sun had failed to reach; the dirty grey of moorland sheep. Nevertheless, it was the green and blue of grass and sky that dominated the landscape.

The scarlet coupé cruising smoothly down the narrow country road stood out like an exotic parrot in an English wood. As the Methodist Chapel came into view on the right, the blonde woman behind the wheel touched the brakes softly. The car slowed gradually and she changed down a gear when she caught sight of a road sign she didn't recall. Pointing to a narrow turning on the left, it read, 'Scardale 1'.

At last, she thought. The unfamiliar road sign was

439

a timely reminder that the world had changed, she realized. Nowadays people who didn't know where they were going had to be able to find Scardale. If she succeeded as well as she hoped, there would be plenty of others who would be seeking that guidance. With a shiver of excitement, she swung the car round the bend. Even though she vaguely recalled the sudden dips and rises of the twisting road, she kept her speed down. The high limestone walls had kept the weak February sunshine off the single-track road and it was still heavily rimed with frost, save where previous traffic had exposed the black tarmac. It wouldn't be an auspicious start to the project if she skidded and damaged her paintwork, she reminded herself.

It came as no shock to Catherine Heathcote when the dry-stone walls suddenly gave way to towering cliffs of streaked grey limestone. What was a surprise was that there was no longer a gate across the road, separating public from private. Now, the only indications that once Scardale had deliberately cut itself off were the stone gateposts and the cattle grid that her wide-profile tyres bumped softly over.

Nothing in the landscape had changed significantly, she realized. Shield Tor and Scardale Crag still loomed above the dale. Sheep still safely grazed, although the dictates of fashion had imposed a flock of Jacob's sheep among the more familiar hardy moorland ewes. The scatterings of woodland were more mature, it was true, but they'd been well maintained, with new saplings replacing the trees that had been cropped or felled by the harsh weather. But it still felt like leaving the world behind and entering a parallel universe, Catherine thought. For all the change in the view, she could have been a child again, peering from the back seat over the adults' shoulders as they drove down into this remote world to find the mysterious source of the seeping Scarlaston on a summer Sunday afternoon.

Only when she drew up on the edge of the village green was real change apparent. In the years since Hawkin's execution, a new prosperity had come to Scardale. She reminded herself of what she'd learned when she'd first written about Alison Carter's murder a dozen years before in a news feature commissioned because a new 'no body' case had hit the headlines. Catherine's research in the local paper archives and among her mother's bridge-playing cronies had revealed that when Ruth Hawkin had inherited the dale and the village from her husband, she had decided to move away from the memories. She had sold the manor house and set up a trust to administer the land and the farms. Tenants had been given the opportunity to buy their homes, and over the intervening years some had been sold to outsiders. Ruth Hawkin had also proved impossible to track down, and had refused all Catherine's attempts to secure an interview via the solicitor who acted for the trust.

Inevitably, the process set in train by Ruth's actions had led to a smartening up of the village. Fresh paint gleamed on windows and doors, gardens had been carved out of nothing and even in the grip of winter, early crocuses, dwarf irises and snowdrops provided splashes of colour. And of course, cars had invaded the village green where once there had only been battered Land Rovers and the squire's Austin Cambridge. A modern Plexiglas kiosk had replaced the old red phone box, but the standing stone still leaned at its familiar angle. Even with the modern cars and the smartened-up cottages, on an afternoon as chill as this, it wasn't hard to picture Scardale as it had been when she'd first visited as a child and later, innocence dispelled, as a teenager.

She'd been sixteen. Two and a half years had passed since Alison Carter's murder, and Catherine had a boyfriend with a scooter. She'd persuaded him to drive her to Scardale one spring afternoon, so they could see for themselves the place where it had happened. It had, she acknowledged with some shame, been nothing more than ghoulish curiosity. She'd been at that age when outrage was the aim of every activity. They hadn't had the stomach – or the footwear – for battling through the undergrowth to find the old mine workings, but their adolescent fumblings in the woodland behind the manor house had held an extra frisson for her because of the very notoriety of the spot.

It had also, she now realized, been a way of exorcizing the horror that had unfolded at Philip Hawkin's trial. Of course, most of the details had been shrouded in the sensational euphemisms of journalese, but Catherine and all her friends knew that something terrible had happened to Alison Carter, the sort of terrible something that they'd only ever been warned could happen at the hands of strangers. It had been all the more frightening because it had befallen Alison at the hands of someone she knew and should have been able to trust. For Catherine and her friends, all from sheltered middle-class families, the idea that home didn't necessarily mean safety had been profoundly unsettling.

On a more mundane level, it had placed constraints on their lives, both parental and self-imposed. They'd

442

been chaperoned and escorted to a stifling degree, just at a time when the rest of Britain's teenagers were discovering the Swinging Sixties. Alison's fate had coloured Catherine's adolescence with hitherto unsuspected darkness, and she had never been able to forget either the case or the victim. More than any other single factor, it had probably influenced her own decision to shake the dust of Buxton from her heels as soon as she possibly could. University in London, then dogsbody work with a news agency and finally a job as a news feature writer had allowed her to sever the bonds with her past, filling her life with new faces, new fascinations, and leaving no loose ends behind.

As she had progressed from one rung of the ladder to the next above it, Catherine had often wondered what Alison's future would have held. Not that she was obsessed, she told herself. Just infected with the natural curiosity that should afflict any journalist who had grown up at one remove from such a strange and unnerving case.

And now, miraculously, she would be the one finally to unshroud the past and reveal the story behind the story. It was fitting, she thought. There couldn't be another journalist better qualified to tell this truth.

Catherine got out of the car and fastened her Barbour jacket, tucking her scarf tightly round her neck. She crossed the green, and climbed the stile that led to the footpath that she knew would take her through the copse where Shep had been found and on to the source of the Scarlaston.

As the frosty grass crunched under her feet, she couldn't help contrasting her walk with the last time she'd been in Scardale. A hot July afternoon ten years before, the sun blasting out of a brassy-blue sky, the trees a welcome respite from the heat. Catherine and a couple of friends had rented a holiday cottage in Dovedale as a base for a walking holiday in the Peaks. One of their trips had been a hike up the Scarlaston from Denderdale to Scardale. Hot and sticky after their expedition, they'd called a taxi from the phone box on the green then sat on a wall and swapped gossip about their London colleagues while they'd waited. Catherine hadn't even mentioned Alison, strangely superstitious when it came to sharing the story with fellow journalists.

It had never occurred to her then that she would be the person who would manage to persuade George Bennett to break his thirty-five-year silence and talk about the case. Although she'd never forgotten Alison Carter, writing the definitive book on one of the most interesting cases of the century hadn't even been on Catherine's agenda.

It certainly hadn't been on her mind the previous autumn in Brussels. But then, in Catherine's experience, the best stories were never the ones you went looking for. And there was no question in her mind that this was going to be the best story of her career.

2

October 1997 – February 1998

The rain poured down in an unrelenting sheet. It might have been bearable if she'd been comfortable and cosy in some glass-fronted bar looking out over the Grand Place, a steaming Irish coffee warming her hands while she gloated over scurrying figures wrestling their umbrellas against the wind. But kicking her heels on a wet Wednesday afternoon in a concrete Eurobox with a view of other office blocks while she waited for a Swedish commissioner to remember their appointment wasn't Catherine's idea of a good time. It wasn't at all what she'd had in mind when she'd planned her little jaunt to Euroland.

Although Catherine was the commissioning editor for features on a glossy women's monthly, she had never lost her taste for the news features that had first earned her a reputation. She liked from time to time to escape the stresses of day-to-day bureaucracy and the pettiness of office politics. Her excuse was the need to remain in touch with her creative side, and to keep abreast with the changing circumstances faced by the writers she employed. So periodically, she would set up a feature that allowed her to do the research, the interviews and the writing.

She'd thought it would be interesting to do a series of interviews with leading women in the EU. She'd reckoned without the endless bureaucracy and the dismal weather. Not to mention the fact that meetings always overran and nobody was ever on time for their interviews. Sighing, Catherine picked up the phone in the conference room and called her minder, a British press officer called Paul Bennett. She'd expected him to be offhand and up himself, like most government press officers, but he'd been a pleasant surprise. Once they'd discovered they'd both grown up in Derbyshire, the relationship had run even more smoothly, and Paul had managed to sort out most of her glitches so far.

'Paul? It's Catherine Heathcote. Sigrid Hammarqvist is a no-show.'

'Oh bugger,' he said with exasperation. 'Can you hold a minute?'

Some classical music shrieked in her ears, the violins angry mosquitoes. Catherine sometimes wished she knew one piece of classical music from another, but she doubted that would be much help to her right then. She moved the receiver far enough from her ear to avoid the irritation but close enough to hear Paul when he came back on the line. A couple of minutes passed, then he spoke. 'Catherine? I'm afraid it's bad news. Or good, depending on your view of Mrs Hammarqvist. She's had to go to Strasbourg for a meeting. Won't be back till the morning, but her secretary promises faithfully she's put you in for her eleven o'clock tomorrow. If that suits?'

'My turn to say, "oh, bugger," Catherine said wryly. 'I was hoping to catch the shuttle back tonight.'

'Sorry,' Paul said. 'The Scandies have a tendency to see journalists as a bit too low down the food chain to lose sleep over.'

'It's not your fault. Thanks for sorting it out for me, anyway. And at least I get another night in sunny Brussels,' she added ironically.

Paul laughed. 'Yeah, right. I don't like to think of you hanging about at a loose end, though. Listen, if you've not got any other plans, why don't you come round to our flat for a drink?'

'No, don't worry, I'll be fine,' Catherine said with professional insouciance.

'I'm not just inviting you out of a sense of duty,' he said insistently. 'I'd like you to meet Helen.'

His partner, she recalled. An interpreter and translator with the Commission. 'I'm sure that's exactly what she fancies after another day in the Tower of Babel,' she said ironically.

'She reads your magazine every month, and she'll kill me if I pass up the chance to bring you home for a glass or three of wine. *And* she's another northern lass,' he added, as if that should clinch it.

Something had, for just after seven, Catherine found herself air-kissing Helen Markiewicz. Not exactly a typical Derbyshire greeting, she'd thought sardonically as she checked out Paul's partner. She certainly looked like she could be one of Catherine's magazine's target group. Thirty-something, her dark hair cut short in a tousled mop, falling forward over a broad forehead. She had a heart-shaped face, with straight dark brows, high cheekbones and a generous smile. Her make-up was subtle but effective, just as the style pages recommended for the professional woman. Helen seemed vaguely familiar, and Catherine wondered if she'd passed her in the corridors of the EU buildings she'd been in over the past few days. Someone so striking and stylish would have caught her eye, however unconsciously. She could see exactly why Paul was eager to show her off.

As Paul poured generous glasses of red wine, the two women settled into opposite corners of a squashy sofa. 'Paul tells me Mrs Hammarqvist stood you up,' Helen said, the traces of a Yorkshire accent still strong in her voice. 'That must be a bit like steeling yourself to go to the dentist only to find he's gone home early.'

'She's not that bad,' Paul protested.

'She'd give Grendel's mother a run for her money,' Helen said obscurely.

'I'm sure Catherine won't let her get away with anything.'

'Oh, I'm sure she won't, love.' Helen grinned at Catherine. 'Did he tell you I'm your number one fan? No bullshit – I actually have a subscription.'

'I'm impressed,' Catherine said. 'But tell me, how did you two meet? Is this a Euro-romance?'

'Watch her, Helen, she's already sussing out the feature for next year's Valentine's Day edition.'

'Not everybody brings their work home with them,' Helen teased Paul back. 'Yes, Catherine, we met in Brussels. Paul was the first person I'd met in the Commission with a northern accent, so we had an instant connection.'

'And I fancied her like hell, so she had no chance,' Paul added, looking over at Helen.

'Where are you from, Helen?'

'Sheffield,' she replied.

'Just over the Pennines from me. I grew up in Buxton.'

Helen nodded. 'My sister's over that way now. Do you know a place called Scardale?'

Catherine recognized the name with a jolt of surprise. 'Of course I know Scardale.'

'Our Jan moved there a couple of years ago.'

'Really? Why Scardale?' Catherine asked.

'Just one of those things. My aunt lived with us for years and she inherited a house there from a distant relative of her late husband. Some second cousin, or something. When my aunt died, it went to our mum. And when she died three years ago, she left it to me and Jan. It had always been rented out, but Jan fancied living in the country, so she decided to give the tenants notice and she took it over. It'd drive me crazy, living out there in the middle of nowhere, but she loves it. Mind you, she does a lot of travelling with her work, so I don't suppose she gets the chance to get too fed up with it.'

'What does she do?' Catherine asked.

'She's got a consultancy business. She works mainly for big multinationals doing psychological assessments of key staff. She's only been doing it a few years now, but she's done really well,' Helen said. 'She'd have to, mind you, to pay for heating that barn of a house.'

There was only one property in Scardale that fitted that description. 'She's not living in Scardale Manor, is she?' Catherine asked.

'You obviously know the place,' Helen laughed. 'That's right. So how come you know a poky little hole like Scardale so well?'

'Helen,' Paul said, a warning note in his voice.

Catherine gave a twisted smile. 'There was a murder in Scardale when I was a teenager. A girl was abducted and killed by her stepfather. She was the same age as I was.'

'Alison Carter?' Helen exclaimed. 'You know about the Alison Carter case?'

'I'm surprised you do,' Catherine said. 'You can hardly have been born when it hit the headlines.'

'Oh, we know all about the Alison Carter case, don't we, Paul?' Helen said, almost gleefully.

'No, Helen, we don't,' Paul said, sounding faintly cross.

'OK, maybe we don't,' Helen said, her voice placating, her hand reaching out to touch his arm. 'But we know a man who does.'

'Leave it, Helen. Catherine's not interested in a thirty-five-year-old murder case.'

'That's where you're wrong, Paul. I've always been fascinated by the case. What's your connection?' She stared at his frowning face. Suddenly, something clicked in her brain. A faint resemblance that had chimed in the back of her head when they'd met, and now his name, connected to the Alison Carter case. Rapidly, she put two and two together. 'Wait a minute . . . You're not *George* Bennett's son, are you?'

'He is,' Helen said triumphantly.

Paul looked suspicious. 'You know my dad?'

Catherine shook her head. 'No, not personally. I know of him, though, because of the Alison Carter case. He did a terrific job on that.'

Paul said, 'Yeah, well, it was before I was born, and Dad's never been one to talk about his work much.'

'It was a really important case, you know. Baby

lawyers still have to learn about it because of its implications in murder cases where there's no body. And there's never been a book about the case. All you can find is newspaper accounts from the time and dry-as-dust legal precedents. I'm amazed your father's not written his memoirs,' Catherine said.

Paul shrugged and ran a hand through neatly barbered blond hair. 'It's not his kind of thing. I remember some journalist turning up at the house one time. I must have been about sixteen. This bloke said he'd covered the case at the time and wanted Dad to cooperate on a book about it, but Dad sent him away with a flea in his ear. He said to Mum afterwards that Alison's mother had gone through enough at the time and she didn't deserve to have it all raked over again.'

At once, Catherine's journalistic instincts were on full alert. 'But she's dead now, Alison's mother. She died in ninety-five. There's no reason why he shouldn't talk about the case now.' She leaned forward, suddenly excited. 'I'd love to write the inside story of the Alison Carter case. It should be told, Paul. Not least because all the reports at the time glossed over the real truth about Philip Hawkin's sexual abuse of his stepdaughter. It was an important case. Not just legally, but in the way it affected so many people's lives.'

Surprisingly, Helen added her support. 'Catherine's right, Paul. You know how unscrupulous some journalists are. And you know how these historic cases are always resurfacing. If your dad doesn't tell his own story, all that'll happen is that some hack with an eye on the main chance will write about it after he's dead too and there's nobody to contradict some sensationalist version of events. And with our Jan on the doorstep, so to speak, Catherine would be able to get right under the skin of the place.'

Paul held up his hands in mock defeat. Clearly Helen had whatever it took to shift him from borderline hostility to eager helpfulness. 'All right, all right, girls. You win. I'll have a word with the old man the next time I call home. I'll tell him I've found the last trustworthy journalist in Europe and she wants to make him a star. Who knows, I might get to bask in his reflected glory. Now, who fancies wandering down to Jacques's Brasserie for a bucket of mussels?'

A week later, back in London, her phone had rung. The son had worked on the father as no outsider could have. George Bennett was playing in a golf tournament for retired police officers near London the following week and he would meet her for a drink to discuss the possibility of her writing an account of the Alison Carter case based on his recollections.

Catherine had dressed carefully for the meeting. Her one Armani suit, low heels. She wanted all the support she could get, and she agreed with her magazine's fashion editor that there was nothing like superb Italian tailoring to make a woman feel in control. She spent more time than her impatience demanded on applying the tinted moisturizer, eye pencil, lip liner and lipstick she needed to feel good about herself. It took a little more with every passing year. Some of her colleagues had had cosmetic surgery, but they had marriages to consider. Catherine knew it was a lot harder to hold someone once the novelty had worn off than it ever was to find someone else's someone willing to share some clandestine good times for as long as it lasted. Not that she had designs of that kind on George Bennett.

But it wouldn't hurt to make him feel flattered that she'd taken trouble for him.

He was still handsome, however, and that made her all the more glad she'd made the effort. Silver-blond hair, crooked smile, eyes that still held genuine good nature in spite of thirty years in the police; like Robert Redford, George Bennett was a man whose best days were a memory, but no one could look at him without knowing that there had been splendour in the grass.

And amazingly, George Bennett was finally ready to talk. She suspected a number of reasons. The one he articulated was that now Ruth Carter was dead, he felt able to talk freely without the prospect of causing her more pain. But she also thought that the dead hand of retirement was weighing heavily on him. After he'd retired from the police as a detective chief superintendent at fifty-three, he'd worked as a security consultant for several companies in the Amber Valley, but his wife's increasing incapacity because of crippling arthritis had induced him to give that up the previous year. George Bennett was clearly not a man who liked to be out of the flow of the world, nor did he relish the obscurity of being just another elderly man to be dismissed as irrelevant. Catherine thought her suggestion had come at the most opportune moment possible.

Four months later, they had a book contract and Catherine had negotiated a six-month leave of absence from her job. And she was in Scardale, a player at last in the drama that had shaped her adolescence.

3

February 1998

George Bennett stared at his reflection in the kitchen window. The ghost of the garden outside floated behind his features, blurring some of the lines that the last thirty-five years had etched. Alison Carter's disappearance had been the first case that had given him sleepless nights, though it had been a long way from the last. But here she was again, stealing sleep from him on a cold winter's night. Half past five and no chance of slipping back into oblivion.

The kettle clicked off and he turned back to the cool fluorescence of the kitchen. He poured boiling water on the teabag he'd already placed in the mug and prodded it with a spoon until it had produced maximum strength. Too many years of police canteens had left him with a taste for the bitterness of tannin-loaded orange tea. He took the milk from the fridge and poured in just enough to cool the tea to the point where he could drink it immediately. Then he sat down at the kitchen table, shrugging his dressing gown closer to his body. He reached for the packet of cigarettes on the table and lit up.

Now the day of Catherine Heathcote's first proper

interview was upon him, George found himself caught in the snarls of regret. He'd always avoided talking about the case. Paul's birth had seemed to him the perfect closure, a fresh start that would allow him to put Ruth Carter's pain behind him. Of course, it hadn't been that clean or that easy. There were too many regular reminders in routine police work for him to have managed to wipe Alison Carter from the easily accessible area of his memory. But he'd managed to stick to his resolution not to talk about the case.

None of his colleagues had understood the reason for his silence over what they would have regarded as a triumph worth boasting about at every opportunity. Only Anne had really grasped that what underlay his decision was his sense of personal failure. Although he'd overcome tremendous odds to solve Alison's baffling disappearance and he'd managed to gather enough evidence to hang the man responsible, George was plagued by the conviction that he'd taken far too long over it. Ruth Carter had gone through long miserable weeks of uncertainty and false hope, clinging to the notion that her daughter might still be alive. Not only that, but Philip Hawkin had known more days of freedom than he had deserved. He'd been eating the meals his wife had cooked him, sleeping at night while she lay awake and afraid, walking his land with the certainty of possession, convinced he'd got away with murder. George blamed himself for allowing Hawkin even that brief interlude of security.

And so he had resisted all attempts to persuade him to talk about the case. He'd turned down offers from several writers who wanted to revisit the case through his eyes. Even that ambulance chaser Don Smart had thought he had the right to come knocking on his door and demand his time and his insights. That hadn't been a difficult request to reject, George thought with a bitter smile.

It was ironic that the very love that had made it possible for him to move forward had been his undoing. He'd known when Paul had first told him and Anne about Helen's sister in Scardale that if his son was as serious about this woman as he appeared to be, then sooner or later he would have to break his resolution never to revisit the scene of the crime. So far, it hadn't arisen. But he knew that Helen's divorce would be finalized soon, and he had a shrewd suspicion that the couple wouldn't wait too long to marry. That would mean meeting Helen's sister, her only surviving family, and he wouldn't be able to avoid Scardale indefinitely.

With that prospect hanging over him, Paul's intercession on behalf of Catherine Heathcote had seemed fateful. It was as if events were conspiring to force him to think about Alison Carter again. He'd decided it wouldn't hurt just to meet the journalist, to see if she was someone he felt he could trust. His first impression had been that she was just another glossy Fleet Street hack, but as they had talked and she had revealed the impact Alison's murder had made on her own life, he had realized that he was never going to find anyone better suited to write a story that now seemed as if it were demanding to be told.

The familiar sound of footsteps descending the stair disturbed his thoughts. He looked up to see Anne appear in the doorway, rumpled with sleep. 'Did I wake you, love?' he asked, reaching across and switching the kettle on again.

'My bladder woke me,' she said wryly, moving slowly across to the chair opposite his. 'And your side of the bed was cold, so I thought you might fancy some company.'

George got up and spooned the malted chocolate brew Anne loved into a mug. 'I wouldn't say no,' he said as he poured the water in, stirring constantly. He returned to his chair and slid her drink across the table to her. She wrapped fingers twisted with arthritis round the mug, savouring its warmth against the constant throb of her rheumatic pain.

'Nervous about today?' she asked.

He nodded. 'As you'd expect, I'm wishing I'd never agreed to this.'

'It would be a lesser man that didn't have cold feet over something as important as this,' she said kindly. 'You can't help wanting to get it right, to do Alison some kind of justice.'

He gave a quiet snort of derision. 'You're implying higher motives than I possess, love. I'm wishing I'd never agreed to it because I don't want to see myself exposed in print for the fool I was over Philip Hawkin.'

Anne shook her head. 'You're the only one that thinks so, George. In everybody else's eyes, you were the hero of the hour. If they had a Freedom of Scardale to give, they'd have granted it to you on the spot the day the jury brought in their verdict.'

He shook his head. 'Maybe so. But you know I've never measured myself by other people's yardsticks, only by my own, and by my standards, I let those people down. I was part of a system that let Alison down in the first place, a system that wouldn't listen to a young girl's claims that she was being sexually abused.'

Anne pursed her lips impatiently. 'Now you're being daft. Back then, nobody admitted there was any such thing as child sex abuse. Certainly not inside families. If you want to make yourself miserable imagining you failed Ruth Carter, that's up to you. But I won't sit by while you beat yourself up over the failings of British society thirty-five years ago. That's just wallowing, George Bennett, and you know it.'

He smiled, acknowledging she was right. 'You could be right. Maybe I should have let all this out years ago. Isn't that what the trick cyclists are always telling us? Letting it out is healthy. Keep it buttoned up and you get all sorts of psychoses.'

Anne mirrored his smile. 'Like paranoia that you're to blame for all the wrongs of the world.'

He ran a hand through his hair. 'There's another thing, too. I've got to lay my ghosts to rest for Paul and Helen's sake. We're going to have to go to Scardale one of these days to meet Helen's sister, and I've let Scardale become the bogeyman for me. I've got to change that or I'll spoil it for everybody. And I don't want to do anything that might ruin the lad's happiness. Talking to a stranger about the whole mess might just make the difference for me.'

'I think you could be right, love, and I can't deny that I'm glad you've finally decided to talk about Alison. Apart from anything else, it happened at an important time in our lives. I've often had to hold back things I've wanted to say, memories I've wanted to share, because I knew that if I talked about when I was carrying Paul, it always reminded you of when you were putting your case together against Philip Hawkin. So I won't be sorry if you opening up to Catherine Heathcote means I'll be able to talk to you about some of the memories I've had to keep to myself. And not just to you, but to Paul too. I know that's selfish of me, but that's what I'd like.'

George's eyes opened wide in surprise. 'I had no idea you felt like that,' he protested, shaking his head. 'How could I not know?'

Anne sipped her drink. 'Because I never let on, love. But now you're properly retired, not doing your security work, it's time we were able to look back on our life together without fear. We've still got a future, George. We're not old, not by today's standards. This is our chance to clear the past away once and for all, for you to see that what you did was good, and right, and it made a difference.' She reached out and put her gnarled hand over his. 'Time for you to forgive yourself, George.'

The sigh seemed to come from the soles of his feet. 'Well, I hope Catherine Heathcote's in a forgiving mood.' He yawned. 'For I'm not going to be at my sparkling best at ten this morning unless I get some more sleep.' He shifted his hand so it gently held Anne's. 'Thanks, love.'

'For what?'

'For reminding me I'm not the monster I sometimes imagine I've become.'

'You're not a monster. Well, except when you wake up with a hangover. It'll be fine, George,' Anne soothed him. 'It's not as if the past holds any surprises, is it?'

4

February/March 1998

Waking for the first time in her rented cottage in Longnor, Catherine had felt a momentary panic. She couldn't remember where she was. She should be sprawled in a warm room with tall sash windows. Instead, her nose was freezing and she was curled into a foetal ball under a strange duvet, the only light seeping round a thin curtain covering a small casement set in a stone wall over a foot thick.

Then memory clicked in with a thrill of excitement that almost banished her irritation at the icy chill of this one-up, one-down stone cottage that she'd taken a six-month lease on. The owners of the holiday cottage had been delighted by her approach. Now she understood why. No one in their right mind would rent this ice-box in winter, she thought as she jumped out of bed, shivering as her long legs were exposed to the air. Sometime today, she'd have to buy some warm pyjamas and a hot-water bottle or she wasn't going to make it out of Longnor without a recurrence of the chilblains that had made her childhood a misery. She cursed the landlords as colourfully as only a journalist can, and ran from the room.

The bathroom was a welcome refuge. A wall-mounted heater blew hot air instantaneously, and the power shower was blessedly steaming. She knew already that the living room-kitchen would warm up quickly too, thanks to an efficient gas fire. But the bedroom was purgatory. In future, she resolved, as she returned there after her shower, she'd remember to take her clothes to the bathroom with her.

As she dressed, she reminded herself that she hadn't slept anywhere this cold since the family home in Buxton before the central heating had been installed when she'd been fifteen. Abruptly, she stopped halfway through pulling her sweater over her head. If she was trying to re-create Scardale in 1963, she couldn't have ended up in a better place. Alison Carter would have grown up only too familiar with frost on the inside of her bedroom windows in the depths of winter. And with a warm, welcoming cottage kitchen, before her mother had exchanged that for life in the manor. Catherine hadn't intended her research to involve quite such a degree of authenticity, but since it was being handed to her on a plate, she'd take it and be grateful. Besides, it was less than a hundred yards from Peter Grundy's home. The retired Longnor constable was bound to be a valuable source, she felt sure. And he would be her entrée into village life. She knew exactly how unfriendly village pubs could be to any-one perceived as an outsider, and she didn't fancy six months of evenings without conversation. Even if it was only the fatstock prices at Leek Market.

Over a breakfast of black coffee and a bacon sand-wich, she flicked through the photocopied cuttings she'd laboriously uncovered in the national newspaper

461

archive at Colindale. She wouldn't have much need of those today; but it didn't hurt to keep going over the ground so she knew exactly how to shape the series of interviews she was about to embark on with George Bennett. They'd agreed that they would meet for two hours every morning. That would give Catherine time to transcribe the tapes of their interviews and wouldn't disrupt the Bennetts too much. The last thing she wanted was for them to grow fed up with her constant intrusion into their life. Nothing would dry up George's flow of reminiscence faster than that.

Half an hour later, she emerged from a tunnel of winter trees into the centre of Cromford village. Following George's directions, she turned right by the millpond and cut up the hill, swinging out to make the sharp left turn into the drive of their detached house. As she killed the engine, the front door was already open. George stood framed in the doorway, a hand raised in greeting. In his dark-grey trousers, air-force blue cardigan and light-grey polo shirt, he looked like a model for a knitwear catalogue for the more mature man. All he needed, she thought, was a pipe clenched between his teeth. Jimmy Stewart meets suburbia in *It's A Wonderful Life* for the over-sixties.

'Good to see you, Catherine,' he called.

'And you, George.' She shivered as she walked into the warm hall. 'I'd forgotten how piercing the weather gets up here at this time of year.'

'It takes me back,' he said, leading the way down the carpeted hall into a living room that resembled a display in a furniture showroom. Everything was smart, stylish, even, but curiously without character. Even the framed Monet prints appeared innocuous rather than indicators of taste. Not a single newspaper disturbed the clinical tidiness of the room, which smelled of floral air-freshener. Wherever the Bennetts displayed their individuality, it wasn't in their living room.

'It was bitter cold like this when Alison disappeared,' George continued. 'It made me hope right from the start she'd been kidnapped, you know. That way, there was a chance we might get her back. I knew in my heart that she'd never survive a night in the open in that weather.'

George gestured towards an armchair that looked both firm and comfortable. 'Have a seat.' He moved to the chair opposite. Catherine noticed he'd automatically taken the seat that put the light behind him and on her. She wondered if it were a policeman's deliberate choice, or something as simple as that being his normal chair. Doubtless she'd be better able to judge after a few of these sessions. 'So,' George said. 'How do you want to do this?'

Before she could reply, an elderly woman walked into the room. Short silver hair framed a face prematurely aged by the lines suffering had carved there. She held herself with the stiff awkwardness of someone for whom movement has ceased to be anything other than a painful necessity. Even from the other side of the room, Catherine could see the fingers knotted and twisted with the misshapen lumps of rheumatoid arthritis. But the smile on her face was still genuine, giving her blue eyes the sparkle of animation. 'You must be Catherine,' she said. 'It's lovely to meet you. I'm Anne, George's wife. Now, I'm not going to interfere with your interviews, except to ask if you'd rather have tea or coffee.'

'It's nice to meet you, too. Thanks for letting me invade your home like this,' Catherine said, calculating the odds on getting a decent cup of coffee in an English home occupied by two people in their sixties. 'I'll have tea, please,' she said. 'Very weak, no milk or sugar.' That should be safe, she reckoned. A couple of months of bad coffee was less than she deserved.

'Tea it is,' Anne said.

'And Mrs Bennett?' Catherine continued. 'You won't be intruding if you want to sit in on any of our sessions. And I'd be very grateful if I could talk to you at some point, to get a picture of what life was like for you as a policeman's wife when your husband was investigating such a demanding case.'

Anne smiled. 'Of course we can have a chat. But I'll leave the interviews to you and George. I don't want to cramp his style, and besides, I've plenty to be getting on with. And now, I'll sort you some tea.'

As Anne left, Catherine took her tape recorder from her bag and placed it on the table between them. 'I'll be taping the interviews. That way there's less chance of me making mistakes. So if there's anything you want to say that's not for publication, that's just for my information, can you make that clear while we're talking? Also, if there's anything that you're not sure about, can you mention that as well? That way I can keep a running list of things I need to check.'

George smiled. 'That all sounds very sensible to me.' He took a packet of cigarettes out of his pocket and lit up, taking an ashtray out of the drawer in the occasional table by his side. 'I hope you don't mind these, by the way. I've cut down a lot since I stopped work, but I still can't manage without them altogether.'

'No problem. I've not smoked for a dozen years now, but I still think of myself as a smoker in abeyance rather than an ex-smoker. You'll always find me with the smokers at parties – somehow, they're usually the more interesting ones,' she said with a smile, not simply flattering. She leaned forward and pressed the 'record' button. 'We're probably not going to get on to the case today. What I'd like to start with is your own background. Most of this will never see the light of day, but it's important for me that I have a picture of who you are and how you got to be that person if I'm going to write about your work on this case with the insight and the empathy I want to bring to it. Also, it's a way of easing gently into the story. I realize you're probably quite nervous about going into the details of the case after all these years, and I want you to feel as relaxed and comfortable about it as possible. And of course, as a police officer, you're much more accustomed to asking the questions than answering them. So is it OK if we start with you?'

George smiled. 'That's fine. I'm happy to tell you anything you want to know.' He paused as Anne walked into the room, moving slowly with a tray that held two mugs. 'One thing I will tell you. This woman is the reason I'm not in the lunatic asylum after thirty-odd years in Derbyshire Police. Anne is my rock, my tower of strength.'

Anne pulled a face as she put the tray down on the coffee table. 'You're such a flannel merchant, George Bennett. What you mean is, Anne is my catering

465

service, my answering machine and my housekeeper.' She looked up at Catherine with a smile.

It was clearly a familiar line of banter. 'She had to develop arthritis so she could get me to lift a finger around the house,' George added.

'I had to do something,' she said drily. 'Otherwise you'd have taken retirement as a cue to stop dead. Now, stop blethering, and tell Catherine what she needs to know. I'll bring some biscuits, then I'll see you both when you're finished.'

So began the pattern of days that lasted through February and March. Catherine would start each day by reading the section of her press cuttings that bracketed the part of the case they would be talking about. After breakfast, she would drive to Cromford, mulling over the questions she needed to tease more truth from her interviewee.

Then she would lead George gently through the case, patiently backtracking to capture a particular detail of weather, of smell, of landscape. She couldn't help but be impressed by his eagerness to make sure they got everything spot on. He proved to have an almost photographic memory for the Alison Carter case, though he claimed not to have a particularly good recall of other investigations in his career. 'I suppose I got a bit obsessed with Alison,' he'd said near the beginning of their interviews. 'Oh, I know it was my first big case, and I was determined to show I could do the business, but it was more than that. It probably had something to do with Anne telling me she was pregnant so near the start of the investigation. I was tormented by the worry of how I would feel if this were to happen to my child, so I wasn't willing ever to let it go.

'That's what it was with me. I don't know what it was with Tommy Clough, but he was as committed to every stage of the inquiry as I was. He worked even more hours than me, and it was his persistence with Hertfordshire Police that got us one of the most crucial pieces of evidence, the linking of Hawkin to the gun that was used to kill Alison.

'You know, it might sound strange, but I never saw him to speak to properly after Hawkin was hanged. Tommy was still in Buxton, but I'd moved to Derby by then. A couple of times, we arranged to meet for a drink, but work always got in the way. And then within a couple of years of Alison's murder, he handed in his resignation and moved away.'

'Where did he go to?' Catherine asked. She'd already asked Peter Grundy the same question one evening in the pub, but he'd shrugged and told her nobody knew. It was as if Tommy Clough had vanished as comprehensively as Alison herself.

But George had known. 'He's in Northumberland. Some little village up there on the coast. He worked for years as a warden with the RSPB, but he's retired now, like me. He never married, though, so he's not got anybody like Anne to keep him going. We exchange Christmas cards, that's about it. I think I'm the only one from the force he bothered to stay in touch with. I can give you his address, though. He might want to talk about Alison. I doubt it, somehow, but then, you got me talking, didn't you?' George smiled.

And so it continued, one strand leading seamlessly into another as the mornings slipped by. After she left George, Catherine soon developed a routine. She would stop on the way back at a pub on the Ashbourne road that did good lunches, then she'd be home by two. The afternoon and early evening were devoted to transcribing tapes, a task she found tedious beyond belief, in spite of her fascination with the material she was gradually amassing. After every half-hour, she allowed herself a short phone call or an e-mail session to save her from complete insanity.

Work over, she'd heat up one of the ready meals she'd bought from the supermarket in her weekly shopping raid on Buxton. Then she'd have an hour by the fire with either her own magazine or a competitor, armed with a notebook. Finally, the day would end with a nightcap in the local pub. This usually involved buying Peter Grundy a drink too, but Catherine didn't mind the small outlay. He'd already provided her with valuable background into Scardale and its families and besides, she'd grown to enjoy his company.

It was, she realized, a curiously satisfying way of life. The work was fascinating, drawing her back into a world that was both familiar and yet alien. The more she discovered about the background to the case, the more her respect for George Bennett had grown. She'd had no idea of what he'd had to contend with to bring Hawkin to justice, both from inside the force and outside. She'd never had a particularly high opinion of the police, but George was gradually transforming that prejudice.

She'd also been nervous of returning so close to home, almost superstitiously afraid that somehow the stifling small-town life she'd struggled so hard to leave behind might swallow her again. Instead, she'd found a strange peace in the rhythm of her days and nights. Not that she'd want to live like this for ever, she reminded herself vigorously. She had a life, after all. This was just a pleasant interlude, nothing more.

What else could it be?

5

April 1998

Catherine had forgotten how springtime came so late out here. For anyone living in the Derbyshire Peaks, April brought relief after the rigours of winter. Bulbs that had bloomed a full month before a mere dozen miles away on the Cheshire Plain finally thrust up through the ground. Trees pushed forth tentative blossom, and the sheep-cropped grass remembered the colour green.

In Scardale, the first leaves were starting to unfurl in copse and spinney as Catherine drove down into the village. Almost with regret, she had completed her initial interviews with George, and today marked the start of the second phase of her project. Catherine had never intended that her book should merely be George Bennett's memoirs. She had always planned to interview as many of the people connected to the case as she could track down. It hadn't occurred to her that so many of them would be reluctant to share their memories of the case. To her surprise, almost all of the Carters, Crowthers and Lomases had refused point blank to have anything to do with the project.

However, she had managed to schedule an interview

with Alison's aunt, Kathy Lomas. Perhaps it wouldn't matter so much that other members of the extended family had turned her down since, according to George, Kathy had been closer to Ruth Carter than anyone else. For that reason alone, Catherine would have wanted to talk to her. But there was a second reason for her eagerness today.

In spite of Helen having prepared the way with her sister, Catherine still hadn't been inside Scardale Manor. Word had come back to her via a letter from Janis Wainwright's solicitor, who reported that his client had several trips planned throughout the late winter and early spring and would be working from home the rest of the time, when she preferred to remain undisturbed. The lawyer had suggested that, since Miss Wainwright could tell Catherine nothing about the Alison Carter case, the best solution that would meet Catherine's needs without disrupting Janis's busy schedule would be for the writer to view the manor on one of the occasions when its owner was away from home.

Catherine was more than happy to agree to the lawyer's suggestion if that was the only way she would get to see inside the manor. Finally, today she would see the interior of Philip Hawkin's inheritance. Even better, she'd have a guide who could reveal which room had been Alison's, which Hawkin's study, and describe the original decor.

She couldn't help speculating about the woman she was about to meet. George Bennett had painted a portrait of a shrewish, pushy woman who had no respect for the police and who constantly nagged and harried at his heels whenever she felt she had cause.

471

Peter Grundy had described her as a woman haunted by what might have been.

From Peter, she had also gleaned some of the bare facts of Kathy Lomas's life. Alison's aunt lived alone these days. Her husband Mike had died five years before in a farm accident, trampled to death by a berserk bull. Her son Derek had left Scardale to go to university in Sheffield and had become a soil scientist for the United Nations. Kathy, now in her mid-sixties, ran a flock of Jacob's sheep in Scardale. She spun the fleeces into yarn which she then turned into expensive designer sweaters on a knitting machine that, according to Peter Grundy's wife, had more controls than the space shuttle.

Kathy and Ruth Carter were cousins, separated by less than a year, connected by blood on both maternal and paternal sides. They had grown into women and mothers side by side. Kathy's Derek had been born a mere three weeks after Alison. The families' histories were inextricably intertwined. If Catherine couldn't get what she needed from Kathy Lomas, the chances were she wasn't going to get it anywhere else. And if she was as awkward as George had predicted, this was one she would have to handle with consummate skill.

Catherine pulled up outside Lark Cottage, the eighteenth-century house Kathy had lived in continuously since her marriage nineteen years before Alison disappeared. The woman who opened the door was still straight and sturdy, her steel-grey hair pinned up in a cottage loaf. Coupled with her coarse red cheeks, it made her look like Mrs Bunn the Baker's Wife from Happy Families. Only her eyes gave the lie

472

to her jolly appearance. They were cool and critical, making Catherine feel she was being appraised and costed in more than merely monetary terms. 'You'll be the writer, then,' Kathy greeted her, reaching to one side and taking a battered anorak from its peg. 'You'll be wanting a look at the manor first, I expect.' Her tone offered no scope for an alternative suggestion.

'That would be great, Mrs Lomas,' Catherine said, falling in beside the older woman as they crossed the corner of the green towards the manor. 'I really appreciate you giving up your time like this for me.' She cursed herself for starting to gush.

'I'm not giving it up for you,' Kathy said briskly. 'It's for the sake of Alison's memory. I often think about our Alison. She were a grand lass. I imagine the life she would have lived if things had gone different. I see her working with children. A teacher, or a doctor. Something positive, useful. And then I think about the reality.' She paused at the door of the manor and gave Catherine a bleak, hard stare.

'If I could turn back the hands of time and change one thing in my whole life, it would be that Wednesday night,' she said bitterly. 'I'd not let Alison out of my sight. There's no point in telling me not to blame myself. I know Ruth Carter went to her grave wondering how she could have changed things, and I'll go into the ground the same way when it's my turn.

'These days, my life seems to be full of regrets. What is it they say? "If might have beens were kings and queens, then we'd have kingdoms all." Well, I've had plenty of years to rue the things undone and the things unsaid. The trouble is, the only place I can say sorry to the people who matter is the grave-yard. And that's why I'm willing to talk to you, Miss Heathcote.'

She took a key from her pocket and unlocked the door, ushering Catherine into the kitchen. Money had clearly been no object when it had been renovated. The pine units and dresser had a patina that indicated their antiquity was the real thing, not some modern reproduction. The worktops were a mix of marble and sealed wood. As well as a dark-green Aga, the room had a matching American-style double-fronted fridge-freezer and a dishwasher. Catherine glanced at the short stack of newspapers on the end of the kitchen table. The top one was dated two days previously. So Janis Wainwright wasn't long gone, she thought. In spite of that, the kitchen had the empty air of a place long unoccupied.

'I bet it wasn't like this in 1963,' she said drily.

At last, Kathy Lomas managed a smile. 'You're not wrong.'

'Maybe you could tell me what it was like?'

'I think I'll make us a cup of tea first,' Kathy hedged.

'I appreciate Ms Wainwright letting me see over the place. You know her sister's engaged to George Bennett's son?'

'Aye. It's a small world, right enough.' She filled the kettle.

'I met Helen in Brussels,' Catherine continued. 'A nice woman. It's a shame her sister's not around.'

'She's away a lot. I doubt she'd fancy being involved in a book about a murder,' Kathy said repressively, clattering two mugs out of a cupboard on to the worktop.

Catherine walked across to the window that gave a view of the village green. She imagined the empty hours Ruth Carter must have spent straining vainly to pick out the rhythm of her daughter's walk approaching the house.

As if reading her thoughts, Kathy spoke. 'Something inside me turned to stone that night when I watched those policemen milling around the village green. If I was ever in danger of forgetting, the nightmares would be reminder enough. I still can't see a police uniform in the village without wanting to be sick.'

She turned back to brewing the tea. 'It changed everything, that night, didn't it?' Catherine asked, surreptitiously switching on the tape recorder in her coat pocket.

'Aye, it did. I'm just glad we had a copper like George Bennett on our side. If it hadn't been for him, that bastard Hawkin might have got away with it. That's the other reason why I was willing to talk to you. It's about time George Bennett got the credit he deserves for what he did for Alison.'

'You're one of the few people in Scardale who seem to think so. Most of your family don't see it like that. Apart from Janet Carter, and Charlie in London, everybody else has refused to talk to me,' Catherine observed, still hoping she might recruit Kathy's help in loosening their tongues.

'Aye, well, that's up to them. They'll have their own reasons for that. I can't say I blame them for not wanting to rake it up again. There's no good memories for any of us from that time.' She poured tea from an earthenware pot into two matching mugs.

'Right then. You want to know what this place looked like?'

They spent an hour going from room to room, with Kathy providing detailed descriptions of the furnishings and decor and Catherine trying to re-create their image in her mind's eye. She was surprised that she felt no sense of the sinister as Kathy walked her through the house. Catherine had imagined that somehow the events that had led to Alison Carter's death would have seeped into the very walls of Scardale Manor, leaving their ghosts in the air like motes of dust. But there was nothing of that here. It was simply an imaginatively restored old house that, in spite of the money spent on it, was never going to be particularly distinguished. Even the outhouse Philip Hawkin had used as a dark-room lacked any atmosphere. Now it was simply a storage shed for gardening tools and old furniture, no more or less.

Nevertheless, it was a productive hour for Catherine, allowing her to set her knowledge of events against a concrete backdrop. She said as much as Kathy Lomas locked the door behind them and led Catherine back to Lark Cottage for their formal interview. 'Aye, well, better you get it right,' Kathy said. 'Now, what did you want to ask me?'

In the end, Kathy's testimony added little to the facts Catherine had learned from George. Its value lay mostly in the inside knowledge the older woman was able to dispense on the personalities involved. By the end of the afternoon, Catherine felt she had finally come close enough to knowing Ruth Carter and Philip Hawkin to write convincingly about them. That in itself had been worth the trip.

'You're seeing Janet after,' Kathy remarked as Catherine wrote the identifying details on the final microcassette.

'That's right. She said evenings suited her best.'

'Aye. With her working full-time, she likes to keep her weekends for her and Alison.' Kathy got to her feet and gathered the mugs together.

'Alison?' Catherine almost yelped.

'Her lass. Our Janet never wed. Wasted her twenties on a married man. Then she fell pregnant when she was thirty-five and old enough to know better. Some Yank she met when she was staying down south in a hotel at a conference. Any road, he was long gone back to Cincinnati before Janet realized she was in the family way, so she raised the lass herself.'

'She called her daughter Alison?'

'Aye. It's like I said. She's not forgotten in Scardale. Mind you, Janet was lucky. She had her mum as an unpaid child-minder so she was able to keep on playing at being the career woman.' There was a surprising note of bitterness in Kathy's voice. Catherine wondered whether she resented her own children for flying the nest and failing to give her the chance to be a hands-on grandmother, or if she despised Janet for resorting to such measures.

'What does she do?'

'She manages a building society branch in Leek.' Kathy glanced out of her window where the curtains were still undrawn in spite of the darkness outside. The headlights of a car swung into sight from the lane end. 'That'll be her now. You'd better be off then.'

Catherine got to her feet, still feeling caught off

477

balance by Kathy Lomas's unpredictable swings from confiding to brusque. 'You've been very helpful.'

Kathy's narrow mouth pursed momentarily. 'Happen,' she said. 'It's been . . . interesting. Aye, interesting. I've told you things I'd forgotten I knew. So, when do we get to read this book?'

'I'm afraid it's not due to be published until next June,' Catherine said. 'But I'll make sure you get a copy as soon as the finished version is available.'

'Make sure you do, lass. I don't want some reporter knocking on my door asking questions about some book I've never read.' She opened the front door and stood back to allow Catherine to pass into the porch. 'Tell Janet she owes me for half a dozen eggs.'

The door was closed behind her before Catherine had reached the end of the path. Stumbling a little in the dark, she turned to her right and walked past Tor Cottage, where Charlie Lomas had lived with his grandmother, and turned into the short path leading to Shire Cottage, where Janet Carter had grown up with her parents and three siblings. According to Peter Grundy, her parents had sold it to her three years before when they decided to retire to Spain because of the climate. Catherine couldn't imagine wanting to live in the house where she'd grown up. She'd been happy enough as a child, but more than ready to make her escape to the freedom and opportunity of London when the chance came.

Whatever had provoked Janet Carter to stay in Scardale, when Catherine saw the interior of Shire Cottage, she realized it probably wasn't sentimentality. The entire ground floor had been stripped out into a single large living space, broken up by the chimney breast. As one of the newer Scardale cottages – probably early Victorian, Janet explained – the ceilings were higher, so opening up the walls had created a remarkable sense of space. One end of the room held a tiny functional kitchen space with stainless-steel units that reflected the variegated greys of the exposed stone walls. The opposite end was a living space, dominated by the rich colours of Indian wall hangings and rugs. Between was a large pine table which seemed to double as dining space and work area. A teenage girl was sitting at it staring intently into a computer screen. She barely looked up as Janet showed Catherine in.

'But it's wonderful,' Catherine exclaimed in spite of herself.

'Brilliant, isn't it?' Janet's features had grown even more feline with age. Her almond-shaped eyes crinkled at the corners as she smiled delightedly. 'It takes everybody by surprise. It's much more conventional upstairs, but I wanted to make it completely different down here.'

'Janet, it's amazing. I've never seen anything like it in an old cottage. How would you feel about my magazine doing a photo feature on it?'

Janet smirked. 'There would be a fee, wouldn't there?'

Catherine's answering smile was wry. 'I think the magazine could manage that. I'm only sorry I can't offer you one for the book interview. But publishers . . . they're so mean with their money.' What she meant was that she had no intention of offering any of her substantial advance to someone as obviously grasping as Janet Carter. She wondered how far she'd managed to screw down the price she'd paid her parents for the cottage.

They settled down on a low sofa and Janet poured red wine into heavy glass tumblers, waving a vague hand towards her daughter. 'Ignore Alison. She won't hear a word we're saying. Comes home from school, sticks a ready meal in the microwave then she's lost in cyberspace. She's the same age now as Ali and me were in 1963, you know. When I look at Alison, I feel all the same anxieties my mother must have known, although my life's so different from hers.

'Everything changed the day Ali disappeared,' Janet recalled, settling down in the manner of a woman who is ready for the conversational long haul. 'I suppose I never appreciated how frightening it was for my aunt and my parents until I had a child of my own. All I could think about was that Ali was missing; it certainly never occurred to me that I should be worried on my own account. But for the adults, right from the word go, as well as the awful anxiety about Ali, there must have been tremendous fear that she might only be the first victim, that none of their kids was safe.

'Back then, remember, children didn't know anything about current affairs. We didn't read the papers or follow the news unless it was about pop groups or film stars. So we were completely oblivious to the fact that there had already been two missing children just up the road in Manchester. All we were aware of was that Ali going missing meant our freedom was curtailed, and that was a very strange experience for us in Scardale.'

Catherine nodded. 'I know exactly what you mean. It had the same effect on us in Buxton. Suddenly, we were treated like china. Everywhere we went, we had to have an adult with us. My mum wouldn't even let me take the dog for a walk in Grin Low woods on my own. Ironic really, when it turned out the danger was so close to home. But it must have been a thousand times worse for you, with all the fear and anxiety right on your own doorstep.'

'Tell me about it,' Janet said with feeling. 'We were used to running free in the dale. We were never indoors in the summer, and even in the dead of winter, we'd be up on the hills, or following the Scarlaston down into Denderdale, or just hanging around in the woods. Because Derek and Ali and I were practically the same age, we were like triplets, never apart. Then suddenly, it was just me and Derek and we were stuck indoors. Like prisoners. God, it was dull.'

'People forget what a drag it was being a young teenager in the early sixties,' Catherine said, remembering only too well how much of a part boredom had played in her own adolescence.

'Especially in a place like Scardale,' Janet said. 'You went to school and all your friends were talking about what they'd been watching on the TV, what they'd seen at the pictures, who they'd got off with at the church dance. We had none of that. They used to take the piss out of us Scardale kids all the time because we never had a clue what the rest of the world was on about. We weren't so much listening to a different drum as stone bloody deaf. Well, you'll remember if you were at school in Buxton.'

Catherine nodded. 'I was the year above you at High Peak. As I remember, it wasn't just the Scardale kids that got the piss taken out of them. We were equally horrible to everybody from the outlying villages.'

'I can imagine. There's nobody crueller to each other than kids. And compared to what happened to us after Ali went missing, being called names was the least of our pains. When I remember the weeks after she disappeared, the most vivid memory that comes to mind is sitting in my bedroom with Derek, listening to Radio Luxembourg on this huge old wireless we had. The reception was terrible, full of static and feedback. It was freezing in there as well – that was long before central heating came to Scardale. We used to sit in the bedroom with our winter coats on. But even now, there are certain songs that take me right back. The Searchers' *Needles and Pins*; Cilla Black's *Anyone Who Had a Heart*; Peter and Gordon's *World Without Love*; and the Beatles' *I Want To Hold Your Hand*. Whenever I hear them, I'm back in my room, sitting on the pink candlewick bedspread, Derek sitting on the floor with his back to the door, his arms round his knees. And no Ali.

'You take so much for granted when you're a child. You spend every day in somebody's company, and it never crosses your mind that one day they might not be there any more. In a way, you know, I feel lucky that you're writing this book. So many of us lose people and there's never anything to prove they were ever there except what's in our heads. At least I'm going to be able to pick up your book and know that Ali really was here. Not for long enough, but she was here.'

6

May 1998

George Bennett paused for breath, hands on hips as he sucked in the mild, humid air. His son waited a few steps ahead, savouring the spectacular view from the Heights of Abraham across the deep gorge carved by the River Derwent to the dramatic profile of Riber Castle on the opposite hill. They'd taken the cable car from Matlock Bath up to the summit and now they were walking the wooded ridge, heading for a winding path that would bring them gradually back down to the river.

Paul couldn't even begin to count the number of walks he and his father had taken over the years. As soon as he was old enough to keep up, George had taken him walking in the dales and peaks of Derbyshire. Some of those days were carved in his memory, like climbing Mam Tor the day before his seventh birthday. Others had disappeared apparently without trace, only surfacing when he revisited the same territory with Helen on one of their occasional visits. When he came home alone, as he had this weekend, he still liked to go out on the hills with his father, though these days George favoured routes that avoided the challenging climbs and reckless scrambles that they'd tackled when he'd been younger and fitter.

Paul turned back to face his father, who had stopped panting, though his face was still scarlet from the effort of the short but steep section they'd just completed. 'You OK?' he asked.

'I'm fine,' George said, straightening up and moving to Paul's side. 'I'm just not as young as I was. It's worth it for the view, though.'

'That's one of the things I really miss, living in Brussels. I got spoilt, growing up with countryside like this on the doorstep. Now, if we want to go for a walk with a decent hill, we've got to drive for hours. So we tend not to bother. And working out in the gym's no substitute for this.' His gesture encompassed the horizon.

'At least it doesn't rain in the gym,' George said, pointing to clouds further down the valley with the shadow of rain beneath them. 'We'll have that to contend with in half an hour or so.' He started walking, Paul falling into step beside him. 'I've not been out as much as I'd like lately myself,' he continued. 'By the time I'd spent the morning with Catherine and done the garden and all the other domestic bits and pieces, I hardly had time for anything more than the odd round of golf.'

Paul grinned. 'So it's all my fault, then?'

'No, I'm not complaining. In a funny kind of way, I'm glad you talked me into it. I'd been bottling it up for far too long. I'd thought dealing with it would be more traumatic than it turned out.' He gave a dry laugh. 'All these years I've been advising my officers to confront their fears, to get back on the horse, and I've been doing the very opposite.'

Paul nodded. 'You always taught me that it's better to face up to the bogeyman.'

'Aye, as long as you pick the ground for the confrontation,' George said wryly. 'Anyway, it turned out that the Alison Carter case wasn't as much of a big bad bogeyman as I'd thought. And Catherine made it very easy for me. She's done her background research, I'll give her that. So a lot of the time, we were concentrating on quite detailed stuff and that made me realize that I'd actually done a pretty good job in the circumstances.' They came to a bend in the path and George stopped and faced his son.

He took a deep breath. 'There is one thing I want to tell you because I don't want you reading it in the book for the first time. It's something your mother and I have always kept from you. When you were little, we didn't tell you because we thought it might frighten you. You know how kids are – all that imagination turns something pretty insignificant into a big deal. And then when you were older, well, there never seemed to be an appropriate time.'

Paul smiled uncertainly. 'Better get it over with, then. Tell me now.'

George reached for his cigarettes and fussed over lighting one in the slight breeze that drifted along the hill. 'The day you were born was the day they hanged Philip Hawkin,' he finally said.

Paul's smile melted into an expression of bewilderment. 'My birthday?' he said.

George nodded. 'I'm afraid so. I got the news that you'd been born just after they hanged him.'

'That's why you always made a big deal of my birthday? To try to take your mind off the fact that you could never forget the other anniversary?' Paul said, unable to keep the hurt from his voice.

George shook his head. 'No, no,' he protested. 'That's not how it was. No, you being born was like – I don't know how to put it – like a sign from the gods that I could put Alison Carter behind me, make a new start. Every year, it wasn't Philip Hawkin's hanging that I remembered on your birthday. It was – listen to me, I sound like some American self-help book – it was the sense of renewal that your birth gave me. Like a promise.'

The two men stood staring at each other, George's face pleading with his son to believe him. A moment passed in silence, then Paul stepped forward and put his arms round his father in a clumsy hug. 'Thanks for telling me,' he mumbled, suddenly aware how much he loved his father, although their physical contact had always been rare. He dropped his arms and grinned. 'I can see why you wouldn't want me to find out something like that from Catherine's book.'

George smiled. 'Judging by your reaction, you'd have been sure to take it the wrong way.'

'Probably,' Paul acknowledged. 'But I can see why you didn't tell me when I was a kid. That would have given me nightmares for sure.'

'Aye. You always were an imaginative little bugger,' George said, turning away to stub out his cigarette under his boot heel. He looked over his shoulder at Paul. 'Oh, and another thing. If you want, next time you come over with Helen, maybe we could take a run out to Scardale and meet her sister.'

Paul grinned. 'Helen would like that. She'd like that a lot. Thanks, Dad. I really appreciate your offer. I know how hard it must have been for you to make it.'

'Aye, well,' George said brusquely. 'Come on, lad, let's get off the hill before that rain comes and drowns us.'

Catherine had expected her return to London to be a relief from the narrow, quiet life she'd been leading in Longnor. It came as a shock to find that the city that had been her home for over twenty years seemed alien: too loud, too dirty, too fast. Even her beloved flat in Notting Hill seemed ridiculously large for one person, its cool pastels and modern furnishings somehow insubstantial compared to the thick stone walls and mismatched furniture of the tiny cottage in Derbyshire.

The idea of rushing round filling her spare moments with social activities seemed strange too, although she did force herself to arrange dinner with a couple of friends and colleagues. It wouldn't do to become too out of touch with the world of work, she told herself firmly. And besides, after two more interviews, a meeting with the editor who had commissioned her book and a brainstorming session with a TV documentary producer who wanted to make a programme based on her research, she reckoned she was entitled to some unrelieved pleasure.

The first of her two interviewees was Charlie – or as he now preferred, Charles Lomas. He was the only one of her cast of characters – apart, of course, from Alison herself – who had shown up in her newspaper searches. She'd found a couple of feature articles about him, though neither of them mentioned the traumatic events of 1963 and 1964.

The reason Charles Lomas had made the feature pages of the national newspapers was nothing to do with Scardale. Rather than remain in the dale where he'd been expected to carry on the family farming tradition, Charles had left Scardale in the winter of 1964. He hitchhiked to London where he found work as a messenger boy for a music publishing company in Soho. He was lucky to arrive at the time when the whole country seemed to be swinging to the Mersey beat. Within a matter of months, his northern accent had earned him a part-time job singing in a group. He ended up organizing their gigs and within five years, he had a profitable business managing rock bands.

By the time Catherine tracked him down, he had an international music publishing empire and still managed half a dozen of Britain's highest-grossing rock musicians. In his reply to her written request for an interview, he'd faxed back that he'd talk to her simply because he believed his family owed a debt of gratitude to George Bennett and he couldn't think of another way to repay it.

When his secretary ushered her into his fifth-floor office with its views of Soho Square, Catherine found herself taken aback. With his neatly barbered silver hair swept back from a high forehead, his manicured hands and his smooth cheeks gleaming from a recent shave, his designer jeans and shirt, it was hard to imagine the Scardale farmer Charles Lomas might have become. But it soon became clear he had inherited his grandmother's legendary storytelling abilities. Before he could bring himself to talk about Alison, he entertained Catherine with gossipy tales of the music business for half an hour.

On the third time of asking, he finally answered her question about Alison. 'That girl was a complete no-shit,' he said admiringly. 'She never had any problem speaking up if she was pissed off with you. You knew where you were with her. Janet was always a bit two-faced, she'd be little miss sweetness to your face and bitch behind your back. Still is, come to that. But Ali couldn't be bothered with all that crap. That's why I never believed she'd been lured away by someone. Whoever took Ali would have had to have forced her, because she wasn't some impressionable, silly little girl.

'Right from the off, I wanted to do everything I could to help. I joined in with the search parties, and of course, it was me who found the place where the struggle had taken place. I can still remember the shock of stumbling across it. We'd developed a rhythm of searching by then, especially those of us who lived in the dale. We knew the ground so well, anything out of the ordinary would leap out at us, much more than it could at the bobbies they'd ferried in from all over the county.

'When I noticed the disturbance in the undergrowth, it literally felt as if someone reached into my chest and grabbed my heart and lungs and squeezed them too tight for breath or circulation. And when I told my gran about it afterwards, the first thing she said was, "Hawkin walks that copse more than anybody else."

'And I told her I'd seen the squire walking the field between the Scarlaston woodland and the spinney the very afternoon Alison disappeared. "Say nowt about it," Gran said. "There'll be a time and a place to tell that copper when he'll pay proper attention. Speak too soon and it gets buried under the weight of everybody else's tittle-tattle."

'Two days later, she said I should tell Inspector Bennett the next chance I got. She was going to take a look at the field herself, to see if she could pick up something the rest of us had missed.' He smiled affectionately. 'She always played to the gallery. She looked like a witch, so she had half the county convinced she had second sight, the power to cast spells and the ability to talk to the animals. In reality, it was just that she was sharper than a block of knives. She was always cottoning on to things that nobody else noticed.

'Looking back at it now, I think all she was doing that afternoon was drawing attention to the field between the woodland and the copse so that when I made my revelation to Inspector Bennett it would have all the more weight. It was probably wrong of us to hold back the information, but you have to remember that we had a very insular life in Scardale. We had no idea who these strangers were, whether they would genuinely try to find Ali or just pick on the likeliest-looking yokel to frame for whatever they decided the crime was. And as Mr Bennett has probably told you, I was the likeliest-looking yokel at that point. Nineteen, all knees and elbows and hormones. Not a pretty sight, I promise you. So of course they had me in for questioning.'

Catherine nodded. 'George told me. That must have been very unpleasant.'

Charles nodded. 'I was torn between being outraged that they couldn't see we were all on the same side and being terrified that they were going to frame me. All I could think of was that I had to find a way of convincing them that I couldn't have harmed a hair on Ali's head without actually telling them what my gran had told me to keep to myself for the time being.

'Of course, as far as the timing of that revelation was concerned, I've suspected for a long time that Gran was motivated by the desire to get the mysterious Uncle Peter off the hook. I was entirely oblivious to that at the time, since I didn't even know he existed until I read about him in the local paper. Remarkable, really, to think the older generation actually did run Scardale as if it were some medieval fiefdom that you could banish undesirables from. But Uncle Peter was still one of the family and Gran always believed blood was stickier than water. So she used the ace she'd kept up her sleeve to divert Inspector Bennett away from the man she was convinced could never have hurt Ali.

'I suppose that means I have to bear some of the responsibility for what happened later. Which is not a comfortable thought, I have to confess.' He sighed. 'My only excuse is that it had never occurred to me in nineteen years to stand up to my grandmother, and this didn't seem like the appropriate time to start.'

Finding the entrance to the Scardale lead mine was Charles's other vivid recollection. Although Catherine found it hard to see that eager young man inside the manicured manager of today, when he spoke about his discovery, all the passion and artlessness of the teenager he had been suddenly became apparent.

'When my mam came to me that morning and said I was wanted to find an old lead mine inside Scardale Crag, I was gobsmacked. I didn't believe such a place could exist and me not know about it. I'd lived in the dale all my life, and nobody had ever mentioned it. But what really convinced me that it couldn't exist was that I would have sworn I knew every inch of Scardale.

'Just because you live in a place doesn't mean you have intimate knowledge of it. Take my cousin Brian. He probably knows every blade of grass in his cow pastures.

'He'll know every step of the path from his house to the cowshed, every inch of the way to his favourite fishing beat on the Scarlaston. But that's all he knows. He never had the instinct to explore. I did, though. When I was a kid, I spent every waking hour that I wasn't at school or working out in the woods and the fields. First time I climbed the crag I was only seven. I used to run up and down Shield Tor a couple of times a week, just for the hell of it. I loved every inch of Scardale.'

For a moment his face closed down as he was transported back to what he had left behind. 'I miss it,' he said abruptly. Then his face cleared, and he was back in memory.

'So you see, I couldn't figure out how the lead mine entrance could still exist without me knowing about it. Still, we were all desperate by that stage. Any chance of finding Ali was worth taking, in our opinion.

'When I found the entrance, I was stunned. I'd never gone that far along the base of the crag before. In the summer, it was too overgrown, and in the winter it looked as if the way was impassable because of the tumble of rocks that obscured it when you were looking up from the river. In fact, it wasn't a hard climb at all, and actually, it was right where the book said it would be.

'What was doubly weird was that somebody else had penetrated Scardale's secret when I hadn't. The realization that my knowledge was so flawed was profoundly unsettling. I lost my trust in my own judgement, and that really shook me.

'Oddly, though, it's stood me in good stead over the years. I never fall for the flannel. I'm always on my guard against the flatterers. I know now that it's possible to be hopelessly wrong about someone you see every day and you think you know. So it's crazy to think you can know anyone on the basis of a few meetings. So, although it didn't feel like it at the time, something good came out of what happened to Ali.'

He passed a hand over his jaw. 'I tell you something, though. I'd happily settle for crap judgement if it meant Ali was still around.'

As far as background information about the players in the drama was concerned, Charles was much less useful than either Kathy or Janet. He gave an apologetic smile. 'I was always a bit in my head,' he said. 'I was always telling myself stories, making up fantasies about how I was going to escape from Scardale and change the world. Half the time, I never really knew what was going on around me. And as for adult relationships – they were a mystery to me. I just knew that I didn't seem to want what everybody else in Scardale wanted.'

He took a deep breath and looked straight into Catherine's eyes. 'I had to come to London to find out why that was. I'm gay, you see. I never had a name for it all those years I was growing up. I just knew I was different. So you see, I'm not the person to ask if I noticed anything odd about Ruth and Phil's relationship.' He smiled. 'I thought everybody's relationships were bloody odd.'

7

May 1998

As she nursed a gin and tonic in the upstairs room of the Lamb and Flag in Covent Garden, Catherine's mobile phone rang. 'Catherine Heathcote. Hello?' she said, praying it wasn't Don Smart calling to cancel their interview.

'Catherine? It's Paul Bennett. Dad told me you're in London, is that right?'

'Yes. I'm down for a few days to talk to some people about the book.'

'I'm in town too. I'm going back to Brussels tomorrow, but I wondered if you fancied dinner this evening?'

Delighted, Catherine said, 'Love to,' and they made arrangements to meet at seven. Cheered by the prospect of dinner with Paul, she looked up to see a gaunt-faced man staring uncertainly across at her. He paid for his pint of bitter, then crossed the room.

'Are you Catherine Heathcote?' he asked.

'Don Smart?' She half stood and extended her hand to shake his as he nodded and subsided into the chair opposite her. She wouldn't have recognized him from the description George Bennett had given her. His red hair had faded to a dirty white, he was clean-shaven and his skin was dry and loose, mottled with age spots rather than freckles. The sharp foxy eyes that George had remembered with such clarity were red-rimmed, the whites tainted with a jaundiced yellow tint.

'Smart by name and smart by nature,' he said. She didn't believe a word of it.

'Thanks for agreeing to talk to me,' was all she said.

He took an inch off the top of his pint. 'I'm cutting my own throat,' he said. 'By rights, this should have been my book. I covered the story from day one, right through to the trial. But George Bennett would never open up to me afterwards. I suppose I remind him too much of his failure.'

'His failure?'

'He desperately wanted to find Alison Carter alive. It was no consolation to him that she was probably long dead before he ever caught the call. I think he's been haunted by her death ever since, and that's why he wouldn't talk to me. He couldn't sit and look at me and not feel like he'd let Ruth Hawkin down.' He reached into his pocket and pulled out a packet of cigarettes. 'Smoke?'

She shook her head.

'I only ever bother offering hacks these days,' he said, lighting up with a sigh of pleasure. 'Everybody else has quit. Even bloody newsrooms are smoke-free these days. So, Catherine, how are you getting along with my book?'

She smiled. 'It's interesting, Don.'

'I'll bet it is,' he said bitterly. 'From day one, word one, I just knew George Bennett was great copy. The man was a bulldog. There was no way he was going to give up on Alison Carter. All the rest of the cops, it was just another job to them. Sure, they felt sorry for the family. And I bet the ones who were fathers themselves went home and gave their daughters an extra-tight hug every night they were out on those moors searching for Alison.

'But it was different with George. With him, it was a mission. The rest of the world might have given up on Alison Carter, but George couldn't have been more passionate in her cause if she'd been his own daughter. I spent a lot of time following George Bennett on the Alison Carter case, but I never did figure out why he felt so strongly about it. It was like it was personal.

'For me, it was a godsend. The job in the northern bureau of the *News* was my first national newspaper job, and I was on the lookout for the story that would take me to Fleet Street. I'd already done some of the *News*'s coverage of the Pauline Reade and John Kilbride disappearances, and I thought if I could get the cops to link them to Alison Carter, I'd have a great page lead.'

'Which you would have done,' she acknowledged.

His look was sour. 'George wouldn't play, of course. He was determined not to hand Alison Carter over to the detectives investigating the other missing children. I don't know if that was a hunch or just pure pig-headedness, but it turned out to be the right decision. Of course, we none of us had any idea that Ian Brady and Myra Hindley even existed then, but George seemed to know by instinct that whatever had happened to Alison Carter, it was a one-off, and it was his.'

'But it was thanks to George you finally did get your crack at Fleet Street, wasn't it?' Catherine asked.

'There's no doubt about that. I got some great stories out of the Alison Carter case. I did those cracking stories with the clairvoyant, I remember. That was my ticket to the big time. Ironically, that meant I never got to write a line of copy about the real Moors Murders revelations.'

Suddenly, Smart was off on the tales of his glory days working as a reporter on various national newspapers, finally returning to the *Daily News* as deputy night news editor. He'd been made redundant three years before, but still worked three nights a week as a casual newsdesk executive on the *News*. 'The reporters they've got working for them these days, they haven't got a clue. That's why they need somebody on the night desk that knows what he's doing.

'I tell you something, though. The Alison Carter case did more for me than help my career,' he confessed. 'Coming on top of the other missing kids, it put me right off the idea of having any children of my own. Unfortunately, my then wife didn't feel the same. So you could say that my marriage was an incidental casualty of what happened to Alison Carter. What took place in that small Derbyshire village one December night had effects that nobody could have predicted.

'It's often the way with cases that involve a genuinely mysterious element. Nobody knows what's really happened, and everybody's life gets put under the microscope. Suddenly all sorts of secrets are forced into the open. It's often not a pretty sight.'

'Any regrets about the way you covered the case?' Catherine asked.

His smile was patronizing. 'Catherine, my love, I was one of the best. Still am one of the best, come to that.

My job as I saw it was twofold. First, I had to provide my editor with good strong exclusive stories that made our existing readers stick with us and brought us new readers. Secondly, I was there to be a thorn in the flesh of the police, so they wouldn't ever get complacent.

'If that meant the odd barney with the bobbies, well, I had broad shoulders. The nearest George Bennett and I came to blows was over the clairvoyant stories. I got the idea for that from a story I'd read in an American magazine. The tabloid press here was much more staid then than it is now, and one or two of the American publications had that bit of edge we didn't have.

'I used to cannibalize them for story ideas all the time. The clairvoyant idea was a classic example of that. I'd read this story about a murder out in the Arizona desert that was supposedly solved by a clairvoyant and that was in the back of my mind when the hunt for Alison Carter started. I put the idea to my editor and he loved it. I knew the British police would never have admitted working with a psychic so my only chance of finding someone with a reputation was to look abroad.

'I called a friend of mine who worked at Reuters and got him to check their files, and that's how I came across Madame Charest. I never met the woman, and it wouldn't have made any difference if I had because she couldn't speak a word of English. We had to do it all through an interpreter. Of course, I never believed a word of it. But it made great copy.

'I know George thought it was irresponsible. He thought the only thing I was interested in was the greater good of Don Smart. But it wasn't just that. The other side of it was that I genuinely wanted her found as much as George did, but news stories die quickly unless there's more fuel to throw on the flames. To keep Alison Carter's name and picture in the paper, I needed a fresh angle. The clairvoyant gave me that, and in turn, she gave Alison Carter a few more days in the headlines.

'In Alison's case, it probably made no difference. But it might have done,' he said self-righteously.

'She was wrong, though, wasn't she? Your Madame Charest?'

Don Smart grinned and suddenly Catherine saw the fox that George had described. 'So? It was a bloody good read. If you can do half as well, Catherine, you'll maybe sell a few more copies of your book than your friends and family can buy between them.'

Don Smart had left a nasty taste in Catherine's mouth that even a decent glass of burgundy in the Garrick Street wine bar couldn't dispel. 'He's such a self-serving shit,' she confided in Paul. 'He's the kind that started British tabloids sliding into the gutter, and he's proud of it.'

'Now you can see why Dad would never talk to him,' Paul said. 'I must say I was surprised when he agreed to your proposal. But I'm glad now I let you and Helen talk me into persuading him to go ahead with it. Working on the book with you seems to have given Dad a new lease of life. He hasn't been this cheerful for ages. It's as if the process of going through it all for your benefit has finally allowed him to let go of the past and move forward.'

'I sensed that too. It's strange, but before I started this project, I was very nervous. I've never done anything on this scale before, and I didn't know if I could sustain

500

my interest or my effort. But it's turned into a real mission, to tell this story properly. And realizing its importance for George has been an added impetus for me to get it right.'

'I can't wait to read it,' Paul said. 'Although, if I'm honest, I do feel a bit apprehensive at the thought of reading about my father, what his life was like before I was around. Almost like spying on someone when they don't know you're there.' He looked down, his face unreadable. 'Most of it will be completely fresh to me, you know. Dad's never been one of those policemen who bores everybody rigid with his war stories. I don't think he'd ever mentioned Alison Carter in my hearing until that journalist turned up on the doorstep.'

He looked up with a reminiscent smile. 'But when I went up there at the weekend, he was full of it. He told me all sorts of things he'd never spoken about before, even though we've always got on well. In a funny kind of way, this project seems to have brought us closer. It's as if working with you has given him an insight into the kind of work I do every day. He was asking me all sorts of detailed questions about the way I do my job, what it's like working with journalists, how they differ from each other, how they go about their jobs. As if he's comparing what he's been doing with you.

'It's been good for Mum too. It was like walking on eggshells for her whenever I asked questions about what it was like when they first got married. She always had to watch her tongue in case she said something that upset Dad. Only, I never understood before exactly what was going on.' He pulled a face. 'I used to think it was something to do with them not wanting to talk about their lives before I came along in case they made it sound like they'd been happier without me. I don't know, Catherine, this has been such a good thing for our family, I almost wish I'd stolen your idea and worked on the book with him myself.'

Catherine laughed. 'He'd never have been able to be as honest with you as he has been with me. Knowing your father as I do now, he'd have been constantly playing down his successes in case you thought he was boasting.'

'And I'd have been turning him into a hero,' Paul said sadly. 'As it is, I seem to be getting obsessed by it. I seem to be talking about it all the time. I'll be doing Helen's head in completely if I'm not careful. Which reminds me. Helen wants one of the first copies off the press to give to her sister. It'll be interesting for Jan to read about what happened in her house.'

Catherine pulled a face. 'Maybe she won't be so keen on living there in splendid isolation after she finds out the whole story. It's not exactly going to be a comfortable read for her.'

'Still, better she knows the real story than gossip and rumour, eh?'

'Well, she'll get the truth from me. That's one thing I'm absolutely determined about.' Catherine raised her glass. 'To truth.'

'To truth,' Paul echoed. 'Better out than in.'

8

May/June/July 1998

Catherine turned off the A1 and found herself immediately on a narrow country lane that wound between fertile fields and mature woodland, the sea a distant glint ahead of her. For some reason she couldn't quite put her finger on, the prospect of meeting Tommy Clough excited her more than interviewing any of the other secondary players in Alison Carter's story. Partly it was because both George and Anne spoke of him with such affection, even after thirty-five years with almost no contact. But the more she thought about it, the more it seemed to her that Clough was the most enigmatic figure of all.

According to George, on the surface, his sergeant had appeared bluff, even brutal at times. Far more than George himself, Clough had seemed a typical police officer of his time. Always one of the lads, always in tune with the rumour and gossip that swirled round every police station, always high up the league table of crimes solved and arrests made, he'd given the impression of being a round peg in a round hole. And yet he had resigned from Derbyshire Police two years after the Alison Carter case was closed and become resident warden at a bird sanctuary in Northumberland. He had cut himself off comprehensively from his past, exchanging camaraderie for isolation.

Now sixty-eight and retired, he still lived in the north east. Anne had told Catherine how she had once visited him for an hour when she'd driven Paul up for an open day at Newcastle University when he'd been making his mind up where to do his degree. According to her, Tommy Clough spent his days watching and photographing birds and his evenings drawing them. In the background, his beloved jazz kept the outside world at bay. As she described it, it was a solitary and peaceful life, strangely at odds with the fifteen years he'd spent bringing criminals to justice.

The road wound gently down the hill to Catherine's destination, a cluster of houses – too small to be called a village – a few miles south of Seahouses. Both excited and apprehensive, she lifted the heavy brass knocker on the door of the former fisherman's cottage.

She would have recognized Tommy Clough anywhere from the photographs George had lent her. He still had a full head of curls, though they glinted silver now instead of light brown. His face was weatherbeaten, but his eyes were still intelligent, his mouth still clearly more accustomed to smiling than scowling. Although he was dressed in baggy corduroy trousers and a fisherman's guernsey, it was clear his broad frame was still well-muscled. He'd supposedly resembled a bull in his youth; now his white curls made him look more like a Derby ram, she thought as she returned his smile. 'Mr Clough,' she said.

'Miss Heathcote, I presume. Come in.' He stood back to let her enter a spartan but spotless living room.

504

The walls were covered with beautiful line drawings of birds, some hand-tinted, others plain black ink on brilliant white paper. In the background, Catherine recognized Branford Marsalis's 'Romances for Saxophone'.

She turned to study the drawings nearest her. 'They're wonderful,' she said, meaning it as she seldom did when she attempted to put interviewees at ease by praising their taste.

'They're not bad,' he said. 'Now, sit yourself down and have a brew. You must be ready for it after that drive up from Derbyshire.'

He vanished into the kitchen, returning with a tray containing teapot, milk jug, sugar bowl and two RSPB mugs. 'I've no coffee,' he said. 'One of the things I promised myself when I left the police was that I was never going to drink another cup of disgusting instant coffee. And there's nowhere around here does a decent roast, so I content myself with tea.'

'Tea's fine,' Catherine said with a smile. Already she trusted this man. She couldn't have said why, but she did. 'Thank you for agreeing to see me.'

'It's George you should be thanking,' he said, picking up the pot and gently agitating it to help the tea brew. 'I decided long ago that it was up to him to decide if the time was ever right to speak about it. I know we worked hand in hand on the investigation, but my take on things is different from George. He's an organizational man, but I was always more of the maverick type. So my version could never be the straightforward story that he'll have told you.

'The Alison Carter case was a defining moment for me, you see. I'd gone into the police because I believed in the idea of justice. The way things panned out on that one, I wasn't so sure the system could be relied on to deliver. I think we got justice in that case, but it was damn close. It could so easily have gone the other way, and there would have been nothing to show for months of work and a girl's life. I came to the conclusion that if a police force can't be depended upon to produce the end result that is its only justification for existence, there doesn't seem a lot of point in being part of it.'

He shook his head and gave a mocking little laugh as he poured the tea. 'Listen to me. Thought for the Day. I sound as pious as a preacher. George Bennett wouldn't recognize me. I used to be one of the lads, you know. I liked a pint, a smoke, a laugh and a joke. It wasn't an act, either. It was just one side of me that happened to fit the job, so I exaggerated it a bit, I suppose.

'But I've always been a thoughtful sort of bloke as well. And when Alison Carter went missing, it was like my imagination went into overdrive. My mind was full of different scenarios, each one worse than the last. I could keep it at bay when I was working, but when I was off duty, I found myself increasingly tormented by waking nightmares. I was drinking a lot too – it was the only way I could get to sleep at night.

'I've often thanked God for George Bennett's obsession with the case. It meant there was always stuff to be getting on with, files to be checked, potential witnesses to be interviewed. Even after we were supposed to have put the case on the back burner. Without either of us ever formalizing it, I became his bagman on the investigation. It made me feel useful. But God, it was hard work getting under the skin of Scardale.

'Do you remember that film in the seventies, *The Wicker Man*? Edward Woodward plays this cop who goes off to this mysterious Scottish island to investigate a missing girl and he gets caught up in the pagan rites of the inhabitants. It's very eerie and there are undercurrents of perverse sexual practices and strange beliefs. Well, that's sort of what it felt like in Scardale in 1963, except we got to go home to normality at the end of the working day. And nobody tried to turn me or George into a human sacrifice,' he added with an embarrassed laugh, as if conscious of having said more than a down-to-earth ex-policeman should admit to.

'And of course, we solved the mystery. Which is more than Edward Woodward got to do.' He put milk in his tea and took a deep draught of it.

'Anne told me that none of your neighbours up here knows you were a police officer,' Catherine observed.

'It's not that I'm ashamed of it,' he said self-consciously, getting up to change the CD. More subdued saxophone, though this time it was unfamiliar to her. She kept quiet, knowing Tommy would pick up where he had left off when he was ready.

He settled back into his chair. 'It's just that people make a certain set of assumptions about you if they know you've been a copper. I wanted to avoid that. I wanted to start again with a clean sheet. I thought that maybe if I could ignore my past, Alison Carter might finally leave me alone.' His mouth twisted into something closer to a grimace than a smile. 'Didn't work. Did it? Here you are, and here I am, going over it all again.

'I was thinking about it last night, getting my thoughts in order. And it's all as vivid as it was going through it the first time,' he added. 'I'm as ready as I'll ever be. Ask away.'

Tommy Clough had been the missing element in Catherine's story. His unique perception had filled the gaps in her understanding, somehow turning a kaleidoscope of jumbled pieces into a coherent picture. He had given her insight into George Bennett as a man as well as a police officer, and he had allowed her to comprehend things that had previously been unclear. At last she had grasped the underlying reasons behind what had sometimes appeared to be a lack of coopera- tion between the villagers and the police. And she could see the overall shape of her story with much greater clarity.

Back in Longnor, she started on the long and com- plex task of organizing her material. Her printer ground away constantly in the background as she stacked separate piles of paper round the living room floor. Transcripts of her long series of interviews with George; a separate pile for her notes and transcripts of each of her other witnesses; a stack of photocopied newspaper clippings; the copies she'd been able to obtain of the trial transcript, thanks to a friend who worked in a law library, and a neat pile of battered second-hand green Penguin editions of famous trials to provide hints and tips as she went along.

Catherine had taken down the innocuous water- colours of the glories of the Peak District that the landlords had chosen and replaced them with photo- graphs of Scardale then and now, including Philip Hawkin's postcards. One wall featured nothing but blown-up photographs of the key players, from Alison herself to a stern-faced George, snapped by a newspaper photographer, emerging from a press conference in mac and trilby. The third wall was taken up with large-scale Ordnance Survey maps of the area.

For the best part of two months, she entirely immersed herself in Scardale. She would rise at eight and work until half past noon. Then she would drive the seven miles into Buxton, park by Poole's Cavern and walk up through the woods to the open moorland above, crossing the open ground to Solomon's Temple, the Victorian folly that overlooked the town. She would descend through the leafy shadows of Grin Low woods and walk back along Green Lane, past the house where she had grown up with her parents. Her father had died five years before and her mother had cashed in the house and moved to a retirement home in Devon where the climate was easier on old bones. Catherine had no idea who lived in the house now, nor did she much care.

She supposed there must still be plenty of people around that she'd been to school with, but Catherine had shed her past like a snake its skin when she'd moved to London. As far as friendships were concerned, she'd been a late developer. As an only child, she'd found the country of her imagination more interesting than the real world of her teenage contemporaries. It was only when she'd started to work with others whose minds ran along the same tracks that she'd found people she could truly forge bonds with. So there were no treasured childhood ties she'd wanted to resurrect. She'd expected to run into half-familiar faces in the supermarket where she shopped, but it hadn't happened. She felt no regrets on that score.

The only part of her past that she cared to be connected to was the stash of memories that allowed her to get under the skin of Alison Carter's life and death.

After her daily walk, she'd drive back to Longnor and have a snack of bread, cheese and salad before returning to her task. At six, she opened a bottle of wine and watched the TV news. Then it was back to work until nine, when she'd stop and eat a pizza or some other instant meal from the supermarket. For the rest of the evening, she'd answer e-mail and read some trashy airport paperback. That, and occasional conversations with her editor about the progress of her book, and with the documentary maker about his timetable, were all she was capable of.

For the first time in her life, Catherine's days had ceased to revolve around a gregarious office and an active social life. She was bemused by how little she missed human company. She had, she thought wryly, become what six months previously she would have categorized as a sad bastard.

When the phone rang one afternoon and she heard George Bennett's voice on the other end, it seemed as if her words had suddenly taken on a life of their own and for a moment, she couldn't take in what he was saying.

'Sorry, George, I was miles away when you rang, can you just run that past me again?' she said uncertainly.

'I hope I haven't interrupted the creative flow at a crucial moment.'

'No, no, nothing like that. How can I help you?' Catherine was back in control, slipping straight into her professional persona.

'I was ringing to tell you Paul is bringing Helen over for a few days next week. Anne and I wondered if you'd like to join us for dinner on Friday?'

'I'd be delighted,' she said. 'I should have the first draft finished by the end of this week. I'll bring it over with me so you can check it over after they've gone back to Brussels.'

'You have been working hard,' George said. 'That'll be a real treat for me. So, Friday at seven it is. See you then, Catherine.'

She replaced the receiver and stared at her wall of photographs. She'd done almost all she could to make them come to life. Now, like Philip Hawkin, she'd have to wait for the verdict of others.

9

August 1998

Catherine ceremoniously handed George the thick padded envelope. 'The first draft,' she said. 'Don't be kind, George. I need to know what you really think.'

She followed him into the living room, where Paul and Helen were sitting on the sofa. 'Here's a cause for celebration,' George said. 'Catherine's delivered her book.'

Helen grinned. 'Well done, Catherine. You've not wasted any time.'

Catherine shrugged. 'I'm due back at work in three weeks. I didn't have any time to waste. That's the beauty of a journalistic training – writing expands or contracts to fill the time available.'

Before they could discuss it further, Anne came through with a tray of glasses and a bottle of champagne. 'Hello, Catherine. George said you had something to celebrate, so we thought we'd crack open the bubbly.'

Paul grinned. 'Not for the first time this week. Helen's divorce finally came through, and we've decided we're going to get married. So we had a couple of bottles the other night to set the seal on it.'

Catherine crossed the room and leaned forward to

kiss Helen on both cheeks. 'That's great news,' she enthused. She turned to Paul and kissed him too. 'I'm thrilled for both of you.'

George took the tray and put it down. 'We're pretty pleased, too. This has turned into a vintage week.' George opened the champagne and filled their glasses. 'A toast,' he said, handing the drinks round. 'To the book.'

'And the happy couple,' Catherine added.

'No, the book, the book,' Paul protested. 'That way we'll have to open another bottle so you can toast me and Helen. And you'll have to come to the wedding,' he added. 'After all, if it wasn't for you, we'd never have got Dad to come to Scardale to meet Helen's sister.'

'You've been to Scardale?' Catherine couldn't hide her astonishment. The one failure she regretted in her research was that she had been unable to persuade George to return to the village and go over the physical ground with her.

George looked faintly sheepish. 'We've not been yet. But we're going to lunch with Helen's sister Janis on Monday.'

Catherine raised her glass to Paul. 'You've pulled it off again. I tried everything short of kidnapping to get him to come there with me.'

Paul grinned. 'You did the groundwork.'

'Well, whoever's responsible, I'm glad you're going,' Catherine said. 'And I don't think you'll find any memories lingering in Scardale Manor, George.'

'What do you mean?' he asked, leaning forward.

'It's been gutted. According to Kathy Lomas, who gave me the tour, there's not a single room that's anything like it was back in 1963. It's not just decorated differently – there's even been a bit of structural work, knocking a couple of small rooms into one bigger one, turning a bedroom into a bathroom, that sort of thing. If you closed your eyes all the way down the Scardale road and didn't open them till you were inside the manor, I guarantee you wouldn't feel a single memory stirring,' she added with a smile.

George shook his head. 'I wish I could believe you,' he said. 'But I've got a feeling that I won't be able to escape the past that easily.'

'I don't know, George,' Helen chipped in. 'You know how houses have an atmosphere? Some places you just walk in and know it's a friendly, welcoming place? And other times, no matter how much money's been spent on it, the house feels cold and hostile? Well, Scardale Manor's one of those houses that feels like home from the moment you cross the threshold. That's what Jan said when she first went to look at the place after we inherited it. She rang me up to tell me she'd known as soon as she walked in that this was the house for her. And I can sense exactly what she means. Whenever I've stayed there, I've always slept like a log and felt totally at home. So if there ever were any ghosts, they moved out a long time ago.'

'So you might be in for a pleasant surprise, love,' Anne said reassuringly.

Still the doubt remained on George's face. 'I hope so,' he said.

'Never mind being worried about memories lying in ambush for you, George. If the remaining Carters, Crowthers and Lomases get wind that you're coming back to the dale, they'll probably roll out the red carpet

514

and decorate their houses with bunting,' Catherine said. 'The only threat to your health and wellbeing might come from an excess of hospitality.'

'Speaking of which, I think it's time for that second bottle,' Paul said, jumping to his feet.

'There is one small thing, George,' Catherine said, smiling as charmingly as she knew how. 'If you manage to survive your return to Scardale, would you consider going back again with me?'

'I thought you'd finished the book,' he said, looking for an excuse to refuse.

'Only the first draft. There's still plenty of time to add to what I've already written.'

George sighed. 'I suppose I owe you that much. All right, Catherine. If I make it out of Scardale alive, I'll go back with you. That's a promise.'

BOOK 2

PART THREE

1

August 1998

Catherine stared at the letter in utter disbelief. Her first thought was that it was a joke. But she rejected that idea before it was even fully formed. She knew George Bennett was far too much the gentleman – and the gentle man – to make this kind of savage joke. She read the letter again and wondered if he was having some kind of breakdown. Perhaps visiting Scardale on top of reliving the Alison Carter case might have caused the crack-up some people would have experienced at the time. She dismissed that too; George Bennett was far too sane a man to lose his marbles thirty-five years on, no matter how traumatic the memories. And he himself had remarked more than once that going over the case had been less disturbing than he had feared.

That recognition left Catherine without a straw to clutch at. Outrage began to burn inside her like indigestion. She had been halfway through a late breakfast when the post had arrived. She'd been expecting a letter from her editor with her comments and requests for any rewrites, not this catastrophe. Her first impulse was to pick up the phone, but before she'd got three digits into George's number, she slammed it down again. Years of journalism had taught her exactly how easy it was to fob somebody off on the phone. This was one she had to deal with face to face.

She left the half-drunk coffee and half-eaten toast on the table. Forty minutes later, she was turning right by the millpond. For every minute of those forty, Catherine had seethed with frustration. All she could see was George's high-handedness and she couldn't understand what had provoked it. He'd never shown the slightest sign that he was capable of such overbearing behaviour. She'd thought they'd become friends, but she couldn't understand how a friend could treat her like this.

In her heart, Catherine knew the book was more hers than it was his, and that he had no right to take it from her. She wasn't daunted by his threat of legal action, knowing what the book contract said. But she was disturbed by the effect his opposition could have on both her sales and her reputation. To have the book repudiated by the one person who knew the case inside out could damage her beyond repair. And that was something Catherine wouldn't accept without a fight. If George had set aside their friendship, then she would have to find it in her heart to do the same, however difficult she might find it.

She edged the car up the narrow road. Both the Bennetts' cars were in the drive, so she had to carry on past their limestone villa and leave the car in a lay-by halfway up the hill. She strode back down to the house and stormed up the drive.

The doorbell echoed, as it does in an empty house. But surely even if George had gone to the village on foot, Anne should be at home. Her arthritis meant that any journey required a car. Catherine stepped away from the front door and walked round the side of the house, thinking they might be in the garden, enjoying the sunshine before it grew too warm for comfort. But she drew a blank there too. There was nothing in sight but manicured lawn and colour-coded flower beds like some miniature Sissinghurst.

It was as she returned to the front of the house that a possible solution came to her. If Paul and Helen had hired a car, it was possible they had taken George and Anne out for the day. The thought simply increased her determination to have it out with George. If she had to wait till bedtime to speak to him, so be it. She was standing in the drive, wondering whether to stake the house out from the car or to browse the bookshop by the millpond for an hour when she heard her name.

The next-door neighbour was standing on her doorstep, looking surprised. 'Catherine?' she repeated.

'Hello, Sandra,' Catherine said, finding a purely professional smile from deep inside. 'I don't suppose you know where George and Anne have gone off to?'

She gaped at her. 'Haven't you heard?' she eventually said, unable to keep a note of glee out of her voice because she knew something Catherine didn't.

'Is there something I should have heard?' she asked coolly.

'I thought you'd have known. He's had a heart attack.'

Catherine stared in disbelief. '*A heart attack?*'

'Rushed to hospital in an ambulance early this morning,' Sandra said with relish. 'Of course, Anne went with him in the ambulance. Paul and Helen followed in their car.'

Appalled, Catherine cleared her throat. 'Is there any news yet?'

'Paul came back to pick up some of his dad's things earlier on and we had a word, of course. George is in intensive care. Paul said it's been touch and go, but the doctors say George is a fighter. Of course, we all knew that.'

Catherine couldn't work out why the woman was so smug about what had happened. She didn't want to think it was because she was hugging to herself the pleasure of knowing something Catherine didn't, but no other explanation came to mind. 'Which hospital?' she asked.

'They've taken him to the specialist cardiac care unit in Derby,' she said.

Catherine was already walking back up the hill to the car. 'They won't let you in,' Sandra called after her. 'You're not family. They won't let you in.'

'We'll see about that,' Catherine said grimly under her breath. Predictably, her fears for George manifested themselves in unreasonable rage. How dare George deprive her of the satisfaction of finding out what the hell was going on by contriving to be at death's door?

It was only as she drove down to Derby that she simmered down and began to realize what a terrible night it must have been for all of them – Anne, Paul, Helen, and of course, George himself, trapped inside a body that wasn't functioning the way he demanded it should. She couldn't imagine anything worse for a man like George. Even at sixty-five, she knew he was trim and fit; his mind too was sharper than most of the serving police officers she'd ever encountered. He could still complete the *Guardian* crossword three days

522

out of four, which was more than Catherine had ever managed. Working so closely with him had provoked respect, but also affection. She hated to think of him diminished by disease.

The intensive care unit wasn't hard to find. Catherine pushed open one of the double doors and found herself in an empty reception area. She pressed the buzzer on the desk and waited. After a couple of minutes, she pressed it again. A nurse in a white overall emerged from one of the three closed doors. 'Can I help you?' she said.

'I'm inquiring about George Bennett?' Catherine said with an anxious half-smile.

'Are you family?' the nurse asked automatically.

'I've been working with George. I'm a friend of the family.'

'I'm afraid we can only allow visits from immediate family,' she said, her voice entirely empty of regret.

'I appreciate that.' Catherine smiled again. 'I wonder, though, if you could tell Anne – Mrs Bennett, that is – that I'm here? Perhaps we could go somewhere for a cup of tea, if that's all right with her?'

The nurse smiled for the first time. 'Of course I'll tell her. Your name is?'

'Catherine Heathcote. Where would be a good place to meet Mrs Bennett?'

The nurse pointed her in the direction of the coffee bar, and as she turned away, Catherine called after her, 'And George? Is there anything you can tell me about George?'

This time, the nurse's voice softened. 'He's what we call critical but stable. The next twenty-four hours will be crucial.'

Catherine walked back to the lifts in a daze. Being in the hospital brought George's personal catastrophe home to her in a way that Sandra's words hadn't. Somewhere behind those closed doors, George was wired up to machines and monitors. Leaving aside what was happening to his body, what was happening to his brain? Would he remember sending the letter to her? Would he have told Anne about it? Should she act as if nothing untoward had happened? Not just in her own interest, she rationalized, but also to keep the family from one extra worry?

Catherine found the coffee bar and settled herself at a corner table with a mineral water. She was so preoccupied with her thoughts, she didn't see Paul until he was practically on top of her. Today, his resemblance to George was spooky. She'd spent so much time staring at a photograph of his father at almost the same age, it was as if the image on her wall had come to life and swapped a mac and trilby for a pair of faded jeans and a polo shirt. He dropped into a chair as if his legs couldn't hold him up any longer.

'I'm really sorry,' Catherine said.

'I know.' He sighed.

'How is he?'

Paul shrugged. 'He's not good. They're saying he had a massive heart attack. He hasn't recovered consciousness yet, but they seem to think he'll come round. Oh God . . .' He covered his face with his hands, obviously overcome. Anxiously, Catherine watched his shoulders heave with deep breaths as he struggled to regain control. Eventually, he recovered enough to continue. 'His heart stopped in the ambulance, and I think they're concerned there might be some brain damage. They're

524

talking about doing a scan, but they're being very non-committal about the prognosis.' He stared down at the table. Catherine covered his hand with hers in a simple gesture of sympathy.

'What happened?' she asked gently.

He sighed again. 'I can't help feeling it's our fault. Mine and Helen's, that is –' He broke off. 'Do you mind if we go outside? It's so oppressive, this hospital atmosphere. My head feels like it's stuffed with cotton wool. I could do with some fresh air.'

They were silent in the lift down. Catherine pointed out a row of benches on the far side of the car park. They sat down and stared unseeingly at a regimented square of rose bushes. Paul tilted his head back and breathed deeply. 'Why would your father's heart attack be your fault?' Catherine asked eventually.

Paul ran a hand through his hair. 'When we went to Scardale, something happened that made him really agitated. I don't really know what it was, exactly . . . He didn't say anything, but I could see he was getting really wound up when we arrived at Jan's. Then when we went indoors, I almost thought he was going to faint. He went pale and sweaty, the way people do when they've got a terrible headache. He seemed distracted. He hardly said a word to Jan, he just kept looking around him as if he expected ghosts to start coming out of the woodwork.'

'Did he say anything about what had upset him?'

Paul rubbed the bridge of his nose with his finger. 'I think it was just the trauma of going back to Scardale again. It's been on his mind so much, obviously, with all the work the two of you have been doing on this book.' His shoulders drooped. 'This is all my fault. I should have realized he wasn't making a fuss over nothing when he said he really didn't want to go to Scardale.'

'There's no reason why you should have thought it would make him ill, though,' Catherine said gently. 'You mustn't blame yourself. Heart attacks don't just happen overnight – it takes a lifetime for the conditions to build up. In your dad's case, years of irregular hours, too many cigarettes, too many greasy-spoon meals eaten on the hoof. It's not your fault this has happened.'

Paul's face was bitter. 'Taking him to Scardale was the trigger.'

'Not necessarily. You've already told me you didn't notice anything in particular that made him especially upset.'

'I know. And I've been through it again and again in my head. We all had lunch out in the garden. He hardly ate anything, which isn't like Dad at all. He blamed the heat, and to be fair, it was warm. After lunch, Jan took Mum round the garden. They were ages, comparing notes, arranging to swap cuttings, all that sort of thing. Dad went for a stroll round the village green, but he was only gone about ten minutes. Then he just sat there under the chestnut tree, staring into space. We left around three because Mum wanted to drop in on the craft fair down in Buxton, and we were home again by six.'

'And George didn't say whether anything special was bothering him?'

Paul shook his head. 'Nothing. He said he had a letter to write and he went upstairs. Helen and Mum put a salad together for the tea and I mowed the lawn. He came downstairs after about half an hour and said he was going to the main post office in Matlock because he wanted to be sure of this letter catching the post and there's no local collection in the evening. I thought it was a bit strange, but he's never been one for putting things off.'

Catherine took a deep breath. It wasn't fair to leave Paul guessing about the letter that had been so important to his father. 'The letter was to me,' she said.

'To you? What on earth was he writing to you about?' Paul was clearly baffled.

'I don't think he wanted to deal with me face to face,' she said. 'I don't think he was up for the argument he knew he'd get.'

'I don't understand what you're saying.' Paul frowned.

'Your father wanted me to cancel the publication of the book. With no explanation at all,' Catherine said.

'What? But that doesn't make any sense.'

'It didn't make sense to me either. That's why I came down to Cromford this morning. Then the next-door neighbour told me what had happened.'

Paul glared at Catherine. 'So you thought you'd come and hassle him here? Very sensitive, Catherine.'

She shook her head. 'No, you misunderstand me, Paul. When I heard what had happened to George, my first thought was for him, for all of you. I wanted to offer my help, my support. Whatever.'

Paul was silent, thinking over what she'd said, his eyes dubious.

'I've grown very fond of your parents over the last six months. Whatever the problem with the book is, it can wait. Believe me, Paul, I'm more concerned now about how your dad's doing.'

Paul began drumming his fingers on the arm of the bench. He clearly lacked his father's gift of stillness. 'Look, Catherine, I'm sorry I snapped at you, but it's been a tough night. I'm not thinking straight.'

She put her hand out and touched his arm. 'I know. If there's anything I can do to help, just tell me – please?'

Paul sighed deeply. 'You *can* do something for me. I want to know what set this off. I want to know what happened yesterday to trigger this heart attack. If I'm going to help him, I have to know what's behind it. You know more about my dad's involvement with Scardale than anybody else, so maybe you can figure out what the hell happened to get him so worked up that his heart packed in on him.'

Catherine felt some of the tension slip away from her shoulders. To have the course of action she'd already decided on endorsed by Paul made her feel easier. 'I'll do my best,' she said. 'Nothing else happened last night that might have upset him? After he'd been to the post, I mean.'

Paul shook his head. 'We all went down to the village pub. They've got a garden out the back and we just sat out there with our glasses of beer and talked about nothing much.' He paused and frowned. 'He was edgy, though. A couple of times, I had to tell him something twice because he just wasn't tuned in to the conversation.'

'Does Helen think there was anything odd in the way he was behaving?'

'She agreed with me, that he seemed to have slipped

a gear. She reckoned he'd been like that since we arrived in Scardale. She'd noticed, but it probably wasn't obvious to anybody that didn't know him. If her sister was offended by Dad's silence, she certainly didn't say anything to Helen . . .'

'George wouldn't have done anything to offend Janis,' Catherine said. 'No matter how upset he was. He's such a kind man.'

Paul cleared his throat. 'Yes. He is.' He glanced at his watch. 'I'd better be getting back.'

'When do you have to be in Brussels?' Catherine asked, getting to her feet.

He shrugged. 'We were supposed to be going home the day after tomorrow. Obviously we won't be leaving now. I'll have to wait and see how he is.'

'I'll walk you back.'

As they approached the hospital, Paul exclaimed, 'That's Helen!' and broke into a panicky run.

Helen swung round at his approach, a can of Coke halfway to her lips. Her face lit up in a smile but he was oblivious to that. 'Has something happened with Dad?' he demanded.

'No, I just needed some fresh air.' She reached out and put an arm round his waist, pulling him to her in a gesture of support.

'Any news on George?' Catherine asked.

Helen shook her head. 'Still the same. Paul, I think we should try to persuade your mum to go and have a cup of tea and a bite to eat.' She gave Catherine an apologetic smile. 'You know Anne – she hasn't left his side since they brought him up to intensive care. She's going to wear herself out.'

'I'll let you go,' Catherine said.

Paul took her hand. 'Find out what he saw. Or heard. Or remembered,' he said. 'Please?'

'I'll do my best,' Catherine said. She watched them walk back into the hospital, glad that she had something to do that might possibly ease the burden of guilt that Paul had assumed. That it would also serve her own interests had become a secondary consideration, she suddenly realized with surprise. George Bennett had clearly become more important to her than she had previously acknowledged. That made it all the more important that a book that would do him justice would eventually be published, she told herself firmly. And that was one service she could certainly provide.

2

August 1998

Whatever had happened to change George Bennett's mind, it had happened in Scardale. Catherine felt certain of that. He'd seen something, but what . . . ? How could so brief a visit have produced so seismic a response? Catherine could have understood it if he had decided she needed to make some changes to her draft in the light of a fresh realization, but what could have been so extraordinary that it derailed the whole project? And if it had been so portentous a moment, how had it passed unnoticed among the rest of the family?

In the shimmering heat of an August afternoon, Scardale was hardly recognizable as the grim winter hamlet she had first revisited in February. Because the summer had been so wet, the grass was lush, the trees more shades of green than any painter could capture. In their shade, even the undistinguished farm labourers' cottages of Scardale looked almost romantic. There was no sense of gloom, no trace of the sinister events of thirty-five years before.

Catherine pulled up outside the manor house, where a five-year-old Toyota estate car sat in the drive. It looked as if Janis Wainwright was at home. She sat in the car for a moment and pondered. She could hardly walk up the path and say, 'What happened to George Bennett yesterday that made him want to scrap our book? What was so terrible about his visit to your house that he collapsed in the night with a massive heart attack?' But what else would work?

She thought about asking Kathy Lomas if she'd seen George the day before. She turned in her seat towards Lark Cottage, but Kathy's car was nowhere to be seen. Exasperated, Catherine got out of the car. When all else failed, she could try the trusted journalistic technique of lying through her teeth. She walked up the narrow path to the kitchen door and raised the heavy brass knocker. She let it fall and heard it echo through the house. A full minute passed, then the door suddenly opened. Dazzled by the sunlight, Catherine could barely make out the woman's shape in the dark interior. 'Can I help you?' she said.

'You must be Janis Wainwright. I know your sister, Helen. My name's Catherine Heathcote. You were kind enough to arrange for me to see round the manor house to help me with a book I'm writing about the Alison Carter case?' She couldn't have sworn to it, but Catherine sensed the woman withdraw at her words.

'I remember,' she said tonelessly.

'I wondered if I might have another look around your house?'

Catherine's eyes were beginning to adjust to the dimness of the kitchen. Janis Wainwright definitely seemed startled, she thought. 'It's not convenient. Another time. I'll arrange something with Kathy,' she said quickly, her words running together in her haste.

'Just the ground floor. I won't be in your way.'

'I'm in the middle of something,' she said firmly.

The door began to shut. Instinctively, Catherine moved closer so Janis would stop closing it. Then she saw what George Bennett had seen the day before. She didn't so much step back as stagger.

'Speak to Kathy,' Janis Wainwright said. As if from a great distance, Catherine heard the lock click, then the crash of bolts being shot home. Dazed, she turned and walked back to her car, stumbling blindly like a sleepwalker.

Now she thought she understood why George had written the letter. But if she was right, it wasn't something she could readily explain to his son. And it wasn't something that made her want to abort the book. It made her realize that there might be a deeper truth behind the Alison Carter case that neither she nor George had so much as guessed at. And it made her even more determined to tell the truth that she had so cheerfully toasted with Paul that night in London.

Catherine sat stock-still in the car, oblivious to the sweltering heat. Now the first moment of shock was past, she could hardly bring herself to credit what she'd seen. It made no sense, she told herself. Her eyes had lied to her. But if that was true, George Bennett's eyes had also lied. The resemblance was remarkable, uncanny even. If that had been all, she could almost have written it off as bizarre coincidence, but Catherine knew that there was no resemblance in the world that stretched to include scars.

She had learned from her reading and her interviews that the one distinguishing mark Alison Carter had possessed was a scar. It was a thin white line about an inch long that ran diagonally through her right eyebrow. It touched the edge of her eye socket and cut up into her forehead. It had happened the summer after her father died. Alison had been running across the school playground with her bottle of milk at playtime when she'd tripped and fallen. The bottle had shattered and a piece of glass had sliced through her flesh. The scar, according to her mother, had always been most prominent in summer when she had a bit of colour from the sun. Just as Janis Wainwright had.

From nowhere, Catherine had a pounding headache. She turned the car around and drove slowly and cautiously back to Longnor. There seemed only one explanation for what she had seen, and that was impossible. Alison Carter was dead. Philip Hawkin had been hanged for her murder. But if Alison Carter was dead, who was Janis Wainwright? How could a woman who could have been Alison's clone be living in Scardale Manor and not be connected to what happened in 1963? But if she were, how was it possible that her own sister knew nothing of it?

Catherine parked the car and walked back to the newsagent's. She bought twenty Marlboro Lights and a box of matches. Back in her cottage, she poured herself a glass of wine so cold it made her teeth hurt. That at least made sense. Then she lit her first cigarette for a dozen years. It made her head swim, but that was an improvement. The nicotine hit her bloodstream and it felt like the most normal thing in the world at that moment.

She smoked the cigarette with devoted attention then sat down with paper and pencil and made notes. After an hour, Catherine had two propositions:

> *Proposition 1. If Alison Carter had not died she would look exactly like Janis Wainwright.*
> *Proposition 2: Alison Carter is Janis Wainwright.*

She also had an action plan. If she was right, it was going to take more than a bit of tweaking and polishing to finish her book. But that was fine by her. If Alison Carter was still alive, *A Place of Execution* was going to be even more exciting than it was already. And somehow she would persuade George to see her point of view, once he was well enough to consider all the implications properly.

The first step was a phone call to her editorial assistant in London: 'Beverley, it's Catherine,' she said, injecting energy she didn't feel into her voice.

'Hi! How's life in the sticks?'

'When the sun's shining like it is today, I wouldn't swap it for London.'

'Well, I can't wait for you to get back. It's a madhouse here. You'll never guess what Rupert wants to do with the Christmas issue –'

'Not now, Bev,' Catherine said firmly. 'I've got an urgent bit of business for you. I need somebody who specializes in computer ageing of photographs. Preferably up in this neck of the woods.'

'Sounds interesting.'

Twenty minutes later, her assistant had rung her back with the number of a man called Rob Kershaw at Manchester University.

Catherine checked her watch. It was almost four.

If Rob Kershaw wasn't escaping the stresses of life in some foreign city, the chances were that he'd still be at work. It was worth a phone call, she reckoned.

The phone was answered on the third ring. 'Rob Kershaw's phone,' a woman's voice said.

'Is Rob there?'

'Sorry, he's on holiday. He'll be back on the twenty-fourth.'

Catherine sighed.

'Can I take a message?' the woman asked.

'Thanks, but there's no point.'

'Is it something I can help you with? I'm Rob's research assistant, Tricia Harris.'

Catherine hesitated. Then she remembered she had nothing to lose. 'Can you do computer ageing of photographs?'

'Oh yes, it's my speciality.'

Within minutes, they were in business. Tricia had nothing more pressing planned than a night in front of the TV, and she suffered from the perennial penury of all graduate students. Once Catherine had dangled the promise of a substantial fee in front of her, she was more than happy to hang on at work while Catherine drove over with her copies of Philip Hawkin's photographs of his stepdaughter.

When she arrived, Tricia efficiently scanned in the two pictures, asked a few questions and then started serious work with keyboard and mouse. Catherine left her to it, knowing how much she hated people peering over her shoulder when she was trying to work. She retreated to the far end of the room where there was an open window and lit her fifth Marlboro Light. She'd give up again tomorrow, she thought. Or whenever she found out what the hell was going on. Whichever was the sooner.

After about an hour and another three cigarettes, Tricia called her over. She picked three sheets of A4 off the printer and spread them out before Catherine. 'The one on the left is what I'd call the best-case scenario,' she said. 'Minimal stress, well nourished and well cared for, maybe about seven pounds over ideal weight. The one in the middle is more typical in some respects – more stress, not quite so much attention paid to looking good, right on the button weight wise. The third one is the one nobody wants to be. She's the one who's had the hard life, the crappy diet, smokes too much – very bad for your lines and wrinkles, you know,' she added with a sly smile at Catherine. 'She's a bit underweight.'

Catherine stretched out a finger and pulled the middle of the three photographs towards her. Apart from the hair colour, it could have been a photograph of the woman who'd answered the door at Scardale Manor. Janis Wainwright's hair had been silver with hints of blonde. Alison Carter, as aged by computer, was still golden, with only a few strands of grey at the temples. 'Amazing,' Catherine said softly.

'Is that what you expected?' Tricia said. Catherine had told her almost nothing, saying she was working on a story about a missing heir who'd turned up to claim a legacy.

'It confirms what I was afraid of,' Catherine said. 'There's somebody walking around who isn't who she says she is.'

Tricia pulled a face. 'Bad luck.'

'Oh no,' Catherine said, feeling excitement gripping her chest. 'Not bad luck at all. Quite the opposite.'

3

August 1998

As she drove away from Manchester University, Catherine felt the hot buzz that burned in her veins whenever she knew she was on the verge of a major story. She was so thrilled she'd temporarily lost sight of the starting point for her exhilaration. That a man was lying on life-support machines in a hospital in Derby had become irrelevant for the moment. Too wound up to eat, she drove back to Longnor with the dizzying possibilities tumbling round in her head.

Catherine decided the first thing she had to do was to find out who Janis Wainwright was legally. That Janis Wainwright had a legal existence she didn't doubt. It would be difficult for her either to own property or to have any significant career without one. Finding it would mean a search through public records for births, marriages and deaths. It would take her days to do it herself, but there were agencies that did that sort of work routinely for journalists. She switched on the laptop and started to formulate an e-mail request to the Legal Search Agency, a company that specialized in tracing information relating both to individuals and to companies.

Catherine was reasonably sure Janis had never married. For one thing, Helen hadn't mentioned a husband. Also, a quick check on the letter she'd had from Janis's lawyer arranging the guided tour of the manor revealed that the lawyer referred to her as, 'Miss Wainwright'. And of course, Helen herself had been married and divorced, which explained why her surname was different.

Somewhere, therefore, there had to be details of Janis Wainwright's birth certificate. To be doubly sure, Catherine decided to ask for Helen's details too. And because, like all good journalists, she had a healthy stock of suspicion, she requested a further check to see if there was a record of Janis Wainwright's death at any point between her birth and Alison's disappearance in December 1963. From the details in the birth certificate, it would be possible to track down the marriage certificate of Janis's parents, and from there, their birth certificates if that proved necessary. That would be the starting point to discover whether there was any real connection between Janis Wainwright and Alison Carter.

Catherine sent off her request, making it clear that she wanted the express option, with results e-mailed to her as well as hard copies sent by post. Even so, she knew it would be late the following afternoon before she could reasonably hope for a reply. She had no idea how she was going to fill the time until then.

Then she remembered George. Feeling guilt at having wiped him from the front of her mind, Catherine phoned the hospital and inquired after him. The intensive care nurse told her there was no change. With mixed emotions, she hung up. She hated the thought of what had happened to George; but the moment of recognition that had triggered his heart attack also seemed to be leading to the biggest story of her life. She had sufficient self-knowledge to understand exactly how much that meant to her. Catherine had always been more committed to her job than she ever had been to another human being. She knew that the commonly held view was that that was sad; but Catherine thought it was sadder to put all your eggs in the basket of humanity when people invariably let you down somewhere along the line. People came and went, and there was a lot of enjoyment to be had from human relationships. She knew that, and she took what pleasure and satisfaction was to be had. But no one individual had ever been as constant as the rush of excitement that came from a well-crafted exclusive.

She poured herself another drink and debated her next move. By the time she'd reached the bottom of the glass, she knew there was only one possible destination.

Three hours later, Catherine was booking into a four-star hotel just outside Newcastle. One of the secrets of good journalism, she had learned, was knowing when to press ahead and when to possess her soul in patience. Her thirst for removing the wraps on this story was tempered by the wisdom of experience. Turning up unannounced on someone's doorstep was always a bad idea late at night. She knew they'd invariably associate it with bad news before she'd even opened her mouth.

But in the morning, people were more optimistic. Long before the invention of the postman with his prospect of good news, everybody knew that. So when she had still been a news reporter, wherever possible she had avoided the late-night knock and gone for the early-morning arrival.

Catherine finally fell asleep to the movie channel, and it was after nine when she woke, grateful that she'd managed a decent night's sleep, given what she had on her mind. The first thing she did was call the hospital. There was, they said, little change, though there were some grounds for optimism. She tried the Bennetts' home number, but only the answering machine responded. She left her best wishes and hung up.

An hour later, she was heading up the A1. She was halfway up the path to the cottage when the door opened. 'Catherine,' Tommy said, his broad face crinkled in a smile. 'You're an unexpected treat. Come through, we'll sit out the back.'

She followed him through the spotless living room and kitchen into his back garden, a paradise of fragrant flowers and shrubs, all chosen, so he'd told her on her earlier visit, to attract birds and butterflies. Today, it was humming softly with bees, and the flutter of multicoloured wings continually snagged the corner of her eye as they spoke.

Tommy pulled up a wooden chair for Catherine then sat on the bench that looked down the garden to the sea beyond. 'So, what brings you up here?' he asked once they were settled.

She sighed. 'I don't know where to start, Tommy. However I say this, it's going to sound like I've finally lost it.' She looked down at the ground. 'Have you heard about George?'

'What's happened?' he asked, alarm in his voice.

Catherine met his stare. 'He's had a heart attack. A bad one, by all accounts. He's in Derby Royal, in the intensive care ward. He's been unconscious since the early hours of yesterday, as far as I'm aware. According to Paul, his heart stopped in the ambulance on the way to the hospital.'

'And you came up all this way to tell me? Catherine, that's really good of you.' Tommy patted her hand. 'I appreciate it.'

'I'm sorry to be the bearer of bad tidings.' For the moment, she was content to occupy the role of concerned friend.

He shrugged. 'At my age, you come to expect it. How's Anne taking it? She must be devastated.'

'She's not left his bedside. Paul's home just now, with his fiancée, and they're with her.'

'Poor Anne. She's lived her life for George. And with her arthritis, she's not fit for heavy nursing, if it comes down to that.' Tommy sighed and shook his head. He gazed out across the garden to the blue sparkle of the North Sea.

Catherine took out her fresh pack of Marlboros. 'Do you mind if I smoke?' she asked.

His bushy eyebrows rose. 'I didn't think you did. But be my guest.' He rose and crossed to the shed in the corner of the garden. He returned with a terracotta plant saucer. 'You can use that as an ashtray. Take your time.' Tommy leaned back, crossing his legs at the ankle and stuffing his hands in the pockets of his baggy corduroy trousers.

'On Monday, George went to Scardale. And on Monday night, he had his heart attack,' she said baldly.

'You got George to go to Scardale?' Tommy's eyes widened in surprise.

'I didn't. I could never manage to persuade him. But Paul did. He's over on a visit with Helen, his fiancée. They're planning on getting married later this year. Anyway, it turns out that Helen's sister Janis moved to Scardale Manor a couple of years back. And they'd arranged to take George and Anne over there for lunch on Monday. I knew George was uncomfortable about going to Scardale, but once he got there, according to Paul, his behaviour became quite odd.'

'Odd how?'

'Paul said he seemed very tense. He had no appetite. Apart from taking a turn round the village green, he just sat in the garden, not talking to anyone. Paul said he was very distracted and wound up for the rest of the day and the evening.' Catherine paused to collect her thoughts. She needed to be careful how she expressed herself to Tommy. He was very quick at picking up nuances of what he wasn't being told.

'Before he was taken ill, he'd written to me, asking me to put a stop on the book. No reason, except that he'd come across some new information that meant the book must be suppressed. Of course, I told Paul about the letter when I saw him at the hospital. I was already convinced that George must have seen something in Scardale that had – I don't know – given him fresh insight into some aspect of the case, or set him worrying about something we'd included in the book. And Paul had come to the same conclusion. He's racked with guilt. He thinks he's responsible for George's heart attack because he persuaded him to go back to Scardale. And he's asked me if I can try to find out what lay behind George's letter to me. So . . .' She shrugged. 'I have to get the answers.'

'You'd have been a good copper,' he said drily.

'Coming from you, I'm not sure that's a compliment.' She fiddled with her cigarette, then firmly stubbed it out.

'Oh, I've nothing but respect for them as could do a job that was too much for me,' he said, pretending a ruefulness she knew he didn't feel. 'And where did you go for your answers? As if I couldn't guess.'

'That's right. I went back to Scardale. I thought I'd ask Helen's sister if I could have another look round the manor, to see if I could discover what had upset George so much.' She shifted in her chair so she could look out over the sea.

'And did you?'

Catherine busied herself with another cigarette. Out of the corner of her eye, she could see Tommy weighing her up, eyes shrewd in his weather-browned face. He knew there was something, but not even in his wildest imaginings could he have come up with what she was about to say, she thought. 'I didn't get to look round the manor,' she said on an exhalation of smoke. 'But I did get to see what must have sent George reeling.' She opened her bag and took out the folder where she'd stashed the computer-aged photograph of Alison Carter.

Tommy held out his hand. She shook her head. 'In a minute. The woman who opened the door, the one who's supposed to be Helen's sister – it's Alison Carter's double. Right down to the scar through the eyebrow.' She handed the folder to Tommy. He opened it gingerly, as if he expected it to explode in his face.

What he saw was worse than anything he could have feared. His mouth fell open. 'I couldn't believe my eyes either. I took Philip Hawkin's photos of Alison to an expert and had them computer aged. That could be a photograph of the woman who answered the door of Scardale Manor. But it's also what Alison would look like if she was still alive.'

The folder was trembling in Tommy's hands. 'No,' he breathed. 'That can't be right. It must be a relative.'

'The scar's the same, Tommy. You don't get identical scars.'

'You must have made a mistake. You can't have seen her properly. Your imagination's playing tricks.'

'Is it? I don't think so, Tommy. It wasn't my imagination that gave George a heart attack. Whatever I saw, I think he saw it before me. That's why I came to you. I need your help. I need you to come and look at Janis Wainwright and tell me and George it's not Alison Carter. Because from where I'm sitting, it looks like I've stumbled across the scoop of the century.'

He covered his face with his free hand, rubbing his leathery skin so it resembled a crumpled animal hide. His hand dropped to his lap and he stared dully at Catherine. 'You know what this means, if you're right?'

She nodded slowly. She'd thought of little else on the long drive north, her mind on a rollercoaster where the high point was the professional effect of the revelation she would make, and the low point was what that would do to George Bennett and his family. Somewhere down the line, she knew she'd have to find a balance between those two consequences. But first she would have to hold the whole truth in her hand. Catherine looked Tommy straight in the eye and said, 'It means they hanged Philip Hawkin for a crime that never happened.'

4

August 1998

Tommy Clough was not a sentimental man. He had always lived in the present, drawing his nourishment from what was around him. His other great quality was persistence. So although he'd never felt particularly enriched by his years in the police, he'd stuck with the job because of the abiding desire for justice that had taken him there in the first place. Even then, however, he'd been able to sustain himself with his twin passions of birds and jazz.

But he'd been telling Catherine nothing less than the truth when he had revealed that it had been the Alison Carter case that had marked the beginning of the end of his police career. He had cared too much about the outcome of a case that was at best shaky. The idea of Alison's killer walking free had tormented him night and day in the lead-up to the trial, and he never wanted to go through that experience again. It had taken him a couple of years to work through what he really felt about the investigation and its results, but once he had made the decision, he'd been out of Derbyshire Police in a matter of weeks. And he had never regretted it for a moment.

Catherine Heathcote's arrival a couple of months earlier had forced him to re-examine the past for almost the first time since he had quit the force. For days before their interview, he had walked the cliffs and headlands near his cottage, turning the Scardale case over and over in his mind.

One of his strengths as a copper had been his intuition. It had frequently made him push even when there was no concrete evidence, and it had paid off more often than not in arrests and convictions. He'd been convinced from the start that Philip Hawkin was a nasty piece of work. All his instincts had screamed that from his first encounter with the man. Long before George Bennett ever voiced the first stirrings of suspicion about Hawkin, Tommy Clough had sensed the squire had something serious to hide.

As soon as George had indicated he wanted them to look more closely at Hawkin, Tommy had been a terrier, running himself into the ground to sniff out any possible shred of evidence that might support the case. No one had worked harder, not even George himself, in the quest to nail Philip Hawkin.

In spite of which, Tommy had never quite been settled in his own mind that Hawkin was a killer. He'd had no doubt that the man had been a vicious sexual predator, and he'd had nightmares over the photographs, which he knew hadn't been doctored, either by George Bennett or anyone else. But even though he despised and loathed Hawkin, he had never been entirely convinced that the man was the killer they had revealed him to be. Perhaps it had been that niggle of doubt that had made him work so hard to build a rock-solid case against the man. He had been trying to convince himself as much as the jury. And the final conviction that his gut instinct had failed him had undermined his confidence in the way he did his job.

And now Catherine had dropped her twin bomb-shell. She believed George Bennett was lying on a life-support machine because he'd realized, as she had, that Alison Carter was alive and well and living in Scardale. In one way, it made no sense. However, if Catherine was right, it vindicated Tommy Clough's own past uneasiness. Nevertheless, this was one time when he would give almost anything to have been wrong all those years before. For if Alison Carter truly was alive, then the repercussions would be appalling. Never mind any possible legal consequences, who-ever Paul Bennett's fiancée was, she was somehow intimately connected to a terrible mistake her future father-in-law had been instrumental in making.

All of this rolled around Tommy's head without reso-lution as he sat in his Land Rover, following Catherine's car down the A1 towards Derbyshire. There had seemed no alternative but to go back with her and do what he could to protect George and his family from the fallout from what Catherine thought she'd discovered. She was, he thought, both headstrong and single-minded, and that was a dangerous combination around such potentially explosive material. She'd wanted to drive him back with her, but he'd been adamant that he wanted the freedom to come and go that he would lack if he was dependent on Catherine to ferry him around. 'I'll be wanting to visit George,' he'd said. 'And it might not always be convenient for you.' Besides, he wanted to be alone with his thoughts.

The five-hour journey seemed to flash past, and suddenly they were drawing up outside a cottage just off the main street in Longnor. Catherine announced that the first thing they had to do was find Tommy somewhere to stay. The pub did rooms, but in mid-August, they were all full of hikers and fishermen. Tommy shrugged, then marched straight up to Peter Grundy's front door and announced that he'd be needing the Grundys' spare room for a few days; would ten pounds a night be fine for bed and breakfast?

Grundy's wife, who'd never liked her husband's bosses and was happy to part one from his money, nearly bit his hand off, though Peter had the grace to look embarrassed. Any questions they had about what had brought Tommy back to Derbyshire were satisfied by the news of George's heart attack. 'You need your friends around you at a time like this,' Mrs Grundy said profoundly.

'You certainly do,' was Tommy's grim response. 'And I intend to do everything I can to help George and Anne.' He'd given Catherine a quick glance, making sure she registered that their interests might not entirely coincide. She inclined her head in acknowledgement, and refused a cup of Mrs Grundy's industrial-strength builder's tea.

'I'll be in the cottage when you're ready, Tommy,' was all she said.

Catherine had no time to ponder exactly what Tommy Clough thought he was up to. She was too impatient to get to her laptop. She went straight on-line and found that LSA had come up with the goods. They'd scanned in the photocopies of the certificates they'd tracked

CERTIFICATE COPY OF AN ENTRY OF BIRTH
GIVEN AT THE GENERAL REGISTER OFFICE, LONDON

Registration District: County Durham

Sub-District of: Consett

Application Number: 7211758

Name: Janis Hester   Sex: Female

When and where born: Twelfth January 1951, Consett

Address: 27 Upington Terrace, Consett, County Durham

Name and Surname of Father: Samuel Wainwright

Name, Surname and Maiden name of Mother:
Dorothy Wainwright formerly Carter

Occupation of Father: Steel Worker

When Registered: Eighteenth January 1951

CERTIFICATE COPY OF AN ENTRY OF BIRTH
GIVEN AT THE GENERAL REGISTER OFFICE, LONDON

Registration District: Sheffield

Sub-District of: Rivelin Valley

Application Number: 2214389

Name: Helen Ruth   Sex: Female

When and where born: Tenth June 1964, Rivelin Valley

Address: 18 Lee Bank, Rivelin Valley

Name and Surname of Father: Samuel Wainwright

Name, Surname and Maiden name of Mother:
Dorothy Wainwright formerly Carter

Occupation of Father: Steel Worker

When Registered: Fourteenth June 1964

down and sent them to her as graphics files.

First, Janis Hester Wainwright. Born January 12th 1951 in Consett. A female child, daughter of Samuel Wainwright and Dorothy Wainwright née Carter. Father's occupation, steel worker. Usual address, 27 Upington Terrace, Consett.

Mother's maiden name, Carter. It was a coincidence, but not much of one. Carter was too common a name to set any store by it, she told herself firmly. This was too important for her to clutch at straws. Concrete evidence was what she needed.

Next, Helen's certificate. Helen Ruth Wainwright. Born June 10th 1964 in Sheffield. A female child, daughter of Samuel Wainwright and Dorothy Wainwright née Carter. Father's occupation, steel worker. Usual address, 18 Lee Bank, Rivelin Valley, Sheffield.

Middle name Ruth. Coupled with Carter, this was starting to look significant, Catherine thought, feeling the excitement stirring inside her.

She hit the <page down> key for the marriage certificate for Samuel and Dorothy Wainwright. The excitement was a physical sensation growling deep in her stomach. Place of marriage; St Stephen's Church, Longnor in the district of Buxton. Date of marriage: April 5th 1948. Samuel Alfred Wainwright, bachelor, had married Dorothy Margaret Carter, spinster. He was 22, she was 21. He was a steel worker, she was a dairymaid. At the time of their marriage, he was living at 27 Upington Terrace, Consett. She was living at Shire Cottage, Scardale, Derbyshire. Her father was Albert Carter, farm labourer. The witnesses were Roy Carter and Joshua Wainwright.

Catherine could hardly trust her eyes. She read the

CERTIFICATE COPY OF AN ENTRY OF MARRIAGE
PURSUANT TO THE MARRIAGE ACT 1836

Registration District: Buxton

Marriage Solemnized at: St Stephens Church, Longnor

In the: County of Derbyshire

Application Number: 87

When Married: Fifth April 1948

Name: Samuel Alfred   **Surname:** Wainwright

Age: 22   **Condition:** Bachelor

Rank or Profession: Steel Worker

Residence: 27 Upington Terrace, Consett

Father's name and Surname: Alfred Wainwright

Occupation of Father: Steel Worker

Name: Dorothy Margaret   **Surname:** Carter

Age: 21   **Condition:** Spinster

Rank or Profession: Dairymaid

Residence: Shire Cottage, Scardale, Derbyshire

Father's Name and Surname: Albert Carter

Occupation of Father: Farm Labourer

In the presence of: Roy Carter, Joshua Wainwright

Solemnized by: Paul Westfield

details again. Janis Wainwright's mother was Dorothy Carter of Shire Cottage, Scardale. One of the witnesses at Dorothy's wedding was Roy Carter. Also of Shire Cottage, Scardale, she wouldn't have minded betting. The same Roy Carter who was Ruth Crowther's husband and Alison Carter's father. So it wouldn't be surprising to find there was a strong resemblance between Janis and Alison. Genetic inheritance could be a strange thing. But that still didn't explain the scar. If Janis wasn't Alison, how did she happen to have the identical distinguishing mark?

The one explanation she could come up with was that the scar had been some bizarre form of self-mutilation that the teenage Janis had inflicted after Alison's disappearance and presumed death. She could imagine them growing up, the family commenting that they could be identical twins, two peas in a pod. And then Alison died and Janis decided to keep her alive by branding herself in the same way, reinstating Alison's uniqueness. It was a grotesque notion, but Catherine knew that teenage girls were capable of the most fantastic behaviour, self-harming included.

The flashing cursor caught her eye. LSA had sent more than the three certificates. She hit the <page down> key again and this time, she sat staring at the screen, slack-jawed and bewildered. She'd submitted her request only out of a routine habit of covering all the bases. But LSA had found the thing she hadn't really believed she should be looking for.

Janis Hester Wainwright had died on May 11th 1959.

Catherine sat staring at the screen for a long time. Only one thing made any kind of sense. She lit a cigarette and tried to imagine any other scenario that would fit the facts, but she came up empty-headed. Nothing fitted unless she started with the assumption that Alison Carter did not die in December 1963. Who was more likely to take on a girl in hiding than a physically distant branch of her family? So she'd assumed the identity of her dead cousin Janis and had grown into womanhood in Sheffield.

A thought struck her, and the hairs on the back of her neck stood on end. All those years ago, Don Smart had persuaded the *Daily News* to consult a clairvoyant who had said Alison was alive and well and safe, living in a house in a street in a big city. Everyone had scoffed at the time. It had been such an unlikely outcome of the picture they were presented with. But it looked now as if that clairvoyant might, against all the odds, have been right.

Catherine was startled out of her reverie by a knock at the door. Tommy had come to tell her he was going to drive down to Cromford to see if anyone was home. If he drew a blank, he intended to continue on to Derby.

'Before you go,' she said, 'take a look at these.' She gestured for him to sit in front of the laptop and showed him how to scroll down. He sat in silence, reading the four certificates with painstaking care.

Then he turned to face her, his eyes troubled. 'Tell me you've come up with another explanation,' he said, his voice a quiet plea.

Catherine shook her head. 'There isn't one that I can think of.'

He massaged his jaw with fingers still strong and thick. 'I need to go and pay my respects to the family,' he said at last. He sighed. 'We need to talk about what happens next. Will you be up when I get back?'

'I'll be up. I'm going into Buxton for something to eat, because these four walls will drive me crazy otherwise,' she said, gesturing at the pictures of Scardale surrounding her. 'I'll be back by nine.'

He nodded. 'So will I, then. Don't worry, Catherine, we'll figure it out between us.'

'Oh, I think we've figured out the crucial fact already, Tommy. It's what we do with it that's a bit harder to work out.'

Tommy smiled at the intensive care nurse. 'I'm family,' he said, with the air of quiet assurance that had seldom failed him. 'George is my brother-in-law.' The metaphorical truth of his words gave him a certain satisfaction.

The nurse nodded. 'His son and daughter-in-law have gone to get something to eat, so there's only his wife with him just now. You can go straight through.' She opened the door for him. 'Third bed down,' she added.

Tommy walked slowly down the ward. He paused a few feet away from the array of life-support machines that sustained his old friend. Anne was sitting with her back to him, her head bent, one hand clasping George's, the other stroking his arm, automatically careful of the drip feeding into a vein. George's skin was pale, with a faint clammy sheen. His lips had a slightly bluish tinge and there were dark shadows under his closed eyes. Beneath the thin sheet, his body looked strangely frail, in spite of the wide shoulders and well-defined muscles. Seeing him like that, the vitality stripped from him, Tommy felt his own mortality like a breath of cold air on his skin.

He stepped forward and laid a hand on Anne's shoulder. She looked up, her eyes weary and resigned. For a moment she looked confused, then the shock of recognition hit her. 'Tommy?' she gasped, incredulous.

'Catherine told me what happened,' he said. 'I wanted to come.'

Anne nodded, as if what he said made perfect sense. 'Of course you did.'

Tommy pulled up a chair and sat down next to her. The hand that had been stroking George's arm reached out and grasped his. 'How is he?' Tommy asked.

'They say he's holding his own, whatever that means,' she said wearily. 'I don't understand why he's still unconscious, though. I thought heart attacks were over and done and you either survived or else . . . But he's been like this nigh on two days now, and they won't say when they think he'll come round.'

'I suppose it's the body's way of healing itself,' Tommy said. 'If I know George, if he was conscious you'd have to tie him to the bed to get him to rest and convalesce properly.'

A faint smile ghosted across Anne's lips. 'You're probably right, Tommy.' They sat in silence for a few minutes, watching George's chest rise and fall. Eventually, Anne said, 'I'm glad you came.'

'I'm just sorry it took this to get me to make the journey.' Tommy patted Anne's hand. 'What about you, Anne? How are you doing?'

'I'm frightened, Tommy. I can't begin to think of what life would be like without him.' She gazed at her husband, despair in the slump of her shoulders.

'When did you sleep last? Or eat?'

Anne shook her head. 'I can't sleep. I went for a lie-down last night. They've got a room for relatives here. But I couldn't get off. I don't like leaving him. I want to be here when he wakes up. He'll be frightened, he won't know where he is. I need to be here. Paul's offered to spell me, but I don't feel right about that. He's already too upset. He blames himself, and I'm afraid of what he'll say to George if he's on his own with him when he comes round. I don't want George set off again.'

'But I'm here now, Anne. I could sit with George while you at least get yourself a cup of tea and something to eat. You look like you're ready to drop.'

She turned and looked curiously at him. 'And what's

he going to think if he sees you sitting there like the ghost of Christmas past?' she said, with a trace of her normal good humour.

'Well, at least it'll take his mind off what's wrong with him,' Tommy replied with a smile. 'You need a break, Anne. Get a cup of tea. Some fresh air.'

Anne bowed her head. 'Maybe you're right. I'm not going outside, though. I'll have ten minutes in the relatives' room. You've got to talk to him, though. They say that's supposed to help. And if he so much as stirs, call the nurse. Send somebody to get me.'

'On you go,' Tommy said. 'I'll keep an eye on him.'

Reluctantly, Anne stood up and moved slowly away. She walked down the ward, casting a backward look every couple of steps. Tommy moved across to her empty chair and leaned forward, elbows on his knees. He began to talk to George in a soft voice about his recent bird-watching experiences. After about ten minutes, a nurse appeared, checking George's vital signs. 'I don't know how you managed it,' she said, 'but Mrs Bennett's sleeping for the first time since they brought her husband in. Even if she only has a nap, it'll do her the world of good.'

'I'm glad.' Tommy waited till the nurse had gone, then he resumed his one-sided conversation. 'You'll be wondering what I'm doing here,' he said. 'It's a bit of a long story, I suppose, and one I shouldn't really be telling you. So never mind what brought me here, just be grateful that my ugly mug was enough to inspire your Anne to go and have a lie-down.'

As he spoke, he noticed George's eyelids fluttering. Then suddenly his eyes opened. Tommy leaned forward, taking George's hand. 'Welcome back, George,' he said softly. He waved his free arm, trying to attract a nurse's attention. 'Don't panic, old pal. You're going to be all right.'

George frowned, puzzlement in his eyes. 'Anne'll be right here,' Tommy said. 'There's nothing to worry about.' As he spoke, a nurse arrived at the bedside. Tommy looked up. 'He's awake.'

As the nurse moved in, Tommy stepped back. 'I'll get Anne,' he promised. He hurried down the ward, following signs to the relatives' room. Anne was sprawled over a sofa, fast asleep. He hated to wake her, but she'd never forgive him if he didn't. Tommy placed a hand on her shoulder and shook it gently. Anne's eyes snapped open, immediately alert, panic in her face.

'It's all right,' he said. 'He's waking up, Anne.'

She struggled to her feet. 'Oh, Tommy!' she exclaimed, throwing her arms round him and hugging his neck. He stood awkward in the embrace, unsure what to do with his hands.

'I'll come back tomorrow,' he said as she released him and turned to go.

In the doorway, she glanced back. 'Thanks, Tommy. You're a miracle.'

He stood for a moment looking after her. 'There's more than one kind of miracle,' he said sadly, making his way out of the intensive care unit.

5

August 1998

Catherine managed to make an indifferent dinner last the best part of an hour and a half. Even so, it was barely half past eight when she got back to Longnor. But Tommy was already waiting, sitting in the warm evening air on the limestone dyke outside her cottage. He looked grey and pale and Catherine felt a pang of concern. She kept forgetting he was an old man, so fit and sprightly did he seem. But he'd driven more than half the day, and he probably hadn't had an evening meal.

He greeted her with, 'Thank God you're back. We need to sit down and talk.'

'How's George?' she asked as she let them both in. 'Drink?'

'Have you any whisky?'

'Only Irish.' She pointed to the sideboard. 'Let me get a glass of wine.' She went through to the kitchen and opened a bottle. When she came back, Tommy had two inches of Bushmills in the bottom of a petrol-station tumbler.

'So how is George?' she repeated, expecting the worst.

'He's recovered consciousness. I was with him when his eyes opened.'

'You were with him? How did you manage to get in?'

Tommy sighed. 'How do you think? I lied. Obviously, he wasn't up to talking. But he seemed to recognize me. I told Anne I'd be back tomorrow morning. Maybe I'll be able to speak to him then.'

'I don't think this is the time to talk about Scardale and Alison with him,' Catherine said.

Tommy gave her a hard stare. He hadn't lost his touch over the years; Catherine felt like a butterfly on a pin. 'You mean you don't want him remembering that he told you to cancel the whole thing.'

'No,' she protested. 'I just think that if whatever happened in Scardale really precipitated the heart attack, he shouldn't be talking about it.'

Tommy shrugged. 'I'd say that was up to George. I'm not going to push it, but if he wants to talk about it, I'm not going to stop him. Better he gets it out of his system with me than he bottles it up and maybe sets off another attack,' he said stubbornly. 'And while we're on the subject, I met Paul as I was leaving. He introduced me to his fiancée. And we have to talk about that,' he said heavily, taking a swig from his glass that disposed of half the whiskey. 'Let's have another look at those certificates.'

Catherine booted up the computer while Tommy paced to and fro in the tiny living room. As soon as she had the first certificate up on the screen, he was at her side. 'Show me Helen's birth certificate again,' he said. She flicked a finger over the <page down> key and her details appeared before them.

'Oh God,' he groaned. He turned away and crossed to the fireplace. He leaned his arm across the mantel and laid his head down.

Catherine swung round in her chair. 'Tommy, are you going to tell me what's going on?'

His big shoulders heaved and he turned back to face her. If he didn't tell her, she was perfectly capable of working it out for herself. At least this way, he could have some control over what she knew and what she did with it. 'You've seen Helen, haven't you?' he said wearily.

Catherine nodded. 'We first met last year, in Brussels.'

'Did she not remind you of anybody?'

'Funnily enough, I did think I'd seen her before. But now we know she's connected to the Scardale clans, I think what I'm seeing is a sort of generic Carter resemblance.'

Tommy sighed. 'Aye, there is a bit of that. A look of her mother. But it's her father she takes after.'

She frowned. 'Tommy, you're not making any sense. When did you ever come across Samuel and Dorothy Wainwright?'

Tommy sat down heavily in the armchair. 'I've never seen either of them in my life. I'm not talking about the Wainwrights. I'm talking about Philip Hawkin.'

'Hawkin?' Catherine echoed, completely lost.

'She's the spit of Philip Hawkin across the eyes. And she's got his colouring. I don't think you'd pick up the resemblance from the photos, but it's clear as day in the flesh.'

'You can't be right,' she protested. 'George would have seen the likeness, surely?'

'He wouldn't necessarily have made the connection

563

until the Scardale link was right in front of his nose. Besides, you said Paul said he'd been uneasy, even before they got to Scardale.'

'It could still be coincidence,' Catherine said stubbornly. If she was going to nail this story, she needed to fight every fact so her defences were already established before she had to persuade an editor. She might as well take advantage of Tommy's experience to help construct her arguments.

'Look at the birth certificate,' he said. 'She's called Helen Ruth. I know Ruth's not exactly an uncommon name, but back then it was usual practice round these parts to give a child a family name for a middle name, usually a grandparent. When you add in all the rest of the details we've got here, Helen's middle name being Ruth is stretching coincidence too far.'

Catherine lit a cigarette to put off the inevitable question. 'So if Philip Hawkin was Helen's father . . . who was her mother?'

'Well, it wasn't his wife, that's for sure. Ruth Carter wasn't having a baby in June 1964 – she was attending her husband's trial. We saw her at least once a week in the run-up to the trial, and she wasn't pregnant.'

'Some women don't show it,' she pointed out. 'They just look like they've put on a bit of weight.'

He shook his head. 'Catherine, when we first met Ruth, she was a sturdy farmer's wife. By the time we got to the trial, she looked like a strong wind would lift her from Scardale into Denderdale without noticing. She could not have borne a daughter in June 1964.'

'So who was it?' Catherine persisted. 'I presume we're ruling out a mad, passionate affair with Dorothy Wainwright?'

'It's always possible, I suppose,' Tommy said. 'Dorothy would only have been in her mid-thirties. But if Hawkin had been sleeping with her, I'd have expected him to bring it out at the trial as evidence that he was a normal, red-blooded male, not some pervert into little girls. We always figured that was the only reason he married Ruth – so that if there was ever any question mark over him molesting Alison, he'd be able to point to his marriage to prove he was just like every other bloke. Anyway, there's no evidence to indicate he ever met the Wainwrights. But if we go with our theory about the real identity of the woman calling herself Janis Wainwright, then we do have a female of child-bearing age in the Wainwrights' house who had a demonstrable connection to Hawkin. A female that we know from photographic evidence was raped by Hawkin.' His words fell heavy as stones.

'Alison Carter is the mother of Helen Markiewicz, née Wainwright,' Catherine said, putting Tommy's circumlocutions into hard unequivocal terms. 'And Philip Hawkin is her father.'

She looked at Tommy and he stared back at her. Nothing else made sense of the solid facts and the physical congruence they had found. But it was a solution that begged so many questions Catherine didn't even know where to begin.

She took a deep breath and said what she knew Tommy would be thinking. 'So George Bennett is about to become the father-in-law of the daughter of a man he was responsible for having hanged for the murder of her mother. Except that Helen hadn't actually been born at the time when her father was supposed to have murdered her mother.' Put like that, she thought, it made Oedipus Rex sound like an every-day story of country folk.

'So it would seem,' Tommy said. He drained his glass and reached over to the sideboard for the whiskey bottle.

'I know this sounds crazy . . . but it looks like Ruth and Alison conspired to have Philip arrested.'

Tommy slowly poured out another stiff Bushmills. He sipped at it, looking directly at her from under his bushy eyebrows. Then he lowered the glass and said, 'At the very least, Catherine. At the very least.'

She tipped more red wine into her glass. Her hand was shaking, she noticed. This was more than the best story she'd ever stumbled across – it was a tragedy with the potential to reach out across thirty-five years and blight a second generation of lives who had no idea their history was so dramatically charged. She was in a position at once terrifying and exhilarating. She didn't think she was entirely to be trusted with the information she already possessed; she was almost glad Tommy was there to act as a brake on her wilder instincts.

'So what now?'

'Good question,' Tommy said.

'Oh, I've got plenty of those.'

'I think there's only one real option. I think we have to walk away right now and forget the whole thing. Leave Alison Carter – if it is her – in peace. Let Helen and Paul get married without a cloud on the horizon.'

'No way,' Catherine protested. 'I can't ignore this. It turns one of the most significant legal cases of the post-war years on its head. It screws up an important legal precedent.'

'Spare me all that, Catherine,' Tommy said angrily. 'You don't give a damn about legal precedents. All you can see is the scoop of a lifetime and the money you can make off it. Can't you see how many lives you're going to destroy if you go public with this? You leave George with his reputation in tatters. You destroy Paul and Helen's future, not to mention shattering Helen's life completely. How's she going to feel when she finds out her sister is really her mother, and the woman she thought was her mother conspired to have her father killed? And then there's Janis, or Alison or whatever you want to call her. You expose her to prosecution for conspiracy to commit murder. All that just so you can have your fifteen minutes of fame?' He was shouting now, his presence filling the room and leaving Catherine breathless.

She swallowed hard and said, 'So I'm just supposed to write off the last six months of my life? I've got a stake in this, too, Tommy. You were the one who talked to me about the importance of justice. How you left the police because you reckoned they couldn't deliver justice. And now you're saying, fuck justice, fuck truth, I'm going to protect my reputation and cover up the fact that me and my boss got an innocent man hanged?' Now she was as angry as he was.

Tommy tossed back some whiskey and tried to suppress his anger. 'This is not about me, Catherine. It's about a good man and his innocent family. None of them deserve to have their lives destroyed over something that should have been dead and buried thirty-five years ago. Listen, you don't have to waste the last six months. You can still publish your book as it is and let sleeping dogs lie.'

567

'But George didn't want to let sleeping dogs lie. He's got more integrity than you have, Tommy. He wanted the book suppressed because it isn't the truth.'

Tommy shook his head. 'He was acting on the spur of the moment. When he's had time to think things over, he'll see the sense in letting it go ahead.'

'You mean when you've talked him into it,' Catherine said savagely. 'That's not good enough any more, Tommy. I can wipe the e-mail off my computer, but I can't erase the knowledge in my head. I'm going to find out the truth, and actually, you can't stop me.'

There was a long silence. Tommy felt his hands bunch into fists and struggled to straighten his fingers. Finally, he took a deep breath and said, 'Maybe I can't stop you. But I can certainly trash you when the book comes out. I can tell the press about how you exploited a man on a life-support machine. I can talk about how you deliberately took advantage of George Bennett's incapacity to stitch up him and his family. You won't look so much like a crusader for justice when I'm finished with you, I promise. You'll look as shabby as Philip Hawkin.'

Neither of them moved, glaring like two dogs in a Mexican stand-off. At last, Catherine spoke. 'Neither of us has any right to make the decision without George,' she said, forcing herself to sound calm. 'We don't even know if we're right. Before we can go any further, we need to speak to Alison Carter.'

Tommy turned from her eyes and stared at the photographs on the wall. Alison Carter, George Bennett, Ruth Carter, Philip Hawkin. In his heart, he knew she was right. It wasn't their choice to make alone. And no choice so important should be made in the dark. He sighed. 'All right. Tomorrow, we'll go to Scardale and get some answers.'

6

August 1998

Tommy stood on Catherine's doorstep at eight the next morning. When she opened the door, he thought she looked as if she'd had as little sleep as he'd managed. 'You're early,' she said, stepping back and letting him in. 'Alison's not going to be thrilled to see us at this time.'

'We're not going to Scardale yet,' he said.

'We're not?'

'No. I promised Anne I'd go back to the hospital this morning. I want to do that first. And I want you to drive me there,' Tommy said, helping himself to the toast on Catherine's plate.

'Make yourself at home, why don't you?' she said, surprised to find herself amused rather than irritated. 'I get it. You don't trust me to wait for you to come back. You think I'll shoot off on my own and get the whole story out of Alison.'

Tommy shook his head. 'Funnily enough, you're wrong. Any more toast?'

'I'll make some.'

He followed her through to the kitchen. 'It's not that I don't trust you. It's something to do with me not being

570

as young as I was. I drove more yesterday than I do in an average month back home, and I never sleep well in a strange bed. The long and short of it, Catherine, is that I'd rather be driven than have to drive all the way to Derby and back.'

She dropped two slices of bread into the toaster and said approvingly, 'Good pitch, Tommy. I almost believe you.' She grinned at the hurt look on his face. 'It's all right, of course I'll drive you to Derby. Whatever Janis Wainwright's got to say isn't going to change between now and then.'

They said little on the drive to Derby, both lost in their own thoughts. Catherine was still racking her brains to come up with a strategy for the meeting that lay ahead in Scardale. She had stayed up long past midnight, smoking, drinking and thinking. She had always believed that a large part of the success of any interview lay in how thorough the preparation had been. But no matter how she turned over in her head what she and Tommy now knew, she couldn't think of a way of approaching this story that would actually produce the truth. Janis Wainwright still had too much to lose.

Their first surprise of the day came when Tommy told the intensive care nurse that he'd come to see his brother-in-law, George Bennett. 'He's not with us any longer,' the nurse said, consulting a clipboard on her desk.

For a moment, Tommy felt his own heart constrict in his chest. 'That can't be right. He'd come round last night. I saw his eyes open.'

The nurse smiled. 'That's right. We've moved him to another ward because he's out of immediate danger now.' She directed them to the cardiac care ward where George had been transferred.

'Tact and diplomacy by the NHS,' Catherine said drily.

They turned the corner of the corridor and found the ward they were looking for. Tommy peered through the window in the door. There were four beds in the room, two unoccupied. By the window, he spotted Anne sitting by a bed, obscuring the occupant, who appeared to be propped up in a half-sitting position. Tommy turned back to Catherine. 'I think you should wait outside.'

Reluctantly, she agreed. 'There's a cafeteria on the sixth floor. I'll wait there for you.' She took her tape recorder out of her pocket. 'I don't suppose . . . ?'

Tommy shook his head. 'This is between me and George. You needn't worry, though. I won't lie to you.'

He watched her walk off towards the lifts, then he squared his shoulders and pushed the door open. As he drew near, he could see George's face. It was hard to believe this was the same man who had looked one step away from a corpse only the night before. Although he still looked exhausted, there was some colour in his cheeks, and the dark circles under his eyes were less prominent. When he caught sight of Tommy, his face brightened in a wide smile.

'Tommy Clough,' George said, his voice weak but recognizably pleased. 'And there was me thinking I'd died and gone to hell when I opened my eyes and saw you staring down at me.'

Tommy reached out and clasped his old boss's hand in both of his. 'I reckon it was the shock of hearing my voice that woke you up.'

'Damn right. I knew I couldn't trust a ladies' man like you around my Anne without me to chaperone.'

'George,' Anne scolded. 'That's a terrible thing to say to Tommy when he's come all this way to see you.'

'Pay no attention to him, Anne, he's obviously still delirious. How are you feeling, George?'

'Knackered, if you want the truth. I've never been so weary in all my born days.'

'You gave us all a bit of a fright,' Tommy said.

'Sorry about that. Mind you, if I'd known this was the way to prise you out of your hermit's existence, I'd have done it years ago,' said George.

Tommy and Anne exchanged looks, both glad that George, weak as he was, hadn't lost his sense of humour.

'Aye, well, I won't be such a stranger in future. It was Catherine who told me, you know. She drove all the way up to Northumberland to break the news.'

George nodded, the light in his eyes dimming. 'I should have guessed,' he said. 'Anne, my love, would you do me a favour? Would you leave me and Tommy alone for a bit? Not long, quarter of an hour or so? It's just that . . . we've things to talk about, love.'

Anne frowned. 'They said you weren't to tire yourself, George.'

'I know. But I'll do myself more harm fretting than I will by talking to Tommy. Trust me, my love. I'm not dicing with death again.' He reached for her hand and patted it gently. 'I'll explain it all, I promise. But not now.'

Anne pursed her lips in disapproval. But she got to her feet. 'Don't you wear him out now, Tommy.' She turned back to George. 'I'll go and phone Paul and tell him they should come over this afternoon.'

'Thanks, my love.' George's eyes followed her to the door. Then, with a sigh, he told Tommy to sit down. 'I was afraid she wouldn't give it up,' he said. 'How much do you know?'

'We don't *know* much, but I think we've more or less worked it out.' Tommy gave a brief outline of Catherine's investigation. 'It doesn't leave a lot of room for doubt,' he concluded.

'It's unbelievable, isn't it? But I knew as soon as I clapped eyes on her,' George said. 'I lived with that face for eight months and it haunted me for years. I knew that whatever she might be calling herself, the woman in Scardale Manor was Alison Carter. And then I realized who Helen had to be.' His eyes closed and his chest rose and fell with his shallow breaths. He opened his eyes on Tommy's concern. 'I'm OK,' he reassured him. 'I'm just tired, that's all.'

'Take your time. I'm in no hurry.'

George managed a faint smile. 'No, but I bet Catherine is. I don't suppose there's any chance of stopping her?'

Tommy shrugged. 'I don't know. She's a tough cookie. Last night, I got her to promise that she would consult you before she made any decisions about what to do. But the promise had a price. I've got to go to Scardale with her to confront the woman we all believe is Alison. Catherine's adamant that we need all the facts, and I can't argue with that.'

'I don't care on my own account,' George said. 'It's Paul and Helen I'm bothered about. We made a terrible mistake before they were even born, but they're the ones who'll end up paying for it. I can't see how they can survive it all coming out. And I don't see how Anne could forgive me for the damage it'd cause them.'

'I know. And it's not just them, George. It's Alison too. Whatever she's done, it's already cost her more than we'll ever know. They could still prosecute her for conspiracy, and I don't reckon she deserves that.'

'So what's to be done, Tommy? I'm no bloody use, lying here.'

Tommy shook his head, unable to hide his frustration. 'I reckon we'll have a better idea once we've heard what Alison has to say for herself.'

'Do what you can.' George's voice was growing weaker. 'I'm tired now. You'd best be off.'

Tommy stood up. 'I'll do my best.'

George nodded. 'You always did, Tommy. No reason to expect any different now.'

Feeling twenty years older than he had a mere day before, Tommy walked out of the room towards an encounter he had never expected that side of the grave. The last time he'd felt this burden on his shoulders had been during the construction of the case against Philip Hawkin. This time, he hoped he'd make a better job of it.

7

August 1998

The weather had swung back to the dismal grey skies and intense showers that had been the hallmark of most of the summer. As they turned down the Scardale road, a sudden torrent of water spilled over the car, turning the tarmac ahead into a swirl of shallow flood water.

'Great day for it,' Tommy said laconically. He felt a turbulent mixture of emotions. His curiosity was stirred by the prospect of uncovering the final truth, but he was apprehensive of the possible consequences of those revelations. He was aware of his responsibility towards George and his family, and uncertain if he could fulfil that obligation. And he felt enormous pity for the woman whose sanctuary they were about to destroy. He wished with all his heart that George had never agreed to break his silence. Or that he had chosen a less intelligent and tenacious writer to work with.

For her part, Catherine refused to allow herself to consider anything other than how she was going to get Janis Wainwright to tell the truth. There would be plenty of time to figure out what she would do with the information once she'd garnered it. Her job now was to make sure that whatever decisions were taken later, they were made in full possession of the facts. She checked her small tape recorder, tucked into the pocket of her linen blazer. All she had to do was to depress the 'record' and 'play' buttons together and she'd have a perfect record of what Janis Wainwright – or rather, Alison Carter – had to say.

They drew up outside the manor, Catherine parking across the drive so Janis couldn't escape except on foot. In silence, they waited for the shower to pass, then squelched across the grass to the path leading to the kitchen door.

Tommy let the knocker fall. The door opened almost at once. Without the handicap of the sun, Catherine was able to take a proper look at the woman who faced them, a guarded look in her eyes. The scar was incontrovertible. Almost beyond question, this was Alison Carter. The woman opened her mouth to speak but Tommy held up his hand and shook his head. 'I'm Tommy Clough. Formerly Detective Sergeant Clough. We'd like to come in for a chat.'

The woman shook her head. The door began to inch shut. Tommy placed his large hand against it, not quite pushing, but preventing it closing further unless she leaned her weight against it. 'Don't slam the door in our faces, Alison,' he said, his voice firm but gentle. 'Remember, Catherine's a journalist. She already knows enough to write one version of the story. There's no statute of limitation on conspiracy to commit murder. And what Catherine's in a position to write now means you could still face prosecution.'

'I've got nothing to say,' she blurted, her face closed

down in panic, the hand that wasn't holding the door creeping up automatically to her cheek.

Sometimes, Catherine thought, brutality was the only effective route left. 'That's fine,' she said. 'I'll just have to see what Helen can tell me.'

The woman's eyes blazed momentary anger, then her shoulders rose and fell in a resigned shrug. She stepped to one side, holding the door open as her mother must have done hundreds of times before her. 'Better I correct whatever rubbish you think you know than you go upsetting Helen without due cause,' she said, her voice cold and harsh.

Tommy stood just inside the threshold as she closed the door behind them. 'You've made some changes here,' he said, looking round at the farmhouse kitchen that could have featured in a period homes magazine with almost no set dressing.

'Nothing to do with me. When my aunt owned it, she had the kitchen done out for her tenants,' she said brusquely.

'I'm not surprised,' Tommy said. Beside him, Catherine surreptitiously pressed the buttons on her tape recorder. 'Hawkin was happy to spend his money on his photography – or on you, Alison, but he never spent a shilling on your mother's comfort.'

'Why do you keep calling me Alison?' she demanded, back to the wall, arms folded over her chest, the smile on her face attempting to demonstrate an ease she clearly didn't feel. 'My name is Janis Wainwright.'

'Too late, Alison.' Catherine noisily pulled out a chair and sat down at the waxed pine table. If Tommy had decided that today he was playing Good Cop, she was more than willing to take up the Bad Cop role.

'You should have trotted out the puzzled act when Tommy called you Alison the first time. You just looked shocked, not confused. You didn't say, "Sorry, you've got the wrong house, there's no Alison lives here."'

Alison glared at her. For the first time, Catherine noticed how much she resembled her mother. In the photographs she'd seen, Ruth must have been ten years younger than Alison was now, though she'd looked older. 'You're very like your mother,' Catherine said.

'How would you know? You never met my mother,' Alison said defiantly.

'I've seen photographs of her. She was in all the papers during the trial.'

Alison shook her head. 'There you go again, talking nonsense. I've no idea what you're on about, you know. My mother was never involved in a trial in her life.'

Tommy walked across the room and stationed himself opposite her. He shook his head with a sympathetic half-smile. 'It's too late, Alison. There's no point in keeping up the pretence any longer.'

'What pretence? I keep telling you, I don't have the faintest idea what you're on about.'

'Are you still claiming to be Janis Wainwright?' Catherine said coldly.

'What do you mean, claiming? What is this? I'm calling the police,' she said, setting off for the phone.

Tommy and Catherine did nothing and said nothing. Alison opened the phone book and looked up the number. Then she glanced over her shoulder to see if they were going anywhere. Catherine smiled politely and Tommy shook his head again. 'You know that's not a good idea,' he said sadly, as her hand crept towards the phone.

'No, Tommy, let her. I really want to hear her explaining how she managed the resurrection,' Catherine said, the epitome of sweet reason. Alison froze. 'That's right, Alison. I know Janis died in 1959. Eleventh of May, to be precise. It must have been hard for your Auntie Dorothy and Uncle Sam. Hard for you too, with you and Janis being much of an age.'

Alison's eyes were fearful now. She must have had nightmares about this moment for years, Tommy thought with a pang of pity. And at last it was unfolding before her. He could only imagine the fear that must be coursing through her right now. Two strangers in her kitchen, one with good reason to want to take revenge on her for making a fool of him thirty-five years before, the other apparently hellbent on exposing her darkest secrets to a sensation-hungry world. And Catherine wasn't making it any easier with her aggressiveness. Somehow, he had to calm things down, to make Alison feel that they were her best chance of salvaging something from this appalling situation.

'Sit down, Alison,' he said kindly. 'We're not out to get you. We just want to know the truth, that's all. If we were planning on destroying you, we'd have gone to the police as soon as Catherine turned up Janis Wainwright's death certificate.'

Slowly, uneasily, like an animal that expects danger, she moved across to the table and sat at the opposite end from Catherine. 'What's any of this to you?' she asked her.

'George Bennett's lying in hospital in Derby because

of what he saw in this house. I'm sure Helen's been on the phone to tell you,' Catherine said.

She nodded. 'Yes. And I'm sorry. I only ever wished George Bennett well.'

'You should never have let him come here, if you wished him well,' Tommy said, unable to keep the edge of anger and pain out of his voice. 'You must have known he'd recognize you.'

She sighed. 'What else could I do? How could I explain to Helen that I didn't want to meet her future in-laws? It had to be better that we got it over with than him coming face to face with me at the wedding. But you still haven't answered my question. What's any of this to you?'

Catherine leaned forward. Her voice was as intense as her expression. 'I've spent six months of my life working with George Bennett to tell a story. Now I find out that we've both been manipulated into believing a lie. George Bennett's paid a hell of a price for finding that out. And I won't be a party to allowing that lie to persist.'

'Whatever the cost to other people? Even if it shames George Bennett? Even if it destroys Paul Bennett and Helen too?' Alison exploded, her composure shattering like a light bulb on a stone floor. 'And it's not just them.' Her hand flew to her mouth in a classic gesture, her eyes widening as she realized she had told them more than they knew.

'If you want me to hold off, you're going to have to give me a better reason than sentimentality. It's time to talk, Alison,' Catherine said coldly. 'Time for the whole story.'

'Why should I say anything to you? This could be

a trick. Everybody knows how far hacks like you will go to get a story. How do I know you know anything about me at all?' It was a last desperate throw of the dice, and everyone in the room knew it.

Catherine opened her bag and took out print-outs of the four certificates. 'This is where we start,' she said, tossing them down the table to Alison. They landed in an unruly flurry. Alison slowly read through them, using the time to regain control of herself. When she looked up, her face was impassive once more. But Catherine could see dark sweat stains forming under the arms of her pale-green blouse.

'So?' Alison said.

Catherine took out the computer-aged photograph and slid it towards Alison. 'According to the computers at Manchester University, this is what Alison would look like if she was still alive. Looked in a mirror lately?'

Alison's lips parted, revealing clenched teeth and she drew in a hiss of breath. The look she gave Catherine made her glad she had Tommy with her.

'What we know is that you are not Janis Wainwright. Thanks to the wonders of DNA, what can probably be proved is that you are Alison Carter. What can definitely be proved is that Helen is not your sister but your daughter. The daughter you had when you were barely fourteen, following the systematic abuse and rape that you suffered at the hands of your stepfather, Philip Hawkin. The man they hanged for your murder. If we went to the police with what we have, they could exhume the bodies and prove these relationships, no bother at all.' Catherine spoke with clinical precision.

'I'm afraid she's right, Alison,' Tommy said. 'But I

meant what I said. We didn't come here to make a case against you. For the sake of everybody involved in this, we need to know what happened. So we can all decide together about the best way to deal with this.'

Without asking for permission, Catherine took out her cigarettes and lit one. Tommy walked across to the draining board and brought her a plate. The activity filled a long silence while Alison stared wordlessly at the computer-aged photograph. Her eyes were glassy with unshed tears.

'Here's what we think happened,' Tommy said gently, sitting down near her. 'Hawkin was abusing you, and we think you didn't know what to do about it. You were afraid of what would happen if you told your mum. Most kids are. But you'd already seen her lose one husband and you were afraid she'd have the same terrible grief if you forced her to choose between Hawkin and you. Then you fell pregnant. And your mum realized what had happened.'

Alison's nod was almost imperceptible. A single tear slid from her right eye and trickled down her cheek. She made no move to wipe it away.

'So she sent you off to live with your aunt and uncle, telling you that from now on you had to be Janis,' Tommy continued. 'And then she set him up. With the information you gave her, she was able to arrange for George Bennett to stumble over the clues she'd planted. She even found where the photographs were kept. And through it all, you kept your silence. You endured the horrors of a pregnancy you didn't want, you lost your childhood and you lost any chance you had of happiness. You didn't even get to bring up your daughter as your own child. For years, the sacrifice was bearable because it meant you all had something approaching a decent life. And now, because of one terrible coincidence, because Paul and Helen met and fell in love, it's all gone tragically wrong.'

Alison took a deep shuddering breath. 'You seem to have managed to work it all out without any help from me,' she said shakily.

Tommy laid a hand on her arm. 'We're right, aren't we?'

'No, Tommy,' Catherine interjected, apparently unmoved by the emotional scene playing itself out before her. 'There's more. We thought before we got here that that was the whole story, but it's not, is it? You gave it away, Alison. When you said it wasn't just Paul and Helen whose lives could be destroyed. There's more to this, and you're going to tell us.'

She looked up at Catherine, her eyes dark with anger. 'You're wrong. There's nothing more to tell.'

'Oh, I think there is. And I think you're going to tell us. Because as things stand, I'm not on your side. You and your mother murdered Philip Hawkin. It wasn't something done on the spur of the moment, under immediate provocation. It took months to achieve, and the pair of you kept your mouths shut all that time. You certainly made a meal of your revenge. But I don't see any reason why you should be protected from the consequences of what you did. If you wanted to avoid the risk of Helen's life being destroyed, you should have told her the truth years ago,' Catherine said, injecting anger into her voice. She was determined not to be diverted by Alison's pain, no matter how genuine it was. 'Now all you've achieved is that you've risked another man's life, a good man's life, all

584

because your mother didn't have the courage to deal with Philip Hawkin head on.'

Alison's head came up. 'You don't understand a damn thing,' she said bitterly. 'You have no idea what you're talking about.'

'So help me to understand,' Catherine challenged.

Alison stared at Catherine long and hard then stood up. 'I have to fetch something. Don't worry,' she added as Tommy pushed his chair back. 'I'm not going to run away. I'm not going to do anything silly. But there's something I need to show you. Then maybe you'll believe me when I tell you what really happened.'

She walked out of the kitchen, leaving Tommy and Catherine staring at each other, wondering what was coming next. 'You're being a bit hard on her,' Tommy said. 'She's been through hell. We don't have the right to make her suffer.'

'Come on, Tommy. She's holding out on us. You have to ask what could be worse than we already know. She's admitted to conspiring with her mother to murder her stepfather, but there's still something locked away inside her that she thinks is even worse.'

Tommy gave Catherine a look that bordered on the contemptuous. 'And you think you've a right to that knowledge?'

'I think we all have.'

He sighed. 'I hope we don't all live to regret this, Catherine.'

8

August 1998

Alison returned, carrying a locked metal file case. She unlocked it with a key from the table drawer, flipped the top open and stepped back as if afraid the contents might bite. Her shoulders hunched protectively as she crossed her arms over her chest. 'I'm putting the kettle on,' she said. 'Tea or coffee?'

'Black coffee,' Catherine replied.

'Tea,' Tommy said. 'Milk, one sugar.'

'I've had my fill of what's in that box,' Alison said, turning her back and crossing to the Aga. 'You look as much as you want, and maybe then you won't be so bloody glib about my past,' she added, turning briefly to glare at Catherine.

Tommy and Catherine approached with the cautious reverence of bomb-disposal experts moving in on a suspect device. The box contained perhaps a dozen manila envelopes, all around ten inches by eight. Tommy pulled out the first. In straggling block capitals, the ink faded, it was labelled, 'Mary Crowther'.

Against the routinely domestic background noises of hot drinks being made, Tommy inserted his thumb under the tucked-in flap of the envelope. He tipped the contents on to the table. There were a dozen black and white photographs, some strips of negatives and two contact sheets. These were not happy portraits of an innocent seven-year-old girl. They were obscene parodies of adult sexuality, lewd poses that turned Catherine's stomach. In one, Philip Hawkin appeared, his hand thrusting between the weeping child's legs.

There were envelopes for Mary's nine-year-old brother Paul; for thirteen-year-old Janet, eight-year-old Shirley, six-year-old Pauline, and even three-year-old Tom Carter; for Brenda and Sandra Lomas, aged seven and five; and for four-year-old Amy Lomas. The horror contained in those envelopes was almost beyond their comprehension. It was a guided tour of a hell Catherine would rather not have known about. Her legs gave way and she slumped into a chair, her face white and strained.

Tommy turned his face away and shuffled the envelopes back into the file box. Now he understood the primeval urge to destroy Philip Hawkin. What had been done to Alison had been bad enough. But this was infinitely worse in its scale and its depravity. If he had seen these photographs thirty-five years before, he doubted whether he'd have been able to keep his hands away from the man's throat.

Alison dumped a tray on the table. 'If you want something stronger, you'll have to go to the pub at Longnor. I don't keep alcohol in the house. In my early twenties, I had a bad patch when the world looked better through a glass. Then I realized it was just another way of letting him win. Damned if I was going to do that after all we'd been through.' Her voice was cold and hard, but her lips quivered as she spoke.

She poured out coffee and tea and sat down at the opposite end of the table from Catherine and Tommy and the Pandora's box she'd gifted them. 'You wanted the truth,' she said. 'Now it's going to be your burden too. See how you like living with it.' Catherine stared dumbly at her, only barely beginning to realize the weight of the curse she had brought on her own head. Images engraved on her mind's eye, she already knew she had condemned herself to nightmares.

Tommy said nothing, his head bowed, his eyes hidden beneath his heavy brows. He knew he was still numb from shock and wished that state would never pass.

'I don't know how to tell this story,' Alison said wearily. 'It's been in my head for thirty-five years but I've had no practice. Once it was all over, none of us ever spoke of it again. I see Kathy Lomas every day I'm in Scardale, and we never mention it. Even with you coming round and digging up old memories, we've none of us sat down and talked about it. We did what we thought we had to do, but that doesn't mean we didn't feel guilty. And guilt isn't something anybody finds easy to share. I learned that from personal experience long before I studied psychology.'

She pushed her hair back from her face and looked Catherine in the eye. 'I never thought we'd get away with it. I lived every day in fear of the knock at the door. I remember my real mum ringing up Dorothy to talk about what was happening with the investigation. Every day she'd phone. And she was on pins because George Bennett was such a good, honest copper. He was so persistent, she said. She was convinced he was going to work out what was really going on. But he never did.'

Tommy raised his head. 'You all lied like you were born to it,' he said stonily. 'Come on, Alison, you might as well let us have the rest of it.'

Alison sighed. 'You have to remember what life was like in the nineteen-sixties. Child abuse didn't exist inside families or communities. It was something that some pervert, some stranger, might do. But if you'd gone to your teacher or your doctor or the village bobby and said the squire of Scardale was fucking and buggering all the village kids, you'd have been locked up for being mentally ill.

'You also have to remember that Philip Hawkin owned us, lock, stock and barrel. He owned our livelihoods, our homes. Under old Squire Castleton, we'd grown up in a feudal system, more or less. Not even the grown-ups questioned the squire. And we were little kids. We didn't know we could tell on the new squire. And we none of us knew about the others, not for sure. We were all too terrified to talk about what was happening, even to each other.

'He was a shrewd bastard, you see. He'd never shown any signs of being a paedophile when he was courting my mother. He never had much time for me before he married her. He was nice enough, buying me things. But he never bothered me at all. I'm convinced the only reason he married my mother was a way of covering his back. If any of us had dared to speak out against him, he could have played the outraged innocent, the happily married man.' She stabbed a finger at Tommy. 'And you lot would have believed him.'

Tommy sighed and nodded. 'You're probably right.'

'I know I'm right. Anyway, like I say, he never came near me before the wedding. But as soon as they were married, it was a different story. Then it was, "little girls have to show their fathers how grateful they are for all he does for them," and all that sort of pernicious emotional blackmail.

'But I wasn't enough for him. That bastard Hawkin was abusing each and every one of us. Except Derek. I think Derek was that little bit too old for him to fancy.' She cupped her hands round her mug of tea and sighed again. 'And we all kept our mouths shut. We were bewildered and terrified, but none of us knew what to do.

'And then one day, my mother asked me why I'd not been using the sanitary towels she'd bought me when my first period had started. I told her I'd not had another period since. She started asking questions, and it all came out. What he'd been doing to me, how he'd been taking pictures of himself doing it to me. And she realized I must be pregnant.'

Alison took a sip of her tea to ease the huskiness in her voice and compose herself. 'Next time he went into Stockport for the day, she ransacked his darkroom. And that's when she found the rest of the pictures, in his stupid bloody safe. She knew then what he was. She got all the adults together and showed them the photographs. You can imagine what it was like. People were baying for Hawkin's blood. The women were all for castrating him and letting him bleed to death. The men talked about killing him and making it look like a farm accident.

'It was old Ma Lomas that talked sense into them. She said that if we killed him, somebody would have to take the blame. Even if he died under a tractor, it wouldn't be written off as just another farm accident. It would be investigated, because he was important. He was the squire, not just some farm labourer who didn't count for anything. One little slip, and somebody from the village would end up in the dock, especially once it became obvious I was pregnant. Besides, she reckoned he wouldn't suffer nearly enough from a quick death.

'The other thing everybody was worried about was that if it came out about the other kids, they'd all be taken into care because their parents hadn't looked after them properly. They reckoned outsiders wouldn't understand life in the dale, how the kids more or less ran wild as they pleased because it was such a safe place with no traffic and next to no strangers, even at the height of summer.

'So they talked about it all that day, and eventually, somebody remembered reading a story in the paper about a missing girl. I don't know whose idea it was, but they decided then that I should go missing and they'd arrange it so that it looked like he'd killed me. Because they knew he had a gun, and because of the photographs of me, they knew he'd hang if they could make it stick. And that way, it wouldn't have to come out about the other kids, so they wouldn't have the pain of going through it all for the police.'

Alison sighed. 'That was the end of my life as I'd known it. The plans were made quickly. It was mostly my mum and Kathy and Ma Lomas who worked it out, but they thought of everything. My Auntie Dorothy and Uncle Sam in Consett were roped in. Auntie Dorothy had been a nurse, so she knew how to take blood. She came over a few days before I disappeared and took a pint from me. They used that to mark the tree in the wood, and to stain one of Hawkin's shirts. They had to delay the discovery of the shirt and my underclothes because they needed his semen. They knew they'd get it eventually because he always used a condom when he went with my mother.' She gave a bitter laugh. 'He didn't want kids of his own. Anyway, my mother eventually got him to have sex with her. She had to plead with him that she needed it for comfort. So they used the sperm in the condom to stain my clothes. They didn't know how much the scientists could tell from the blood and the semen, but they wanted to make sure they didn't trip up on the details.

'And of course, everybody had to be clear about their stories. They all had their roles to play, and they had to get it right. The little kids were kept in the dark, but Derek and Janet were in on it too. Kathy spent hours with them, making sure they knew how important it was not to let anything slip. Me, I wandered round in a daze most of the time. I kept taking Shep out for walks, trying to memorize everything I knew I was going to lose. I felt so guilty all the time. All this upheaval, everybody wound up like clock springs, and all I could think was that it was all my fault.' She bit her lip and closed her eyes momentarily. 'It took me a long time and a lot of therapy to understand that I wasn't the one to blame. But at the time, I really, really hated myself.' She hesitated briefly, her eyes glistening with tears again. She blinked hard, brusquely rubbed a hand across her eyes and continued.

'While all this was going on in the dale, Dorothy and

Sam arranged to move house from Consett to Sheffield the same week the disappearance was planned so the new neighbours wouldn't realize I wasn't really their Janis. It was pretty easy in 1963.' Alison paused for a moment, her eyes looking inward as if searching for the next chapter in her tragic tale.

'The glory days of full employment,' Tommy muttered.

'That's right. Sam was a skilled steel worker and it wasn't hard for him to walk into a new job. And back then, houses went with jobs,' Alison said.

'The day it was all set for, Sam waited for me up by the Methodist Chapel in his Land Rover. He drove me to Sheffield, and I moved in with them. They put it about that I'd had TB and I had to stay indoors and not mix with folk until I was completely better again, so nobody would find out about the pregnancy. As time went on, Dorothy padded herself up so she'd look pregnant.'

Alison closed her eyes and a spasm of pain crossed her face. 'It was so hard,' she said, looking up and meeting Catherine's eyes. It was the writer who looked away first. 'I lost everything. I lost my family, my friends, my future. I lost Scardale. Strange things were happening to my body, and I hated it. My mum couldn't even come and visit until after the trial because nobody in the village had mentioned the existence of the Wainwrights to the police, and she didn't want to have to explain where she was going. Dorothy and Sam were really good to me, but it never made up for what I'd lost. It was drummed into me that I had to go through with it for the sake of all the other children in Scardale; that we were doing it so

Hawkin could never hurt another child the way he'd hurt me.'

'It made a kind of sense, I suppose,' Catherine said dully.

Alison sipped more tea and said defiantly, 'I'm not ashamed of what we did.' Neither Tommy nor Catherine said anything.

Alison pushed her hair back from her face again and continued her story. 'Helen was born in my bedroom one afternoon in June, just a couple of weeks before that bastard Hawkin's trial. Sam registered her as being his and Dorothy's child, and they brought her up like that, thinking I was her big sister and Dorothy was her mum. A couple of years went by, then I got a job in an office.' A wry smile appeared for the first time that morning. 'A solicitor's office, would you believe? You'd think I'd have had my fill of the law, wouldn't you? Anyway, I went to night classes to catch up on the stuff I'd missed at school. I even did an Open University degree. I did some training in occupational psychology and eventually set myself up in business. And every step of the way felt like a spit in the eye to that bastard. But it was never enough, you know?

'My real mum came and lived with us after Hawkin was hanged. I was glad of that. I really needed her. She didn't want to go back to Scardale, so she set up the Scardale Trust to administer the estate. She kept this place, though. She knew I'd want to come back one day. We kept Helen in the dark about the Scardale connection. She thinks to this day that Ruth and her husband lived just outside Sheffield. Ruth told her that Roy had been cremated, so there was no grave for her to visit. Helen never questioned it.

'When my mother died, the manor went to Dorothy on the understanding that it was meant for me and Helen, and when Dorothy died, it came to us. Helen thinks I'm mad, living in this backwater. But it's my home, and it was lost to me for so long, I just want to enjoy it now.'

She stared into her tea. 'So now you know.'

Catherine frowned. She knew there must be so many questions she should ask, but she could think of none.

'And every time you look at Helen, you must see him staring back at you,' Tommy said.

The muscles along Alison's jaw bunched as she clenched her teeth. 'When she was little, it wasn't so obvious,' she finally said. 'By the time she'd really started to resemble him, I'd learned that I could use that to help me. That bastard destroyed my childhood, he deprived me of my family and friends. He would have killed me if he'd discovered I was pregnant, I know he would. He was the powerful one, I was the weak one. So I never want to forget the way I helped turn the tables. Let me tell you, taking your own life is a very powerful thing. And that's what I did. But it's a lot easier to lose control over your life than it is to win it. That's why I wanted to make sure I never got complacent, never lost sight of my past. So I learned to be glad Helen was there as a constant reminder that we'd fought back against the man who tried to strip us of everything that made us who we were,' she said passionately. After a long pause, she said, almost in a tone of wonder, 'And you know, there's nothing of him in her. She's got all my mother's strength and goodness. As if everything that made my mother special jumped a generation into her skin.'

Tommy cleared his throat, obviously moved by Alison's story. 'So the whole village was in on the conspiracy?'

'All the adults,' she confirmed. 'Ma Lomas said everyone had to pretend they didn't trust the police to begin with, and only let stuff trickle out gradually. You and George Bennett were a bonus, really. They couldn't have predicted that they'd get a pair of cops who'd become so obsessed by the case that they wouldn't give up. It meant the villagers really could hold back and know that they wouldn't have to go chasing the police to get them to pick up the threads after things had gone quiet initially.'

Tommy shook his head, bemused by the terrible irony. 'We were the victims of our own integrity.' He gave a half-smile. 'It's not often you can say that about coppers. But if we'd been less determined to get a result, to see justice done, you'd never have got away with a conspiracy on this scale.'

For a moment, nobody said anything. Alison got up and walked over to the window. She stared across the village green into the dale she'd set out from on a December night thirty-five years before and had obviously never stopped loving. Now she possessed it again, Catherine thought, but she'd paid a terrible price. Eventually, Alison dragged her eyes away from the view, straightened her shoulders and said, 'So, what now?'

'That's a hell of a good question,' Tommy said.

9

August 1998

Catherine and Tommy bought another bottle of Bushmills on the way back to the cottage. Suitable equipment
for a wake, she thought. Tonight they would bury once
and for all the ghost of Alison Carter. Tomorrow they
would each have a hangover, though that would be the
least of their worries, Catherine suspected. But tonight,
she wanted to be insensible by the time her head hit
the pillow. Anything to escape that parade of horror
and degradation that Philip Hawkin had bequeathed
to the world.

When she closed the door behind them, Catherine
spoke for the first time since they'd left Alison Carter
to her memories. 'Well, that's it,' she said. 'We got the
truth.' She crossed to the sideboard and poured them
both stiff whiskeys.

Tommy accepted his glass in silence. He was staring at
the wall of photographs, facing the bitter knowledge that
Ma Lomas and her clan had managed to fool the world
long enough to send Philip Hawkin down the terrible
road that led to judicial murder. It gave him no satisfaction to realize that his own gut instinct had been right
about Hawkin. The man hadn't been a killer, after all.

Faced with the photographs Alison had devastated them with, Catherine could not resist the conclusion that the villagers of Scardale had had right on their side when they turned their sleepy backwater into a place of execution. They had known that nothing but death would stop Hawkin and save the other children he would lure into his grasp. Even sending their own children away would not have prevented him from continuing. He would have found other children to destroy; he had both the power and the money to do what he would with witnesses who would not be believed even if they could bring themselves to speak. 'It never occurred to me that there would be others,' Catherine said bleakly.

'No.' Tommy turned away from the accusing photographs and slumped into a chair.

'I can't find it in me to blame them for what they did,' Catherine said.

'In their place, I wouldn't have had second thoughts about joining in,' Tommy acknowledged.

'The terrible irony is that compared to what Alison's gone through, Philip Hawkin's suffering was blessedly brief. She's lived with it every day of her life since then. She lost so much, and always at the back of her mind there must have been the fear that one day she was going to open the door and find somebody like me on the other side.' Catherine picked up the whiskey bottle and put it on the table between them.

They sat in stunned silence, like the survivors of a terrible accident who can't quite take in their lucky escape. Both remained locked in their thoughts for the time it took them to smoke a handful of cigarettes apiece. 'George was right,' Catherine finally said. 'I can't go ahead with the book. Sure, I'd get all the glory for revealing that such a famous case was built on lies and deceit. But I can't do that to George and Anne. It's not just the shame it would bring to George, but the pain it would give him to watch Helen and Paul disintegrate. And all the surviving Scardale villagers would face prosecution for conspiracy, not just Alison.' Like a Greek tragedy, she thought, the reverberations of what had happened in Scardale thirty-five years before would shake apart other lives far distant from that afternoon, innocent lives who deserved protection from a past that was no fault of theirs.

Tommy drained his glass and refilled it. 'I'll drink to that,' he said. 'I don't think anybody would argue with you.'

'You can go and tell George in the morning,' Catherine said.

'Don't you want to tell him yourself?'

She shook her head. 'I've got enough to do, trying to get us out of the book contract without explaining the real reason. No, Tommy, you tell him. It's only right. If it hadn't been for you, I don't know if I'd ever have worked out that Helen was Alison's daughter by Hawkin. And then I wouldn't have had the leverage to get her to talk. Or any reason to keep silence now. So you deserve the credit.'

He snorted. 'Credit? For taking the lid off this can of worms? I'll pass, if it's all the same to you. But I'll be happy to tell George that nobody's going to blow Paul and Helen's lives to bits. I know how much it will mean to him. I'll spare him the details, though.'

Catherine reached for the bottle. 'That'd be a good idea,' she said, pouring another inch of whiskey into her tumbler. 'And then I suggest we all do our best to forget the last few days ever happened.'

10

October 1998

George Bennett stared through the windscreen. It was late October, and now the leaves were off the trees, the field gateway he had pulled into gave a clear view down the dale to the village of Scardale. The familiar grey cottages looked like an organic part of the landscape from this distance, reminding him how the peculiarities of topography had shaped the social world of the village he'd first entered thirty-five years before. He gazed across the fields to Scardale Manor and thought about the woman who was about to become his son's official sister-in-law. Some might think she – and the others who had taken part – deserved to be punished for the conspiracy that had hanged a man who, whatever his other crimes, had been innocent of murder. But George didn't care about retribution. He cared about the future more than the past. There was nothing like staring his own death in the face to make a man value his life.

That was why he was making this trip today. Only three days before, the doctor had agreed that he could start to drive again, provided he didn't undertake any long journeys. Cromford to Scardale wasn't a long journey in terms of distance, he had reasoned. The distance here was all emotional and psychological, a span of thirty-five years and a compass of passions too complex to be calculated. Four days ahead lay the wedding that could finally resolve this dreadful history, and George was determined to do all he could to make sure the ghosts were laid to rest at last. And so he had phoned the woman he would never be able to call by her real name after today and asked for a meeting.

Thirty-five years ago, he had first travelled this narrow road. Even then, his feelings had been mixed. He remembered with bitter irony his excitement at the possibility of taking charge of his first big case, a guilty excitement mixed with his concern both for the missing girl and her family. Not even in his wildest imaginings could he have foreseen how the disappearance of Alison Carter would come back to threaten not only his own peace of mind, but also the future happiness of his beloved son.

One of the deeper ironies of the events of the last year had been the replacement of one guilt with another. He had always carried the conviction that he had somehow failed Ruth Carter until the process of working through the case with Catherine had finally allowed him to understand that he had done the best he could have done in the circumstances. But now he knew what had truly been happening in Scardale over that bitter winter, he was oppressed by a fresh burden. Surely there were points in the investigation at which he could have realized something was going on that went far beyond the surface he was being shown? Had he been so blinded by his arrogance and his obsession with getting a conviction that he'd missed pointers that a more experienced detective would have picked up on? And if he had uncovered the truth, would it have given Alison Carter a better life than she'd otherwise endured?

Tommy Clough had assured him that wasn't the case, that he'd been taken in every bit as much as George himself. But that was no real consolation. Tommy, he felt sure, would have said that anyway as reassurance to a sick man.

Whatever his past failings, he had to find a way to reconcile himself to them. Whether his damaged heart would give him months or years to live, he didn't want that time to be contaminated with self-recrimination beyond bearing. He needed to forgive himself, and perhaps the first step on that journey was for him and Alison Carter to forgive each other for pains real and imagined.

With a deep sigh, George put his car in gear and slowly edged back on to the Scardale road. No matter what the future might hold, it was time to take the first step on the road to burying the past, this time for ever.

Also available from HarperCollins*Publishers*

The Mermaids Singing

Val McDermid

You always remember the first time. Isn't that what they say about sex?
How much more true it is of murder . . .

Up till now, the only serial killers Tony Hill had encountered
were safely behind bars. This one's different – this one's on the
loose. In the northern town of Bradfield four men have been
found mutilated and tortured. Fear grips the city; no man feels
safe. Clinical psychologist Tony Hill is brought in to profile the
killer. A man with more than enough sexual problems of his
own, Tony himself becomes the unsuspecting target of a battle
of wits and wills where he has to use every ounce of his
professional skill and personal nerve to survive.

A tense, brilliantly written psychological thriller,
The Mermaids Singing explores the tormented mind of a
serial killer unlike any the world of fiction has ever seen.

**Winner of the 1995 CWA Award for
Best Crime Novel of the Year**

'Truly, horribly good' *Mail on Sunday*

ISBN: 978-0-00-734467-3

Also available from HarperCollins*Publishers*

A Darker Domain

Val McDermid

Twenty-five years ago, the daughter of the richest man in Scotland
and her baby son were kidnapped and held to ransom. But
Catriona Grant ended up dead and little Adam's fate has remained
a mystery ever since. When a new clue is discovered in a deserted
Tuscan villa – along with grisly evidence of a recent murder – cold
case expert DI Karen Pirie is assigned to follow the trail.

She's already working a case from the same year. During the
Miners' Strike of 1984, pit worker Mick Prentice vanished.
He was presumed to have broken ranks and fled south with
other 'scabs' . . . but Karen finds that the reported events of
that night don't add up. Where did he really go? And is
there a link to the Grant mystery?

The truth is stranger – and far darker – than fiction.

'A searing piece . . . McDermid orchestrates the tension with
authority' *Daily Express*

'Val McDermid sends you to bed with lights blazing' *Sunday Times*

'Scotland's queen of crime uses the Miners' Strike as a
backdrop to murder and abduction . . . a novel as intelligent
as it is tightly plotted' *Independent (Books of the Year)*

ISBN: 978-0-00-724331-0

Audio book available on CD or download, read by Valerie Grogan

The Grave Tattoo

Val McDermid

A 200-year-old-secret is now a matter of life and death. And it could be worth a fortune.

It's summer in the Lake District and heavy rain over the fells has uncovered a bizarrely tattooed body. Could it be linked to the old rumour that Fletcher Christian, mutinous First Mate on the *Bounty*, had secretly returned to England?

Scholar Jane Gresham wants to find out. She believes that the Lakeland poet William Wordsworth, a friend of Christian's, may have sheltered the fugitive and turned his tale into an epic poem – which has since disappeared. But as she follows each lead, death is hard on her heels. The centuries-old mystery is putting lives at risk. And it isn't just the truth that is waiting to be discovered, but a bounty worth millions . . .

'Grips from the first page until the final deeply satisfying sentence' *Daily Express*

'Absorbing . . . the mix of historical and literary elements with modern detection is handled with panache' *The Times*

'A cleverly plotted thriller with oodles of atmosphere' *Guardian*

ISBN: 978-0-00-734460-4

Audio available on CD or download,
read by Dervla Kirwan and Rupert Penry-Jones

Also available from HarperCollins*Publishers*

The Distant Echo

Val McDermid

SOME THINGS JUST WON'T LET GO
The past, for instance.
That night in the cemetery.
The girl's body in the snow.

On a freezing Fife morning four drunken students stumble upon the body of a woman in the snow. Rosie has been raped, stabbed and left for dead in an ancient Pictish cemetery. And the only suspects are the four young men now stained with her blood.

Twenty-five years later the police mount a 'cold case' review of Rosie's unsolved murder and the four are still suspects. But when two of them die in a suspicious circumstances, it seems that someone is pursuing their own brand of justice. For the remaining two there is only one way to avoid becoming the next victim – find out who really killed Rosie all those years ago . . .

'McDermid's capacity to enter the warped mind of a deviant criminal is shiveringly convincing' *The Times*

'A classic . . . McDermid pulls out all the stops. Impeccable' *Guardian*

'A powerful story of murder and revenge . . . an exciting page-turner' *Sunday Telegraph*

ISBN: 978-0-00-734465-9

Audio book available on CD or download, read by Peter Capaldi

Also available from HarperCollins*Publishers*

Killing the Shadows

Val McDermid

A killer is on the loose. His prey – crime writers. And he hunts with a bloodlust that shatters all the conventional wisdom on how serial killers operate.

Professor Fiona Cameron is a psychologist who uses computer technology to track serial offenders. She vowed never to work for the Met again after they went against her advice and screwed up an investigation as a result. But when her lover, thriller writer Kit Martin, tells her a fellow crime novelist has been murdered, Fiona can't help taking an interest.

With the killer striking again, Fiona is caught up in a race against time, not only to save a life, but to bring herself redemption, both personal and professional.

'McDermid is our leading pathologist of everyday evil . . . the subtle orchestration of terror is masterful' *Guardian*

'*Killing the Shadows* exerts the dangerous pull of a rip tide, drawing us towards its unsettling resolution' *Independent*

'A multi-layered novel, as hauntingly strung together as a hangman's noose' *Sunday Express*

ISBN: 978-0-00-734464-2

Audio book available on CD and download, read by Emilia Fox

Also available from HarperCollins*Publishers*

Beneath the Bleeding

Val McDermid

The race is on to uncover the identity of a murderer with
nothing to lose – and everything to kill for.

When Robbie Bishop, star midfielder for the Bradfield Vics, is
poisoned by a rare and deadly toxin, profiler Dr Tony Hill and
trusted colleague DCI Carol Jordan have their work cut out for
them. Robbie was adored, so the public want answers – but the
answers aren't coming, and trails are running cold.

Then a bomb explodes in the football stadium, causing massive
casualties – and another man dies from poisoning. Is there a link
between the cases? And what are the motives for these crimes?
The clock is ticking for Tony and Carol – and the
death toll keeps rising . . .

'Outstanding . . . lock the door and prepare
to read in a sitting' *Guardian*

'McDermid is the queen of serial killers . . . few can scoop
her on throat-catching narrative' *Daily Mail*

'Compelling . . . McDermid is a consummate plotter
and this is a first-rate story' *Observer*

ISBN: 978-0-00-734469-7

Audio book available on CD and download, read by Shaun Dooley

Also available from HarperCollins*Publishers*

The Torment of Others

Val McDermid

For some, there is nothing so sweet, so thrilling, as the torment of others . . .

A dead girl lies on a blood-soaked mattress, her limbs spread in a parody of ecstasy. The scene matches a series of murders which ended when irrefutable forensic evidence secured the conviction of one Derek Tyler. But Tyler's been locked up in a mental institution for two years, barely speaking a word – except to say that 'the Voice' told him to do it.

Top criminal psychologist Dr Tony Hill is prepared to think the unthinkable – this is not a copycat murder but something much stranger. While DCI Carol Jordan and her team mount a desperate and dangerous undercover police operation to trap the murderer, Hill heads towards a terrifying face-off with one of the most perverse killers he has ever encountered . . .

'One of McDermid's finest, which is saying a lot' Marcel Berlins, *The Times*

'A disturbing, high-tension book, unstinting in its portrayals of psychological distress. One of McDermid's best, which is saying a lot' *The Times*

'An especially taut and inventive thriller – McDermid on top form' *Daily Mail*

ISBN: 978-0-00-734475-8

Audio book available on CD and download, read by Colin Buchanan